Welcome TO THE
Garden Club

Welcome to the Garden Club

A Novel

JENNY B. TILBURY

WELCOME TO THE GARDEN CLUB
A NOVEL

iUniverse books may be ordered through booksellers or by contacting:

iUniverse
1663 Liberty Drive
Bloomington, IN 47403
www.iuniverse.com
1-800-Authors (1-800-288-4677)

ISBN: 978-1-4917-6457-2 (sc)
ISBN: 978-1-4917-6456-5 (e)

Library of Congress Control Number: 2015905093

Print information available on the last page.

iUniverse rev. date: 6/18/2015

To all the clubs that have embraced me, all the women who have inspired me, and to my mother, who always impressed me.

To my sweet silver fox; I love you.

In Loving Memory of Dorothy Lee Wood
1954 - 2009

CHAPTER 1

— Stephanie —

Thursday, September 9

Ah, the sunlight is in abundance now. It was raining cats and dogs when I woke up. I kept thinking I'd need a pirogue to get anywhere today. I step out on to Royal Street to hear the jazz band playing "You Are My Sunshine." I love that song. It reminds me of one of many treasured memories I have of my mother. She would sing a couple of bars and ask, "Do you know who sang this?" I would proudly answer, "Yes, ma'am, Governor Jimmy Davis," and then she'd smile and continue to sing.

It's a challenge in any weather to navigate the cracked, broken, and often wobbly sidewalks in heels, as I'm trying to do now. I don't know why in the world I chose these shoes. I remember my grandmother saying, "You must suffer to be beautiful, *mon chéri*." But must I really chance breaking my leg?

I need to go only a few blocks, but after only one I decide not to walk and I wave like a crazy person at a passing taxi whose driver ignores me. Wearing a wide-brim hat the size of an extra-large pizza, I feel less like Carrie Bradshaw hailing a cab on Central Park North and more like the Mad Hatter, for surely if any city in America qualifies as a wonderland, it's New Orleans, specifically here in the area known as the French Quarter, where my husband, Louis, and I live.

With parking at a premium in the Quarter, you'd think there would be more taxicabs, like in Manhattan; but alas, that isn't the case. When I do manage to secure a ride, I can see the driver staring at me in the rearview mirror—or at least at my hat, which is completely understandable, as it's a one-of-a-kind creation from Fleur de Paris, a custom millinery boutique on Royal Street. The odds are extremely high that I will not be the only fashionable woman in the Quarter wearing a captivating chapeau today from this well-known shop.

Opening day of the Fleur-de-Lis Ladies Garden Club of the French Quarter is our chance to express our inner southern divas.

Yes, I'm in a club. Who would have ever thought? And such a highfalutin one at that.

Highfalutin or not, I must say I have met some of my dearest friends at the garden club (which is how most of us refer to it). The club was started in 1840 by Lisette Prieur and Isabella Bronzinelle, who originally developed the club to focus on the "Beautification of the City of New Orleans." (My best friend, Gloria Bronzinelle Vincent, is a direct descendent of Isabella Bronzinelle.) With a focus on flowers, fragrance, and finery, the Fleur-de-Lis Ladies Garden Club became a French Quarter institution that operated for nearly its first century with little formal organization.

Things changed in 1946 after the war. The club added food, wine, and guest speakers, and it adopted loosely written guidelines according to which it has operated to this day. The most significant changes over the years have been the incremental increases in membership fees.

The "official" garden club rules and regulations are short and unashamedly stringent: Membership is limited to fifty women, meeting attendance is mandatory, members must maintain French Quarter residency, annual membership fees are $200. The final rule—no guests allowed—gives *exclusive* a whole new meaning.

Many women have waited, begged, pleaded, and, yes, paid to get in. Very few members *ever* drop out. I became a member at thirty, when my name finally came up on the list after two women died that year from old age. Very old age.

This is a club that has stood the test of time and has made very few, if any, changes. It is what it is—prestigious and a tad haughty, with copious amounts of tradition, such as wearing hats on the first meeting in September. I'm really not a hat person, but like I said, it's tradition. Anyway, who's going to notice the hat when the dress is so loud?

The taxi drops me at the corner of Decatur and Toulouse just as a young couple smooching in a horse-drawn buggy passes by, which makes me smile. Our luncheon meetings are typically held in area restaurants and business establishments every second Thursday of the month, but today's meeting is unusual, as it is being held in a private residence in a not-so-private location.

More than 110 years old, the Jackson Brewery is a historical landmark in the heart of the French Quarter. The Shops at JAX have become quite a tourist attraction and include several floors of attractions, stores, kiosks, restaurants, bars, and cafés. The uppermost floors comprise private condominiums.

Often touted as having the best location and views in the city, the Jax Brewery penthouse where we're meeting is on the Crescent City bend of the Mississippi River, with breathtaking views day and night of the river, ports, French Quarter, and downtown Central Business District (CBD) skyline.

The penthouse is private, accessible only by a private elevator, and today there is a handsome young man in a pristine white jacket standing nearby to allow entrance to those whose names appear on the guest list he holds, and who can also provide at least one piece of corroborating identification, such as a driver's license.

After a quick ride to the top, I step out of the elevator and into one of the most luxurious condominiums I have ever seen; and trust me—I've seen my share.

There is a beautiful serving station greeting guests, where two white-gloved servers are pouring equal parts champagne and juice into exquisite crystal goblets. My favorite—mimosas! I'm all for champagne and orange juice. Actually, I'm all for champagne and anything, particularly Moet champagne, Rémy Martin cognac, and a dash of lemon juice, which are the components of the famous French 75 cocktail served at Arnaud's French 75 Bar.

I approach the table and nod affirmatively.

"Not too much; I have to walk home." I laugh as the server stops pouring. "I was just kidding. You can fill it up."

I can smell the aroma of food. Something is cooking with fresh basil—perhaps a tomato basil soup. The scent of herb-rubbed pork tenderloin is also distinct, and I think I detect asparagus as well. I didn't realize I was this hungry, but my growling stomach is quickly forgotten as I take my drink and walk farther into the room. The visual sensation trumps anything my acute olfactory senses are transmitting to my brain as I am stopped in my tracks by a view that is literally breathtaking.

The entire space is encased in glass, and all the french doors are wide open to a lush and redolent garden balcony that rivals anything I've seen on a ground level. Tables bedecked with crisp linen tables dot the patio, and crystal water goblets catch the glint of the late-morning sunlight. The delicate bone china at all the place settings is most definitely Royal Copenhagen's Flora Danica pattern, the most expensive china in the world; the astonishing detail of the floral pattern and gold serrated edge is unmistakable. I've never seen so many place settings of this pattern in one place. I look out to see a cruise ship pulling out of the port, while the historic Natchez paddle-wheel riverboat filled with tourists passes by.

In the French Quarter, you have Mississippi views or monumental views. This opulent condominium has both. The huge rooftop balcony overlooks the river and the most famous landmarks in the Quarter: Jackson Square, the Pontalba Apartments (the oldest apartments in the country), and the St. Louis Cathedral, which all are located right across the street.

I'm still stunned by the entire sensory overload when I suddenly become aware that I'm basically alone. Other than the uniformed servers, I don't see any of the garden club ladies, and I look at my watch. I'm uncharacteristically early, which offers me a small window of time to relax and relish the surroundings before the social swirl begins.

I'm startled by the voice behind me.

"Spectacular, isn't it?"

The familiar gravelly voice makes me smile as I turn and see Miss Dolores Delacroix in all her strappy spandex glory. Dolores is one of those women who believe the lie that one size fits all. An avid Stein Mart shopper, she seems to think she is one size smaller than she really is.

"I arrived early to help Miss Oleta. Not that she needed any help; she's hired half the staff of Galatoire's to serve today." She glances full-circle around the room. "I don't know where the mistress of the house is. I haven't seen her for a while, but I put down place cards for you, Gloria, and me over there." She points to a table near a potted lemon tree. "Is that spot okay?"

Truthfully, there isn't a bad seat in the house, but Dolores has selected one of the best tables on the elegant patio for people-watching, adjacent to the head table and the lectern.

"Thanks, it's perfect."

I really can't say more because I'm still floored by this utterly extravagant presentation. We each sip our mimosas and stare at the expansive view.

"Where's Gloria?" Dolores looks around. "Didn't she come with you?"

"She's running late." I check my cell phone but don't see another text from her.

"She flew in last night, right? She's probably sleeping in," Dolores says.

"Gloria? Not a chance. She never gets jet lag, no matter how many hours she's been in the air. She texted me a half hour ago; something came up on her way out the door. I don't know what."

"So where was she this time?" Dolores asks.

"Paris."

"Wow, must be nice." Dolores reaches down and plucks a dead leaf off a nearby hibiscus and gently rotates the entire pot. "Much better," she says.

"You know—it's not like she was vacationing, Dolores. I'd be surprised if she even left her apartment."

"I know, but you have to admit, having offices in both the French Quarter *and* in France *is* quite glamorous." She sighs.

I know what she means, but personally I think all the back-to-back international travel is taking a toll on Gloria. I finish my drink, and before I can put the glass down, a server swoops out of nowhere and surreptitiously takes it from me.

"May I bring you another?" she asks graciously.

"No thank you," I say.

When I'm sure we are alone again, I ask Dolores to spill the beans. "Okay, girlfriend, I've got my second wind. Give me the lowdown on this place; what's it like?" I ask. "I can't believe she landed this location right out of the gate!"

We were stunned when the new incoming president of the garden club announced that opening day was going to be here, at a location few of us had ever seen, at least from the *inside*.

"You have no idea, Steph," Dolores whispers, even though no one is within earshot. "It's like walking through the frigging Louvre! I had no idea Oleta, or anyone for that matter, lived this way!"

Oleta Atwood is a very wealthy and somewhat reclusive widow, and the only time we see her is at our monthly meetings; otherwise, she is taking her private jet to one of her equally private residences around the world. In fact, the only reason we see her at all is that one of the longstanding rules of the club is that if you miss more than three unexcused meetings per season, you are *out*—as in finished, *fini*, hasta la vista. Your name goes off the list faster than graffiti off a cop car, and another moves up. Although it's a rule that has been somewhat lax the past few years, it's one that is treated with a modicum of respect.

"It's totally amazing," Dolores gushes. "There are six bedrooms, ten bathrooms, a library, a den, a media room, and two full kitchens, one inside and out. See that?" She points toward the far end of the patio. "That's a Viking commercial kitchen. It has a barbecue center and cooking station, and that's a seafood/crawfish boiling station next to it." She continues to point out amenities as though she's a Gray Line tour guide as more women in hats begin to appear. We meander around the balcony, where I'm stopped in my tracks at the sight of a full-size rooftop swimming pool, hot tub, and what appears to be a sixty-inch outdoor TV.

"Look there." Dolores points. "That's a cabana with *three* bathrooms. Can you believe it?"

I'm speechless.

"Wait until you see the master bathroom; you'll pee your pants."

"Dolores!" I poke her gently in the side with my elbow.

"Sorry." She laughs heartily—a deep, throaty laugh that bespeaks years of cigarette smoking and an affinity for dirty martinis with lots of salty olives.

Dolores isn't your typical garden club kind of gal; this is one of the many reasons I adore her. After years on the list, her name finally came to the top a few years after mine when a couple of members moved out of state. I distinctly recall Dolores's first garden club meeting because it was the start of Gloria's second term as president, and because her flamboyant fashion style made her stand out. Since coming on board a decade ago, Dolores has had almost as many ex-husbands as years of membership (okay, maybe I'm exaggerating a bit, but it's no secret this woman has horrible taste in men). She's a magnet for losers who appear to have potential.

Dolores Delacroix has been dealt more than a few bad hands, yet she's a fighter. The last divorce cleaned her out and sent her into bankruptcy, forcing her to move from the "big house" they had on Esplanade to the nine-hundred-square-foot pied-à-terre she leases in the heart of the Quarter today.

"Hey, I own my own business, have a roof over my head, running water, air-conditioning, a courtyard garden, access to a swimming pool, and some of the best gal pals in the Quarter; what more do I need, besides a good bottle of wine now and then?" she often says, the latter of which she thoroughly enjoys with abandon. She can drink like a sailor.

Dolores maintains her garden club membership mostly as a way to stay connected with clients. Unlike the majority of garden club members, Dolores works because she *has* to, not because she *wants* to. However, there is no doubt she is doing what she was born to do.

As tenderhearted as she is coarse, Dolores has made her small business a tremendous success. Beautiful Bloomers is a one-woman operation that caters specifically to French Quarter property owners. She has completed a number of master gardening educational programs and is a member of the American Horticulture Society.

"You've really outdone yourself, Dolores. This is an incomparable masterpiece. Bravo!"

The spacious rooftop patio is furnished with obviously high-end outdoor furniture that is functional and beautiful, and the lush landscape could rival any five-star luxury hotel with its mature palm trees placed symmetrically in all the corners, and colorful pots of various sizes artistically placed around each tree, filled with ivy and layered with wave petunias of rich purple and crisp white.

"Thank you. It's been quite a challenge getting everything up here." Dolores sighs. "I'm glad she's my only Jax Brewery client. They have so many damn rules for parking and hauling things through the lobby, like it's the freaking Taj Mahal or something. It's a pain in the butt. Even so, it does look pretty fabulous, if I do say so myself."

"Is Oleta pleased?"

"More than pleased. She's hired me to do her lake house—or one of them, I should say." Dolores grins and gives a thumbs-up.

"That's wonderful! Don't forget us little people on your way up, okay?"

"Never." She wraps me in a big bear hug, almost spilling her drink.

"Oops, sorry."

"You know what's crazy?" Dolores says. "I doubt she's here but a few weeks every year."

It doesn't surprise me that Oleta doesn't live here full-time; many New Orleanians have two homes, usually one in the suburbs and one in the Quarter or on the lake. There was a time when Louis and I kept two homes, one here and another on acreage in Texas, but the quantity of living space wasn't increasing the quality of our lives, so we made the decision to liquidate our Texan holdings and have never looked back. Louis and I are very content with one fabulous home that is centrally located in the Vieux Carré, on Rue Royal.

"Can't get any better than this," Louis always says.

We have the quintessential monumental view, as our wraparound balcony overlooks St. Anthony's Garden, directly behind the St. Louis Cathedral. One of the most engaging and spiritually powerful aspects of our location occurs late at night when the sun goes down and the strategically placed spotlights illuminate the huge marble statue of Jesus.

The friendly neighborhood Savior statue defines the Big Easy, as well as the rest of the state, as an image of resilience and strength in the face of adversity and obstacles. This is true particularly at night, when the lights on the statue cast an enormous silhouetted reflection of Jesus with outstretched hands on the cathedral wall. The magnified image eerily resembles a referee jubilantly announcing a game-saving touchdown to the masses who pass by.

Every night, the famous "Touchdown Jesus" looms larger than life over St. Anthony's Garden, our virtual backyard. It's a constant reminder that we are being watched over by God.

Dolores is our official groundskeeper and has been instrumental in developing and maintaining our lush potted plants and hanging baskets of plumbago and ivy. There was a time when we had real competition with St. Anthony's Garden, but Hurricane Katrina diminished that rivalry.

It was a sad day when we watched the final pruning and excavation of century-old trees in the garden from our balcony.

We would be lost without Dolores, and I know many of her Beautiful Bloomer clients feel the same way, even if they find it difficult to get beyond her edgy exterior and her raw sense of humor. Personally, I find her refreshing. You always know where you stand with Dolores Delacroix.

Dolores interrupts my reverie. "So do you know who the guest chef is?"

"No, tell me … who is it?"

"Kevin Belton."

I'm speechless at her announcement.

"He's actually quite funny; he could be a comedian. Did you know he once played professional football?" Dolores asks.

I did know that. Louis and I once attended one of his classes at the New Orleans School of Cooking. We had a great time, and he was very informative.

"How did *she* manage to get him? *He's a very busy man.*"

"I think her husband has some sort of connection with him," Dolores says. "I'm sure Gloria knows. Ask her."

I intend to do just that, as soon as she arrives.

CHAPTER 2

— Stephanie —

The space is filling up as I visit with several of the ladies and find myself wandering in and out of conversations, catching up from our summer hiatus. There are many events to attend during the summer months, so it's a good thing the garden club takes a reprieve in July and August.

I take a seat at our table, chat with Dolores and the other ladies sitting with us, and watch the activity closely.

Wow, what a crowd. Look at all the hats—look at all of these influential women. This moment really brings back memories. It seems like just yesterday I attended my first opening day and met one of my dearest friends.

Gloria, where are you? I look at my watch. She's still got a few minutes before we start.

When we first met, I was so enthralled with all the cultured and confident women, and their colorful hats, that I didn't even notice the striking woman standing right in front of me.

"Hello, my name is Gloria Vincent, what's yours?" she asked with a slight hint of a French accent.

"Stephanie Lewis." We shook hands firmly, yet warmly.

"Oh! You're Stephanie! I was so looking forward to meeting you; Gracie has said so many wonderful things about you."

Gracie was my mother's best friend who placed my name on the club waiting list when I was just a little girl, enabling me to seize this coveted place in my thirties. It's strange to say, but Mom was never a garden club member, yet Gracie always thought I should be.

"Welcome to the Garden Club," Gloria said. "I hope you enjoy your membership for years to come. Please make sure you pick up your handmade name tag. A lot of thought and love went into them."

Thought and love? Into a name tag? What have I gotten myself into?

That was almost three decades ago, but it's a memory that always makes me smile, as we became best friends almost overnight.

Gloria has served as president of the garden club a record three times. As an ancestor of Isabella Bronzinelle, one of the two founding members, her membership was guaranteed at birth, just like all the matriarchs in her family tree.

Today she owns her own business, where she presides as editor-in-chief of *NOLA 2 NOLA*, a popular bimonthly magazine that has infiltrated the world. And although she's no longer involved in daily operations, she's still on the masthead of her family's international business, Bronzinelle Steel, as the CAO, chief administrative officer. She also sits on several prestigious boards.

Gloria Bronzinelle Vincent is equal parts drive, dedication, and delight, and she has donated more time, energy, and money to French Quarter causes than anyone sitting in this room today, I imagine.

While I share in her penchant for philanthropy, I prefer the behind-the-scenes worker-bee areas of operation. I wouldn't be caught dead as the president of this (or any) club; you couldn't pay me enough, and this job is strictly volunteer!

This year we have the youngest president in the history of the club, not to mention the most unconventional. To say Elizabeth LeBlanc is somewhat of a dark horse is an understatement; she's been a garden club member for only two years and has managed to snag the presidency because of the rule that enables heirs of the founding board members the ability to independently appoint a president when a previously elected president is unable to fulfill her duties. The only person with that distinction and authority is Gloria, and I have absolutely no idea what she was thinking when Sylvia Anderson informed her at the beginning of this past summer hiatus that she would be unable to serve as president because of unexpected family circumstances, and out of the blue Gloria appointed this ditzy thirty-nine-year-old ex-cheerleader as our club president.

The entire situation has been the talk of the town for months, and folks are clearly on two sides of the fence: those who think she can handle it; and the majority of us, who know she doesn't have a snowball's chance in hell of making it. Odds have her gone before Christmas.

Gloria is also the honorary director of our executive board, a position that by nature of her ancestry and 170-year-old rules and regulations affords her incredible latitude and power. Fortunately, Gloria is very big on delegating, personal empowerment, and individual growth, so she doesn't wield that power too often.

Just then I see Gloria exit the elevator, grab a glass of champagne, and quickly scan the group who are beginning to take their seats.

"Thanks for saving my seat." Gloria drapes her Chanel bag on the back of her chair, gives me a quick hug, blows an air kiss to Dolores, and glides into the seat on my right. The scent of Creed Fleurissimo wafts around her like an expensive invisible bubble.

"Coco has been sick all morning; I didn't want to leave her," she says.

"Sick how?" I ask.

"Maybe a flu bug. I don't know. Maria is watching her, but the vet is stopping by later today."

How a ninety-pound Doberman exhibits flu symptoms is more than I want to discuss at lunch, but I can see Gloria is concerned. It doesn't surprise me that she has a vet who makes house calls, especially for her "baby."

A gift from her late husband, Charles Vincent III, Coco has been around for years. The dog is old—gray whiskers and creaky bones old. This "flu bug" thing doesn't sound good. With no children of her own, Coco is like the perfect child for Gloria's enabling parenting gene. I do love the woman, but she gives the term "control freak" a completely new meaning.

"You left her in good hands; Maria will know exactly what to do," I say.

Maria Salvador is Gloria's full-time live-in housekeeper, a gem of a woman whose Spanish ancestry in the Quarter dates back to the 1800s (and whose former job as a cocktail mixologist makes her all the more valuable). I can picture her and Randy taking care of Coco like a baby. Randy is Maria's husband, also employed full-time by Gloria as caretaker of her estate, driver, and all-around handyman. Although they've been married for ages, they still act like young kids in love; it's always sweet to see them together. Randy came to work for the Vincent family when Charles and Gloria were first married. He met and married Maria, and the duo have been an integral part of the family ever since.

"What did I miss?" Gloria says, placing the napkin in her lap.

"Not much, just the typical posturing and lots of summer Botox. Look at Tracy's lips; she looks like Daffy Duck on steroids."

Gloria glances at the woman sitting at the table next to ours.

"Oh my, that's a bit frightening." She tries not to stare.

"Welcome back to the not-so-real world. Hey, I love your hair; *tres chic*," I say.

"*Merci*. I met a fabulous hairdresser at Salon Bonaparte who didn't immediately want to cut it off—very refreshing for a change. He had a clever way of knotting and winding that I can actually replicate on my own. Does it look okay in the back?" She turns her head.

"It looks great; I'm impressed," I say.

"It doesn't make me look like a dowager empress?"

I laugh and shake my head. As if the über elegant Gloria Vincent could ever look bad.

I often see Gloria at home, where she wears her nearly waist-length hair in a thick plaited braid, or sometimes in a ponytail, which oddly enough doesn't look at all dated on a woman her age. However, when she goes out, her hair is always tied back in a classic knot or chignon updo, a trademark look that complements her Katherine Hepburn–esque style. She is one of the most no-nonsense, authentic, and attractive women I know, inside and out.

"You look wonderful, and that hat! Parisian couture, no doubt?" I admire her fabulous accessory.

"*Oui oui*, madame. You like?" She tilts her head.

"It's stunning. Just like everything else today, especially these appetizers." I pick up the small silver tray of delicate pastry puffs. "Try one of these and tell me if you recognize the spice; I can't figure it out."

"I think I'll pass; I'm not very hungry right now." She turns up her nose.

"Don't worry about Coco," I say, "I'm sure she'll be fine. She was just excited to see you after a week's absence, that's all." I put the tray back down, but not before popping one more of the delicacies into my mouth. "So did you have time for shopping on the Champs-Elysees? Find anything worthwhile besides your new hat?"

We all have our hobbies. I love French Quarter history, specifically that which is documented about history-making French Quarter women. Dolores has her plants; my husband, Louis, has his cooking and guitars; and Gloria is an ardent collector of antiques—very expensive antiques. She has a fortune in priceless art and antiquities in her home, and she acquires new pieces on virtually every trip.

Just a few streets over from my place, Vincent Manor is one of the grand homes on Esplanade that people drive by and point at from their car windows. A breathtaking mansion that for over a century was known as the Bronzinelle Estate, it has been in Gloria's family for generations and comprises a main house, guesthouse, carriage house, slave quarters, and some ancillary smaller buildings that are used to store garden tools and such. The home is listed as a national historic landmark, and some of her antiques are even older than the house.

"I didn't stop in a single antique store this time; too much work to do. So how is our fearless leader faring?" She asks.

The fact that Gloria refers to Elizabeth as a leader confounds me. As for "fearless," that's even more mind-boggling.

"Just peachy." I take a sip of my mimosa and motion for another. "Tweety bird is over there," I nod toward the only woman standing.

Flitting among the group like an annoying fly, she is wearing impossibly high Christian Louboutin heels and a delicate canary-yellow rhinestone-and-feather fascinator hat. The first thing one notices about Elizabeth LeBlanc is her teensy tiny waist, above which sits the most expensive pair of flotation devices this side of the Mississippi—a fact well documented in a recent article about her husband in *GQ Magazine*.

Married to Jake LeBlanc, a kicker for the New Orleans Saints, Elizabeth is part of the new breed of "power couples," and she's the epitome of nouveau-riche chic. He's sport-star handsome, and she's Hollywood gorgeous. Her trademark violet eyes are immediately distinctive and disarming, and she's got long, thick, chestnut-colored hair, creamy olive-tone skin, and more money than sense. She's from new money in Atlanta; her family owns a fleet of garbage trucks or something to do with waste management. Her husband has made millions kicking a ball. Personally, I think she virtually bought her way into the club two years ago. Gloria calls her voluptuous; I call her vacuous. She's the proverbial bad apple spoiling our bunch.

It's no secret Elizabeth LeBlanc rubs me the wrong way, but she's like forty-grit sandpaper to Dolores. To say they don't get along is an understatement. Keep them apart or sparks will fly.

Elizabeth was responsible for the loss of one of Dolores's key clients. The fact that she even has the nerve to show her face here, let alone serve as president, is most decidedly a burr under Dolores's saddle.

Gloria is unusually quiet as everyone chitchats at our table, but it's understandable considering the circumstances with Coco. I hope her dog is going to be okay.

I'm looking around with relish at all the smart, savvy, and sassy women in attendance, and making mental notes of their outfits and wondering if Francis Doyle, like Tracy, got her lips done this past summer—*They seem plumper*—when I'm startled by Dolores, who leans over to whisper in my ear.

"Have you seen Lady McBitch's new Louis Vuitton handbag? Word has it she spent close to nine thousand on it."

"Seriously?" I give her arm a slap and scold her for using the private nickname we have given to our president. I try not to stare at the bag covered with the legendary LV monogram sitting on the floor under Elizabeth's chair. "I believe that qualifies as luggage; you could smuggle a small child in that," I say.

How can someone spend that kind of money on a purse? I think everyone should be able to buy what they want, what they can afford. I'm far from a socialist, but I do have an issue with that kind of extravagance.

Dolores is filling me in on more of the juicy gossip surrounding Elizabeth when Gloria is unable to contain herself and interrupts.

"Ladies, play nice," she admonishes, and then she reaches for one of the floral three-ring binders in the center of the table.

I love my friend, but I hate it when she acts so righteous.

"Ooh-la-la, very fancy." She swoons. "She's made quite a first impression," Gloria says as she pages through the notebook.

I've already reviewed this year's notebook, and it's all I can do not to scoff at Gloria's misdirected admiration.

"I see you don't agree." Gloria takes a sip of her champagne while turning the pages. "Your displeasure is showing like a bad haircut, Stevie. It's very unbecoming."

Gloria is the only friend I have who uses the nickname given to me by my husband when we met at a Fleetwood Mac concert years ago.

"You remind me of Stevie Nicks," Louis said, "but prettier."

He's always been a man of few words.

Decades later, I'm still Stevie in his eyes.

"I'm not displeased, Gloria," I say, "I'm just being cautious. There's something about her I don't trust. Something isn't right. I can't believe you don't see it."

"What I see is someone who has done a great deal of work and should be commended," Gloria declares. "I predict this is going to be a monumental year!"

The September meeting is the formal unveiling of our season outline for the next ten months. The new incoming president spends the summer months lining up all the locations, speakers, and menus for the coming year, and it's her sole responsibility to get everything printed for these annual garden club notebooks, which are distributed at this ceremonial first meeting. Yes, Elizabeth's notebooks are quite fancy, I'll grant you that; but everyone knows you can't judge a book by its cover.

Although I hate to admit it, I have to agree that it appears our new president has done an outstanding job on the upcoming season, at least on paper. I do suppose landing this prime location for opening day is commendable, plus she did manage to get Chef Kevin to be our speaker today.

"Look who she's managed to get for February." Gloria taps the page. "John Besh."

"I know, I know, but I'll believe it when I see it."

John Besh is a very famous chef and the owner of several fabulous restaurants in New Orleans.

"Why so cynical, *mon chéri?*" Gloria asks.

"I'm not being cynical, just realistic."

"I see. Well, considering she accepted the position only two months ago, I say she's done a superb job, and I think this notebook looks wonderful." Gloria's tone is decidedly succinct as she continues. "Elizabeth asked my advice on printing options, and I connected her with one of our vendors. I like her initiative, the garden club needs fresh blood."

"What are we, vampires?" I joke.

"Very funny, but that is possible, considering how stuck in time this group is. We need some modern ideas; we need some change." She shakes her head and reaches for an appetizer.

"Earth to Gloria." I wave my hand in front of her face. "We're not about changing the world; we're about keeping the Quarter beautiful and preserving the history of a community. We're a venerable social institution, like the Fraternal Order of the Masons," I declare.

"You do know that the Masons have been solidly involved in philanthropic endeavors for ages, and that's hardly the case with us, Stevie. It's not like the garden club is really doing anything significantly life-changing." Gloria leans back in her chair and sighs.

"That's not true! We're keeping the Quarter beautiful one garden, one balcony, one courtyard at a time," I say. "That's our job, that's why we exist, plain and simple. We have centuries of tradition and core values that must remain intact. And don't forget our cookbook. It's preserving recipes for generations to come!"

The fact is, one of my favorite reasons for belonging to the garden club is that I love collecting recipes (and Louis loves cooking, so it's a partnership made in heaven). Throughout the year, a person selected by the president at the start of her term collects recipes from members, and at the end of the year she compiles them into one collection, and we print and sell the book to our members. It's the official *Annual Garden Club Cookbook*, and it's our only fund-raising venture for the club. The money raised is used for our annual Christmas party held in lieu of our meeting in December.

Gloria's next comment jerks me back to reality; it shouldn't surprise me, but it does.

"Our cookbook is usually seen only by the women in this room, and maybe a few of their family members. That's hardly mass-distribution, Stevie." Gloria reaches into her handbag for a tube of Elizabeth Arden lipstick in Luscious Flame and, without using a mirror, applies it perfectly. "What we do is hardly a fund-raising effort, as we barely break even on costs every year."

"We're not *The Joy of Cooking*, Gloria."

"Well, you've got that right; we're not a lot of things."

"What's that supposed to mean?" I ask.

"All I'm saying is that we're not taking advantage of the opportunity to do more, to be more," she sighs. Her frustration is palpable, although I don't fully agree with it.

Coming from the owner/editor of a ritzy lifestyle magazine, it's not unexpected that Gloria would want our cookbook to be more than what it is. But it is what it is. The fact is, she can't control everything, and she's not always right. Gloria has great ideas; she's a born leader and exudes confidence. But she's often bossy, impatient, demanding, and, yes, sometimes irritatingly opinionated. But I'll get over it, because truth be told, I love her like the sister I never had. In fact, this entire group is like family to me; they are my roots.

I spend two days a week volunteering at the Williams Research Center for the Historic New Orleans Collection. Louis and I are Bienville Circle members and are large supporters of the organization. It was there I first began to learn about Gloria's ancestors.

Gloria's roots are well documented from the late 1700s. She is a descendant of the Bronzinelle and Medina families, making her somewhat royalty in the Quarter.

As I've gotten older, not old, I have come to realize how important friendships are and how they can affect our lives in so many ways. Women need women, plain and simple.

Gloria and I were born in the same year, Gloria being the eldest by a few months. We are both only-children. However, I have Louis, two great kids, and two equally wonderful grandchildren. Coco and her magazine are her children, and along with Maria and Randy, the ladies of the garden club are her family. I would do just about anything for Gloria Vincent, and I know she feels the same way about me.

Let's just pretend we are vampires, since there are so many in New Orleans, and you can give only one person eternal life. Who will it be? A child, a husband, or a best friend?

Hmm, that might be a harder question to answer than you think. Anyway, I'm not a vampire, although I think my sister-in-law could be, but that's another story. What I'm saying is that women understand each other. We understand love in all its forms, from the respectful love for our parents, to the endearing love for a husband, to the unconditional love for a child.

Sitting here on opening day of the garden club with some of my best friends, I feel the warmth of love. I am so blessed to have these wonderful women in my life. I know without a shadow of a doubt most of them would be there in a heartbeat if I needed them, and vice versa. They are true friends, soul mates. I think this is why the fifty-member rule has held up for centuries. We are family—a delightful, dysfunctional, and dependable family.

Chances are we'll have our share of high drama with Elizabeth as president. If her notebook is any indication, she has a lot of changes planned for the club, and that won't bode well for her longevity. Perhaps Gloria will agree to step in when Elizabeth is asked to leave, something I predict will happen sooner rather than later.

Instead of responding to Gloria's comment about "doing more and being more," I figure maybe it's best to change the subject.

"Are you up for a little afternoon delight tomorrow?" I lean close to Gloria and seductively bat my eyelashes, which makes her laugh. "Louis will be back by tonight; we can make it a threesome."

"That sounds tempting." Gloria smiles and reaches for her water. "I'm always ready for a date with you and your darling, but I have to pass this time; I've got a stack of papers I must address from my trip."

For many of us in the Quarter, "afternoon delight" is not to be interpreted as a roll in the proverbial hay before returning to the office; it's a special time of fellowship we fondly refer to as "drunch." Drunch in the Quarter is a historic event. Contrary to urban legend that it is merely a late-morning or early afternoon meal where folks have an excuse to gather at a local hotspot to consume more alcohol than food, in the Quarter drunch is an institution and is seen as a precursor to a dinner, most specifically on Friday afternoon. While it's true that some may experience their afternoon delight in a plush hotel suite, we most often prefer ours at Galatoire's, one of the most famous culinary destinations in the Vieux Carré.

Thanks to the mirrored walls, you never have a bad seat for people-watching. The grand room, also known as the gymnasium, meshes celebrities and locals together as if they were relatives. The food is exquisite, served as though it comes from a revolving-door kitchen, continuously, and never disappoints. Despite the worst acoustics of any restaurant known to mankind, Galatoire's offers a meal and experience not soon forgotten. Everyone is family when they dine at Galatoire's. One of the Galatoire family members is a good friend and often provides us with special family recipes for our coveted annual cookbook.

I wonder what our annual cookbook will look like this year, with Miss Ra-Ra at the helm.

Ding-dink-ding, ding-dink-ding. The familiar sound of our infamous broken bell calls us to attention. Despite all the wealth in this room, no one has ever replaced it. Everyone stops talking as a reverent hush falls over the patio.

Then, in a sweet, soft British accent we hear "Good morning, ladies. Welcome to the opening day of the Fleur-de-Lis Ladies Garden Club of the French Quarter. The meeting will now come to order."

Miss Alma Stokes has called to order every meeting of the garden club for the past two decades, and her opening spiel is one of the few times the club is ever referred to by its formal name. I listen carefully as she introduces our new leader.

When I lean forward to prepare for Elizabeth's opening speech, I find myself gaping with incredulity. "Oh my God! Do not tell me she is about to lead us in a cheer."

My voice is louder than I intended. No sooner are the words out of my mouth than, after being introduced, our new club president launches into a combination hip-hop song, rap, and some sort of bizarre collegiate cheer. We will learn later that it's a poem she wrote just for the club, but right now it's just ridiculous.

"What a spectacle! Is she serious?" I say, looking around the room to see a mixture of horror and delight on the faces of the other women.

Now I know this woman won't make it past Christmas. In fact, I give her until Thanksgiving. This behavior is way out of line. Her husband might make a living kicking a ball around a field and pushing people around in life, but we won't put up with it. There's far too much tradition here to tamper with. Some things are better left unchanged, and the

Fleur-de-Lis Ladies Garden Club of the French Quarter is one of those things. Then I notice Gloria is laughing.

"You think this is funny? Seriously?" I ask.

"I think she's got gumption. Look around, Stevie; we look like an audience from an old Ed Sullivan show. We need more spitfires like Elizabeth LeBlanc," Gloria staunchly says. "She is just what the doctor ordered."

I'm speechless as this pathetic excuse for a club president finishes making an absolute fool of herself and Gloria leads in the smattering of applause.

"Whose side are you on?" I ask.

"Didn't know there was a war." Gloria pats my leg lovingly.

CHAPTER 3

— Gloria —

Friday, September 10

"Would you care for another?"

Maria startles me as she picks up the empty champagne flute from the Chippendale side table on my left.

"I don't know; how many have I had?" I remove my reading glasses, allowing them to dangle around my neck on a beautiful Swarovski crystal chain Stevie gave me for my birthday a few years ago.

"Only one, Miss Gloria"—Maria smiles—"and I mixed it with a lot of orange juice."

"Okay, one more, but that's it."

"Will you be attending drunch today with Dr. Lewis and Miss Stephanie?" Maria asks.

It was difficult not to accept Stevie's invitation yesterday, but having been out of the country for over a week, I just couldn't spend today eating and drinking, no matter how much I love doing just that.

"Not today. I've decided to stay in and attack this mountain of paperwork from my meetings in Paris. I'd rather not start next week with all this still on my plate," I tap the inch-thick file on my lap. "In fact, I really should take this work up to my office, but I do love the den this time of day."

Maria nods. "*Si*. I agree. It is a lovely room."

I look at the Louis XVI clock on the mantel and realize Stevie and Louis are most likely sitting at Galatoire's now, and I smile. Socializing and party throwing are significant aspects of their life as a couple, and they are so much fun to be around. Their relationship road is hardly without bumps, but they've stayed the course; and like a bottle of fine Bordeaux, they keep getting better with age, as does their reputation for being one of the premiere host-and-hostess couples in the Quarter.

The fact is, Stevie hates to be alone, while I, on the other hand, long for stretches of solitude that are almost impossible for me to achieve, especially with my responsibilities on the advisory boards of three organizations and with the increasing success of *NOLA 2 NOLA*.

When Charles died, I thought a part of me died, and back then self-induced solitude was the only way I could survive the loss, loneliness, and longing for my one true love. Keeping his memory and our time together alive was my sole focus for months, until I felt a calling to launch the magazine.

It wasn't like I had an actual visit from God, nothing quite as spiritually significant as that, yet I can recall the day as if it were yesterday. Something in my spirit told me that while it was perfectly acceptable and understandable to mourn my husband, I couldn't continue to mourn forever. I couldn't shut myself off from the world.

And so I stopped.

However, I never stopped loving my sweet Charles.

Today what began as a self-published newsletter thirteen years ago has mushroomed into a multimillion-dollar business and the entire second floor of my historic home now comprises the *NOLA 2 NOLA* editorial offices and production space.

All in all, the entire publishing enterprise has been a phenomenal success. We recently celebrated two hundred thousand subscribers to our hard-copy edition, with numbers climbing for the online version. Last year we launched a French edition that took off like lightning, far exceeding our expectations.

Not bad for someone who didn't know a thing about magazine publishing and distribution when she began.

Thank you, Charles, for watching out for me down here.

Maria returns with a fresh mimosa, a tray of pastries and fruit, and a special dog treat biscuit for Coco, who is feeling much better today but nonetheless barely moves from her plush doggie bed next to my chair. When I returned from the meeting yesterday, Maria was excited to inform me that Coco was feeling better and the vet couldn't find anything wrong.

"I am so blessed to have you in my life, Maria; thank you for taking such good care of Coco and me." I put my arms out to give her a hug.

"Someone has to, Miss Gloria." She takes my hands in hers. "You work too hard; you need to relax."

"Thank you, Maria, but there's such so much to do with work and at home. I have a to-do list a mile long. Perhaps this weekend you can take my fall and winter clothes out of storage and move them to my master closet?"

"Of course." She takes a soft chamois out of her smock pocket and begins to dust the furniture. Maria seldom stands still.

"Where do you suggest I hang them?" she asks. "I suppose I could use the curtain rod ..."

"Very funny," I say. However, Maria isn't laughing. She stops dusting, crosses her arms, and gives me "the look," which makes me feel like a little girl being scolded.

Maria has been after me for weeks to address the situation in my closet.

The truth is I've lost a little weight and some of my clothes have subsequently lost their ability to fit properly. This past summer when I got tired of strategically positioning safety pins, notching my belts tighter, and at one point actually using duct tape to secure the inside seam of a Chanel jacket I desperately wanted to wear, I finally broke down and began to buy clothing in a smaller size.

Now rods are crammed, stacks of garments line the floor, and my shelves are starting to resemble the aftermath of a sale at Nordstrom Rack. I'm usually very organized, as is Maria, but this is one area I can't seem to get a handle on.

A couple months ago I got all hyped up to go through every closet and drawer in my master suite, including the overflow in the two adjoining guest bedrooms, but no matter how hard I tried, I never managed to get to it.

However, the bottom line is that here we are, several months later, and I have even more of a mess in my closet than I did then.

"Okay, you win; let's get this done!" I throw my hands in the air in surrender, grabbing my file just in time before it falls off my lap. "Why don't you start by putting a few of those clothing donation bags in my room, the ones the shelter provides, and maybe that will motivate me. I promise, cross my heart, I will work on it this weekend."

"Yes, ma'am, I will do that. Speaking of the shelter, I believe someone called while you were gone. I think it is something about the silent auction. Charlotte left a message on your desk."

Charlotte is my full-time assistant at *NOLA 2 NOLA*, and without her and Maria, my life would be unmanageable.

"Yes, I saw that. The auction committee is getting a head start on acquiring items for next year's gala. I'm thinking of donating the sideboard; it doesn't quite fit since we got the new dining room set."

Hardly new, the mahogany table is a rare eighteenth-century Georgian accordion table, extended to its full ninety-five-inch length, with twelve ornately carved mahogany chairs. It was a spectacular find at Ida Manheim Antiques on Royal Street, one of the premier antique shops in the French Quarter.

"That would be a very generous donation," Maria says.

"It is a rather unusual item for the silent auction, but a few more donations like it will help us raise enough funds to rent bigger office space."

"Are they still working at that tiny place next to the Bottom of the Cup Tearoom on Chartres Street?" Maria asks as she continues to dust and straighten things up.

"Unfortunately, yes, and it's beginning to wear on Emme, bless her heart."

Emme Masterson is the executive director for Grace House, a nonprofit organization that started with one transitional living home for women in the Quarter and now includes four separate homes. I have been an advisory board member since the organization began.

With the capacity to meet the needs of forty single women with or without children, Grace Houses are more than places of refuge for women and children struggling through difficult circumstances. They are places where futures are born and dreams are realized; places where women learn the skills needed to support themselves and gain the self-confidence and self-respect that are critical aspects of transitioning into their own apartments or homes.

Residents are accepted into the program only after a rigorous interview process and can stay at no cost for a full year, during which they actively participate in what is called Grace Camp, a.k.a. boot camp for life.

There is always a waiting list, which prompted the board to adopt a more aggressive development strategy, starting with moving the administrative team off-site, which opened room for six additional residents. This provided Emme the space she needed to develop and implement many of the fund-raising efforts that have enabled the organization to grow.

The office space is less than ideal, and we need to raise a lot of money to move the administrative operations elsewhere.

This sideboard donation could play a significant part in raising funds at the silent auction.

"Maria, would you ask Charlotte to call Ms. Masterson to let her know we'll have Phillip photograph the sideboard, and to also remind me to get the insurance appraisal from the safe. Let's hit the ground running and set the tone for next year's auction."

"Consider it done." Maria jots a note on a little pad of paper that she always keeps on hand.

"Let's see if we can double the amount raised at the last gala," I say.

"From your mouth to God's ears." Maria grins. "If that is all, Miss Gloria, I am going to work in the kitchen now. Can I get you anything else?"

"I think I'm good; thank you, Maria."

Before leaving, she stops by my chair.

"Miss Gloria, I worry that you are doing too much. You always tell me there are only so many hours in a day; we all have the same: twenty-four."

She smiles and pats me warmly on the shoulder as she leaves the room.

CHAPTER 4

— Gloria —

I'm not sure how long Maria has been gone, but even in the focused silence I don't seem to be making any headway on the papers in my lap. Brushing away the crumbs that have fallen on one of the pages, I realize it seems as though I've read the last paragraph several times. Just then, Maria returns.

"Miss Elizabeth is here to see you."

I thought I heard the bell. "Elizabeth LeBlanc?"

Maria nods affirmatively.

Hmm, Elizabeth LeBlanc, on a Friday afternoon, uninvited and unexpected. This could be interesting. "Please show her in, but take these with you." I hand her the tray of pastries and fruit. "And can you let Coco out?"

Without much prompting, Coco follows Maria out of the room.

I set down my papers just as Maria escorts Elizabeth into the room.

Every time I see her, I'm still stunned by Elizabeth LeBlanc's beauty. Other than her well-documented breast implants, a fact unfortunately made public by an overambitious docujournalist, her breathtaking beauty is natural and untouched by human hands. She's the French Quarter equivalent to a young Elizabeth Taylor. Most people see her as one of those sultry, sophisticated, and sexy women who make history by marrying a famous athlete; however, she is much more than that. The fact she graduated summa cum laude and is the descendant of one of the founding members of Mensa is not something she promotes or the press pursues. While others may see her as aloof, I've always seen the gears in her brain working overtime.

Her natural beauty is only surpassed by her heartfelt desire to make a difference in our garden club, especially as the youngest president in the club's history. I'm aware the majority of the garden club doesn't take kindly to her, but I appreciate her commitment and zeal. She is greatly needed, even if many of my garden club sisters aren't yet aware of that fact. She's been an active volunteer at Grace House for years and is one of our best advisory committee members.

As the wife of a well-known sports star, she must always be aware of how she looks in public—a burden that she carries with aplomb and sensibility, as she is also the mother of four very active teenagers: Michael, seventeen; Michelle, fifteen; and twins Mariann and Marissa, thirteen.

"What a pleasant surprise," I say as Elizabeth greets me warmly with a hug and a European kiss on each cheek.

"I'm so sorry to drop by unannounced, but I drove by and there was an empty parking place in front of your house, and I found myself pulling in. I sat in my car and tried calling you on my cell phone, but your voice mail picked up. Is there any chance you have a few minutes to talk? I know you just got back in the country; if this is an inconvenience, we can make it another day."

"This is perfect timing; I was giving myself excuses for not getting to work. I've got so much to do, but for some reason I just can't seem to get myself started. Would you care for a mimosa?"

"No thanks, I've got a ton of errands to run this afternoon; probably shouldn't drink and drive. Are you sure I'm not interrupting?"

"Not at all." I shake my head to Maria, who has waited quietly outside the door to see if she would be needed.

"So what brings you by?"

"I was wondering what you thought of the meeting yesterday—what the ladies thought of the program, what you thought of the program. Was it—was I—okay?" She twists a lovely ruby ring on her pinky finger and bites her bottom lip.

This type of leadership position is new for Elizabeth. Her husband is out of town the majority of the time, between training camp and games, and now that her children are older and Michael is driving, she has found herself with more available time to devote to her own hobbies and passions, of which gardening is one. She shares my thinking that the garden club could be so much more, and I was thrilled when she agreed to step in as president, especially on such short notice.

"You did a wonderful job. Your notebook was the crème de la crème. The best I've seen. Chef Kevin was fabulous! His demonstration of using fresh herbs was inspiring. The location was over the top, and I got several calls yesterday about how wonderful everything was. The food, program, everything."

I didn't have the heart to tell her how upset Stevie had been, especially about the almond tea, or that our conversation after the meeting yesterday was filled with anything but compliments.

I can still hear Stevie complaining. "Come home with me and I'll serve you a real glass of tea!" Stevie said to me yesterday as the garden club meeting adjourned. "Can you believe she had the gall to bring special attention to that concoction by complimenting Phyllis on the almond tea she brought, when it was completely made with instant everything? Instant tea, Crystal Light, and God knows what other artificial ingredients. I was so embarrassed."

"Stevie, please, Elizabeth is young, and I think she did a very good job for her first meeting."

"Are you serious? Opening with a college cheer. And thirty-nine is hardly young. Why do you keep making excuses for her?"

"Why do you keep crucifying her?"

"I'm hardly crucifying her. I'm just calling it as I see it, and I see an accident waiting to happen. I suppose we should just give her enough rope and sit back to watch her hang herself with it."

"That's very kind of you, Stephanie, very nurturing."

"Give me a break; I'm not Mother Teresa."

"No, you're not. But you could be a tad more supportive; she could learn a lot from you."

"I highly doubt that. She thinks she knows everything already. What's to learn?"

We ended our somewhat tense conversation about Elizabeth's first day with one of Stevie's typical eye-rolling "whatever" declarations.

I'm not sure why Stevie has such disdain for this young woman who is now sitting across from me in my den, but I do know she would be less than happy to find Elizabeth asking my opinion of her first day as president of the garden club.

I smile just a little as I think about it.

"Do you really think everything went well?" she practically whispers.

"You did an excellent job, dear."

"Thank you, Gloria; that means a lot coming from you. I can't believe I'm actually president." She reaches for my hand. "You are the reason I'm here. Thank you."

"No no, dear. You are the reason you are here. This coming year is going to be exhilarating, and I for one can't wait to see what's going to happen. You are a very capable and creative young woman."

"Not so young, I'm afraid." She looks down at her shoes. "Jake called me his 'Old Lady' the other day." She laughs without smiling.

"Surely he was joking."

"No, I don't think so."

It makes me sad that someone so beautiful and blessed could judge herself so harshly, especially on a callous comment made by her equally callous cad of a husband—an opinion I keep to myself. I've never actually met the man, but several of my editors have worked on photo shoots with him, and word has it that he's a player on more than the ball field. Who knows if it's actually true, but I've seen him at several press junkets, and I wasn't impressed. For her sake, I hope I'm wrong.

Suddenly I find myself in one of those rare moments where you know exactly what to say.

"Elizabeth, up until the day she died, my mother had a penchant, a passion, for quoting memorable women. She had a steel-trap brain, an amazing memory. I wish I could say I inherited that gift, but unfortunately that is not the case. However, there are many words of wisdom she frequently repeated that I have no doubt changed the way I approached my life. She often quoted First Lady Eleanor Roosevelt, who said, 'Remember that no one can make you feel inferior without your consent.' I remember looking up the word 'inferior,' and I didn't like it, so I decided I was never going to feel that way."

"Is it that easy?" Elizabeth asks quietly.

"It's never too late to change your mind and your choices."

I can see that this bright, beautiful, and bold woman is fighting back tears, and I reach out to take her clasped hands in mine.

"Elizabeth, may I be frank with you?" I ask quietly.

"Of course." She raises her perfectly arched eyebrows.

"There has never been a doubt in my mind that you are going to do amazing things in your life. I felt that from the moment I met you, and it has nothing whatsoever to do with how you look, what you wear, or who you're married to."

Tears spill from her eyes, and she quickly wipes them away.

"Sweetie, I'm not sure what is going on in your life, but I want you to know that I believe in you and in your dreams, whatever they may be."

She excuses herself to go to the powder room, and although a small part of me hopes I haven't said too much, a larger part feels confident in having spoken up. There seem to be more and more young women these days who don't appear to have older women role models in their lives, whether mothers, grandmothers, aunts, or even mothers-in-law.

My mother believed that women must always encourage one another because there are enough negative forces at work to discourage and defeat them. I've tried to do that in all my friendships. I hope I can help in some small way to encourage Elizabeth to embrace her potential; she has so much to offer.

Elizabeth returns from the powder room wearing a smile, fresh lipstick, and a determined look in her eyes as she sits down across from me.

"I have something important I'd like to ask you," she says as she pulls some folded papers from her large purse. "This is really why I wanted to talk with you."

"Yes?"

"These are the garden club rules and regulations you gave me when I started. I've been reading them, along with reviewing archive registration and attendance rosters for the past several years, and it seems there is a problem. Two problems, actually."

"What might those be?" I ask.

"Well, the first problem is that archival information about the garden club is all over the place, and very few documents include dates. I was surprised that a group of this significance and longevity doesn't have one central repository where archived material, such as meeting minutes, cookbooks, membership rosters, financial data, and such, is stored." She shakes her head in amazement. "Do you have any idea where I might find past documentation?" She tilts her head.

"I think I may still have a couple of file boxes in the storage closet;

I'll have Randy get them to you. And I can give you the names of a few women who might have old documentation."

"That's great." Elizabeth looks pleased. "I think it's important to collect as much information as we have, and then to develop some standard practices for document revisions. We also need a database to catalog members, recipes, and meeting locations. There's a lot that needs to be done from an administrative perspective to bring us into the current century, and I'm prepared to get the ball rolling." She leans forward and takes a deep breath. "However, the problem I think we need to address now is that our official rules and regulations state that when members miss three or more meetings over the course of a year without documented excused absences, their membership is revoked. It seems there are several women, most specifically two members, who have consistently broken that rule for the past few years. In fact, the last written documentation for excused absences was during your last term as president." She shows me a photocopy of one of my notes. "How do you think I should handle this?" she asks.

Well, well, well. She wants to actually enforce the rules, what a novel idea! I'm flattered she has sought my counsel, but I wonder what she has in mind.

"Sweetie, how do *you* think you should handle it? And tell me why you think it should be handled at all."

When Maria shows Elizabeth out over two hours later, I have to admit I'm even more impressed by the level of commitment and professionalism this woman demonstrates, and I can hardly wait for our members to see her leadership skills at the October meeting.

CHAPTER 5

— Stephanie —

Thursday, October 14

We still have over a month until the end of hurricane season, but I do believe the weather is already starting to change. The cool spells are becoming more frequent. Today I'm wearing my irreverent pin that says "Practice Safe Hex," as it's almost Halloween, a very special occasion in the Quarter.

It is an easy walk from my place to Muriel's Restaurant. Elizabeth certainly has my approval on this meeting location. Great food, and a perfect place for people-watching. This historic building is one of my favorites, for the rich colors on the interior as well as the exterior. With a stunning 140-foot wraparound balcony, it's the only public balcony overlooking historic Jackson Square. Today's weather is perfect for diners on the first floor to enjoy the sounds on the street with the large glass double doors open to the sidewalks on Chartres Street.

As I enter the side door on Chartres, I pass the ever-present table for one, set daily with food and wine for the house ghost. The story has it that Pierre Antoine Lepardi Jourdan renovated this as his dream house, and after losing it in a poker game, the realization of what he had done was too much to bear and he committed suicide. It is believed that his ghost lives on in the beloved house, and keeping the table set fresh every single day is part of the rich fabric of history that surrounds Muriel's Restaurant.

"Right this way," the hostess says, and she leads me to the base of a winding staircase. "It's the room on your right at the top," she says, pointing. I don't blame her for not leading the way, especially in three-inch heels.

"Thank you." I take a deep breath and start the climb. No matter how many times I've ascended this staircase, I'm never prepared for how many stairs there actually are. It's like hiking up Mount Everest. Okay, maybe that's a bit dramatic, but you get my drift.

"Oh my God, how many steps are there? I'm getting too old for this," I say aloud. Some of the ladies following behind laugh and agree.

As I reach the top of the staircase, I can see our "Welcome to the Garden Club" sign sitting on a tabletop easel on the sign-in table set up just inside the beautiful Cotillion Room. Before I join the masses already assembling, I take a quick peek into the adjoining Séance Room to see if Gloria is there, which she isn't. I type her a speedy text message and hit send.

> Should have called you before I left the house, at Muriel's now, will save you a seat.

As I sign in and reach for my name tag, Miss V. greets me warmly with a hug and whispers in my ear.

"Welcome, my dear. Guess what? They are serving puppy drum today!"

"Yum, I was hoping that would be on our menu; you know it's my favorite."

"Yes, I know, that's why I wanted to share the news with you. But don't tell anyone I snitched; you know the menu is always a surprise."

"My lips are sealed." I pull an invisible zipper across my lips, but my mouth is starting to water in anticipation of the lunch. Pecan-crusted puppy drum is one of Muriel's signature dishes and is the best fish in town.

After securing my hand-decorated nametag, I look up to see crazy Dolores waving from across the room, wearing a big black witch hat.

"Shouldn't Elizabeth be wearing that?" I ask as I greet her.

Dolores looks at me with mock surprise, her eyes wide as she feigns horror, "Oh my! shame on you," she says; she then gives me a devilish smile. "What, no Gloria?" she asks, glancing over my shoulder.

"Not yet."

"That's okay, I've saved two seats."

Dolores has become our go-to gal for seat saving, and I love it.

"Thanks." I slip into a chair and reach inside my purse for my lip balm and whisk it quickly across my chapped lips, at the same time taking in the grand and richly decorated room. It has been freshly painted in a deep, luxurious cranberry, with crisp white wainscoting and gold accents.

"Gloria is going to love this new wall color," I say, and I take a delicate cucumber sandwich appetizer from a silver tray on the table. "Excellent!"

"It's white bread, cucumber, and cream cheese, for crying out loud," Dolores says. "Kind of hard for anyone to mess that up."

"My, my, isn't someone testy today?" I tease.

"Don't ask," she says, her eyes throwing daggers at Elizabeth. "Look at her; she's got something up her sleeve. I can feel it."

She doesn't seem any different to me.

As starting time nears, I see ladies begin to reach inside their handbags and jacket pockets to turn off their cell phones.

We have an unwritten rule in the garden club that technology of any kind is off-limits during our luncheon meetings. That means we do not use cell phones, notebooks, iPads, or any other newfangled communication devices that may come down the pipe. Members of the garden club have made a solemn promise to be fully present in the moment from the moment the starting bell rings; no ancillary activities are permitted.

However, that doesn't include Mabel Ingersoll, who is sitting nearby, oblivious to the activity around her. Mabel is one of our older members and is almost completely deaf. She is an absolute joy who is beloved by virtually everyone, and she has been given special dispensation to keep quietly occupied with her embroidery during our meetings. However, she is no ordinary needleworker. In her day, Mabel was the founder and president of one of the foremost cross-stitching guilds in the country. Mabel Ingersoll's counted cross-stitch needlework hangs in some of the most prestigious museums and private collections all around the world. To watch her fingers in action is like watching da Vinci paint a masterpiece.

We have members who are accomplished women from many fields: the arts, health care, business, politics. Of course there are also the original "women behind the men," who have been responsible for maintaining a lifestyle and legacy for their family for years.

Although there is no age minimum listed in our rules and regulations, the structure for how new members are inducted into the organization generally precludes that young women will join the ranks, simply because of how many names are in front of theirs on the list. This is a structure that I, for one, wholeheartedly agree with.

It seems as though I have just arrived when Alma starts ringing the bell. *Ding-dink-ding, ding-dink-ding.*

A quick call to order sends members scrambling to their seats, and still no Gloria.

Though she is usually one of the first in attendance, this is the second month in a row Gloria has been late; she's typically waiting for me. I make a mental note that I'm going to have to get on her case about this. After all, she's the one who taught me to treat these garden club meetings with great reverence and respect.

Just as everyone gets settled, Elizabeth takes to the podium and in a rather cocky tone says, "Good morning, ladies. Welcome to the garden club, and to Muriel's Restaurant."

"We all know where we're at; give me a break," I whisper to Dolores, who nods in agreement as Elizabeth pauses to take a sip of water from a nearby crystal goblet. "Oh, that's not a good sign. She hasn't said more than one sentence and already needs water." I settle back, cross my legs, and reach for another appetizer. "This could be a long lunch."

Elizabeth takes a deep breath and continues her welcome. "For our first order of business, I'd like to introduce three new garden club members."

What the heck?

I almost choke on the bruschetta, and the surprise is palpable as members collectively gasp and begin to crane their necks to more carefully peruse the tables for who is missing, just as three very stylish women are escorted into the room.

"How did this happen?" someone at our table whispers.

"Where does she get off bringing in new members without an election?" another person from a nearby table asks.

"How could she let three members quit?" I say, unconcerned about my volume.

I assume that for those who were on the fence about Elizabeth being president, this should send a clear signal that she needs to go. This announcement has more than a few heads spinning when Alma leans over from the table behind me to speak.

"They didn't quit, my dear; she kicked them out."

"Why? How? When?" I stammer.

"They broke the rules," Alma says matter-of-factly.

"Which rules?" I ask.

"Linda didn't pay her dues on time, Anne missed too many meetings without a valid excuse, and Tracy left in protest to kicking out her best friend."

"I can't believe it!" Clearly I'm not alone in my shock.

"Ladies, ladies," Elizabeth continues, "I understand your surprise. However, I'm sure you'll agree that maintaining the integrity of our group structure is paramount, which is why our founding sisters developed the rules and regulations we follow today. Rest assured our executive board deliberated carefully, and these changes were implemented with the utmost discretion and sensitivity."

"Discretion and sensitivity? Are you serious?" I say aloud.

"Are you telling us the board knew about this and approved it?" Dolores shouts.

"Yes, Miss Delacroix. I personally met with all three of our executive board members to discuss our options, and this was our collective decision. So, without further ado, please join me in giving a warm garden club welcome to …"

As she introduces Andrea so and so, and Janie so and so, and Natalie so and so, the members gently clap while most are still in total shock.

As far as I know, this has never happened in the history of the club. I'm mentally preparing for a tribal war after the meeting.

Obviously, this all took place days before the meeting by the executive board behind closed doors, in some sort of covert meeting. Otherwise, there would have been an uproar and this travesty would never have taken place.

"Should we all protest?" Dolores asks.

"Should we all quit?" someone else suggests.

"Quit? Not on your life!" I say. "I wouldn't give that little twit the satisfaction. It will be a cold day in hell before I sit back quietly and let her ruin this institution by starting her own little nouveaux riche sorority club!"

"Hear, hear!" Dolores raises her glass. "I second that sentiment!" She downs the rest of her vodka martini and motions for another. She then leans close and asks, "So, do you think Gloria knew about this?"

I snap back at her, "Of course she knew; who do you think is in charge of the executive board, Dolores!"

"Well sue me for asking. So why isn't she here?"

"That's a good question."

Where is she? Why didn't she give me a heads-up? I look across the table, and Miss V. looks as if she is about to have a stroke as she frantically fans herself with a folded piece of paper. Before any of us can catch our breath or gather ourselves, Elizabeth proceeds with business as usual.

"We have a special guest speaker today, all the way from Argyle, Texas. Mr. Jim Barker is a buyer for the Iris Farm of Argyle and is also the cousin of our longtime member ..."

I have completely zoned out, but I can see a tall, good-looking man walk forward, and I can hear his smooth southern drawl, but I can't really comprehend his words as the lights dim and he starts his forty-five-minute presentation, complete with a slide show.

I'm still in shock when the lights go up, and as I look around the room, the majority of ladies look like deer caught in headlights. I'm not sure if it's the lighting change or the change in membership that has stunned them. New members are few and far between, and they *never* come three at once!

Jim thanks us for inviting him to speak, makes a joke about the upcoming Halloween holiday, and gives everyone a ceramic tile coaster with a picture of a lovely very dark purple iris appropriately named Dracula.

Owing to all the preceding drama, I can't remember what this southern gentleman told us about the Dracula iris. I'm glad he left his card; I slide it into my purse.

The restaurant staff is stirring around getting ready to serve us, and there is still no sign of Gloria. There is also no sign that the group is willing to embrace the recent change in membership with open arms, as some women walk out after the presentation. The growing tension among those remaining is made obvious by the eerie silence that has fallen on the room.

When lunch is served there is an unusual hush as the sound of utensils cutting food and ice water being poured into glasses fills the room like background musical accompaniment to a dramatic theatrical production. Except this isn't make-believe. Effusive table talk is clearly on a moratorium, but cell towers will be on fire this afternoon, mine included.

I glance at my watch. Gloria would never come this late, so it's safe to say she's going to be a no-show today.

The restaurant has graciously allowed us to bring in our own homemade desserts, something that more and more restaurants are refusing to allow us to do as health code restrictions change. Our food committee has done a fantastic job baking and decorating a red velvet cake to look like Dracula—the character, not the flower. I'm starting to see a theme, or maybe a resemblance to our new bloodsucking leader. The committee members have also prepared a sock-it-to-me cake, also appropriate.

I'll admit, the meal was fantastic; the meeting, not so much. No need to linger today. I gather my belongings, and before I can completely stand up, Miss V. grabs my arm.

"Stephanie, you have always been such a dear to take me to the cemetery on All Saints' Day. Can I count on you again this year?"

"Uh, sure, Miss V., glad to help. I'll call you later in the week to coordinate things, okay?"

"Thank you, darling." She hugs me warmly.

On one special day a year, the craftsmanship and artistry of cemetery planners, designers, and artisans can be said to be on display. That day is commonly celebrated in south Louisiana and New Orleans. November 1, All Saints' Day, is the one day every year when cemeteries are sure to have visitors.

Every year, the work of construction and maintenance goes on at a feverish pace through September and October at cemeteries all over the south. And as All Saints' Day dawns, the cemeteries present a panorama of beauty and order. In the early days visitors came in horse-drawn carriages, and today they come in long lines of automobiles. All Saints'

Day is still observed, people still come in large numbers, but now it has also become a time of year when the personal maintenance of family plots is conducted in a reverent and special way, and tombs blossom with elaborate floral tributes.

However, it's not always easy to get up after Halloween night and go clean up gravesites.

Nevertheless, taking Miss V. to Metairie Cemetery on All Saints' Day has become as much my own tradition as it is a historically religious tradition. Even so, while it's an honor to be asked, right now I can't wrap my brain around anything except this recent membership debacle.

That's why I'm headed straight for Gloria's house, as soon as I stop home and change my shoes.

When I finally get there, Maria answers the door and ushers me inside.

"Miss Gloria is expecting you."

"How nice. Did someone call to warn her to batten down the hatches? That Hurricane Stephanie was on her way?"

Maria looks at me with a startled expression.

"I'm sorry, Maria; I didn't mean to snap at you."

"No, you meant to snap at me." Gloria walks into the grand foyer the way a CEO enters a board meeting. She's wearing a flowing gossamer silk caftan in a brilliant iridescent bluish green shade reminiscent of an exotic bird, with a turban to match. "So here I am. You can snap away, but let's get a drink first, okay? Maria, we may need something stronger than iced tea this afternoon. Can you prepare us a couple of cosmos? Is that okay with you, Stevie—a cosmo?"

"Don't think you're going to smooth this over with your Southern hospitality and a cold drink! Why didn't you tell me about this beforehand? I can't believe you let me get blindsided!"

"Where would you like your refreshments?" Maria asks Gloria.

"In the study. Thank you, Maria."

"That's brave of you," I say. "Mrs. Peacock, in the study; sounds good to me."

"*Clue!*" Gloria laughs and claps her hands. "Charles and I so loved that game! Pray tell, which weapon shall you choose?"

"Let me think about it," I say as she leads me down the hallway toward the back of her grand home, the afternoon sunlight glistening through the lead-crystal panes.

"What took you so long? I expected you an hour ago."

"And I expected you at the meeting. Where were you?"

Gloria stops at the doorway to the study and turns to me.

"I was on my way; trust me. I certainly didn't want to miss this meeting, but I've been trying to get in to see my doctor, and they had a last-minute cancellation. It was the only day this week he could see me. They called as I was walking out the door. I sent you a text; didn't you get it? Anyway, I was in and out of the office, but I got stuck in traffic and then it was too late to get to Muriel's. I'm sorry, Stevie. I'm sorry I didn't tell you."

"You don't need to tell me everywhere you go," I snap. "I'm not your personal assistant. I don't need to keep track of your whereabouts."

"I didn't mean that. I'm sorry I didn't tell you about the changes in membership, but I couldn't."

"Couldn't or wouldn't?"

"Couldn't. Please, let's sit down so we can talk about this."

We enter the room Gloria calls her study, which is actually a glass-enclosed courtyard area near the pool, and I'm immediately struck by the scent of gardenias and the rich tapestry of green foliage that abounds from every corner. Gloria takes a seat in an oversize white wicker rocker, motioning for me to sit in an identical chair next to it. Frankly, as much as I'd like to storm around the room and pace wildly, I need to get off my feet.

"I would have gotten here sooner, but I had to stop by my house and crowbar my feet out of my shoes." I sit, slip off my shoes, and stretch my aching toes.

"I see," Gloria chuckles. "Breaking in new pumps, are we?"

"Yes, and I couldn't walk another block without my flats, but my feet are still killing me. I should know better."

In record time—which has me certain she was already prepared—Maria walks into the room carrying a silver serving tray with two chilled glasses of what I know will be the best cosmos in town, or at least on this block, since there are quite a few excellent bartenders in the Quarter given the history of the Obituary Cocktail Tour and annual Tales of the Cocktail convention.

"Thank you, Maria," Gloria and I say almost in unison.

"You are most welcome. Can I bring anything else?"

"How about a candlestick," I say. Maria furrows her eyebrows in confusion, and Gloria laughs.

"Thank you, Maria; we're good," Gloria says, raising her glass to me as Maria leaves.

"Let's toast to the brand-new members of the garden club. Here's to fresh blood!"

"Cut out the fresh blood nonsense before I draw yours, and tell me what the hell happened!" I take a long sip of my refreshing cocktail; the cosmopolitan is smooth and strong, and I'm glad I'm not driving.

"Ooh, touchy, touchy, aren't we? Elizabeth is doing exactly what you said the garden club should be doing."

"What are you talking about?"

"She is simply following our rules. You know, those rules that 'preserve the tradition and core values' of the club. I know you don't want to lose our tradition and core values. Correct?"

"But why weren't we informed about the status of the rule-breaking members first?"

"Because that's not how our rules and regulations work, Stevie. Elizabeth met with all the executive board members first, and then she personally contacted Anne and Linda. These ladies were not first-time offenders. In fact, they had totally disregarded the rules for the past few years. Elizabeth followed the rules to a T. She did her job; nothing more, nothing less. Actually, it was a very brave thing to do."

"What? Use her title for a power play?"

"No, Stevie, she did her job as president. She acted as a leader. It took guts, and I'm proud of her."

"Whatever, Gloria, if that's the way you choose to look at it. But you might want to start keeping a good record of your own absences; otherwise, you might find yourself kicked to the curb as well."

Gloria daintily places her cocktail on the table and responds slowly.

"No one has been kicked to the curb. What's really bothering you, Stephanie? I know you've never cared for Anne or Linda, and Tracy's voluntary resignation in protest is a plus for everybody, and you know it, so what really has you ticked off?" Gloria calmly takes a sip of her drink while keeping her cerulean-blue eyes focused like a cat on mine.

"You should have told me. I thought we were friends. Where is your loyalty?"

"We are friends, but the executive board is sworn to secrecy. This isn't personal, Stevie; it's business."

"Not personal? You're more than my best friend; you're like family. Doesn't that mean anything to you? How can you say it isn't personal? You know how important the garden club is to me." I fight back tears.

"Our friendship means the world to me as well; you know that," Gloria says quietly. "And the garden club is important to both of us. The garden club has been a family legacy since 1840; it's not just a socializing hot spot for me. I have more than a vested interest in this group; please don't ever question my loyalty to it or to you. If you really want to know what goes on behind the scenes, you should get more involved and become an executive board member. We're going to have an opening soon when Kay moves."

Here we go again. Gloria knows how I feel about this; I have no desire to be involved in the leadership politics of any organization. Period. But she thinks everyone needs to *do* more, *be* more. I stand, gulp the last of my drink, and set the glass on the end table a bit harder than I intended, thankful it doesn't break.

"I have to go. Thanks for the drink and the enlightening conversation."

"Wait, Stevie. Can we please talk about this? You've been an amazing asset on more committees than I can count over the years. There isn't an organization that wouldn't jump at the chance to have you championing their program or event."

"Your point is?" I cross my arms.

"My point is"—Gloria stands and points a well-manicured finger at me—"you've been unofficially leading in some capacity or other for years; why can't you commit to an official leadership role? You would be a fabulous executive board member! What happened that has made you so unwilling or unable to be more involved?"

"Nothing happened! I simply choose not to waste my time in pathetic power play meetings! And my not being on the garden club executive board has nothing whatsoever to do with this, and you know it, so stop trying to change the subject!"

"Why are you yelling, Stephanie?"

I hate it when she uses my full name in that condescending know-it-all tone.

"I'm not yelling!" I yell. "Never mind; this is obviously a waste of time. Now I really need to go. Louis is probably wondering why the garden club meeting has lasted almost six hours today. He wasn't at the house when I stopped to change my shoes, but I imagine he's home now, probably preparing dinner."

"Dependable Louis, bless his heart, give him a hug from me," Gloria says.

"Yes, he is dependable, trustworthy, *and* loyal. Like family is *supposed* to be."

As I storm out of Gloria's house, I fight the urge to go back and apologize, but damn it, I'm right! She is way off base. I would never have blindsided her like this. What is friendship without loyalty?

CHAPTER 6

— Gloria —

Thursday, October 21

It's been a crazy morning upstairs in the offices, as Charlotte, my assistant, is on a file-purging mission, editors are proofing stories and asking for feedback, Phillip is preparing for a major photo shoot in the carriage house, and Randy is conducting cord control behind a new computer and printer. Emme called and wants to meet to discuss the Grace House Gala and some ideas she has for developing a website to feature the silent auction items, a great idea I fully support.

Plus I've received a follow-up call from a publishing colleague I met for lunch earlier in the week, who posed a rather intriguing business opportunity—a proposition that sounds interesting, but one I've had no time to seriously consider or explore.

All in all, it's been a crazy week, and I have escaped to the kitchen to collect my thoughts and make a cup of tea when Maria appears and diplomatically confronts the elephant in the room in a way only she can.

"Is Miss Stephanie well?" she asks. "I have not seen her all week."

I've been so involved in business that it never really dawned on me that it has been a week since Stevie stormed out of my house and we have yet to talk.

"I'm sure she's just fine. Where are my tea bags?" I ask, rummaging through the pantry.

"Sit down." Maria gently guides me to a bar stool at the gleaming black granite countertop. "I will make you some tea." She magically plucks the box of herbal tea from the shelf.

I thrive on wearing many hats; however, considering all that I'm juggling, maybe this added conflict with Stevie is bothering me more than I care to admit. We really are quite close, and it's rare to go this long without speaking.

"If you ask me, I think you have too much stress; it is not good." Maria puts a Pyrex glass cup of water in the microwave and touches the buttons almost without looking. "Why don't you call Miss Stephanie and you two go to lunch? You don't eat. It's almost one o'clock; you need to eat." She reaches for the cordless phone, sets it on the counter in front of me, and quickly turns to grab a teacup from the cupboard.

"I guess you're right; someone has to make the first move, and it might as well be me. She's too stubborn."

Maria doesn't say a word as I hit the speed dial button, but her raised eyebrows and gentle chuckle lead me to believe she thinks maybe I'm just as stubborn.

I'm glad when Stevie agrees to meet me in a half hour.

"Sorry, Maria, tea will have to wait; I'm going to lunch as ordered." I lovingly salute her. "Please let Charlotte know I'll be back in a bit," I say as I hurry to my room to change shoes and put on some lipstick.

I have just been seated at our regular table when I see Stevie walk through the door and immediately bypass the hostess and a line of waiting patrons, much to their chagrin.

With a very relaxed atmosphere, the Napoleon House is one of our favorite lunch spots. We come here often. It's only a few blocks from Stevie's house, which makes it one of her favorite go-to places.

Stevie plops her big Brighton handbag on the interior chair and gives me a kiss on the cheek, a good sign that she's not still angry.

"Hi, girlfriend, I'm so glad you could make it," I say. "It's a madhouse at the office, and General Maria said I had to call you and go eat."

"Wise woman. It was great timing; I was standing in front of the refrigerator waiting for something to call out my name, but the silence was deafening."

Leave it to Stevie to make me laugh.

"In fact, I've been thinking about the shrimp avocado salad since you called."

"Think no more; I already told Nick that's what we would have, and as soon as I sat down, he brought two iced teas."

"Ya gotta love this kind of service." She picks up her tea and tips the glass at Nick, our server, who blows her a kiss.

"He is too cute for words," she says, as always.

"Stevie, I'm sorry I didn't tell you ahead of time about the executive board's decision. You know I usually tell you everything; we are the original Ya-Ya sisters, but this time I just couldn't. I'm sorry I hurt your feelings. Please forgive me."

"Forgive you? Always. Forgive Elizabeth? That's highly unlikely. Maybe she should have kicked one member to the curb at a time. It might have been easier to swallow, but three at once? Trust me—I'm not the only one who thinks so. But whatever. Time will tell."

I resist the urge to remind her once again that Elizabeth didn't kick anyone to the curb—they broke the rules, something she can't seem to grasp—but I don't want to get into it again. Time to change the subject.

"Maybe this is where we should throw our sixtieth birthday party," I say. "I can't believe it's next year; seems like just yesterday we celebrated our fiftieth. Time is flying. We probably should reserve a space somewhere; did we ever decide on the date?"

It seems I found just the right topic to change the subject. Give Stevie a new party to plan or a successful old party to discuss, and she's first in line.

"Well, I don't know if it feels like yesterday, but it doesn't feel like a decade, that's for sure. But as much as I like it here, I think we need more room. Why don't we go back to the Foundation Room? It's a beautiful place. I can call and see what dates they have available between our birthdays, maybe in July? What do you think?"

Our fiftieth birthday party took place in the Foundation Room, a luxurious private club in the House of Blues building on Decatur Street. I love the room, the service, and the food.

"That sounds good to me. Go for it and let me know the date so I can get it on my calendar."

Nick brings out two very large split avocados filled with a beautiful shrimp rémoulade—one of the best in town, and definitely Stevie's favorite.

We take our first bite just as a woman who looks vaguely familiar walks by our table.

"Can't wait for the pirate party; I got a new wench outfit. TTFN." She continues to walk without stopping for an introduction. Stevie waves with her mouth full and looks at me with her eyebrows raised.

"So how many are coming to your soiree this year?" I ask.

"Not sure." She reaches for her iced tea. "Probably around seventy or so."

"You know, if that party gets any bigger, you're going to need a parade permit to walk from pub to pub."

"You are coming, right?"

"Wouldn't miss it," I say.

Only Stevie can get an increasing number of ageing adults to dress up in pirate and wench outfits and act like wild teenagers with no inhibitions.

The annual Lewis pirate party is one of the most talked-about parties in the French Quarter. It starts with each pirate being given his or her choice of an ounce of gold or an ounce of silver upon arrival, meaning shots of Goldschläger, a clear cinnamon schnapps with flecks of gold in it, or Patrón tequila. Some people shouldn't be allowed to drink. And oh, the costumes; some go to extremes, and some show the extremes. This party always goes into the wee hours.

"Looks like you could use a good party," Stevie says. "You look beat."

"Gosh, don't hold back; why don't you tell me what you really think?"

"Seriously, what's up?"

"Nothing I can't handle; just a few more irons in the fire than usual. We never expected the French edition to take off so quickly, and the growth is creating some challenges, combined with the general stress of running a business. Not to mention the tension in the garden club."

"There's tension?" Stevie bats her eyelashes.

"You know very well there has been tension. I've been fielding calls all week from members."

"What did I tell you? I knew there would be fallout. Elizabeth is all wrong for us; you'll see. Hey, maybe there will be mutiny among the pirates and we can get rid of her. That would relieve some of the tension for everyone." Stevie chuckles.

"Stevie, that's just plain mean. What has she ever done to you? She really admires you and wants your acceptance. You did invite her to your party, right?"

"Of course I did; my mother taught me manners. I wouldn't invite the whole club and intentionally leave one person out. I'm not that bad. Can we not talk about her while we're eating?"

"Fine, but I hope she comes to the party."

"So what's the general stress at the magazine actually about? You are the boss, aren't you?"

"I am, but I have an opportunity to change that."

"Like how? What do you mean?"

"Can you keep a secret?"

"Of course." She continues to eat but leans closer.

"Carlyle Communications is expanding their European operations to the States. I had lunch with one of their partners on Monday. They would like me to consider a total buyout. We went to a great little Asian place on the *World* to talk about it."

Stevie almost chokes on a bite of her salad.

"You were on the *World* and didn't call to tell me? Louis and I tried to finagle an invite from someone to get on board before it pulled out of port yesterday. You snake!" She lovingly hits my shoulder. "So what was it like?"

"Unbelievable! You would never know you were on a boat. He sure picked a great place to talk about a buyout; I could almost picture myself sailing around the world."

"First of all, the *World* is hardly a boat, and second, are you seriously considering selling the magazine? What would you do? I never thought you would retire."

"Who said anything about retiring? I've got plenty to keep me busy. Anyway, I haven't really explored the idea; we've only begun to talk about it, but we're continuing our discussion next month. Please keep this confidential, Stevie."

"I totally understand."

I hope she does. Word travels fast in this town, and this is a big deal. Carlyle Communications is an eponymous company much like that of the Hearst family.

"Don't look now, but there is a scrumptious specimen of Greek godlike humanity approaching at three o'clock," Stevie whispers.

"I thought that was you. Bonjour, Gloria," the breathtakingly handsome man says, extending his hand.

"Anthony, what a surprise; I thought you were heading back to Paris."

"I was, but my father asked me to look at some property we're considering for the expansion and I got held up a few days. I'm heading to the airport now. Did you get my message?"

"Yes, I did. I'm sorry; it's been a rather hectic week. Anthony, I'd like you to meet Stephanie Lewis. Stephanie, this is Anthony Carlyle."

"*Enchante*, Ms. Lewis."

"Mrs. Lewis," Stevie says, shaking his hand. "And call me Stephanie."

"Stephanie it is." He smiles radiantly. "May I say that is an exquisite Weiss brooch you're wearing."

"Why thank you, Mr. Carlyle," Stevie coos. "I've had it for years; my husband gave it to me."

"He has excellent taste. Please, call me Anthony."

I'm watching this pleasant exchange with amusement as I notice Stevie blushing and—*Could it be?*—yes, flirting!

"How is it you know vintage jewelry, Anthony? Are you in the business?"

"I'm afraid not. I had an aunt who collected only the best vintage pieces from Weiss, Eisenberg, and the like. I guess I paid attention. Please don't let me interrupt your lunch, ladies; I was just on my way out when I saw you. I do hope we can visit again soon, Gloria."

"I look forward to that. Safe travel, and please, tell your father I said hello."

"I will do that." He bows ever so slightly and reaches into the pocket of his charcoal-gray Armani jacket for a business card that he places on the table in front of me.

"Just in case," he says as he shakes my hand once again and says a few words in French before turning to Stevie. "It was a pleasure to meet you, Stephanie."

"Likewise," she says like a dumbstruck teenager.

"Be still my beating heart!" Stevie says, watching him walk out the door. "I need to satisfy my sweet tooth after that." She reaches for the dessert menu and uses it as a fan. "How do you know him? I didn't notice a ring; is he single? Dolores would flip over him—unless he's gay?"

"Take a breath, Stevie, before you hyperventilate," I laugh. "He's a business associate. Yes, he's single, and his sexual orientation is none of our business. Do you really think he's attractive?" I ask.

"Hello? Add 'going blind' to your list of personal problems to address." She reaches over, picks up his business card, and slaps her palm against her forehead.

"Duh! Carlyle, as in Carlyle Communications! *That's* who you had lunch with on the *World*? I didn't connect the name. Why didn't you say something?"

"And what, stop you from fawning all over him like white on rice? Not on your life."

"I was not fawning."

"Then what do you call it?"

"I was merely having polite conversation, but jeez Louise, it was tough to concentrate with that face, that body, that accent. So sue me; I'm a red-blooded American girl." She fans her face with her hands. "So what did he say before he left? I hate it when hoity-toity people slip into another language; it's actually quite rude."

"Just that his father is really serious in discussing a possible acquisition and they want to know if I'm even interested. Guess I should really stop long enough to give it serious consideration, and let them know one way or the other."

"Is daddy-o single?"

"I told you this is business, and yes, he's a widower."

"That sounds promising. So who says business can't be pleasurable? I'd say you need to meet with papa and son a few times and talk it over before you decide whether or not you want to explore the possibilities further, just to make sure the fit is right. How old is Daddy Warbucks?"

"Stevie, you are insufferable, and I think Francois just celebrated his seventieth."

"Francois, eh? Ooh-la-la." She whistles. "Tell me more."

"There's nothing more to tell, and I came here to get *away* from business, so let's see what we can do about satisfying that sweet tooth of yours." I pick up a menu.

We're reviewing dessert options when my phone rings.

"Oops, sorry, forgot to silence the ringer."

When I reach into my jacket pocket to shut it off, I glance at the name on the screen.

"Sorry, Stevie, I have to take this one."

I hold the phone to my chin and softly say to Stevie, "It's loud in here; I'm going to step outside for just a second."

Stevie rolls her eyes and reaches for the last piece of bread in the basket. I wonder how she can stay so thin, because that girl can eat.

I'm gone for only a minute or two, and as I sit back in my chair, I prepare myself for what's to come; I know this girl so well.

"I hate it when people take calls during meals."

"I know you do, but that was my doctor. I've been waiting to get the results back from my lab work since you and I had our last discussion. Seems they ran the wrong test. I need to go back again and give another blood donation."

"What a baby; it's only a little pinprick. What do they need, a vial or two? Hardly constitutes a donation."

"Easy for you to say; you know I hate needles. But it's more about the inconvenience; I really don't have time for this. It took me months to get in to see Doc Creswell, and I had to miss a garden club meeting to do it. I don't know when I can get back. Looks like it's more Tums and Maalox for me. Oh well."

"Indigestion?" she asks.

"You have no idea. I think my days of rich and spicy foods are over."

"Well, suck it up and deal with it. Go get your blood test and quit complaining. I'm not fond of needles either. Thank God we're both natural beauties; no Botox or new boobs for us. Nothing looks worse than new boobs on an old lady. Just ain't right."

"Stevie, you are too much."

"Louis would disagree; he says you can never have too much of a good thing." She winks.

We agree to split a slice of cheesecake, and after placing our order I decide once again to navigate waters that still need to be calmed.

"Speaking of old ladies, Elizabeth told me that Jake has started calling her an 'old lady,' and not in a playful way. Can you imagine? We *can* talk about her now, since you've finished eating, right?"

"Do we have to?"

"Yes. I don't exactly know what it is, but there's something very sad about that entire situation. She could use your help, not your constant criticism. Her life is not the walk in the park you seem to think it is; she really needs strong and supportive sisters around her."

"Then she should go back to her cheerleader buddies."

"Stevie." I glance down at the clock on my cell phone and jump.

"Oh my goodness, I can't believe we've been here for two hours! I really must scoot; I've got an afternoon meeting with Tim."

Tim McNally is a local wine expert who hosts a weekly radio program and writes a monthly column for the magazine. He's having a winemaker from Oregon on his show this week and has agreed to do a special feature story for us.

We get our cheesecake in a to-go box and split the check, and as we start to leave, Stevie grabs my arm.

"Thanks for calling; I've missed you. Sorry for my bad behavior."

I'm shocked. Stevie, apologizing? That rarely happens, but that's who she is and I love her anyway.

"Whatever," I say.

She throws her head back and laughs, then wraps her arms around me in a big hug.

"Okay, let's hit the road. I'll walk with you as far as Violet's; I'm just going to peek my head in." She links her arm in mine as we head out of the restaurant and begin to walk.

Violet's is a lovely boutique on Chartres Street about halfway between the Napoleon House and my place on Esplanade. Stevie is addicted to the dresses they sell. Funny thing—I never see her wear them. Louis makes her cross the street when they walk past the shop. He tells her she can go in but her credit card can't. They're a cute couple.

I leave her at the storefront door and hurry down the street.

When I finally make it back to my house, I'm exhausted; my back and feet are killing me. When I sit down at the granite countertop that I left a few hours earlier, Maria comes in.

"Oh! I did not hear you come in. Did you have a good time with Miss Stephanie?" Before I can answer, Maria takes a pink Post-it note off the refrigerator. "Oh yes, Dr. Creswell's office called while you were out. They wanted you to call and schedule some test."

"It's nothing special," I say. "Another simple blood test; they flubbed something up at the lab. But obviously they're being very thorough; the receptionist also called on my cell while I was at lunch."

"What day is your new appointment?" she asks.

"I didn't make one—said I'd call back when I could look at my calendar."

"How about if you do it now?" She reaches for the phone.

"No, Maria. That is sweet of you, but I can handle it on my—"

"I know you can handle it on your own. You can handle everything on your own! But Maria says to call now and reschedule your appointment!"

I always know something is up when she speaks of herself in the third person, but Maria very seldom raises her voice.

Then she boldly places the house phone none too gently in front of me, and before I realize what's happening, she reaches into my jacket pocket, where she knows I keep my cell phone, and practically slams it on the counter next to it.

Truthfully, I'm a bit taken aback. It's like I'm having an out-of-body experience as I pick up my cell phone, call, and make the appointment.

"There, are you satisfied?" I slide my phone back into my pocket. "I have to be at the lab first thing in the morning. Please ask Randy to have the car ready at seven thirty. Now, I'm going to freshen up so I can make my four o'clock meeting. Is that okay with you, boss?"

Maria furrows her brow and starts to wring her hands.

"I meant no disrespect, Miss Gloria."

"None taken. Thank you for caring, but I'm fine." I give her a quick hug before heading to my room.

I manage to get through a very long afternoon, and it's close to midnight when I fall into bed exhausted. Nonetheless, I make it to the lab bright and early Friday morning for my eight o'clock appointment, where the technician is a pro and painlessly draws my blood on the first attempt. I'm in and out in under ten minutes and back home before nine—a good thing, because there's a lot to accomplish as this month comes to an end, what with ongoing deadlines, Stevie's pirate party, and Halloween night dinner at the Rib Room. Then there's the ongoing garden club drama and the uproar about Elizabeth.

Perhaps most important, however, are the further discussions I've had on the phone with Anthony Carlyle about a possible acquisition. Frankly, the more I think about the possibility of selling the business, the more attractive the idea becomes. I didn't expect to feel this way, but I begin to realize that I have the same strong feeling in my spirit to close this chapter in my life as I had when I opened it.

If I accept the generous seven-figure offer the Carlyles have verbally placed on the table, *NOLA 2 NOLA* will become part of a huge international publishing conglomerate that will allow it to grow in ways it never could under my ownership.

What sounds even more attractive is that I could usher in a new season of possibility in my own life as well. I'd like to be more involved in Grace House and in the transitional living programs they are developing for women in the community.

I believe I'm ready to do something different.

And that's why I've scheduled a three-day trip to Paris just after Thanksgiving to meet face-to-face with Francois and Anthony Carlyle.

CHAPTER 7

— Stephanie —

Monday, November 1

I can't believe how fast October passed. Once again, our annual pirate party was a smashing success. It's always held the Saturday night before Halloween, and Louis really gets into the event. He's in charge of ordering the lighted swords for everyone. We are quite a sight—seventy plus pirates parading through the Quarter yelling, "Arrrrrgh!"

We do have a great time!

This year the pirate party fell on October 30, which meant the next night—last night—was Halloween, when we dressed up again, walked around celebrating with the masses, and then had dinner at the Rib Room, where nearly everyone was dressed in flamboyant and utterly creative costumes. After all, it is the French Quarter, and we take dressing up very seriously.

Partying that hard two nights in a row isn't as easy as it used to be. What was I thinking? Gloria was smart and called it a night much earlier in the evening. I should have taken her lead.

I can't believe it's November 1, All Saints' Day.

"I need coffee, strong coffee!" I moan as I reach over, shut off the alarm, and sit up on the side of the bed. Louis grabs my pillow and puts it over his face. "Oh my gosh, my feet hurt as much as my head," I groan. It's going to take an act of God to get through this day. "Lord, give me strength," I say as I look out the window at the comforting statue and shuffle toward the bathroom. "Louis, will you please call for my car?"

Parking can be a nightmare in the Quarter, and luckily we have an arrangement with the Bourbon Orleans hotel, just a few doors down. We call, and their valet gets our car from the parking garage and pulls it up in front of the hotel. I just walk across the street and get in. It can't get more convenient than that.

"Hmm," he mutters, not moving.

"Louis! Please? Will you please call for my car? Then you can go back to sleep for the rest of the day. Lucky you."

"Yeah, well whose fault is it that you're busy?" he says, reaching for his cell phone. "You're the one who always volunteers. I don't know why anyone visits a cemetery. Those people are long gone; there's no one in those tombs."

Louis and I don't share the same sentiment for the dead. I love driving around in the famous New Orleans cemeteries, admiring the crypts—or villas and estates, as they are called here. Our cemeteries contain some of the most exquisite examples of stone carving and ironwork you'll ever see. My fascination with these somber places of reflection took on even more meaning after I met Gloria and learned that a great deal of the opulent and ornate designs I admired most were those created by artisans from Bronzinelle Steel and Stone, the family business founded by Gloria's ancestors.

Even with his disdain for the eternal resting place of our bones, Louis agreed to buy our plot a few years ago when a coworker died and he saw the stress that planning a burial put on his wife and son. But the dirt portion of burial is only that, a portion, and I secretly hope that he will splurge on a lavish resting place for us one day—fancy digs, as they say; excuse the pun.

I have my basket of cleaning supplies and a to-go cup of hot strong coffee, and I'm out the door. It appears Miss V. and I will have a good climate for cleaning and decorating today. It's funny how the weather can change so unexpectedly; last week we were freezing, and today we might get a sunburn.

Heading down Chartres Street, I make a wide turn into the tiniest of driveways. I stop my car, and as I get out I see Miss V.'s huge, beautiful, full-bloomed hibiscus, potted just inside the gate. Lush vines cover the brick walls that surround the courtyard at the back of her house.

"Good All Saints' morning, dear!" Miss V. shouts, locking her back door and hurrying to the car. She is 89, looks 69, and has the wisdom of someone 199. She's a great lady to know, and one of the oldest surviving members of the garden club. She's been a widow for many years and has a grown daughter living in Dallas that is the author of a children's book series. Miss V. is extremely proud of her.

"Good All Saints' morning to you as well," I say.

She is holding a piece of paper in her gnarled hand as she embraces me in one of her famous bear hugs.

"Here is that recipe I promised you. I taped it to my door so I wouldn't forget it today!" She laughs and thrusts into my hands what appears to be a photocopy of an old magazine page. My confusion must be visible.

"It's the no-bake turkey cookie recipe I said I'd give to you for your neighbor's children."

"Oh yes, I forgot all about that. I'm sure they will enjoy making these. Thank you!"

"My granddaughters think this is the best part of Thanksgiving dinner."

"I bet they do. My kids used to love these, but I lost the recipe years ago."

I help her up into my car, an SUV that's a bit high for her tiny frame to navigate. As always, she's a trooper, and we're on the road in no time.

The Metairie Cemetery isn't far, but every time I drive through the entrance gates, I thank God just for getting me there. I'm always afraid I'll get killed turning in. Coming from the Quarter, you have to maneuver across oncoming traffic under the interstate, executing a precarious turn that makes you feel like you're headed the wrong way onto an entrance ramp. It's very scary under normal circumstances, and when you add a lack of sleep and a leftover blood alcohol content that's probably very near to the legal limit, it's nothing short of a miracle to arrive in one piece.

As soon as we make the first turn onto the expansive grounds, we see the management has set up a tent to purchase fresh flowers with attendants ready to assist so you don't even have to get out of the car. Now that's service.

I come here often to walk and meditate, and it can be hours before I see another living soul, but not on this day. Although the early morning

Mass for All Saints' Day is over, the expansive grounds are still teeming with people. The majority of burial sites in this historic cemetery, in this City of the Dead, are what they call independent aboveground entombments. The crypts, tombs, and mausoleums vary in architectural style from Classic, to Gothic, to Egyptian, to Modern. They are made of concrete, marble, brick, stone, and polished granite. Wrought iron plays a predominant role in many of the styles, as does attractive landscaping.

Today people are weeding flower beds, polishing stone, carefully cleaning custom designed stained-glass windows, and trimming hedges. Some visitors are placing fresh flowers in urns, and some are sitting on benches or folding chairs, silently talking to their loved ones, or to God.

Being here on this special day is always a powerful experience.

There is so much rich history and tradition in New Orleans, and I once again feel incredibly blessed to call this place my home.

"Tell me, dear, how is my sweet Dr. Lewis? I miss him so."

"He's doing really well, Miss V. He misses you too. He said to make sure to tell you hello."

Louis sold his practice and retired as a full-time allergist the same year I turned fifty, and we didn't question whether or not to remain in our little bit of French Quarter heaven. I'm glad we did, because we had no idea that in addition to consulting on exceptionally complicated cases, Louis would become a much sought-after guest lecturer at medical schools and universities all over the world, and he's often away on travel several times a month. At first I traveled with him, but the sheen quickly wore off that new experience as I spent far too much time alone in hotels and way too much money on shopping, to relieve the boredom. That's when I really began to get more involved in the garden club and in my volunteer work, and while I may be alone when Louis travels, I am never lonely.

Many of his old patients, like Miss V., ask about him often.

Louis loves what he does, I love what I do, and we love each other and our unconventional and thoroughly enjoyable life together.

We've been wholeheartedly cleaning the ornate wrought iron doors to her family's marble crypt and talking about Mr. V, Louis, and our lives as "women in the Quarter" when, after several hours, Miss V. finally says, "I think that will do it."

I'm exhausted and stiff as I stand, stretch, and give my neck a chance to crack by turning it from side to side. Just then, someone familiar catches my eye.

Is that Gloria?

I start to shout her name but remember the solemnity of the place and reconsider.

"Miss V., would you mind if I took a couple of these fresh flowers to put on a friend's tomb?"

"Of course not, dear; I have plenty. Take what you need. Please don't rush; take your time. I'm going to sit for a while and rest, and visit with my sweetheart."

That she still calls her husband "sweetheart" makes me choke up, and I nod, giving her the space to commune with her beloved in solitude.

I weave my way between the maze of crypts and tombs, being careful to walk respectfully on this sacred ground. As I get closer, my curiosity is rewarded, as this is most assuredly Gloria, but I stop before she sees me and stand quietly behind a large obelisk monument.

It seems strange to me now that after all these years of friendship I've never been to Gloria's family tomb. When Charles passed away, they had a memorial service. He was to be cremated, and his ashes were going to be placed in the tomb at a later date in a private ceremony with just his family in attendance.

I wonder why she didn't mention that she would be here today. She knows I take Miss V. every year, and I'm sure we talked about it last night. Maybe this is why she left the Rib Room early. She's a smart woman— went home early and got a good night's sleep.

Today Gloria is sitting alone on an elaborately carved stone bench, staring into the distance. Although our friendship gets tested from time to time, I have never doubted her love and loyalty, and I want so much to call out a greeting to my friend, to reach out and give her a warm hug, but I suddenly feel like an unwelcome voyeur. As I turn to walk away, she stands and without hesitation strides off in the opposite direction, her silk neck scarf gently floating in the breeze behind her.

I wait until she is out of sight before approaching a massive structure that can only be described as magnificent. I sit on the bench Gloria has just vacated, one of two flanking the entrance to a breathtaking Greek Revival vestibule mausoleum, where the polished granite shimmers like glass in the early afternoon sunlight. I don't know why it never dawned on me that her family resting place would be bigger than a small single-family home, or why she's never shared this place with me, her closest friend. I'm struck once again by all the things I don't know about the friend I thought I knew.

I know Gloria's ancestors came to New Orleans from France and Spain; I'm always coming across tidbits of her history at the Williams Center. I've always known Gloria's family fortune was made from importing marble, granite, and stone, and from building burial vaults, mausoleums, and tombs in what are now the oldest historic cemeteries in Louisiana.

Yet that is an aspect of Gloria's life I seldom consciously consider. She is my buddy, my girlfriend, my soul sister.

I quietly walk up the tiered steps to the entrance of the structure, where I find myself standing in a vestibule interior chapel area clearly designed for visitors. Two more carved benches are centered between vaulted walls where the remains of what appear to be dozens of family members are interred. I read the names and dates carved on the walls.

I see "Charles Alexander Vincent III" carved into black granite.

Born September 2, 1945
Died August 31, 1997

To the right of Charles's resting place is Gloria's name and birth date carved in stone, with a gaping space on her marker waiting for a second date. It sends a shiver up my spine, and I wonder what Gloria feels when she looks at it. While Louis and I have a plot of land, there is nothing carved in stone just waiting for our final departure date.

I find this more than a tad creepy.

I realize I'd better get back to Miss V. before she gets worried, and I'm about to leave when I notice an alcove toward the center of the structure. What I find there is difficult to wrap my brain around at first.

Intricately carved in a beautiful pink granite stone is

Abigail Louise Bronzinelle Vincent
Born October 19, 1971

Died October 2, 1972
Our beloved angel has gone home.

I feel the breath sucked out of my lungs as the reality sinks in. Gloria had a daughter who died before her first birthday. We've been best friends for almost thirty years, and I had no idea.

CHAPTER 8

— Gloria —

Tuesday, November 9

I'm reading the e-mail that has just arrived from Elizabeth and glance at the time on the lower right corner of my computer monitor.

Okay, Stevie, I know you're online. I wonder how long will it take for you to get fired up about this recent message?

Just then a live chat request window pops up on my Skype screen from Stevie.

I click on the "accept" button, and as I wait for our laptops and cameras to sync for our Skype chat, I quickly read the e-mail again.

From:	Elizabeth LeBlanc [EL@aol.com]
Sent:	Tuesday, November 9, 2010 8:05 a.m.
To:	'Undisclosed Recipients'
Subject:	Last-Minute Change in Plans for Garden Club Meeting

Dear Members,

I regret to inform you that due to circumstances beyond my control, the location for our Thursday garden club meeting is being moved from my home on Governor Nicholls to the Old Absinth House at 240 Bourbon Street in the Jean Lafitte Bistro, on the second floor. The meeting time remains the same. However, we are unable to bring in prepared food, and there will be an added cost for lunch and drinks. The good news is that we will be able to use the room after lunch for our craft project session.

I apologize for any inconvenience this change in plans may cause, and I look forward to seeing all of you this Thursday.

Elizabeth LeBlanc, President
Fleur-de-Lis Ladies Garden Club of the French Quarter

Stevie's face no sooner pops up on my screen than she launches into yet another tirade about Elizabeth.

"Is she serious? We're going to meet in a bar? This is not the kind of crowd that meets in a bar! We are not her little cheerleader chums. Surely you know this is totally inappropriate, Gloria."

"Slow down, Stevie; catch your breath. We're not meeting in the bar; the Bistro is upstairs. It's actually quite a charming room and you know as well as I do they will serve great food."

"So what has happened to your new BFF this time? What circumstances are beyond her control?"

I ignore her sarcastic "best friends forever" comment.

"She's had quite a situation to deal with. A waterline to the dishwasher broke and completely flooded the kitchen and dining room. The poor thing has been a wreck over this, handling the emergency while accommodating the needs of the club as well."

"Which is exactly why she has no business being the president; it's too much for her to handle."

"Au contraire, madame, she has done a stellar job. It's not easy to find somewhere in the Quarter to put fifty women who want to dine like royalty and then brandish glue guns and sequins. Luckily, her husband is good friends with the manager of that other restaurant located in the Old Absinth House building, what's it called again?"

"Tony Moran's."

"Yes, that's it, why can't I ever remember the name of that place?

Anyway, with one call, he was able to reserve the Jean Lafitte room for the entire afternoon. We owe Jake LeBlanc for that favor."

"I don't owe that man anything; he's a snake."

While I tend to agree with her, I keep silent on that count.

"Really, Stephanie, accidents do happen, and you have to be flexible. Aren't you the one who always says to 'ride the wave'?"

"Whatever. So, what about all the food the committee has prepared?"

"I'm sure they'll think of something. Perhaps they can freeze it for Thanksgiving. Which reminds me, I know your kids are coming into town for that weekend and you haven't decided whether to stay in or go out, so I'd love for you and your family to come to my house for Thanksgiving this year. You always have me, and this year I would be honored if you'd let me reciprocate. Please, would you at least consider it?"

"I don't know. Let me talk to Louis; he was paging through cookbooks last night."

"Tell him he can plan the menu with Maria. We'll get whatever ingredients he needs, and he can come over early to help her cook if he'd like."

"That just might sway him; you know he loves your kitchen—and Maria. I'll let you know, okay?"

"Sounds good."

"Speaking of kitchens, I just have to say this whole thing with Elizabeth sounds a bit far-fetched. I mean really, it's not like we're even cooking in the kitchen, for crying out loud! The food committee takes care of it all; we bring everything in. Surely she can entertain a few ladies for a couple of hours. All she has to do is hire a plumber and get the damn pipe fixed; what's the big deal? What a lame excuse."

"You're home on your laptop, right?" I ask.

"Yes, I'm home, why?"

"Okay then, do me a favor. Walk out to your balcony and get the hose that Dolores uses when she waters your baskets, drag it into your kitchen, and set it down on the floor by the refrigerator and go back on the patio and turn the water on. Then I want you to forget that the water is running for about two hours and call me back and tell me that a flooded kitchen is a lame excuse."

I click the disconnect button on Skype and the chat box goes black.

★ ★ ★ ★ ★

Thursday, November 11

The management of the John Lafitte Bistro has done everything in their power to accommodate our garden club at the last minute. The tables in the room are dressed in crisp white linen with napkins of the same material in a brilliant shade of red. Table centerpieces consist of two single long-stemmed roses—one red, one white—in tall, narrow clear glass vases. Elegant white dinnerware sits atop high-gloss black charger plates, which altogether makes for a stunning presentation when the ladies begin to arrive.

Miss Alma is telling everyone who enters how this unusual luncheon will be conducted.

"The restaurant has provided a limited menu with a choice of two meals, and servers will be taking individual orders as soon as you are seated. Everything will be prepared fresh while we conduct the general business of the meeting."

This time I've saved seats for Stevie and Dolores, and they're both surprised.

Stevie doesn't mention the abrupt disconnection of our recent Skype call—a good thing, because I'm just about at my breaking point concerning her negativity regarding Elizabeth.

Today our server is a young lady whose name tag reads "Chloe."

"What a pretty name," I say. "Chloe, I will have the baked chicken. Could you please remove the skin and skip the potatoes? I'll just have the chicken and the dinner salad, with the dressing on the side, please."

"Really, Gloria, that's all you're going to eat? Why bother eating at all? Miss V.'s parakeet eats more than you do."

"I'm trying to eat healthy; that's not an easy task when you live in the French Quarter."

"Well, you've got that right," Stevie says as she orders the beef medallions with au gratin potatoes and extra vegetables. I have no idea where she puts all the food she consumes, because it never shows up on her body.

The truth is I'm watching what I eat very carefully because after all these bouts with indigestion and nausea, I think that when all is said and done, I'll find that what I'm really dealing with is either an ulcer or a bad gallbladder. My repeat blood work came back fine, which seems par for the course and speaks to an issue Charles was passionate about.

"One test always seems to lead to another; it's all part of a systematic scheme to keep medical professionals and insurance companies in business," he used to say.

Looks like he was right, because now I'm scheduled for yet another test the day after Thanksgiving that will take several hours, and I'm not a very happy camper about that prospect, especially given my plans to leave for Paris the next day.

Doctor Creswell has been painting in broad brushstrokes insofar as diagnosis possibilities, and he wants to "take a peek inside my stomach," he says, as if it's a simple matter of opening a door and taking a look. "We will know a lot more after the endoscopy," he says.

So until I get an official diagnosis, I'm eating very basic foods and seem to be doing much better.

Chloe takes orders from everyone at our table, and Stevie and Dolores are busy discussing what to plant in some new ceramic pots she bought in Texas when Alma stands and taps her fork on the side of her water glass to let us know it's time to begin.

Elizabeth opens the meeting after Alma rings the bell. *Ding-dink-ding, ding-dink-ding.*

"I want to tell you all again how sorry I am for any inconvenience this change in venue may have caused you." After making a few jokes about the plumbing situation in her home, and commending the Bistro for coming to the rescue at the last minute, she continues with the club business.

"As you know, we've had some membership changes in the garden club, and I'm proud of the way you have embraced these changes and our newest members." She nods to where Andrea, Janie, and Natalie are sitting and gently applauds. "These membership changes came about after a much-needed review of our 170-year-old rules and regulations by our executive board. I believe it goes without saying that what worked 170 years ago may not work quite as well today." I notice a few of the ladies are getting fidgety about what may come next.

"That said, this recent issue concerning a venue change speaks to another issue that our executive board would like to bring to the table for future discussion. We won't spend time today discussing this as a group, but rest assured we'll all have the opportunity to share our thoughts over the coming months as we explore our options."

She has the attention of everyone as she continues.

"It's important for us to address the growing difficulties we've had not only in securing locations but also in our ability to provide our own desserts or specialty dishes, and to have ample room for conducting cooking demonstrations, or our occasional craft projects. We have also had challenges in being able to readily access prior documentation and vital business of the club, as there isn't a standard location for storing archival information. All that said, it may be time for us to consider a somewhat more permanent space for the club, somewhere we can conduct monthly meetings if we choose, somewhere to have an administrative office that could be used by the executive board and the current committees, including a space for the development and distribution of the annual cookbook, a project with untapped potential."

She lets her words sink in. "Ladies, the garden club has been in existence since 1840; isn't it time we had some type of permanent home?"

The room begins to hum with activity as questions are asked and opinions are voiced. I'm surprised to see that Stevie doesn't look overly disturbed by this announcement. In fact, she and Dolores are relatively quiet as Elizabeth reins in the mixed response outcry.

"Ladies, ladies, I know this is a lot to think about, and I'm certain that when the time comes to address these concerns more fully, we'll be prepared to do so. All the executive board asks is that we begin the open dialogue to discuss our possibilities, and I encourage any of you to call me, or to put your thoughts in writing."

She completes the business portion of our meeting by reminding everyone to bring unwrapped toys to our December luncheon at the Omni Royal. "And we've got some wonderful entertainment lined up, so please make sure to join us next month for our very special annual Christmas celebration luncheon."

She talks a bit about today's craft project and then wraps up the meeting. At that moment, like a well-timed orchestral movement, the servers flamboyantly enter the room balancing large trays of dinner plates, each with a silver cover. Piping-hot steam is released as each cover is removed with a dramatic flourish. The food is exceptional, the table conversations appear lively, and everyone seems to be having a good time when Miss V. announces that craft time will start in ten minutes.

Once a year, instead of a speaker presentation, the club does a craft, and it's no secret that I'm not a fan of crafts.

"Well, if you ladies will excuse me, I need to get back to the office." I stand.

"Ha ha! I win!" Stevie smacks Dolores on the shoulder and holds her hand out, palm up. "Fork it over, you owe me twenty bucks."

"Fine, fine," Dolores reaches into her handbag and pulls out a twenty-dollar bill and thrusts it into Stevie's hand. My raised eyebrows must command more respect than I realize as Stevie folds the bill, tucks it into her cleavage, and explains through her laughter.

"I bet Dolores ten bucks that you'd find some kind of excuse to get out of staying for craft time, and double or nothing if you did it within sixty seconds of Miss V.'s announcement. Do I know you, or what?" She smiles.

"Yes, my friend, you know me," I say, and give her a quick kiss on the cheek so I can leave before the glitter has a chance to fly. "I'll see you on Thanksgiving, if not before. Are you sure you won't join us, Dolores?" I ask.

"Thanks, but no can do. I'm driving to Houston to visit with the kids."

"Well, if your plans change," I say, "there will be a seat for you." I give her a hug.

"You're absolutely sure you don't want to stay?" Stevie jokes. "We're actually making something cute and useful, a pumpkin candle holder. Don't you want one?"

"Make an extra one for me, Stevie," I say over my shoulder as I make my way across the room to say good-bye to Elizabeth and congratulate her on a job well done.

CHAPTER 9

— Gloria —

Thursday, November 25–Thanksgiving Day

Attracting more than 3.5 million people to the streets of Manhattan in New York City each year, the Macy's Thanksgiving Day Parade has been a Big Apple tradition since 1924. The annual parade has become synonymous with Thanksgiving tradition, and over 50 million TV viewers nationwide will be watching the live broadcast from Times Square today. Normally I would be one of them, but not this year.

After watching the parade on TV, I usually go out with Stevie and Louis to one of the many fabulous restaurants in the Quarter that are open on Thanksgiving, or over to their place, where Louis cooks. This year I am entertaining at my home, something I haven't done on Thanksgiving Day in a long time.

Maria and I have enjoyed ourselves shopping, preparing, and cooking over the past few days, and Randy has been extremely accommodating in running back and forth to Whole Foods more than a couple of times for things we either forgot or decided at the last minute we couldn't do without.

"There's going to be enough food to feed a small army," I said to Maria the day before the grand event. "But I want to make sure Stevie and Louis have plenty of leftovers for the weekend with the kids in town."

I was thrilled when Louis and Stevie accepted my invitation, especially knowing the kids would be coming as well.

"Louis said he's fine not cooking this year," Stevie said when she called to confirm. "It's going to give him more time to spend with the kids and grandkids."

As with a great many busy families today, it's hard for the Lewis clan to all connect at one time. I've watched Stevie struggle with this over the years, resigning herself to the fact that her grown children have lives of their own.

I have to say I'm more than a little excited to have all of them coming here. After all, Stevie is my closest friend, and I didn't just watch her precious children grow up; we all grew up together. I hung their artwork on my refrigerator; attended their school events, recitals, ball games, graduations, and wedding; and even sat in the waiting room for the birth of Melissa's first child. At seventeen, Luke was the youngest pallbearer at Charles's funeral, and Melissa cried for days when her dear Uncle Charlie died.

Today Luke Lewis is a professor at Stanford and is in from California for the long weekend. He's still single at thirty, a fact that bothers Stevie more than it does Louis. Melissa is their thirty-one-year-old daughter, an accomplished artist who lives in Austin with her husband and two children; Jaden is three and Lila is one. Carter, her husband, is a lobbyist and planned to be back from a business trip in Germany the day before Thanksgiving, but his return flight was cancelled, and now he won't be back until the day after. He will be greatly missed at dinner.

Also in attendance for dinner will be Randy and Maria—not as employees, but as friends, dear friends. I was hesitant at first about inviting them—not because I didn't want to, but because I didn't want them to feel obligated.

"You and Randy always have that long weekend off, and I know you spend that time with your family, especially Thanksgiving Day, so I want you to know that it's completely fine if you can't—"

"You *are* family," Maria assured me. "We have not had Thanksgiving dinner here at Vincent Manor for many years; we would not miss this for all the tea in China! Randy says the same thing."

Maria was especially excited when I told her of my plans not only to host the dinner but also to prepare some of the signature dishes my mother used to make myself.

Cooking is another thing I could look forward to doing again if I decide to sell *NOLA 2 NOLA*. I've thoroughly enjoyed the years spent developing the magazine, but between the business and volunteer obligations there hasn't been much time to do anything else. Who knows, I may even get a social life.

★   ★   ★   ★   ★

Thanksgiving Day

When the sumptuous feast is set before us and all are in their seats at the elegant dinner table, I'm overwhelmed by emotion as I address my guests.

"I've asked Randy to say the blessing before we begin." I extend my arms, and everyone clasps hands around the table. "But first, I want to thank all of you for being here today. I look around this table and see the most important people in my life, and I am thankful for the blessing of friends who have become my family. You have all enriched my life in so many ways. I pray God will continue to bless each of you as we enter this Christmas season, and throughout the coming new year as well."

Stevie squeezes my left hand, and Maria my right, as Randy begins to say a grace-filled prayer that seems to touch everyone at the table in a special way. When he utters his heartfelt "amen," I brush back the tears of emotion that threaten to cascade down my cheeks, and see several others do the same.

I reach for the serving spoon that sits beside the sweet potato casserole (with melted marshmallows, a southern must).

"Shall we?" I say joyfully.

Dinner is a culinary carnival and a cavalcade of communication as dishes are passed, food is enjoyed, and multiple simultaneous conversations are conducted, creating the kind of civilized mayhem that transpires only when nine people come together at one dinner table—at least when nine people *like these nine people* come together at one dinner table.

I grab my cell phone and ask one of the servers I've hired to take a picture of the group.

"I'm just so sorry that Carter isn't here with us."

"Me too," Melissa says.

"Don't worry, Aunt Glo; we'll just Photoshop him in," Luke says.

After an hour and a half of nonstop eating and talking, we finally start to wind down.

Randy and Maria leave early as planned, headed to their oldest son's home, where a huge family gathering of about fifty relatives is taking place. It was such a joy to have them begin the holiday season with me.

When dinner started, it was all Maria could do not to get up and take care of us, but once she saw that the two servers I hired from a very reputable agency were doing just fine, she relaxed and enjoyed herself. When she and Randy excused themselves just before dessert was served, we were all sorry to see them go.

Now, as we finish the perfect dessert of homemade pumpkin pie topped with fresh whipped cream, the adult conversation shifts into a satiated silence while the children seem to be getting their second wind. Melissa is bouncing the baby on her knee while trying to keep her toddler from tormenting Coco, who is being quite a sport at having the pint-size ball of energy invading her space.

"Here, pony; come here, pony," Stevie's grandson says, convinced that he can ride Coco like the pony at the petting zoo he recently visited.

"Jaden! Don't jump on the doggie, honey; she's not a pony. Coco is a doggie; we don't jump on doggies," Melissa says calmly.

Stevie and I laugh as we comfortably lounge back in our chairs, both of us savoring the moment.

"That cornbread dressing was amazing, Gloria," Stevie says. "The turkey was incredibly moist, and your mother's sweet potato casserole is a hit as always. For someone who hardly cooks these days and barely eats, I'm impressed." She holds up her glass of wine in a salute. "Bravo to the chef!"

Everyone joins in the compliments, and I wish Maria were here to receive the accolades as well, because I couldn't have done it without her.

Soon Louis begins to fidget and glances at his watch.

"Well, we don't want to overstay our welcome. Can we help you guys clear the table and clean up?" he says to the servers as he and Luke jump up in unison, begin to stack empty plates, and disappear into the kitchen.

"Someone's in a hurry." I smile. "Is there a ball game calling your name, Louis?" I say loudly.

"Can't imagine anything could be more inviting than to just sit here, have a glass of wine, and let your food digest," Stevie says while rubbing her stomach. "Actually, can you pass me that clean bread plate? I may pick at that bird some more."

"If we could market your metabolism, we'd make a fortune," I joke. "Where do you put it? Has she always been like this, Melissa? Refresh my memory."

"Like what, a human garbage disposal?" Stevie's daughter jokes.

"I hadn't thought of it quite that way," I laugh, "but yes, I guess that's what I meant."

"She's been like this for as long as I can remember, but you've known her almost as long as I have. I do remember when I was a teenager I made the mistake of thinking it was hereditary, but I can gain weight just looking at some foods. Unfortunately, I don't share the same gene." Melissa winks at her mom and stands up as Lila squirms in her arms. "I need to change this little girl; be right back. Can you keep an eye on Jaden?"

"I go with Mama," the toddler says, trotting after her before either Stevie or I can grab him.

"He's following you," Stevie shouts after Melissa.

"Got him," Melissa calls out from the hallway.

"Guess we know how to clear a room, eh, girlfriend?" Stevie reaches for the bottle of Silver Oak. "May I refresh your glass, madame?"

"Oui, oui. Merci!"

"I have an idea. How about if we give Louis and the kids a reprieve and let them go back to our place to get into their comfy clothes and watch the game while you and I hang out here and visit. Unless you've got other plans?" Stevie asks.

"Actually, I do have a tentative date, but I think I'll play hard to get for a while. Give me a minute to call him," I tease.

"Let him down easy; send him a text instead," she advises as we head to the kitchen to deliver the good news to Stevie's family.

"Are you sure?" Louis says, trying valiantly to hide his enthusiasm.

"We don't want to abandon you," Luke adds.

"Don't believe either one of them," Melissa laughs. "You know they're both dying to put on sweatpants with elastic waistbands and become one with the sofa in front of the TV. I'll be the only honest one here, Aunt Gloria. I love you and I love being here, but I need to get these two back to Mom and Dad's so I can get them ready for bed; it's been a long day for them—and me."

"I understand, sweetie." I give her a big hug, grateful to still be her "Aunt Gloria."

"So you kids really don't mind if I hang back and visit a bit with Gloria?" Stevie asks.

With a unanimous decision that all is well, Louis and Luke load the car in record time.

"It's times like this I'd love to have a driveway," Louis says, helping his daughter and grandkids get settled into the backseat.

It's only a seven-block trip back to their house, but once they get there, it's a dance of coordination to unload the car and get everything and everyone loaded into the elevator and upstairs, and then Louis has to drop the car at the hotel valet so they can park it before he can walk back to the house. I love their place, their view, and their luscious balcony, but I love the convenience of my home more.

Luke hops into the front seat balancing a casserole dish and two Tupperware containers of leftovers that didn't fit in the trunk. They won't have to cook for the next several days.

"See you later, gorgeous." Louis wraps me in a big bear hug.

"Stay safe, my sweet silver fox."

I wave good-bye and stand outside until their car disappears from view before heading back inside.

While I've been saying good-bye, Stevie and the servers from the agency have been like superheroes. In no time the table is clear, the dishes are loaded into the dishwasher, the table linens are in a basket in the laundry room, and the kitchen is clean. Although they haven't said a word to indicate they would rather be elsewhere, I can sense the two young men are just as anxious as Louis and Luke to go watch the game that is already in progress. They are visibly excited while maintaining a professional decorum when I give them each a generous and well-earned gratuity and tell them they can leave early.

It's not quite four in the afternoon when I close the door behind them and turn to Stevie, exhausted but elated.

"Let's finish this wine out by the pool; the weather is so nice," she says.

"Lead the way." I grab my glass and a corkscrew—and another bottle of wine, just in case.

As we pass the den on our way out, Stevie stops to admire a recent art acquisition.

"Stunning! I absolutely love this piece, Gloria! It doesn't have the sharp edges of a Picasso, but it looks a little like his work, is it?"

"Not quite, but you're close. It's by Françoise Gilot; she was Pablo Picasso's artistic muse and the mother of his two children, Claude and Paloma."

"I'm not sure I've ever seen any of her work." She peers closely at the canvas.

"There aren't too many of her pieces in private collections. I was lucky to get this one from the Mann Gallery; Mr. Weathers helped me acquire it. Gilot had quite a fascinating life; met Picasso when she was twenty-one and he was sixty."

"Yikes, that's quite a jump—forty years older."

"I know; can you imagine? They were only together for a decade, and ten years after that she wrote *My Life with Picasso*."

"Well, I absolutely love it, Gloria."

"You have excellent taste. I'll make a note in my will to leave it to you," I laugh.

"You do that. While you're at it, you can leave me the art deco dressing table in your boudoir and the pair of oriental chairs in your foyer."

"Anything else?"

"Nah, I think that'll do it. Oh, wait! I've always coveted your Waterford collection; you could throw that in too," she laughs, "and I'll make sure to leave you my collection of vintage jewelry if I go first. That's about all I have that your money can't buy." She puts her arm around my shoulders and leads me out the door.

"Don't say that, Stevie; you have a great deal that money can't buy."

"Whatever." She rolls her eyes.

We sit in wicker rocking chairs poolside and both exhale at the same time. The melodic sound of water gently flowing from the stacked marble waterfall is like comforting music.

Stevie reaches over and puts her hand on top of mine. "You did good, girly-girl, maybe too good; we might have to start coming here every year."

"That would be fine with me."

It's only when the sun goes down enough to trigger all the outdoor lights in the landscaping, pool, and waterfall that we realize a few minutes has turned into hours.

"Let's do drunch at Galatoire's next week when I get home from Paris," I suggest as Stevie heads out for home.

"Sounds good to me, if I'm back in time from the Kremlin," she jokes.

When Stevie leaves, I let Coco out in the dog run while I make a quick tour of the house to close blinds, turn off overhead lights, and make sure everything is secure. The entire house is wired with timers that turn nightlights on inside almost every room, so the house always looks occupied; but when Maria and Randy are gone, I like to take the extra precaution of checking everything. Coco is waiting for me when I open the door to let her back in.

I see the Post-it note stuck to the high-tech electronic keypad on the wall when I go to set the alarm.

> Good job! You are setting the alarm! I am proud of you!
> Happy Thanksgiving, Miss Gloria! The coffeepot is ready
> to go in the morning; have a good trip. Please call if you
> need us! We will see you when you return on Wednesday.
> Randy will be at baggage claim to meet you.
>
> Love,
> Maria and Randy

The overabundance of exclamation points in her sweet message makes me smile.

Maria and Randy weren't happy that I hired a driver to take me to the airport on Saturday, but I insisted. These wonderful people are always there for me; they deserve some time off.

What they don't know is that I've also hired the same driver to take me to the Imaging Center tomorrow for my endoscopy and upper GI test. I tried to reschedule the appointment for when I returned from France, but they were booked until the first of the year and my doctor was pretty insistent. It's a relatively easy procedure, and I might as well get it over with so we can begin to officially treat this ulcer or whatever it is.

"Come on, Coco; let's go to bed. It's been a long and wonderful day."

She looks up at me with warm and trusting eyes and lumbers beside me to the bedroom. She's getting so old and weak, and I slow down my pace so she can keep up.

CHAPTER 10

— Stephanie —

Friday, December 3

It's been a little over a week since Thanksgiving and I'm still full; nonetheless, Louis is headed to Galatoire's to hold our spot for a table for Friday drunch. The kids left earlier in the week, and as much as I love having them here, I'm not as young as I used to be, and all the activity wore me out. All I've wanted to do is curl up with a good book and hang around the house, which is unusual for me. I'm finding it difficult to get started today, but I need to get ready; Louis will have a fit if I'm late.

Getting dressed for drunch is the kick in the pants I need to revive my energy, and my anticipation for the start of the holiday season increases with every step I take toward Galatoire's. I haven't seen Gloria since she returned from Paris on Wednesday, I'm anxious to hear how things went with the Carlyle cuties. To be honest, I have no idea if the elder Carlyle is cute or not, but with sonny boy being a ten plus on the Richter scale of looks, I'm thinking he could balance any deficit his papa might possess— unless Dad is an absolute troll, like Onassis. But then again, Jackie did marry him, and it wasn't like she was financially destitute.

My mouth starts to water as I get closer to Galatoire's. December is a very busy month for this restaurant, starting with the first Monday, when they hold their Galatoire's Annual Christmas Auction, with proceeds benefitting several charities, such as the Galatoire Foundation, Operation Homefront, the Hermann-Grimm and Gallier Historic Houses, and the Youth Empowerment Project. They also host an annual Mardi Gras Auction.

Whether conducted silent or live, auctions are part of the fabric of philanthropy. Gloria tries every year to get me involved on the silent auction committee for the Grace House Gala, and although that leadership aspect doesn't interest me, I do love the thrill of the chase, the acquisition of unique auction items, and putting together auction packages. I've agreed to help her in this area. "But don't expect me to sit on any committees," I told Gloria firmly. "I work alone; take it or leave it." She took it.

However, the Galatoire Annual Auctions are different—unique—in that the items in their auction never change; they remain the same year after year. In fact, their auction items never leave the confines of the restaurant. You see, the items going up for bid are dinner reservations and select table locations at two of the most talked-about events in the French Quarter: the huge party on the Friday before Christmas, and another on the Friday before Mardi Gras—two "sold out" events where everyone in the restaurant is there because they won their reservations at the annual auction. Seats can go anywhere from $300 each to well over $3,000 for a table for eight in one of the prime locations on the main floor. My plan today is to convince Louis that we must attend the annual auction, scheduled for this Monday.

It appears that diners are just being seated for Friday Drunch when I arrive, and it's standing room only at the door. I see Louis wave from the front of the line just as Gloria gets out of a cab in front of the restaurant.

"Great timing, girlfriend!" I give her a big hug. "Welcome back; let's go eat."

"That's my girl, a one-track mind that's always on food; sounds good to me," she says, linking her arm in mine. "I feel like my feet haven't touched down since my plane landed on Wednesday; it's been one thing after another. Seriously, it's a virtual madhouse."

"You love it and you know it."

We make our way through the crowd to reach Louis. "I want to hear all about your trip," I say. "How is that hunk-a-hunk-a burning love?"

Gloria smacks me on the arm and says, "Shh," and then turns to Louis. "Hello, my sweet silver fox." She reaches her arms out to Louis and kisses him on both cheeks.

"Hello back atcha, gorgeous; glad you could join us. Stevie wasn't sure if you'd be able to make it. Hey, thanks again for dinner last week; we had a great time. The kids sure loved seeing you."

"You are so welcome, and it was good to see them too."

"Looks like you've been getting some sun. From what I gather, maybe it's *not* all work and no play, eh?" Louis winks mischievously.

Gloria furrows her brow at me. "Stephanie, what have you been telling this man?"

"Nothing, nothing. Just that you're doing some business with two single guys—one who stepped out of GQ *Magazine*, and the other straight from the Forbes Top Ten."

"You are insufferable."

"Yeah, but that's why you love me."

Louis is right, Gloria does look rather tan, but I can't tell if it's real or sprayed on. I've never known her to get a fake tan, but then I've never known her to get a real one either. She's always maniacal about wearing sunscreen and big-brimmed hats whenever she's in the sun—one of the reasons she looks so amazing at her age.

"Bon appétit!" David Gooch greets us at the door, looking especially handsome today with his dark pinstriped suit and festive holiday tie, and personally escorts us to our seats.

Let drunch begin!

Holiday spirit is definitely in the air, and almost everyone is table-hopping. Gloria and I usually don't budge an inch from our seats; Louis table-hops enough for the three of us. Don't get me wrong; it's not that we're snobs, but no matter how often we talk, there's always so much for Gloria and me to catch up on when we attend drunch. We know that our dear friends and neighbors will come by our table to say hello.

I'm hoping I'll have the opportunity today to broach the subject of the discovery I made at the cemetery on All Saint's Day, but this might not be the time or place. I still can't believe she had a daughter she has never spoken of. I wanted to bring it up on Thanksgiving, but that timing didn't feel right either. I'll just have to play it by ear as I've been doing.

True to form, we no sooner receive our drink orders than Louis is out of his seat and visiting with folks across the room, and friends begin to stop by our table in a steady stream.

It's great to see Tim McNally, our local wine aficionado and his lovely wife, Brenda, also a writer. Brenda is never without her fabulous digital camera and is always snapping candid shots of folks she meets and greets throughout the Quarter. Even better, she never fails to upload the pictures and send them to us. Were it not for Brenda, I wouldn't have half the film memories I do today; she's a gem.

"So, tell me, have you made a decision? Are you selling out?" I ask Gloria just as our server stops by and tops off our champagne from the bottle chilling in the ice bucket.

"Stevie, please, not too loud; I really don't want to field questions from anyone this early in the game, and I surely don't want my employees to find this out from anyone before they hear it from me."

"So you have made a decision! Was there any *physical coercion* needed, courtesy of Monsieur Carlyle?" I tease.

"Stevie, you're being absolutely ridiculous; this is business and nothing more. Besides, he's fourteen years younger than me."

"I meant the senior Carlyle, not the boy-toy Carlyle. Sonny is easy on the eyes, but it's dad who is ripe for picking. He's a ba-jillionaire widower; what's not to like?"

"I'm going to pretend I didn't hear you say that." Gloria shakes her head.

"So what's with the tan?" I peer close. "Looks real, but I know better."

"Do you like it?"

"It's different, but yes, I think I like it."

"It was a whim. We're featuring a new salon day spa that's opening on Royal, and I met with the owner yesterday to discuss the layout. We finished up early, I had an hour between appointments, and the next thing I know I'm standing naked in a chrome cubicle, being sprayed like a '57 Chevy. It was surreal."

"Now that's a mind picture I've never had before. A bit scary." I laugh.

"You can say that again!" We toast our glasses, amazed that we can actually hear the ding of the crystal against the din in the room.

We've only been here an hour and a half and we've gone through nearly two bottles of some incredibly delicious champagne, and the salads are just being served, which is all part of the restaurant's master plan—giving the chef and cooking crew time to prepare orders, and guests time to visit. Louis is now standing by a table near the front window talking to Kenny Charbonnet, a local attorney, and his beautiful wife, Janie, a premiere French Quarter power couple.

"I'm heading to the ladies' room; be right back." I grab my purse.

"I'll alert the media," Gloria responds with a repartee we've used for years that always cracks me up.

"You do that, girlfriend," I say as I head toward the back of the restaurant.

I'm within a few feet of my destination when I see him. I keep walking, and thanks to the mirror-lined walls it doesn't look like I'm staring, but I am.

There's no mistaking Jake LeBlanc, just as there's no mistaking that the woman he's sitting next to isn't Elizabeth. He has one arm draped around her shoulder and the other draped around a highball glass. Their heads are close together as they talk, and he must be saying something witty, as she throws her head back in laughter. *Oh boy, if Elizabeth could see this.* I'm tempted to click a pic with my cell phone camera, but I left it on the table.

Wait until I tell Gloria.

After the quickest visit to the ladies' room ever, I prepare to head back to my table, determined not to stop and visit with anyone on the way. I take one last look at Jake to make sure my mind isn't playing tricks, and it's not. In fact, it appears the two lovebirds are sitting even closer together now—if that's possible, considering if she were any closer, she'd be in his lap.

I can't believe what I'm seeing. It sure takes balls, or a lack thereof, for a married man to carry on like this in public. Can't he be more discrete? Who raised him? What a jerk.

I look up to see I'm not the only one witnessing this spectacle. Evelyn Schwartz, a writer for the *Times Picayune*, is sitting in the opposite corner with her cronies, watching Jake's every move; and honey, he has some moves. I notice the man sitting on her left is holding his cell phone as though he's checking something, when clearly what he's doing is secretly taking photos.

I hurry back to my table, thankful that Gloria is alone as I sit quickly in the chair next to her and spill all the dirty details.

"Her photographer didn't fool me with his act; I know he was taking pictures, and Evelyn looked like someone about to get a medal at the Olympics," I say.

Just then we look up to see Evelyn walking toward us with her clutch tucked under her arm, on her way to make a quick exit. She nods at us with a hint of a smile.

Suddenly, Gloria stands and extends her hand, blocking the aisle.

"Hello, Evelyn. How nice to see you. Leaving so soon?" They shake hands.

"Oh, hello, Gloria. I didn't see you over here; this isn't your usual table. I'm accustomed to seeing you in the center of the room, holding court where all the action is."

"Ah yes, but these seats along the wall do afford one the opportunity to people-watch in a rather surreptitious way, don't you agree?" Evelyn tilts her head and raises her chin, and I can almost see the wheels turning in her brain as she tries to figure out her next move when Gloria places her hand on Evelyn's shoulder and gently turns her toward me.

"Have you met my dear friend Stephanie Lewis? Stephanie, this is Evelyn Schwartz. Evelyn writes for the *Picayune*." We nod a polite hello. "Why don't you join us for a glass of holiday champagne, Evelyn? I'm sure Henry won't mind if you're late; tell him you were with me."

I have no idea who Henry is, or what Gloria has up her sleeve, but I know she's become quite protective of Elizabeth. *This could get interesting.*

"Thank you for the invitation, but I have to run; it seems like my Christmas just came early," she says with a smirk on her face. She steps around Gloria and heads quickly toward the exit.

Gloria gives me a determined look and immediately takes out her phone. Within seconds she has the editor of the newspaper on the line. She holds the phone away from her mouth and whispers to me, "It's a small world."

Oh, how I love the way this woman operates! The Henry she was referring to is Henry Paxton, the editor of the *Picayune*; you can't get any higher on the food chain at the paper than him. Gloria is well-respected in the industry and knows just about everyone in the print business.

With the phone to her ear, she walks outside to continue the conversation.

When she returns, she has a look of disgust on her tanned face as she puts her phone on the table and sits down.

"I can't stop them from running the story, but he'll hold it until Sunday. I hate to see a family destroyed, especially at Christmas. I had a feeling Jake was a snake, but his children don't need to find out this way; Elizabeth doesn't need to find out this way."

"You think she doesn't already know? From what I saw, it looks like that marriage has been on the rocks for some time. You don't suddenly feel free enough to carry on in such a public place with another woman when you're happily married, unless you don't think of yourself as married."

"Thank you for your insight, Dr. Phil. Just because you have a front-row seat doesn't mean you have the best view in the house."

I'm taken aback by her tone and am thinking how to respond when there's a temporary lull in the boisterous volume and she picks up her phone to make another call.

"I'm so glad you answered, Elizabeth; I was wondering if I could stop by today and talk to you. Slow down, sweetie; I can't understand you," Gloria looks worried.

"What's the matter?" I ask.

Gloria holds the phone away from her mouth and says, "She's crying; she's hysterical."

Although it's impossible to make out the words, the fact I can hear Elizabeth's voice at all from where I'm sitting surprises me. She's clearly upset.

"Elizabeth, listen to me. I know it's hard, but try to calm down, honey. I'm on my way now. I'll be there in a few minutes and we can talk, okay? No, sweetie, it isn't putting me out. Remember—I called you first; I want to see you. It's going to be okay. Take a deep breath; I'll be there soon." She hangs up, stands, and reaches for her sweater and purse.

"So she already knows?" I reach for my champagne.

"No. St least not about this. Seems they had a fight this morning; he packed a bag and said he was going out of town for the weekend. She said it wasn't like their 'usual' fights; she thinks he means it this time. She's worried sick about him and blaming herself."

"Some 'out of town' he chose, eh?"

It's no secret I don't think much of our Madame President, but I wouldn't wish this kind of situation on anyone—especially at Christmas, and especially on someone with children.

Gloria opens her handbag, takes out a one-hundred-dollar bill, and sets it in front of me. "Please give this to Louis in case I don't see him on my way out; and tell him I said good-bye, okay?" She gives me a quick hug.

"What are you going to say? How do you tell someone about that?" I nod my head toward the table where Jake and company are still sitting, seemingly oblivious to the world.

"I don't quite know. Say a prayer for me. Someone has to tell her before it's splashed all over every cotton-picking newspaper in the country, and I'm not going to do it over the phone."

CHAPTER 11

— Gloria —

Friday, December 3

The taxi drops me off in front of Elizabeth's grand and somewhat gaudy home in Old Metairie, a rather prestigious—and some say pretentious—area, not too far from the Quarter. The little community of Old Metairie, part of the vast suburban expanse of Metairie, is located between New Orleans and Kenner. The LeBlanc home is in the two-hundred block on Mulberry Drive, a very distinguished location. Many of the homes in this area were flooded by Hurricane Katrina, and all but one or two have been completely rebuilt. It's an old neighborhood that is a mix of old and new money as well as old facades and new construction.

Their weekend home on Governor Nicholls Street in the French Quarter is gorgeous—a true example of sophistication and elegance. This home is much bigger, but no less elegant; it's just the kind of home where you'd expect a sports star to live with his beautiful wife and four lovely children. However, I know things are about to change considerably for this family, and my heart breaks for them.

"Thank you for coming, Gloria. I feel like such an idiot for the meltdown I had on the phone; I'm sorry." Elizabeth looks worn and haggard when she answers the door.

"Don't be silly, dear; there's no need to apologize."

"I've called Jake several times to apologize," she says, sniffling, "but either he's ignoring my calls or has his phone turned off. I've got a fresh pot of coffee in the kitchen; let's sit in there, okay?" She leads me through the luxurious foyer into her great room kitchen, where coffee mugs and a plate of homemade cookies await us.

"Are the children home?" I ask as she pours us piping-hot coffee.

"No. Since Michael got his license, he uses any excuse possible to drive. He's taking the girls shopping at the mall after school. He's a good driver, very careful and conscientious, so I don't worry—at least not too much." She tries to smile, but the sadness in her eyes makes me want to weep, which is the last thing she needs right now.

"Do they know about your argument with their father?"

"No, thank God. They had already left for school before Jake came downstairs. I could tell he wasn't feeling well. I should have left him alone, but I didn't. You know, he's one of the oldest players on the team, and every year he worries that this is the year he'll get cut. I can't imagine what that kind of pressure must be like. Plus he's in physical pain almost every day. He really needs surgery on his knee again, but he keeps putting it off; says he has to work through the pain for the sake of the team until the end of the season. Oh, Gloria, I don't know what got into me. I should never have pushed him so hard; he's going through so much stress right now."

"Pushed? How so?" I take a sip of coffee.

"Not physically, nothing like that. It's just that things have been a little strained for us over the past few months, and I told him I thought we should see someone."

"Someone—as in a marriage counselor?"

"Yes."

"I take it he didn't embrace that suggestion?"

"Oh, he embraced it all right. For me. He said *I'm* the one who needs a shrink, *I'm* the one who has the problems, and as soon as *I* can get it together, he'll think about *us* getting back together. That's when he went to his room and started throwing things into a bag."

"*His* room?" My question opens a floodgate of emotion as Elizabeth pours out her heart.

"We haven't slept in the same room for months. If he's not on the road with the team, he's at the gym or out with the guys. When he is home, we barely talk. Some nights he doesn't come home at all. He has zero time for the kids; it's like they don't exist. I keep making excuses for him to the kids, but that isn't working anymore; they know something's wrong. We've been married for nineteen years, but it's like we're strangers now. I just don't want to live this way anymore, Gloria, and instead of helping, I pushed him too hard. I nagged him too much that things had to change, and now look what I've done."

"I'm sorry, honey." I reach over and take her hands in mine. "No one is perfect; we all make mistakes, and marriage is hard. I don't know all the dynamics of your relationship with your husband, but I do know that you want the best for your children and those you care about. You are not responsible for the choices Jake makes. Do you understand that?"

"Yes." She looks at me sadly as the tears roll gently down her cheeks, and I grasp her hands more firmly in my own.

"Elizabeth, you are only responsible for the choices you make, and I'm here because you're going to need to make a whole lot of difficult and painful choices in the next twenty-four hours. There's no easy way to say this, but I want you to know that I'm here for you and I will help in any way that I can."

"What do you mean?" she whispers.

By the time I finish telling her what I know, she's run the gamut of emotions from shock to anger, betrayal, grief, humiliation, and now fear.

"Oh my God, it's going to be all over the newspapers! What am I going to do? How do I tell the kids? Where should I go? Should I stay here? What should I do first?"

"First we develop a strategy."

She decides it will be best if the kids don't have to deal with the nightmare of the initial media blitz, so Elizabeth calls her parents in Atlanta to arrange for the children to fly out and stay with them for the next two weeks and then books early Saturday-morning flights for them. She tells her parents the truth and decides to tell her children the truth as well when they get home later tonight—at least what she knows of the truth at this point: that their father was in a restaurant earlier today with another woman and a newspaper photographer took pictures of them, that there will most likely be a lot of media attention, and that not all of it will be true.

"Sending them to Mom and Dad's is for their own protection; they don't need to be here if the press decides to make a field day out of this. Is there any chance the story might not run at all?" she asks.

"Well, as far as I know there really isn't a story, just photos. But that's all they need; they'll make up the rest as they go along. As soon as the Sunday morning paper drops, this will go out over the AP newswire; and if I were you, I'd prepare for the worse. If it passes under the radar, it will be a blessing, but I don't think that will happen."

At this point she's stopped beating herself up for any mistakes she has made and is too angry to even think about what to say to Jake if he calls.

"He said he was going away for the weekend. For his sake, I hope he doesn't change his mind, because his face is the last thing I want to see right now!"

She makes a call to her best friend, who is also an attorney—not to talk about divorce, it's too soon for that, but just to talk about her options right now insofar as protecting her children. We go over every possible scenario, including her statement to the press, which is really a nonstatement. It is so much better that she will be prepared, not blindsided.

"Okay, now let's talk about next week's garden club meeting. Is everything set for the Christmas party? How can I help?" I ask.

"Oh my gosh, how can I face the club members? I'm so embarrassed."

"Young lady, have you not been listening to anything I've said? *You* have nothing to be embarrassed about! It was Jake who made the choice to behave in a reprehensible manner, not you. Hold your head high and, like the song says, *you will survive*."

We go over the luncheon party plans, and it's clear that everything is on track. We agree that I will handle all the last-minute details, and she hands me the file.

"Sweetie, all you have to do is show up looking beautiful as always. Until then, you have my cell phone number, and if you need anything—and I mean anything—do not hesitate to call me."

Our good-bye hug lasts considerably longer than usual as she fights valiantly to keep herself together.

"Thank you, Gloria, for everything. I love you."

"Love you too, kiddo. And I mean it—you *will* survive."

The kids pull in just as my taxi pulls out, and I say a silent prayer for this family whose lives are about to change.

* * * *

Monday, December 6

Just as expected, the photo of Jake LeBlanc and his mystery woman at Galatoire's was front and center on the Lifestyle page of yesterday's Sunday paper. The mystery woman is Mitzi Branch, and it turns out he's been seeing her for quite some time—and not only her; other women and photos begin to surface in record time. I've talked to Elizabeth several times since yesterday, and she's hanging in there. It's going to be another busy week.

I head to the kitchen, where the aroma of fresh-brewed coffee calls my name.

"Good morning, Maria."

"Good morning, Miss Gloria. Would you like some breakfast?"

"Hmm, how about some toast?"

"Coming right up. Those were delivered a few minutes ago." I follow the nod of her head to see a very beautiful, and very big, arrangement of two-dozen long-stemmed red roses.

"My goodness, did someone die?" I laugh. "That's huge! Who is it from?"

"The card is addressed to you, Miss Gloria; I did not open it," she smiles.

"Well, well, why don't we just find out." The card is from Don & Bill's Florist, one of the most elegant shops in the Quarter. "Ooh-la-la, someone has good taste."

Bonjour Gloria,

Wishing you a fresh new week filled with opportunity, blessings, and joie de vivre!

Anthony

"They're from Carlyle Communications, how sweet." I slide the card into my pocket and take my toast and coffee up to my office, where I hit the ground running.

I didn't think it was possible, but calls from garden club members about Elizabeth and this breaking news are even more intense than they were when she made membership changes in October. I love these women, but some of them really need to get a life outside of this club. Stevie has checked in a few times, and I have assured her that the Christmas party this Thursday will proceed without a hitch.

The receptionist from Dr. Creswell's office calls to schedule an appointment to discuss my test results from the endoscopy I had the day after Thanksgiving. The soonest I can get in is this Friday.

After lunch, Charlotte comes to my office to tell me her husband will be transferred out of state and they will be moving in the spring, and she sadly gives me her notice. I'll be sorry to see her go, but I can't help but think of this as a good sign. If I accept the offer, the *NOLA 2 NOLA* staff will be kept on as part of the acquisition, but their offices will be moved to the Central Business District, an area just outside the Quarter. I know Charlotte dislikes driving every day; she walks to work. But the CBD is a bit too far to walk. I was worried about how she would take the news and was planning to ask her to remain as my personal assistant. Sadly, that is no longer an option, as her last day will be May 1.

With a seven-hour time difference, it's after eight o'clock at night in Paris when I call Anthony to thank him for the lovely flowers, and I'm surprised when he answers the phone in his office.

"Our team has been working overtime to incorporate your requests into our proposal. We are sending the first draft for your review via courier tomorrow. Please do not hesitate to add or revise anything you wish. The only way this will work is if you are 100 percent happy; that is our goal, my goal."

His sincerity feels completely genuine, and I am once again amazed at the ease with which we communicate.

It's almost an hour later when I hang up. I then carve out time to focus on the garden club Christmas party and place a call to the Omni Hotel to finalize our plans. Elizabeth's notes indicate she has reserved the Joséphine Bonaparte Room, but when I call I'm informed that the room was never reserved.

"I'm sorry, Mrs. Vincent; our records show that Mrs. LeBlanc never confirmed this arrangement. The Joséphine Bonaparte Room is occupied by a conference until this coming weekend."

I speak with the general manager, who is the son of a close associate and he graciously arranges for us to have our Christmas luncheon in a blocked-off section of the Esplanade Ballroom, a beautiful area that faces the decorated courtyard. This is one mistake that will turn out for the best, and the members need never know.

Before the day ends, Emme Masterson stops by to discuss the Grace House Gala, and I'm excited to hear that significant donations are coming in for the silent auction, including a 1964 Ford Mustang convertible donated by Mr. and Mrs. Patrick Marshall, the owners of one of the largest private collections of classic automobiles in the country. Clearly, my sideboard started the ball rolling.

"Stevie has some great ideas for the auction packages," Emme says. "I just wish she would agree to lead some of these willing volunteers who really need direction. We need to leverage our assets, but she's insistent that she work alone. Can you talk to her?"

"I've been talking to her about this for years. I'll see what I can do, but I'm not promising anything."

I'm the last to leave the *NOLA 2 NOLA* offices, and when I finally get downstairs it's after nine, I'm thoroughly exhausted, and my back is killing me. I can't sit like that all day, no matter how ergonomic my chair is. I stare into the refrigerator, but nothing looks good. I grab a small container of Greek yogurt, eat a few spoonfuls, and toss it into the trash. I let Coco inside from the dog run, and we head back to my master suite, where I swallow a few ibuprofen, take a swig of liquid antacid, and crawl into bed.

CHAPTER 12
— Gloria —

Thursday, December 9

The local hotel lobbies are beautiful during the holiday season. Stevie's favorite is the Royal Sonesta, with their Christmas-tree-lined halls, great for family photos. However, the Omni Royal Hotel has outdone everyone this year. The holiday decorations and lights at the entrance and in the lobby will transport you to a sparkling Christmas wonderland. If this breathtaking display doesn't put you in the spirit, nothing will.

The annual Christmas meeting of the garden club is always a festive occasion. We don't conduct any general business at this meeting. There is no formal agenda, just good food, good friends, and a dash of entertainment, most often in the form of Dolores Delacroix, who is unfortunately unable to make it today because of an unexpected business emergency. She will be sorely missed.

Stevie comes up behind me and wraps her arms around my shoulders.

"Merry Christmas, my best friend; you look beautiful today."

"Thank you, but my goodness, it's you who looks beautiful! Turn around and let me get a look at you!"

Stevie is wearing a tight-fitting off-the-shoulder red satin dress, with lipstick that is a perfect match. Her strappy red shoes are encrusted with crystals, and she looks amazing.

All the ladies look elegant. This is the only holiday event for some of our older members, and they make sure it counts.

Unfortunately, looks can be deceiving. I recall some of the judgmental and juvenile phone conversations I've had over the past few days about

Elizabeth with more than a few of the women seated in the room today, many of whom have tried and convicted her without a hearing. Jake is a sports legend in this town, and it's incomprehensible for some folks to think that he could actually be to blame. Surely he sought refuge in the arms of other women because his wife, our club president, is seriously flawed in some way. This mind-set boggles me.

When Elizabeth enters the ballroom, she is wearing a gold-sequined gown that I have no doubt is from the Dior couture collection. Her luxurious hair is swept up into a mass of curls on top of her head, with gentle tendrils hanging down on each side. The room gets noticeably quieter as she bravely crosses the floor to join us, her head held high, and it doesn't take long before the volume returns.

"Stephanie, what a gorgeous gown. You look absolutely fabulous in red; that's definitely your color," she exclaims sincerely, and then she turns and gives me a hug. "And you, madame, look stunning as well. Is that an Oscar de la Renta?"

"Good eye. Yes, it is. How are you doing, sweetie?" I take her hand.

"I'm hanging in there."

Although her makeup is impeccable, it's clear she has been crying. Her eyes are red and slightly puffy. This is her first public appearance since her husbands' indiscretions were disclosed on Sunday. Since then, the press has descended on her like vultures; they've been having a feeding frenzy. You can barely turn on the television or surf the Internet news sites without seeing photos of Elizabeth along with ridiculous headlines and fabricated stories of grossly inaccurate conjecture.

Things have gotten especially messy over the past twenty-four hours, as it's come to light that Jake has hired a very high-profile divorce attorney who is launching a definitive smear campaign against Elizabeth to deflect the light from his client.

Although I'm sure most of the ladies are unaware of their presence, there are private security guards stationed at the entrance doors to the ballroom as well as in the hotel lobby, at my expense, maintaining a watchful eye to keep paparazzi, reporters, and tourists from ascending on Elizabeth. I'm not sure how this afternoon is going to turn out, and I say a quick prayer that all hell doesn't break loose today.

There is an awkward silence between Stevie and Elizabeth.

"This room is absolutely beautiful; don't you agree, ladies?" I ask.

"Ah, yes, yes it is," Stevie says, and she takes a glass of champagne from the tray offered by the server who walks by. Both Elizabeth and I decline.

"Well, it's thanks to you and your team that we're able to have our celebration here at the Omni this year, Stephanie," Elizabeth says. "You folks sold a lot of cookbooks last year to raise the funds for this. I'm wondering if you would consider doing it again, if you would be in charge of collecting the recipes and working with me to develop the next cookbook?"

Stevie is bumfuzzled, and I'm a bit surprised myself, but it's a rather brilliant strategy. A line by Vito Corleone from *The Godfather* echoes in my mind: "Keep your friends close and your enemies closer."

"Ahh, sure?" Stevie replies, and she takes a gulp of champagne.

"Excellent! As you know, things in my life are a bit … hectic … right now, but let's get together after the first of the year and talk about this, okay? I think we have an untapped resource in this cookbook, and I have some new ideas I'd like to run by you for your feedback, okay?"

"Okay." Stevie looks at me to say something, and I just smile.

I must say, it's rather a pleasure to see Stevie a bit off kilter; it doesn't happen often. She excuses herself to take a seat. Elizabeth begins to circulate among the tables and visit with members, but I'm disappointed to see no one is making an attempt to talk at any length with her. Nonetheless, she continues to hold her head high and joins in the gleeful applause and appreciation as Miss V. begins to distribute her gifts to the members.

An annual tradition, Miss V. makes old-fashioned tea cakes wrapped in bright colored cellophane; we usually get four or five cookies each. As we've agreed upon, this is the only gift that members will receive today. For once it isn't all about us, because this is the one time every year that we give back to the community in a big way as we participate in the local toy drive. This is a competitive group of women, and every year they try their best to outdo one another in toy donations.

While it's true that many of our members are involved in their own philanthropic endeavors and charities, the garden club as a whole doesn't sponsor any community outreach projects, and I for one would like to see the club adopt a more community-minded spirit throughout the entire year. However, I don't let that diminish the pride I feel as the ladies enter the ballroom and place their unwrapped toys in the collection boxes that are now overflowing.

If only they could demonstrate that same generosity of spirit and love to their sister. I'm saddened to see that some of the women are greeting Elizabeth reluctantly, and in some cases, rudely.

It's about fifteen minutes before the meeting starts when I have an idea—just enough time to put the plan in place.

Like clockwork, Miss Alma rings our broken bell—*Ding-dink-ding, ding-dink-ding*—and approaches the podium.

"Ladies, we have a special surprise today. This doesn't happen often, but one of our most distinguished members has asked to say something, so it is with great honor and pleasure that I introduce to you someone who needs no introduction: Gloria Vincent."

I'm humbled at the applause as I walk to the podium, and do my best to ignore the surprised looks on Stevie's and Elizabeth's faces.

"Thank you, Miss Alma; and thank you, ladies. What a joy to look out and see so many friends—friends who are truly like family.

"It's hard to believe another year has come to an end—a year that has been filled with a lot of changes, a lot of ups and downs. However, rocky roads aren't new to most of us. Over the years, our members have experienced situations and circumstances of great trial and tribulation, and yes, even of great controversy. I personally know every lady in this room today; we've been through a lot together, and there isn't a one of us who is exempt from the pain of poor choices, our own or those made by others."

I stop for a moment to let my words sink in.

"However, we are fighters, and many of us have blossomed in spite of, or perhaps because of, where we were planted. We understand that some truly beautiful flowers can spring forth from less-than-ideal places as long as the soil is rich and the plant is properly nurtured. I'd like to think of our garden club as the rich soil that has nurtured all of us through painful seasons of growth and pruning. As we prepare for this new year, we must prune away old thinking that keeps us from being all that we can be."

I pick up a folded piece of paper that I asked Miss Alma to place on the lectern.

"Even though we are not a religious group, I know we are all spiritual women, and I'd like to read a verse from Ecclesiastes." I unfold the paper and read the scripture on the page. "'A person standing alone can be attacked and defeated, but two can stand back-to-back and conquer. Three are even better, for a triple braided cord is not easily broken.'

"Ladies, today we stand together not as a triple-braided cord, but as a cord of fifty strands, a cord of strength that cannot be easily broken." I take the cordless microphone from the stand and continue to talk as I walk toward Elizabeth, who is trying valiantly not to cry.

"When I was faced with selecting someone to fill the position of president of this venerable institution, I did not take the responsibility lightly. The woman I chose was, and is, of strong character, good ethics, and an indomitable spirit. Since coming on board this past September, she has given our garden club new life." I hold out my hand to Elizabeth, who stands up beside me.

"On this, her fourth meeting as our president, Elizabeth LeBlanc faces a challenging time in her life, as she is walking through one of those painful life experiences each of us has experienced in some form or another over the course of our lives. She didn't ask me to speak; in fact, I didn't know I was going to speak until a few minutes ago." I can feel Elizabeth shaking as I hold her hand and address her directly.

"Elizabeth, I know it wasn't easy for you to come here today, and I'd like to speak on behalf of this remarkable group of women who are gathered here now." Hoping to bring a bit of levity to the heaviness of the message, I put my arm around her shoulders and glance shyly at her ample chest. "While some of us, myself included, are envious that we don't have your front"—I pause briefly for the giggles to subside—"I want to assure you that together we most assuredly have your back. You are not alone in the difficult journey you are facing. You can depend on us, all of us, to be the rich soil of protection that you need, to help you grow into the person the almighty Creator has intended for you to become."

Tears stream unashamedly down Elizabeth's cheeks as Miss Alma reaches over from her chair and places a lovely folded lace hanky into her hand.

"And so, my dear sisters, without further ado, let's begin this Christmas celebration as we always do, by having our garden club president greet us and introduce the wonderful musicians she has arranged for our enjoyment today. Ladies, let's give a warm and nurturing welcome to our esteemed president, Elizabeth LeBlanc."

As I hand the microphone to Elizabeth, I am so proud of my sisters as a brief moment of surprise and silence passes and they rise to their feet in thunderous applause.

*　*　*　*　*

Friday, December 10

My doctor's office is about seven miles from my house on Veterans Highway, a drive that on a good traffic day can take all of fifteen minutes. But today is not a good traffic day, and it takes Randy over forty-five minutes. I hurry to catch the elevator and slip in, gliding up to the sixth floor, where I dart down the hall to the oversize glass door, happy to find it still unlocked. There isn't a soul in the waiting room or in the office from what I can see as I walk to the window and gently tap the bell on the counter.

I'm surprised when I see Dr. Creswell appear instead of the receptionist or one of his nurses.

"I'm so sorry I'm late; there was an accident on the—"

"Don't worry about it, Gloria. I knew you wouldn't stand me up without a call; that's why I waited." He shakes my hand on his way across the waiting room to turn the deadbolt on the glass doors. "Come on back; can I get you anything? Water, a Coke?"

"No thanks, I'm fine."

Then it dawns on me—maybe I'm not fine. It's almost six o'clock on a Friday night, my doctor has waited for me after everyone has left the office and has offered me refreshments like a dinner party host. When he leads me into his private office and takes the seat next to me, I know I'm in trouble.

Dr. Creswell wastes no time in giving me the results of my recent test.

"This scope only allowed me to see the upper part of your digestive tract, stomach, and the first part of the intestine, and visually everything looks clear in this region. I couldn't see any unusual masses, but the needle biopsy we took affirms the presence of cancerous cells in the area. I'm just not certain where the cells originated. You need a complete CT scan and more specialized tests, Gloria. I can recommend several excellent oncologists who work out of the Ochsner Medical Center. It's imperative that you see a specialist as soon as possible. This could be very serious."

"How serious?" I whisper.

"Very."

"Are you telling me that I could die?"

"We're all going to die someday, Gloria. That's the nature of the beast: birth, life, and death. It's an inevitable progression," he responds gently, and I can see how hard this is for him.

"Curtis, I appreciate the philosophical truth, but please cut to the chase; we've been friends for a long time. You know me; you know I don't do well with sugarcoating. Lay *all* my cards on the table; I can handle the truth."

"The truth is that in your case we simply don't have enough information yet. It's impossible to predict anything at this point, Gloria."

"Curtis, please," I plead.

"I wish there was more I could tell you. A full CT scan will reveal where the cancer is," he says quietly. "There are all kinds of treatment options for cancer these days, Gloria, and there's a good chance we've caught it in time. We'll know how to proceed once we know what we're dealing with. Let's cross that bridge when we get to it, okay? Right now, you need additional tests."

I'm not sure how I get to the lobby, or how long I've been standing by the floor-to-ceiling windows that face a beautifully landscaped front entrance, but I'm staring mindlessly when I hear my name.

"Gloria?"

"Yes?" The voice is familiar, but I don't recognize the rather mysterious woman standing in front of me.

"It's me," she says, briefly removing her glasses to reveal her unmistakable violet eyes.

I would never have recognized Elizabeth with her hair wrapped in a beautiful silk scarf, wearing oversize sunglasses and rather nondescript clothing. Clearly she's traveling incognito.

"It's been awful, Gloria; I haven't slept in days. Did you see what they're saying now about yesterday? That I was at the Omni for some clandestine meeting with a foreign lover from Istanbul or somewhere? They took a picture of me leaving the building with some man walking behind me who I didn't even know! They're making it up as they go along! My doctor just gave me something to calm my nerves and help me sleep."

"I'm so sorry, honey, but please be careful about leaning too heavily on medications. You're a fighter, and you're going to get through this, but drugs aren't the answer. Promise me you'll use them briefly to cope and not escape. Okay? Promise me."

"I promise. Thank you for caring, and thank you for what you said yesterday. I've had a lot of calls from members; a couple of them even helped me get here today. It's like running an obstacle course getting from my place with the press corps camped out on the sidewalk."

"If you need Randy to take you anywhere, let me know; I'm certain he'd love to help."

"Thank you. So what brings you out this way?" Elizabeth asks.

"Just a routine checkup. I'm heading home right now; do you need a ride?"

"No thank you. My friends are waiting in the parking garage, manning the getaway car, but I'll stay in touch."

When she hugs me, I find it difficult to let her go, and I fight back the tears with every ounce of fortitude I can muster, afraid of releasing an avalanche of emotion.

Randy sees me coming down the walkway and jumps out to open the back door. I'm extremely glad that my own car is waiting at the curb. I slide into the comfort and privacy of the space that beckons me like a warm embrace. The soft leather of the seat feels good.

"Thank you for waiting; I'm so glad not to be taking a taxi today."

"My pleasure, Miss Gloria; you know we aim to please."

It's business as usual until he merges into the traffic that will return us to the Quarter, and I'm finally able to give voice to the cacophony of words that are screaming from my heart.

"It turns out I don't have some wildly exotic disease I picked up in France. It seems I might have some type of cancer, Randy, or at least the 'presence of cancerous cells,' whatever that means. I need to see a specialist, an oncologist."

I can barely say the *C* word, as though speaking it aloud will unleash an uncontrollable monster.

Our eyes meet in the rearview mirror, and our years of working together transcend time as I see his eyes well up with tears.

CHAPTER 13

— Stephanie —

Wednesday, December 15

"**A**re you sure you don't mind if I take on the cookbook project? Truthfully, I can't believe she even asked me; it's not like we're the best of friends."

Louis laughs as he reaches for a slice of grilled flatbread topped with blue cheese and figs that the waiter has just placed on our table.

"What's so funny?" I ask.

"You are, Stevie," he says, and he takes a big bite of the appetizer.

"Why am I funny?"

"Because you know perfectly well that I don't mind if you handle the cookbook project. You've been involved in some form or fashion with the garden club cookbook project for years, and I've listened to you whine and complain about it for ages. You're the perfect person to handle it. They should have asked you years ago. Try this; it's great." He nudges the plate toward me as I shake my head.

"I don't whine and complain."

"In the words of my one true love, 'Whatever,'" he says, laughing even louder as he peruses the menu. "So what are you going to order?" he asks.

"The baked chicken, what else?"

"I'm thinking about trying the crab ravioli; it looks good," he says, eyeing the plate being served to an attractive blonde at the next table.

"Everything looks good to you." I can't help but smile at Louis, who is peering at dinner plates all over the restaurant to see something that catches his eye.

Located just outside the Quarter, Luke's is another one of our go-to spots. With a menu that features a really interesting blend of German, French, and Cajun influences, it's one of the restaurants owned by John Besh, who is perhaps the city's most famous restaurateur after Emeril Lagasse and Chef Paul Prudhomme.

The waiter refills our wineglasses, and we place our order just before a large party of holiday revelers enters.

"What does Gloria think?" Louis swirls his wine around the inside of the goblet.

"About what?"

"The cookbook. About you handling it."

"I'm not actually handling it; I'm helping our fearless leader handle it. And I have no idea what Gloria thinks. She's been swamped every time I call. I think she's avoiding me."

"Don't be silly. She's not avoiding you; she's a busy lady."

"And I'm not?"

"I didn't say that, Stevie. But she runs a very successful magazine and sits on the board of quite a few powerful organizations. I don't know how you two spend as much time together as you do. I think she's managed to juggle things pretty darn well over the years, especially since Charles died."

"I don't know, Louis; something's up. I feel it. I haven't seen her since the garden club Christmas party at the Omni last week. I wonder if Elizabeth has seen her; they have become rather chummy."

"Yeah, well I imagine Elizabeth can use a few friends right about now; Jake the snake is all over the news. How is she doing?"

"Beats me. She doesn't confide in me."

"Did she know he was seeing so many women? Last I heard it was three girlfriends in three states. How can a guy keep that kind of thing quiet for so long?"

"Obviously he couldn't."

When the news first broke about the woman Jake was caught with at Galatoire's, it didn't take long for his other girlfriends to get jealous and come forward. It's been a media circus around their place in the Quarter on Governor Nicholls, where Jake retreated, while Elizabeth has remained in their bigger home a few miles away in Old Metairie. In my mind's eye, I can still see him sitting at that table with an aura of invincibility.

"The morning news said he's still on the team, at least for now, but some of his corporate sponsors are pulling back. Looks like he can kiss all his fame and fortune good-bye," Louis says. "I feel bad for their kids."

"Dolores said Alma told her that Elizabeth sent the kids to Atlanta to be with their grandparents. At least they don't have to be exposed to all of this. Rumor has it Elizabeth's afraid Jake will clean her out if she leaves right now. Personally, I wonder if maybe she's enjoying the spotlight."

"You can't be serious," Louis says, reaching for the salt. "She doesn't seem like that kind of person. Gloria obviously thinks highly of her, and she's a pretty good judge of character."

"Yeah, whatever." I hold out my empty glass for Louis to refill it.

"You should call her."

"I told you, I've been calling her. She's too busy to talk," I say.

"Not Gloria—I'm talking about Elizabeth. If you're going to work on the cookbook together, you might as well figure out how to get along with each other."

"I get along with her just fine."

Louis is quiet while the waiter serves our dinner, but he speaks up quickly as soon as we're alone again.

"Stevie, it's the Christmas season, and the president of your garden club has just found out that her husband, the father of her children, has been having multiple affairs over the past decade. She's home alone. Where is your mercy?"

"I doubt she's alone; she's probably got an entourage of ex-cheerleader girlfriends camping out with her. Can we just change the subject?" I ask. Clearly, Louis isn't grasping this entire situation.

"Gladly. So what should we have for dessert?" Louis asks as he takes the first bite of his dinner. I shake my head and laugh.

It's quite a bit later when we leave the restaurant. After an amazing meal, including a shared dessert of vanilla cake with blueberries and crème fraîche, we need the long walk home.

"I'm stuffed!" I say, wishing I could unbutton the waistband on my pants.

Luke's is located a few blocks on the other side of Canal on St. Charles. Quite a hike from our house, but the weather is perfect for a long stroll. We cross Canal and can't help but stop to gaze at the Christmas Oasis. This section of the city has outdone itself with all the lights. Everything that can be wrapped in lights is, including the light poles, palm trees, balconies, and buildings. The businesses have decorated like never before. What a sight.

We cross Iberville on Royal, and Louis pauses to look in the windows at the Monteleone Hotel and sees the jazz band playing in the Carousel Bar.

He turns to me and says, "Let's go in for one drink."

"Let's not and say we did. My feet are swelling, and there is no more stretch in these jeans."

We walk on, admiring the holiday decorations that beckon from every angle.

"I want to finish hanging that green stuff tomorrow; did you pick up what we need?" Louis asks.

Truthfully, I forgot all about getting the rest of the garland for the balcony.

"I'll head over to Perino's tomorrow to pick it up," I assure him, and I reach into my pocket for my cell phone. "I'll see if Gloria wants to go with me."

Once again, my call goes to voice mail. Louis stops to peer into another shop window as I stop walking to leave a message on her phone.

"Hey, girlfriend, it's me. Where the Sam Hill are you? I'm starting to get worried; you know what they say about all work and no play. I'm driving to Perino's in the morning to pick up the last of the Christmas decorations and garland for our balcony; can you join me? And are you coming with us this weekend to do City Park? I promise I won't make you ride the minitrain this year. Call and let me know about mañana and this weekend. Love you. Bye."

City Park has the best Christmas light display in New Orleans. People come from miles around to see it, and we have made it an annual tradition with Gloria to see the lights and go for dinner afterward.

Louis and I are just about home when my cell phone chimes to inform me of an incoming text message from Gloria.

> Thanks, but I have to pass on shopping tomorrow. I'm swamped. Forgot all about City Park this weekend. Promised Elizabeth I'd go with her to see the Nutcracker. Please forgive me.

I want to shove the phone back into my pocket, but I'm staring at the message like an idiot. "She's not coming to City Park with us this year. She's avoiding me, Louis. I know it."

"Don't be ridiculous, Stevie. Is she still coming over on Christmas Eve?"

"I have no idea. I'll see." I type out a quick text message to ask her and hit send.

> R u joining us and the kids on Christmas Eve, or did you get a better offer elsewhere?

I feel bad when I read her reply.

> Of course I'll be there! Can't wait to see the kids. Please don't be mad about this weekend. You know how much I love you and Louis. It's just that Elizabeth really needs a friend right now. I can't give you specifics, but she needs me.

Yeah, well so do I.

We continue to play phone tag over the next week, but truth be told, I'm just as swamped as Gloria. I'm thankful we have text messaging; otherwise, we wouldn't be talking at all. There is always so much to do during the holidays.

Christmas Eve

Our annual Christmas Eve celebration is a big deal, and it seems to have gotten even bigger this year. Some folks stop by for a few minutes, and some stay for hours. Over the years we've even had a few who needed to spend the night, but that hasn't happened in a while.

The kids and grandkids are home for the holidays, and as dinnertime approaches, friends from all over the city begin to stop by for some of Louis's famous shrimp Creole and baked rice. Delicious on its own, but I also provide my favorite salad with spring greens, candied pecans, purple onions, avocado, sun-dried tomatoes, seasoned croutons, and a couple of sliced boiled eggs, topped with crumbled feta cheese and tossed with olive oil and balsamic vinegar. Our daughter makes the best homemade rosemary bread.

Music is piped into every room. Wonderful aromas swirl around us, laughter and chatter abound, and glasses overflow with some of the finest champagnes and wines, the best once again provided by our friends Tim and Brenda.

After dinner, we have pie—lots and lots of pie: pecan pie, sweet potato pie, and my mother's famous chocolate pie.

Mom was an incredibly busy and very accomplished woman, but baking was not her forte, and when she made her chocolate pie, Louis always said he never knew if he'd need a fork, a spoon, or a straw to eat it. Her recipe has outlived her, and I'm not ashamed to say that my version is a bit more consistent in its consistency. However, she did know how to make a perfect meringue topping that I've yet to master.

Tomorrow, things will be more peaceful. Christmas Day is much quieter than Christmas Eve, especially now that we have grandkids. It's a day primarily reserved for our immediate family and the people Louis lovingly refers to as strays or orphans—people who are alone during the holiday season for whatever reason.

Tomorrow, folks will begin to arrive at two, and Louis will prepare a huge beef tenderloin on the grill. And at some point in the afternoon he will hold his arms wide and brandish a pair of tongs like a sword as he mimics the famous Leonardo DiCaprio line from the movie *Titanic* and shout from the balcony, "I'm king of the grill!"

But tonight, on this beautiful Christmas Eve, he's king of the kitchen as he spoons out shrimp Creole and warmly greets everyone who arrives.

I'm on the other side of the dining room when I see Gloria and our dear friend Alan from the gem and lapidary store enter. She returns my wave when I manage to catch her eye, but it seems to be forever before we can make our way over to each other.

Louis and I are saddened when she informs us she might not be joining us tomorrow.

"I have simply got to show up at Earl and Sylvia's place," she says sadly. "I will try to stop by later."

Earl Hughes is the CEO of Bronzinelle Steel, and he and his wife, Sylvia, host an exclusive Christmas Day brunch every few years at their home for some of their key shareholders and VIPs. Because she's an extraordinary businesswoman and juggles her responsibilities so well, I sometimes tend to forget that Gloria is the only living heir to an industrial empire and there are times when she can't delegate, when she has to make an appearance. Nonetheless, I'm disappointed she might miss Christmas Day with us.

New Year's Eve

I know I've gained ten pounds in the last two weeks. Cookies, cakes, and pie, pie, and more pie! And now it's New Year's Eve, and back to Galatoire's we go.

Tonight we are merging our party with a mutual friend's group, and the rest of the patrons are not happy. We end up with a party of over thirty, and downstairs to boot! That means more booze, more noise, and more fun!

We arrive at six thirty for drinks in the bar until our tables are ready at eight, and we hope to finish up by eleven thirty. Then, after dinner, some will go to Alma's house for more celebrating, and a few of us will go to the Omni Royal rooftop bar to ring in the new year with hotel guests and other club members.

Louis and I are club members, and we are each allowed to bring one guest whenever we visit the club, including special events like this. For years we always brought Charles and Gloria as our guests, and then it became just Gloria and a guest of her choice, usually an employee of the magazine or a business associate. This year Gloria made a last-minute decision to surprise Randy and Maria by flying in several of their older relatives from Mexico, and tonight she is playing hostess at her home for the Salvador family. I'm happy for Randy and Maria, but I won't lie; I was a bit peeved that Gloria waited until a few days ago to tell us about her change in plans.

"I'm so sorry to upset the apple cart at the last minute, but I just know you'll find someone to take with you. Besides, you'll be so busy enjoying yourself you won't even miss my old fuddy-duddy self," she said when she called.

It's almost midnight, and servers are scattered around the pool pouring rosé champagne and serving chocolate-covered strawberries as the anticipation in the crowd mounts. We invited our neighbors Mark and Carol to join us, and although it's been a great evening, it doesn't seem the same without Gloria. She was wrong; I do miss her.

As if reading my mind, Louis whispers in my ear, "I miss her too, and we'll just have to lay down the law and tell her she has no other option next year but to be on this rooftop with us. Period. End of story." He crosses his arms firmly.

I smile and take his hand as we look toward the river with excitement. The rooftop bar at the Omni Royal has an excellent view of the Jax Brewery, where the countdown officially begins. Louis puts his arm around me as everyone on the roof collectively shouts "Ten, nine, eight, seven, six, five, four, three, two, one … *happy new year!*"

In many cities around the world, life is all about lifestyle: who you know, where you go, and what you wear. But here in New Orleans, our lifestyle is all about life: how you enjoy it, how you live it, and how you love it, especially on holidays. Holidays throughout the year are celebrated on an entirely different level in the French Quarter, especially on New Year's Eve. The air is electric, filled with a magical sense of awe and wonder that seems to illuminate the heart and soul with a charging volt of power and passion. It is almost like a spiritual jolt that supernaturally prepares us for another year of festive celebrations, while at the same time causing us to be deeply thankful for the blessings we have had throughout the year.

The fireworks are dwindling and the shouting is subsiding when Louis looks at me lovingly and whispers, "Let's go home, baby," and then gives me a wink.

"Oh, for heaven's sake."

CHAPTER 14

— Gloria —

Thursday, January 13

I have a far better understanding of how valuable autopilot and cruise-control systems are, as I'm not sure how I would have made it through Christmas or New Year's Eve if my brain hadn't engaged its own God-given navigation system, and if Randy and Maria hadn't been here to lend much-needed (and deeply appreciated) support.

Randy and Maria have always been a blessing to me, but the way they've handled this situation with my health over the past several weeks has been exceptional.

I was a blubbering mess of emotion when Randy brought me home from the doctor's office that day, so it was impossible not to tell Maria what Dr. Creswell said. I wasn't in the house but ten minutes when she shifted into mother mode and sent me to bed as if I were a sick child with the flu, hovering over my every need. I willingly accepted that role for a couple of days, shutting out the world and knowing I was safe in Randy and Maria's care.

There's never a good time to get news like that, but there couldn't be a worse time than two weeks before Christmas. After the initial shock wore off, the three of us spent several days and nights discussing a game plan.

"It's impossible to get an appointment at this time of year unless you're dying, which I'm not, so I'll see the oncologist Dr. Creswell has recommended after the first of the year. In the meantime, we'll take it one day at a time. Agreed?"

"Agreed," Randy and Maria said.

"And I've decided not to tell anyone else just yet, including Stevie, until I get more tests."

"If that is your wish," Randy said, "you know your secret is safe with us. Our lips are always sealed when it comes to your life, Miss Gloria."

"I know that. Thank you. But it's not like we're lying to her; there just isn't anything to tell her yet. Dr. Creswell is a GP; even he said he wasn't *exactly* sure what it was, so let's be optimistic and refuse to let a little health glitch spoil our holiday season!"

As an eternal optimist, my mind is telling me that having the mere "presence of cancerous cells" certainly isn't a death sentence. Medical science has come so far, and a great many people win the battle with cancer, if indeed that's what this is, and I have no doubt I'll be one of them.

And thus the "business as usual" campaign began, which unfortunately turned out to mean limited time with Stevie during the holidays, because I just couldn't be around her without feeling guilty for not telling her; but there really wasn't anything concrete I could tell her yet.

The last-minute change in plans for New Year's Eve was nothing short of an answer to prayer. Being able to arrange for the Salvador family to visit from Mexico gave me a valid excuse for missing New Year's Eve with Stevie and Louis. I couldn't bear to keep up the hoax all night, and I surely didn't want to put a damper on the festivities.

Today is the first meeting of the garden club in the New Year. It's a beautiful New Orleans day, and I'm feeling much better, especially since I made the decision not to let the presence of some mysterious cells that may or may not exist dictate my outlook on life.

We are midway into the garden club season, and the January meeting is notorious for having the lowest attendance, but I'm feeling energized in meeting with the ladies who have meant so much to me for so many years, including Stevie. I've truly missed her over the past few weeks.

When it's time to leave for the garden club meeting, Maria is in the kitchen shining my mother's sterling silver ice bucket and talking to Randy, who is sitting at the island counter, waiting for me. He stands when I enter the room.

"Your chariot awaits you, senora," Randy says, with an intentional dramatic theatricality that makes me laugh.

"Gracias, Senor Salvador." I nod. "I'm not sure when I'll be back, Maria, so don't plan on me for dinner."

"Are you going to talk with Miss Stevie today?" Maria says nonchalantly without making eye contact as she continues polishing.

"Of course I'll talk with her. She never misses a garden club meeting, and Broussard's is one of her favorite restaurants in the Quarter."

"Every restaurant in the Quarter is Miss Stevie's favorite," says Maria. Randy smiles and I agree as Maria stops working and gives me the look—the look that says, "You know that isn't what I meant."

"Maria ..." Randy says to his wife with a stern tone he seldom uses.

"I'm sorry, Miss Gloria," Maria says as she returns to her task.

Maria knows that Stevie is going to be really angry and hurt that I didn't tell her about my health issue as soon as I found out, but she also knows why I've kept it quiet. There still isn't anything conclusive to report, and Stevie would drive me crazy with her worrying in the interim, so it really is better this way.

"You don't have to apologize, Maria. I know I have to tell her, and I will when the time is right." I give her a quick hug and head out the door to the waiting car.

Randy opens the back door with his usual pomp and circumstance. He loves this part of his job, and I've learned over the years to intentionally make it a point to allow him to do this from time to time.

I slide into the roomy backseat as he gently shuts the door, and I watch as he practically sprints around the front of the car.

"I do still know how to drive, Randy." I smile as he gets behind the wheel.

"I know that, Miss Gloria." He leans over the seat and grins. "Would you like to drive the Baby? If so, she's all yours; just say the word." He raises his arms in surrender.

The Baby, as he has called it for years, is a Rolls Royce Ghost, a behemoth of a car compared to my sporty Lexus, which is at the dealership for a tune-up, and he knows quite well I hate to drive it. Actually, the driving part is rather enjoyable; what I really hate is to park it.

"No thank you, Randy. I'll entrust my life to your vehicular virility."

"Ah ... beautiful and brilliant!" he says as he starts the ignition and the powerful engine purrs to life, and he winks at me as he pulls out of the driveway.

I can't recall a time when a Ghost wasn't parked at the Bronzinelle Estate, or at Vincent Manor for that matter. Charles loved this car. Part of owning a luxury motor car is being comfortable with the incredible ostentatiousness of it all, something Charles and every generation of Bronzinelle men have been able to do, going as far back as 1913, when a Rolls Royce Ghost won the Spanish Grand Prix.

I loved riding in the back as a child, but not as much in the years after, when there were times I felt like a bug under a microscope whenever we drove down the street. These days, however, I do love the opportunity to get work done during travel time, as the backseat is really an amazingly efficient office on wheels, with a laptop computer and a center console filled with the accouterments of my trade, such as red ink pens, Post-it note flags, highlighters, and paper clips. Besides, Randy enjoys carting me around town, and as long as he doesn't call me Miss Daisy, I humor him.

It's not a very long drive, but it is rather tricky with several streets closed for construction. Randy expertly navigates the detours, and I manage to make a couple of important business calls and find myself hanging up the phone just as Randy pulls to a stop at 819 Conti Street. He gets out and quickly runs around the car to open my door as I glance at my watch.

"I can't believe I'm so early; this hardly ever happens these days," I say as Randy offers his hand to help me out of the car, a gesture he has graciously extended for decades, but one I'm taking less for granted these days. He is a precious soul, as protective as a father and as loving as a brother, even back when Charles was alive.

"What time should I return?" he asks, gently closing the door and using his shirt sleeve to wipe off fingerprints only he can see.

"I think I'll take a cab home today, Randy. I'm not sure how the afternoon will play out."

"Are you sure, Miss Gloria? It's a bit chilly today."

"Yes, Randy, I'm sure. Besides, I've got my coat." I'm thankful for the trench coat I'm wearing as I wrap it snugly around me. "I'm going to be okay; everything's going to be okay," I say, gently touching his arm. "Please stop worrying about me."

"I have been worrying about you for many, many years, Miss Gloria; why would I stop now?" he says quietly as he squeezes my hand. "I will be working on the bricks in the courtyard today; you will call me if you change your mind, *Si?* I can be here *uno momento.*"

"Yes, Randy, I will call you if I change my mind. Now get out of here before they give you a ticket." I point toward the two women on foot patrol who are a few doors down and heading our way.

I watch him drive away and turn on Bourbon Street before I head into the restaurant.

I'm so glad we are having our garden club meeting at Broussard's. I was ecstatic when Elizabeth chose it as one of our locations for this season.

The building is lovely, with classic charm and historical elegance. Beautiful hand-painted Italian tile greets you in the foyer, and several of the dining rooms have french doors opening into a lush, tropical courtyard patio.

At Broussard's, a deep respect for the historical fabric of New Orleans and a passion for life's finer elements come together. It's one of the many places in the Quarter that feels like home to me. And the food is never disappointing, especially the corn, shrimp, and sweet potato bisque, a favorite dish of mine.

"Hello, Mrs. Vincent," the hostess greets me warmly after I've checked my coat. "You're here for the garden club meeting, right?" I nod affirmatively. "It's in the Magnolia Room today, right this way."

I know the room well, and as we round the bar area, I get a quick glance into the serene cobblestone courtyard with a soothing fountain. The courtyard once served as the home's carriageway, and *NOLA 2 NOLA*, as well as *New Orleans Magazine*, voted it as "the most beautiful courtyard in the French Quarter."

When I enter the Magnolia Room, I'm surprised to see several women already there, including Stevie, who waves wildly from her table, as though I could miss seeing her in the near-empty room. It's another forty-five minutes before Alma will ring the starting bell, and the waitstaff are still setting the tables. It's a testimony to our history, our longevity, that we have been permitted entrance early, while the hustle and bustle of preparation is still going on around us.

"Sound the trumpets and record this historic moment; Gloria Vincent is early for a garden club meeting!" Stevie shouts as the other gals at the table applaud. She grabs me in a bear hug.

"Guilty as charged!" I laugh as hugs and hellos around the table ensue.

We're all sharing holiday updates and playing catch-up as more women trickle in and get seated when Stevie leans in and gently elbows me.

"I'm glad to *finally* get a chance to hang out with you, but tell me again why we even bother to have a January meeting when the turnout is always so low?"

She's right; our numbers are traditionally low in January, but this is worse than usual.

"Increasing attendance is one of the things Elizabeth wants to address at a special meeting," I say. "She's got some wonderful ideas about membership, Stevie."

"Is that so? What kind of ideas?"

"I'll leave that up to her to disclose; she's been rehearsing her announcement for the past two weeks. I could recite it in my sleep!" I laugh.

"I see, so you've been chatting it up with Lady Mc … President?"

"I would hardly call our conversations 'chatting it up.'" I'm surprised at Stevie's abruptness.

It's true, I've seen Elizabeth a few times, and although I've come to adore her, our friendship isn't the same as what I share with Stevie.

"Stevie, as you may recall, I am one of the executive board members, and as such it is entirely within protocol for her to be communicating with me about proposals she'd like to present to the membership."

Stevie squeezes a lemon slice in her water and takes a long sip. "How special. Is it also protocol for her to be so late?" she says, craning her neck to scan the room. "It's less than a half hour before we start. Where exactly is your new BFF? Will she be gracing us with her presence today? Will we have the supreme honor of being privy to the special secret you two share? Or perhaps the weather is just a little too cold, kind of like her?"

I'm stunned by her vitriolic diatribe.

"She isn't cold, Stevie; she's going through hell right now, but she'll be here."

"Yeah right, she's going through hell in a Louis Vuitton handbasket." Stevie rolls her eyes and laughs sardonically.

"Stevie, you have no idea what Elizabeth is dealing with. It's bad enough to be humiliated by someone you trust, but she has to do it on national television, not to mention being splattered all over every social media platform known to man. Why are you being so hard on her? For one minute try to put yourself in her shoes."

"No such luck; I can't afford them."

"Why are you being such a little snit? You agreed to handle the annual cookbook; I heard you at the Omni. But from what I gather, you haven't returned any of her calls."

"You know as well as I do that she wasn't being serious when she asked. Give me a break."

I'm not sure where she got that idea, because I know for a fact Elizabeth is very serious, and I'm genuinely puzzled at what is happening.

I sit quietly for the next several minutes and listen to Stevie vociferously berate Elizabeth as she calls her a "gold digger," a "spoiled brat," and a "socially inept dilettante."

Clearly we don't know the same woman, and I'm not sure what has happened since the Omni event that has turned her so vehemently against Elizabeth.

Before long, her verbal assault is picked up by the other ladies at our table as they all begin to gossip openly about what they *think* they know about Elizabeth's circumstances.

The fact is, I've spoken with Elizabeth many times since the news broke about Jake, and the conjecture being bantered about is so far from the truth it isn't even mildly amusing.

I love Stevie, and I treasure our friendship, but I'm disgusted at the direction her conversation has taken, and also with how willing the ladies are to jump on the character-assassination bandwagon with her.

I feel a wave of anger as I abruptly stand, grab Stevie's hand, and say, "Will you please come with me for a minute? Excuse us, ladies, we'll be right back; just running to the powder room before things get started."

I'm sure we appear like the good friends we are as we walk across the room, but inside I'm screaming as I practically drag her to a more private place in the restaurant just outside the ladies' room in the hall, away from prying eyes or ears. My voice is controlled but far from calm when I turn and face her.

"Stephanie Lewis, I am ashamed of you! What has that poor girl ever done to warrant your cruel judgment and condemnation? You talk as if you know what's really going on, but the truth is you don't; you're clueless! Those women listen to you and respect you, and they believe the things you say, even when those things are based on fallacy and fiction!"

"Take it easy, Gloria; don't get so riled up. Little Miss Priss isn't exactly Miss Congeniality around here, even if she's got you wrapped around her spoiled little diamond-clad finger. I can't do her any more damage than she's already done for herself."

"Riled up? Is that what you think I am?"

"Well, yeah. I can appreciate that you see the world through rose-colored glasses and you embrace change and innovation, but the Fleur-de-Lis Ladies Garden Club is based on time-honored history and tradition, and the fact is, you don't mess with history and tradition. Little Miss Lizzy needs to leave well enough alone. You know what they say: 'If it ain't broke, don't fix it.'"

"Stevie, we're not just talking about the garden club; we're talking about someone's character, reputation, and future! But since you've brought it up, the garden club *is* broken, and Elizabeth has bent over backward to help fix it! And if you want to talk about facts, the fact is that her bold ideas and strategic leadership may ensure the club is around for another one hundred seventy years! She's a good person—a decent soul—and you are disparaging her name unjustly!"

"And you have no loyalty, Gloria Vincent! We've been best friends for decades, long before Miss Whatsherface came on the scene, and if anyone needs to get a clue, it's you! Quit talking about her like she's some kind of savior. What on earth is the matter with you?"

Suddenly the truth hits me like a sucker punch in the gut. How could I have been so blind? She's jealous of Elizabeth. She's afraid of losing our friendship, but that has never been an option. I couldn't imagine my life without my dearest friend, even when she behaves reprehensibly like this.

"Is that what this is about? You think I'm being disloyal to you because I've befriended Elizabeth? Oh honey, I could never replace you; no one could take your place."

"Clearly that hasn't been the case. Who have you spent more time with over the past several weeks?"

Before I can respond, Elizabeth comes barreling around the corner like a bat out of hell. She sees us and stops dead in her tracks, a look of abject terror on her face.

"Well, speak of the devil," Stevie says, and looks at her watch. "You're cutting it a bit close, wouldn't you say? Gloria and I were just heading back to our table. The meeting starts in less than fifteen minutes."

"I know, I know. I've been on the phone trying to get another speaker. Our speaker called a half hour ago and cancelled; he said there's too much construction and couldn't carry all his supplies from the parking garage!"

"Well, that doesn't surprise me," Stevie pipes in. "If I wasn't able to walk here, I probably wouldn't have shown up either; not all of us have chauffeurs." She pats me condescendingly on the arm and continues, seemingly oblivious to her rudeness. "Apparently they're doing something underground, and they have streets blocked all over the Quarter."

"I know," Elizabeth says, "that's why I was here ahead of time to meet him, but he didn't even bother to try coming in! How could he do this at the last minute? What are we going to do?"

"Don't worry, Elizabeth; we'll think of something—won't we, Stevie?" I say.

"Ah … sure … we'll just cross our arms and blink like Jeannie to make a speaker appear."

No sooner do the words leave Stevie's lips than we hear Dolores's loud, joyful, raspy voice in the bar.

"Do y'all have drinks in the Magnolia Room—real drinks?" she booms.

"Yes, ma'am," someone replies meekly.

"Good, 'cause I'm parched. Please bring me a vodka martini—a little dry, a little dirty—with a lot of extra olives."

She rounds the same corner Elizabeth just traversed and runs into the three of us staring at her.

Dolores has always marched to the tune of her own fashion drum, and today is no exception. She's wearing a black pencil skirt, hot-pink stiletto heels, and a skin-tight sweater in a shade of chartreuse that could stop traffic. Even more outrageous, she has several dollar bills hanging from two large safety pins strategically placed on her chest like matching brooches.

Stevie bursts out laughing, and even Elizabeth smiles.

"Do you think anyone will notice?" Dolores puts her hands on her hips and shakes her chest provocatively. "Tomorrow is actually my birthday, but I thought I'd start early with the garden club. You gals don't mind, do you?"

A New Orleans tradition is to pin a dollar to your chest on your birthday, and throughout the day, people (including many, many strangers) wish you a happy birthday, and some add money to your pins. Leave it to Dolores to keep tradition alive.

Leave it to Dolores …

We're on the same page when Stevie blurts out, "Dolores, do you still teach that class on container gardening?"

"Well, yeah. I just did one in Shreveport last week. Why?"

Elizabeth and I laugh as Stevie crosses her arms, blinks firmly, and says, "Voilà! Your wish is granted!"

"Come with us," I say, and we lead the visibly surprised but compliant birthday girl into the room and quickly tell her what we need her to do.

A little more than half the club has made it today when, a few minutes later, Elizabeth gives a nod to Alma and she rings our broken bell. *Ding-dink-ding, ding-dink-ding.*

"Greetings, ladies; thank you for joining us. We only have two special announcements today. First, Dolores is celebrating her birthday tomorrow and has decided to collect today."

Dolores stands at the front of the room and shimmies, waving the dollar bills pinned to her chest as everyone begins to clap. We may be a seasoned group of stoic ladies, but this French Quarter tradition never fails to bring smiles and laughs. And in spite of her raw edge, Dolores and her crazy ways are beginning to grow on the ladies.

"Thank you, Dolores," Alma says. "As for the second announcement, we've got a very special treat for you today. Let's welcome our club president to tell us all about it." Alma leads the applause as Elizabeth comes forward.

"Thank you, Alma, and thank you, ladies, for braving the ever-challenging obstacle course that our city streets never fail to provide. Unfortunately, our speaker wasn't as successful as you in navigating the course and is unable to join us, but as Alma shared, we have a very special surprise today."

Elizabeth glances at her notes and folds the paper in half.

"Our guest speaker is no stranger to the special needs we have in the Quarter to maximize the beauty of minimal outdoor space. As a master gardener, she is also a member of the American Horticulture Society, the Society of Garden Designers, and the Professional Gardeners' Guild. As the owner/operator of one of the premier boutique gardening services in the Quarter, her award-winning courtyard and balcony designs have made her one of the most sought-after landscape wizards in the city. Here to talk about container gardening in the way only she can, it is with deep appreciation that I give you our own garden club sister and birthday girl extraordinaire, Ms. Dolores Delacroix."

"Wow, that was some introduction," Stevie says over the applause as Dolores makes her way to the podium while quickly removing the safety pins from her sweater.

"Don't y'all worry, I'll put these pins back just as soon as I'm done, so prepare your offerings," she teases. She then launches into an enthusiastic thirty-minute presentation that has everyone enthralled.

She speaks with ease and expertise about the unique challenges of container gardening, and discusses flowers, plants, trees, shrubberies, and even bulbs. She talks about soil, temperature, feeding, placement, and watering. She's truly an expert, and I'm so proud of her for doing this without the slightest hesitation at the last minute. There isn't a doubt in my mind that she has surprised quite a few people today; we sometimes forget just how knowledgeable she is.

After an exceptional presentation, Dolores returns to her seat to the accompaniment of a standing ovation as lunch is served, and boisterous chatter begins to fill the room.

"What's the name of her business again?" Miss V. asks from across our table.

"Beautiful Bloomers," Stevie says. "Remember those pots of agapanthus you admired on our balcony last week? Dolores is responsible for suggesting and procuring them. She's been taking care of our plants for years; Louis and I would be lost without her."

"I know exactly what you mean," I add. "Dolores has been taking care of the courtyards and balconies at Vincent Manor for more years than I can count."

"We could use a new gardener," Natalie says. "Our ivy never seems to grow beyond a couple of feet."

"Then Dolores is who you need, but she's far more than a gardener," I say. "Don't get me wrong, some gardeners are very good; but for the most part their job is to get in, cut down, trim up, and get out. They don't necessarily have the expertise to look at the aesthetics of a landscape design and take all aspects into consideration concerning ongoing maintenance. I think of what Dolores does as being like the difference between hiring a concierge doctor or going to the clinic. Personally, I'd take the concierge doc anytime."

This starts a new round of conversation, and I predict that Beautiful Bloomers has definitely turned a corner today. I'm so proud of Dolores as I catch her eye and give her a wink.

"I wish more people could have heard this presentation," I whisper to Stevie.

"Yeah, it's a rather pathetic turnout," she says. "So when do we get to hear Madame President's brilliant new ideas for holding our members accountable to their attendance?"

"That's just it, Stevie—it's not just about getting the current members to show up to meetings; we've got to share the great information we have every month with more women. We need more members, including younger members. We've got to get some new perspective in this group. Something has to change; can't you see that, Stevie?"

"The only thing that has to change is our president; she's the reason we're going downhill, and when you finally realize that, I'll try not to say I told you so," Stevie says. "And I do agree with you, Dolores did a great job, but I never thought I'd see that." She nods toward Dolores, who is seated next to Elizabeth at the head table, where they appear to be having a great time.

"See what?" I ask. "Two grown women behaving like adults and enjoying themselves?"

"Give me a break, Gloria; you know they can't stand each other."

"I don't know any such thing, and neither do you—not really." I take a sip of water, hoping to calm my suddenly queasy stomach.

"Gloria, you know as well as I do that Elizabeth's big mouth cost Dolores the Colette account last summer. They haven't said more than two words since the garden club season started last September, and now they're what, best buddies? And don't tell me you haven't heard the things coming to light in the news about Elizabeth; it can't *all* be conjecture and innuendo."

As much as I'd like to counter her false perspective, I'm suddenly more concerned about settling my stomach, and all I can muster is a disgusted look. *Maybe I'm just hungrier than I thought.* I force myself to take several spoons of the ever-popular bisque.

"What's up with you, Gloria?" Stevie asks. "I don't see you for weeks, and you've been acting like a nasty nun with a ruler since you got here; look at my knuckles." She holds out her hands. "And I'm not being jealous, just truthful."

She is being jealous and rude, but I don't have the energy to argue.

"I'm sorry I was hard on you; it's just that there really is more to Elizabeth's story than meets the eye, and even if you don't want to admit it, the garden club *is* in trouble, but I shouldn't have snapped at you. There's a lot on my plate right now, but I'm fine, really. Once I make a decision whether or not to sell, things will get much better."

"Are you really still considering the acquisition?"

"I got the first written offer last week. There are still a ton of things to negotiate if I decide to accept it, but I must say it's a rather attractive deal."

"I can't believe you're actually considering it." Stevie shakes her head.

"I know; it is rather surreal at times, but it feels right, Stevie. All the pieces seem to fit."

"Speaking of surreal, how are the pieces fitting with Daddy Warbucks Carlyle?"

"Francois?"

"Yes, Francois, and don't be coy; you know your secret is safe with me. It would be like Aristotle and Jackie, the unity of two dynasties. Our own NOLA royalty!"

I reach over and feel her forehead with the back of my hand. "You're sick, dear. You really need to see a doctor."

"The only thing I need to see is Gloria Vincent admitting that she's been secretly dating the owner of the company that wants to acquire her magazine," she says.

I'm speechless at the thought. "You're kidding, right? There's nothing whatsoever going on between Francois Carlyle and me!"

"Whatever," Stevie says, and I manage to smile in spite of the fact that suddenly my favorite bisque is talking back to me like a rebellious child.

I look around the room, mainly to see if anyone else can hear the rumbling in my stomach. I've known most of these women all my life. As I was an only child, many of these women have become sisters to me. I can disagree with them, and they can call me stubborn, but at the end of the day, we love each other. I just hope they know how much they mean to me. I'd like to think I'm always appreciative for the abundant blessings God has given me, but I find myself being especially thankful today. Thankful and increasingly nostalgic, as even the wallpaper in this room is bringing back memories. I have met with Louis and Stevie in the bar for drinks, come here for the Obituary Cocktail Club, and had dinner here with Charles more times than I can count.

Suddenly I feel like a young pregnant woman as a wave of nausea comes over me, and I quickly realize I've got to get out before I lose what little lunch I've had.

I reach into my purse and glance at my cell phone, which is turned off. "Oh gosh, I'm sorry, ladies. I hate to leave, but I just got a text message, and something's come up at work. I need to run."

I remove the napkin from my lap and place it on the table.

"You barely ate anything." Stevie looks at my dish.

"Actually, I'm still stuffed, Maria fixed me a huge breakfast. Why don't you have them put this in a container for Louis? He loves their bisque as much as I do."

"Yeah, he's a regular, Mikie; he'll eat anything," she laughs as I slide my chair back and stand.

Uh oh …

I feel a bit dizzy, and my stomach leaps as I hold on to the back of my chair and pretend to adjust the ankle strap on one of my shoes. Most of the ladies are chatting and pay no attention, but Stevie seems to be watching my every move as I steady myself with one hand and reach into my purse with the other for the coat-check ticket and casually ask the waiter to retrieve my coat.

I pretend to listen to Natalie rattle on about her new puppy, and in record time the young waiter brings my coat and graciously holds it open for me as I let go of the chair and slide my arms into the sleeves. He looks like the college-age son of a friend, and I can smell his overly-spicy cologne as I notice the glistening gold name tag.

"Thank you, Carl." I grasp his hand as though I've known him for years. "Why don't you walk me to the door and tell me how your mother is doing." He's visibly surprised as I link my arm into his as though we're old friends and allow him to lead me out of the room with little suspicion from anyone, the young man included, that I'm actually holding on to him for dear life.

Maybe I should have called Randy after all.

The nausea passes, and I'm on far steadier feet when I head out the front door and slip into the cab waiting at the curb. I'm feeling exhausted as I sink into the seat and give the driver my address. I'm sorry I won't hear Elizabeth's announcement about the special meeting she wants to conduct, but I'm sure Stevie will call later to tell me all about it.

CHAPTER 15

— Stephanie —

The meeting has wrapped up, and Dolores and I visit at the bar while Elizabeth settles the bill at the corner table with the manager. It's quiet. The evening rush won't start for a couple of hours, and the cutie-pie bartender, Ken, is at our beck and call. He takes our drink orders and turns to get cocktail glasses and ice.

"Well, in spite of the low turnout, I still managed to collect twenty-seven dollars. Not bad for an old broad. That should buy me two packs of cigarettes and a decent bottle of wine," Dolores says, counting the dollar bills that are still affixed to the pins on her chest.

"You do know that smoking can kill you, right?" I ask.

"Yeah, right. So can a speeding car when you cross the street. I had a client once who never smoked a day in her life and she died from lung cancer. When it's your time to go, it's your time to go."

I lean my arms on the bar and watch as Dolores stares at Ken like he's a shiny new toy.

"You seemed rather friendly with Lady McBitch, what's up with that?" I ask.

"Nothing. I was sitting at the head table, in case you didn't notice. I couldn't very well ignore her. Besides, she's not as bad as I thought. Kinda funny, actually."

The bartender serves our drinks and winks at Dolores. "Your side shot is on the house; happy birthday."

She winks back at him. "Well thank you, sweetie pie, that's mighty thoughtful of you."

"Funny? How so?" I ask, swirling the ice around inside my glass.

"Let's not waste our breath talking about Elizabeth, okay? Rumor has it Gloria is dating someone. Spill the beans. Who is it?"

"I have no idea what you're talking about. Gloria, dating? Really?" I take a long swallow of my drink.

Suddenly everything makes sense; that's why she's been avoiding me! I bet Gloria really has been seeing Francois! But why the secret? Why lie to me?

"Fine. Have it your way." She downs the shot of Patron tequila the bartender gave her as a birthday gift and stands up. "It's time for me to go anyway. I've got people to do and things to see … or vice versa. See you later, alligator." She gives me a kiss on the cheek.

"You were really great today," I say. "Thanks again for coming to the rescue."

"No problem. I aim to please." She winks at the bartender and wiggles away provocatively.

"She's quite a character," Ken says, and we watch Dolores head out the door with her birthday dollars waving in the breeze.

"You can say that again! She's going to milk this weekend for all it's worth."

He nods, and I notice his gaze move as I follow his eyes to see Elizabeth walking toward the door. Her skin-tight Victoria Beckham dress sends mixed messages between business and pleasure, a fact that has made the young designer a multimillionaire, conquering both the boardroom and the bedroom with her edgy fashion. Elizabeth is texting on her cell phone with an angry fervor that culminates when she suddenly stops and drops her phone into a classic Chanel handbag hanging from her shoulder. I watch as she closes her eyes and takes a deep breath, as if to center herself in a swirling storm.

She opens her eyes and looks up to see me staring at her, and she crosses the room toward me.

"Hello, Mrs. LeBlanc. What can I get for you?" The bartender is practically panting like a puppy as Elizabeth takes the barstool vacated by Dolores and places her bag on the empty stool next to it.

"Please, it's Elizabeth, and I think I'll have a Chivas and soda, but hold the soda."

"Hmm, never took you for a scotch kind of girl," I say.

"Make that a double," she tells the bartender, ignoring me.

"That bad, eh? I thought the meeting went rather well, considering the circumstances. Dolores did a spectacular job; I think the ladies were impressed."

"Yes, she did, and yes, they were. Thanks for conjuring her up on such short notice. Can you make people disappear as easily as you make them appear?" she says, taking a large gulp of the drink that puppy-man has set in front of her at lightning speed.

There's no sense asking who it is she might want to get rid of.

She takes another gulp and looks directly at me. Her voice is calm and steady.

"I'll make it easy on you, Stephanie. I know you don't like me. I'm not exactly sure why, but this isn't about me, or us; it's about the annual cookbook and raising much-needed funds for the garden club. Are you still interested in handling the cookbook? Yes or no? You haven't returned my calls. If you don't want to do it, just tell me, okay?"

I surprise myself with my response. "Gloria yelled at me today for dissing you in public."

She unexpectedly laughs. "You can't get away with much around her, can you? She's one of the few good and honest people left in the world. So ... were you?"

"What?"

"Dissing me in public."

"Yeah, I guess I was."

"Well, join the crowd." She tips her glass toward me and sips the golden liquid.

"Gloria accused me of being jealous because of her friendship with you."

"Are you?"

"I didn't think so, but now I don't know; maybe I was, am."

We both nurse our drinks quietly for a moment before she breaks the awkward silence.

"Can I ask you something?"

"Uh, sure ..."

"I know you and Gloria are very close, and I respect that. When she first approached me to consider being the president of the garden club, I wondered why you weren't stepping in to be the leader. Everyone knows how close you two are and how involved you have been in the club."

"What did Gloria tell you?" I ask.

"She said you aren't comfortable in leadership roles, and I didn't press her, but I've watched you these past months, and that simply isn't true. You *are* a leader. Women look up to you; they respect you."

"Yeah, right, that's what Gloria says, but I don't happen to agree with either of you," I say.

"Well, you're wrong. And if we make it another year, I think you would be an excellent garden club president."

"What do you mean, *if* we make it?"

She tilts her head and creases her eyebrows together, and I think of something Gloria once said about Botox and try not to laugh.

"What's so funny? Do I have something on my face?" She peers into the mirror behind the bar.

"No." I shake my head. "It's just that you, Gloria, and I might be the only women left in the garden club who can actually move our eyebrows." We both laugh. "So tell me, really, what do you mean by 'if we make it'?" I ask.

"Nothing. I mean if *I* don't make it; if *I* have to leave, drop out."

I don't think she's being entirely truthful with me; I don't think that's at all what she means. But just as I'm about to call her on the carpet for the deception, I have a profound feeling of compassion as I notice that her usually vibrant, violet eyes look vacant and haunted as she stares down into her glass and tries desperately to blink back tears.

At that moment, if sadness were a scent it would be an overpowering stench.

It's no secret I'm not her biggest fan, but I'm even less of a fan of her adulterous husband, and I'm surprised by my words. "Jake LeBlanc is a jerk. Don't let him win."

Her look of despondent surrender invokes a history of torments and conflicts that far surpass ordinary understanding as she whispers, "He always wins. That's what he does. Everything is a game to him; our marriage is no different. I lost a long time ago; I just wasn't smart enough to get out of the game."

Typically, I'm not the person folks come to for advice. Words of wisdom don't usually flow from my lips, at least not like they do from those of Dame Gloria—and I mean her no disrespect when I say that. She's an icon of stability and the editor of a famous magazine, for crying out loud; words are her world. But nonetheless, in the back of my mind I can hear her voice as clearly as if she were standing in front of me now. *"There are no coincidences, Stevie, so when you find yourself in a position to shore up a shattered soul, or offer comfort to the weary, you must believe that God has placed you there for such a time as this. Choose your words wisely. You can make a difference."*

Okay, my friend, what would you say? Give me the words.

"Elizabeth, have you ever heard of a woman named Dorothy Dix?" I ask.

"Um, no, I don't think so."

"Louis and I were just talking about her a few days ago. Back in the late 1800s the *New Orleans Daily Picayune* had a popular advice column written by her called "Dictates for a Happy Life." She admonished that we had to make up our mind to be happy. She said, 'If you are ever to be happy, it must start now, today.'"

"Do you think it's that simple, Stephanie?" She swirls the ice around inside her glass, which is now empty of liquid. "That we can will ourselves to be happy?"

"I think it can be if we let it. We can't do anything about the past; it's over. All we can do now is move forward. I think being happy is a choice. It's also a choice for you to admit that your soon-to-be ex-husband is an idiot. That neither you nor your children are going to get the support you need from the 'Great Jake LeBlanc' because he's too busy making a fool of himself. It's going to be up to you to get everybody's life back on track."

"I'm not sure I can do that on my own."

"But you're not on your own." I surprise myself as I hear the words. "You have Gloria; she's the queen of positive living and personal empowerment, and you have us, your garden club sisters." I raise my glass and call out to the bartender. "Ken, will you please refresh our drinks so we can appropriately toast?"

"My pleasure, ma'am," he says while pouring and smiling like a Cheshire cat.

Gloria will be over the moon that Elizabeth and I are actually talking civilly. Maybe she's right; maybe it is time for the garden club members to pull together and help this woman out. If I can begin to warm up to her, maybe a few others will too.

I'm giving this heretofore absurd possibility thoughtful consideration when she suddenly sits up straight, takes a deep breath, and says, "I was prepared to make a special announcement at the meeting today about membership, but the sudden change in plans threw me off my game; I didn't get the job done." she sighs.

"Yeah, Gloria was saying something about that."

Elizabeth raises her eyebrows in surprise.

"Don't worry—she didn't divulge any specifics, just a cryptic inference that you have some great ideas that you want to share."

"Every idea is great to Gloria, even if it turns out not to be after further exploration. She encourages creative thinking and initiative like no one I've ever met before. She makes you believe you can do anything."

"Yep, that's Gloria." I can almost see the wheels turning inside Elizabeth's head, and I ask, "So what's on your mind?"

"I found a building we can lease for the garden club, somewhere we can hold meetings from time to time, a place for an administrative office and real file cabinets, not cardboard boxes. There's going to be a lot of opposition to this idea, mostly because we don't have the money. But we could have the money, and a lot of it."

"What exactly are you proposing?"

"Stephanie, I have an idea about the recipe book for this year—a big idea. But this idea isn't worth a hill of beans if you don't get behind it, if it doesn't have your full support. That's why I asked you to take the lead on the cookbook this year; that's why I wanted to talk with you. Will you listen to me with an open mind if I tell you what I'm thinking?"

"I'll try."

"In a nutshell, I think we need to raise the bar on our annual cookbook. Change the layout and format, use more professional publishing, and increase the distribution. Turn it into an annual fund-raiser that actually makes money, and not just something to cover the expenses for the annual Christmas party."

"Gloria has been saying that for years."

"And she's right! So are you in?"

The concept is growing on me, although I'm not ready to admit that to her.

"How do you propose that we increase the distribution?" I ask.

"We need a website. We need an Internet presence, including someone to conduct marketing and promotions."

"This is beginning to sound like a lot of work."

"It is a lot of work, but if something doesn't change, the garden club will become extinct. We need a new and improved vision, a defined strategy, and a written plan of action." She glances at her watch and jumps. "Oh my goodness, I have to get going." She reaches into her handbag and places two twenty-dollar bills on the bar and says, "Thanks, Ken, you can keep the change. She looks at me and says, "Don't make a decision now; just promise me you'll think about it and let me know soon, okay?"

"I will."

We both get up and gather our things, and I put my hand on her arm and say, "And promise me you'll call if you need additional counseling; my services are free."

She laughs with a genuine abandon that feels, dare I say it, honest and vulnerable.

"I will."

We give each other an awkward but nonetheless comforting hug, head out the door, and go our separate ways. I'm not ready to admit that Gloria may be right about Lady Mc … Liz, but I am willing to admit there might be more substance to her than meets the eye.

Walking back to my house, I give Gloria a call, and I'm surprised when she answers after the first ring.

"Hey, girlfriend, I need to call you back," she says hurriedly. "I have someone on the other line, and it may be after dinner before I can get back to you, okay?" Her voice echoes, and I wonder where she is.

"Yeah, but make sure you call me back, I have a lot to tell; you will never believe what happened after you left. I had a special one-on-one with the prez."

"Honestly can't talk right now. I promise I'll call you back." And then she hangs up.

I'm sure whatever she's handling must be pretty significant, because

I know Gloria, and she's always ready to talk about epiphanies or coincidences or anything to do with Elizabeth. I guess my news will have to wait, but I have no doubt she will be surprised, and pleased, when she hears that Elizabeth and I have actually had a "real" conversation.

As I exit the elevator into my kitchen, Louis is standing at the counter, stuffing one of his favorite cookies left over from the holidays into his mouth.

"Are those still good?" I ask as I drop my purse and keys on the counter.

"Of course they're still good. Here, try one." He thrusts one out to me.

I shake my head as he continues to eat the simple little sugar cookies with a dollop of strawberry jam pressed onto the top. He makes them every year. I just wish he would cut the recipe; we really don't need five dozen cookies. I'll be glad when they're all gone.

"It's been a long day, honey; I need to rest my eyes for just a while, okay?" I head for the sofa without waiting for a response.

It feels like my eyes have been closed for just a few moments when Louis gently nudges me and I look up to see his smiling face. He is holding two glasses of wine. "It's happy hour."

"Already?" I sit up and take one of the chilled glasses.

"Yep, you took a little nap. Well, not a little nap; a long nap."

We clink our glasses before he sits down and reaches for the remote control to turn on the television.

"Did Gloria call? What time is it?" I ask.

"No phone calls since you got home, and it's well after five o'clock."

"Seriously? Wow, I really conked out. Guess I must have needed it."

CHAPTER 16

— Gloria —

After a somewhat hurried and urgent exit from our garden club meeting, the taxi driver gets me home from Broussard's in record time, and I make it to my powder room before losing what little lunch I managed to eat—or "tossing my cookies," as Charles used to say.

The fact I'm now sitting on the floor in my bathroom and leaning on a glistening porcelain bowl that smells of citrus disinfectant while thinking fondly of my late husband is not without humor, and the audible sound of my laughter surprises me, as does the reverberating echo it makes in the room.

I'm even more surprised, startled, as the quiet is abruptly interrupted by the familiar disco song "We Are Family" by Sister Sledge that signals a call from Stevie. I reach into my pocket for my cell phone, intending to send her call directly to voice mail, but I hit the wrong button and realize I've answered the call instead, so I give her my "I need to call you back; I have someone on the other line" excuse. I feel bad for fibbing and then hanging up on her, especially after she tells me she's had a "special one-on-one moment" with Elizabeth.

Truthfully, I do wonder what happened between them, but frankly I think I'm having my own special moment as I scroll through the contact list on my phone to search for the specialist Doc Creswell recommended. I know that I entered the phone number from the business card he gave me. I find the number and call it, and I'm surprised when the receptionist says I can come in tomorrow afternoon. After I hang up, I turn the phone off and slide it back into my pocket.

I'm sure Maria isn't home; otherwise, she would be in hover mode, as would Coco, who must be out in the dog run, or maybe with Randy in the garage.

I pull one of the plush monogrammed towels from the towel rack and bury my face into the soft folds. The gentle scent of lavender fabric softener is comforting. I pull my legs up to my chest and rest my head on my knees, thankful my back isn't aching today, and for the flexibility that comes from years of exercise, yoga, and stretching.

I'm not sure how long I've been sitting quietly on the bathroom floor when I hear the kitchen door open, followed by the gentle click of Coco's nails on the tile floor. She instinctively knows I'm home and makes a direct beeline to the bathroom.

"Are you home, Miss Gloria?" Maria calls out.

I quickly pull myself up from the floor and shut the bathroom door.

"Yes, Maria, I'll be out in a jiff," I call through the door as I turn the faucet on full blast, splash water on my face, and use my cupped hands to take a sip of water and rinse my mouth as quietly as possible. I lean on the sink and look at my reflection.

Well, aren't you a sorry sight?

I smooth back my hair, take a deep breath, open the door, and shout a hello to Maria as I head straight upstairs, bypass the activity of the NOLA 2 NOLA team, and retreat to the privacy of my office, where I seem to have renewed energy and manage to plow through quite a bit of work on my desk in a couple of hours.

Before the day comes to an end, I give the NOLA 2 NOLA staff tomorrow off.

"Take a long three-day weekend, and I'll see you all on Monday," I say.

Randy and Maria already have plans to head out of town tomorrow afternoon to visit with family in Alexandria for the weekend, and later that evening, I assure them all is fine and give them Friday off as well.

* * * * *

Friday morning, January 14

The house is deliciously quiet as I sit in the study with a mug of hot, fragrant coffee and call Stevie. She answers on the first ring.

"Hey, girl, so much for calling me back yesterday, what happened to you?" Stevie asks.

"I'm sorry, I got swamped, and by the time I finished I was too tired to even watch the news, much less talk on the phone." There's no way I'm going to tell her I was sitting on the bathroom floor when she called yesterday, or that I'm going to see a doctor this afternoon.

"So what happened after I left?" I inquire. "Tell me about your 'special one-on-one' with Elizabeth—and how did her announcement go? I'm surprised no one has called me about it. What did the girls think?"

"She never gave her grand speech, but I had drinks with her in the bar afterward. We talked for a long time. But as much as I want to fill you in on all the juicy details, I can't talk now. I'm working at the Williams House today, and I'm running late. It seems that piece you did on their new collection has really increased their traffic; they asked if I could come in a bit earlier than usual."

I love that Stevie volunteers for an organization that is not only near and dear to my heart but also has a tremendous impact on preserving and sharing the extraordinary history of the French Quarter. Some of the most powerful philanthropists in the country are members of the Historic New Orleans Collection, an umbrella organization that comprises several significant outreach arms, of which the Williams House is but one.

I have no doubt Stevie is a tremendous asset to that organization, but her gifts and talents are often wasted on collecting tickets at the Courtyard Concerts. While I deeply appreciate and respect that every volunteer is significant to a nonprofit organization, I know that Stevie is so much more than a worker bee.

"Okay, so when can we connect?" I ask.

"We can talk more tonight at the Obit. You are coming to this one, right?"

Darn, I forgot all about the weekly get-together of the Obituary Cocktail Club.

"Where is it this week?" I ask.

"Sylvain. See ya at six?"

"I'll try to make it, Stevie."

"Remember what you always tell me, Gloria: 'There is no trying, just doing.' See ya later, gator," she says, and she hangs up.

Maybe a drink is precisely what I'll need after I meet with this new doctor. Then again, I'm feeling so much better today, and after I get off the phone with Stevie I briefly contemplate cancelling my appointment, but then I remember kneeling to the porcelain goddess yesterday and reconsider.

★   ★   ★   ★   ★

Friday afternoon, January 14

The Ochsner Medical Center is on Jefferson Highway, a short taxi ride from the house, and the driver is a pleasant young man from Uganda. His accent complements an excellent command of English, and before I know it he's dropping me off at the front door.

I review the directory to find the office, and when I check in, I'm surprised to be immediately escorted to the doctor's private office, where she is working at her desk.

"Thank you for seeing me on such short notice," I say.

She stands and offers her hand in a warm greeting. "I've been waiting for your call, Mrs. Vincent. Please, have a seat." She motions to a leather chair in front of her expansive desk, which is neatly stacked with several medical charts and books.

Dr. Eva Lucerne is nothing like what I expected. She is a petite woman with a shoulder-length pageboy of thick, naturally blonde hair. I know women who pay a fortune to get that shade of blonde. Her eyes are brownish-hazel, she wears very little makeup, and I wonder if the arch in her perfectly plucked eyebrows might be permanent ink—not that her brows look fake, just incredibly perfect.

The timbre of her voice is soothing, and she has a deep and refined articulation as she continues. "Curtis, Dr. Creswell, gave me your file last month. When I didn't hear from you, I thought perhaps you had found another specialist."

"With it being so close to Christmas and all, I figured it would be best for everyone if I just waited until after the first of the year. Plus, I've been feeling so much better … and please, call me Gloria."

She pauses for a moment, as though calling me by my first name is a completely foreign concept. "Okay then, if you're feeling so much better, Gloria, tell me why you called yesterday to see if I could squeeze you in today. My receptionist said you seemed a bit anxious."

Touché. Chalk one up for the doc.

In the writing world, what happens next is often referred to as a "pregnant pause," when the silence that follows a statement is full of uncomfortable or ironic implications and no one responds right away.

The good doctor is the first to break the silence. "Gloria, as you know, the results from your endoscopy and upper GI were inconclusive; there were no apparent masses in your throat or upper gastrointestinal area, but the tissue biopsy did show the presence of cancerous cells. This could mean any number of things, including that these cells may be the origin of the problem, or that they have spread here from another location. That's why it's absolutely critical that we conduct additional tests so we can clearly see what we're dealing with in order to make an accurate diagnosis and commence appropriate treatment."

She clasps her hands together and leans her arms on the desk in the time-honored pose that countless professionals adopt when they deliver serious or very important news, and it makes me smile. That she notices me noticing her body language and shifts her position without losing eye contact tells me a great deal about her, and although I think she's sincere in her concern, I can't help but think she may be feeling a sense of urgency relating more to pleasing a colleague than my need to undergo additional tests this quickly.

"Dr. Lucerne, I'm not refuting what the lab results indicate, but I'm also not entirely convinced we're talking about cancer," I say, "because I've been noticing a pattern, and it appears the episodes I have all relate to times when I eat spicy or overly rich food. It sounds more like an ulcer, or perhaps my gallbladder, or some type of digestive issue."

She interrupts gently. "If that's the case, these tests will reveal it without question and we can get you started on a treatment path that will address the issue."

"I understand. So what is the next step?" I ask.

"We need to do a complete CT scan and a fine-needle aspiration from any mass we may find. The results of these tests will definitively tell us where the cancer is centralized, if it has spread, and if we're dealing with something benign or malignant. These tests will also dictate the treatment plan options available, including whether you are a candidate for surgery."

I take a deep breath. "Well, you certainly don't pull any punches."

"Do you want me to?" She leans back. "I didn't take you for a beat-around-the-bush kind of gal."

"No, you're right, I do prefer straightforwardness. So what you're saying is that if you do happen to find something, there's a chance you can just remove it, is that right?"

"Yes, there is that possibility, but we have to take it one step at a time. We can get you in the first thing on Monday for a thorough exam, a CT scan, and a biopsy, but you can't eat or drink anything after midnight on Sunday, and you need to plan on being here for about three to four hours."

Three to four hours? On a Monday morning after a long three-day weekend? Oh my.

She smiles, stands, and extends her hand. "I'm glad you called, Gloria, and that I was able to see you today, but I'm afraid I have to be at the hospital in fifteen minutes." As our right hands connect, she maintains a firm grasp and says, "In spite of the circumstances, it was good to meet you, Gloria. My team will take good care of you on Monday; you are in excellent hands."

Traffic is a nightmare getting back to the Quarter from the Ochsner Center, and I have one of those psychopath taxi drivers, the kind you see in Bruce Willis or Mel Gibson action movies. As soon as I get home, I hang my purse from the finial on the staircase and walk directly to the bar in the study, where I pour myself a glass of cognac. I'm nursing my drink and checking messages on my phone when I'm startled by its ring and see Anthony Carlyle's name appear. I'm especially surprised since it's seven hours later in France.

I quickly manage to forget all about my harrowing cab ride and recent appointment with Dr. Lucerne as I anticipate Anthony's melodic and, dare I say, comforting voice. We've become unexpected friends, good friends, and I've come to look forward to our frequent and often lengthy phone conversations.

"Bonjour, Monsieur Carlyle. *Comment allez-vous?*"

"Bonjour *belle femme*, have I caught you at a good time?"

"That depends on how you define 'good time.' You know what they say; one man's pain is another man's pleasure. 'Good' is highly subjective."

Oh my God, did I really just say that? How lame. And did Anthony Carlyle just call me a beautiful woman?

★ ★ ★ ★ ★

Friday night, January 14

It doesn't look like I'll be able to make the Obit gathering at Sylvain tonight, because Anthony Carlyle will be in town and is coming over for dinner. Actually, he's coming over to talk business, but because of the last-minute nature of the meeting, he suggested we make it dinner as well and has insisted on bringing it himself.

"I'm sorry to cancel on you again, girlfriend," I told Stevie when I called, not disclosing anything more specific, "but I have a last-minute business meeting I need to handle." She was disappointed but understanding.

Although I'm certainly looking forward to visiting with Anthony, this truly is business.

It's important to me that my creative team at *NOLA 2 NOLA* isn't forced into sacrificing the space they need to perform their responsibilities. One of the acquisition terms we are still working on is an agreement that my team are not merged into corporate-style, cracker-box cubicles. We have talked numerous times about Anthony seeing the *NOLA 2 NOLA* office space to get an overall feel for the current staff environment.

"I don't expect Carlyle Communications to duplicate the rather unique office environment my team enjoys," I said to Francois and Anthony Carlyle when we met together in Paris back in November. "But I do think it's important that you see where this group of professionals has worked for so many years to make the publication the success that it is today."

Since I'm a firm believer in providential appointments, I'm guessing this unexpected last-minute visit from Anthony is really a kick in the pants from the Almighty to encourage me to make the decision to either go ahead with this acquisition or cancel it entirely.

I'm dripping wet and stepping out of the shower a couple of hours later when Anthony calls back.

"We just landed. As soon as Jeffrey parks this crate, I'll be on my way."

Jeffrey is Anthony's pilot, and "the crate" is a private Gulfstream jet owned by Carlyle Communications.

I take a deep breath when the doorbell rings and silently thank God that I don't have to pretend to Randy or Maria that this is just another typical dinner meeting and I'm not nervous, because, for some reason, I am.

When I open the heavy front door with its beveled glass, it's like I'm looking at a scene from any number of sappy romantic comedies, when the unbelievably handsome man is standing on the stoop with flowers, food, and a fabulous face that could launch a thousand ships.

This really is a business dinner, and I'm not fooling myself that it's anything more, but there's no denying that Anthony Carlyle is a charmer. He looks like a French Greek god, and I pray I don't appear like a simpering fool.

"Welcome to Vincent Manor." I do my utmost to look utterly nonplussed by his dashing appearance as he greets me European style with a kiss on each cheek and hands me a bouquet of cut flowers. The familiar fragrance of Stargazer and Casablanca lilies is impossible to ignore as I inhale the luxurious scent. Charles always gave me lilies.

"They're beautiful, Anthony, how thoughtful."

"Beautiful flowers for a beautiful woman."

"You are too kind." I usher him inside and close the door.

"My goodness, those are some sizeable doggie bags!" I laugh as he holds out not one, but two decorative logo-emblazoned shopping bags.

"Dinner is served, mademoiselle."

He has brought take-out from Delmonico's, of all places, and delicious aromas drift from the bags.

"I've set places for us in the dining room, but how about if we open some wine and I give you the quick twenty-five-cent tour before we sit down, if that's okay with you? And I'd like to put these flowers in water."

"That sounds perfect; lead the way."

He follows me to the kitchen and sets the bags on the counter.

"I've pulled several bottles of wine I think you will enjoy. Why don't you select one and pour us a couple of glasses while I get a vase for these? The opener is right there." I point toward the wine and the Waterford goblets.

"Your wish is my command." He comments on the various wine selections I've made and chooses a lovely sauvignon blanc from the Loire Valley to begin the evening. His family home is on a vineyard in France, and this man knows his wine. We visit like old friends as he fills our glasses and I use a sharp knife to trim the ends off each floral stem.

"You were raised in this home, is that correct?" he asks.

"Yes. My ancestors came from Spain and France—Isabella Medina and Henri Bronzinelle. They built this home in 1825."

"This is some kitchen." He whistles as his eyes seem to drink in the surroundings.

"Thank you. It does tend to be a gathering spot."

"Am I correct to assume it didn't look quite like this back in 1825?" He settles himself on one of the kitchen stools and appears genuinely interested as I begin to arrange the trimmed flowers in a Lalique vase.

"That is an accurate assumption. Actually, when Bronzinelle Manor was built, kitchens were never inside the main home, which is strange to think of today; but back then it made sense, as wood-burning cook stoves were dangerous, and cooking was not something that "respectable" people conducted themselves. Many of the large estates in New Orleans, especially here in the French Quarter, had slave quarters directly adjacent to or behind the home, where all the cooking was done."

"I didn't know that." Anthony nods with interest as I continue.

"In the last few years Charles was alive, he orchestrated a major renovation. We practically gutted the lower level of the house and most of the slave quarters in the back and built this beautiful gourmet kitchen and the adjacent master suite that overlooks the courtyard. The master suite can be accessed from the main hall, the glassed-in study, and from there." I point to a closed door just off the kitchen.

"Ah, I would love to see that renovation," Anthony teases seductively. At least I think he's teasing, but I skip by his none-to-subtle innuendo and continue.

"The second story of this main house is where the *NOLA 2 NOLA* offices are located, and the second story of the former slave quarters above the master suite is the apartment where Randy and Maria live. They have about two thousand square feet; their balcony also overlooks the pool and courtyard."

"Are Randy and Maria here this evening?" Anthony asks.

"No, they are out of town until Monday."

"How unfortunate," he says as he takes a sip of wine and smiles.

"There, all done." I step back and look at the finished floral arrangement. "Anthony, can I get you to carry this into the dining room for me? Then we can take a quick walk-through and come back to eat. Unless you'd rather have dinner now?"

"No, your plan is great; I'd like to get our business out of the way so we can move on to the pleasure part."

Is he flirting with me?

He carefully picks up the vase, follows me to the adjacent dining room, and places it carefully on the table where I indicate, commenting on my antique furniture.

"I do love mahogany," he says, gently running his fingertips over the surface. "This is an exquisite set."

"Thank you."

I proceed to quickly walk him through the lower level, answering his questions and espousing the history along the way.

"We've had a team of professionals over the years who have been so sensitive to maintaining interior and exterior integrity that you'll need a detective to determine what is new and what is original. We copied the balusters, pilasters, dentil work, soffits, weatherboards, and corners of the original house."

"Quite an undertaking," Anthony says as he visually inspects his surroundings. "And your papa was raised here as well?"

His French accent on "papa" makes me smile. "Yes, my father grew up in this home."

He stops to look more closely at the crown molding. "Wow!" he says, and I shake my head and laugh.

"Am I really considering the sale of my beloved magazine to a man who says 'Wow?'"

"What's wrong with 'wow'? It's a perfectly good word. So tell me, when did you meet your husband?"

We continue our tour of the lower level, including a very quick walk-through of the master suite, as I respond.

"We were childhood friends. After college, he came back to work for the Bronzinelle family."

"And that's when your friendship blossomed into something more?" Anthony asks.

"Much more. We got married in 1968; within two years both of my parents were dead of natural causes." I swirl the wine around inside my glass and lead him toward the grand staircase.

"Leaving you as the only heir," he says quietly. "I'm sorry for your loss. That was a lot of responsibility for a young woman, inheriting this home and an international business of that size."

"Yes, it was. Fortunately, my father had an excellent infrastructure in place, and I didn't have to actually oversee the day-to-day operations. And Charles was a godsend. I couldn't have done it without him. He basically handled all the company business while I went back to school and then got involved in the garden club and in the other charities we supported. We began renovation projects within a few months."

"And you never had children?"

"No children."

We walk quietly up the staircase together. It's been a long time since I've talked about my life so personally, and I'm afraid my emotions will give me away as Anthony places his hand on my arm.

"You and Charles have done an amazing job with this place, Gloria. It's truly beautiful."

"Thanks, but it was amazing to start with. It had good bones."

"Here's to good bones!" Anthony raises his glass and I do likewise, one hand on the balustrade, as we reach the top of the stairs and enter the NOLA 2 NOLA offices.

We conduct a brisk and basic walk-through of the administrative offices and my personal office, which includes a private powder room, before we take the elevator down to the main floor.

"I hardly ever use the elevator, but it's been a godsend to Maria and

Charlotte. It's directly off the old butler's pantry adjacent the kitchen, and we conduct a great many business luncheons in the conference room."

The elevator doors open, and we cross through the butler's pantry and back into the kitchen, where we started.

"Voilà! There you have it, the entire main house."

"I am monumentally impressed, Gloria. I have read about your home, and naturally I've seen photos of it, but none of that does justice to the incredible beauty and spirit of the home."

"Thank you, Anthony. It's sometimes hard to believe it's been designated as a National Historic Landmark; to me it's just home."

We refill our glasses and cross through the kitchen and go outside. I point to the carriage house.

"The lower level is the garage and Randy's workroom. Before renovating the upstairs, it was basically used for storage. Phillip, our staff photographer, is in seventh heaven with the new studio. We were spending a fortune renting studio space. Now we have our own studio and a state-of the-art photo-editing suite. Plus he has his own office. We are really pleased with how it turned out."

As we return to the main house for dinner, instead of entering back through the kitchen door, I take him around through the courtyard. I can't wait to see his expression. He has seen views of the courtyard from several rooms on the lower level, but it's not quite the same.

"What do you think?" I ask as we turn the corner.

It's clear he doesn't know what to look at first, as his eyes dart over the courtyard like a bumblebee in a garden of honeysuckle.

"I'd like to say 'wow,' but I'm afraid you'll beat me up." We both laugh. "This is absolutely stunning, Gloria."

"Thank you. I do love this space, especially in the evening like this when the lights and sounds are so soothing." I walk to the edge of the shimmering water. "This is one of the largest private swimming pools in the French Quarter." He is speechless as he stands at my side staring at the pool, which sits perfectly in the center of the courtyard, surrounded by fountains and lush trees with up-lighting. The music playing through the outdoor sound system is a mix of classical, jazz, and easy listening.

"You must do a great deal of entertaining in such a beautiful place," he says.

"We do," I nod. "We host many fund-raising events."

Anthony once again holds up his glass. "These renovations are brilliant, and your home is a literal showcase. Absolutely *magnifique*! I can understand how difficult it will be for your staff to leave it if you decide to accept our offer. But if you do, I want you to know that we will take excellent care of them; you have my word on that."

"Did you ever come to terms on the building you and your father were looking at downtown?" I ask.

"We actually closed on it last week. Carlyle Communications now owns a three-story building in the Central Business District, and we are prepared to delegate an entire floor to the *NOLA 2 NOLA* division, giving your team, as well as any new staff, ample room."

"That's good to know, Anthony. These people are important to me, and to the magazine." I glance at my watch and see that it's been almost an hour since Anthony arrived. "Perhaps we should eat now, and open another bottle of wine? I don't know about you, but I'm famished!" I say as we walk back into the house.

When we sit down to eat, I devour a delicious and tender slice of prime rib, along with roasted vegetables with almond slivers. My appetite is back with a vengeance, although I'm eating slowly and being careful not to eat anything that looks too rich or appears at all spicy.

We sit and talk for what seems like hours about food, wine, music, Bronzinelle Steel, and Carlyle Communications. I'm not sure I've ever met anyone who understands the unique nature of my life, and I find myself telling Anthony things I haven't shared in many years. Our families have so much in common.

At the end of dinner, he leans in close and I can smell the familiar scent of Aramis. For once the queasiness in my stomach is not related to nausea—not by a long shot.

"I can't tell you how gratifying it is to see a woman actually eat!" he says after we've finished. "How do you stay so trim? Do you exercise a great deal? Please tell me you are not like so many American women who are addicted to exercise and who only pretend to eat or are bulimic." He shakes his head. "I simply cannot understand that."

"Trust me—I like to eat, seldom work out, and no, I don't have anorexia or bulimia. I've been having some slight issues with certain foods, so I am curtailing spicy foods and creamy sauces. I've always tried to eat healthy, and I guess I'm blessed with good genes, but who knows, it could all backfire on me when I hit sixty this year. I could end up getting old and fat."

"Somehow I doubt that." He smiles. After a few moments of comfortable silence, he speaks. "Gloria, may I ask you a personal question?"

"Of course."

"You are a beautiful woman—sophisticated, savvy, and sexy, a very lethal combination. Why have you remained single? Surely you must be fighting off admirers."

"Oh, absolutely. It's a veritable boxing match around here most times." I put my fists up in a mock display of throwing punches.

"I'm serious." He reaches out and gently covers my clenched fists with his hands. "My father acts like a doting puppy around you, and I have to say it's rather embarrassing how some women behave around him, but not you."

I have to remind myself to breathe as he stares at me with his piercing blue eyes and continues to hold on to my hands.

I abruptly pull my hands back, take a sip of wine, and stand. "Your father is a sweet man. As for women behaving foolishly around him, surely you are not blind as to your effect on the opposite sex?" I pat him somewhat condescendingly on the shoulder, a fact he will scold me for later. "I'd like to show you something else I think you'll appreciate, if you'd care to take a short walk?"

"Lead the way," he says. "I'm right behind you." He stands and follows me to the adjoining room, where I show him a huge family tree that has been hand painted on a six-foot-by-nine-foot canvas framed in carved mahogany that takes up an entire wall.

"This was just delivered a few days ago. It's the complete Bronzinelle lineage, going back as far as we can trace it. You're one of the first to see it."

"My, oh my," he says quietly, and he begins to study the information.

As Anthony continues to look closely at my family tree, I can see him doing the math in his brain as he says, "It appears many of the men in your family have had the wisdom to marry older women."

"Oh, that was smooth, Anthony." I smile.

He takes the wineglass from my hand, places it on a nearby table, and takes my hand in his. "It is true that you are slightly older than me," he says, with a hint of a smile.

"Fourteen years is hardly 'slightly.'"

"The numeral is irrelevant," he states matter-of-factly. "And we have another truth to address." He looks into my eyes.

"And what might that be?" I raise my eyebrows.

"It is also true that your husband has been gone for many years, which makes you technically a widow, and that I have never been married, which makes me technically, what?"

"Single?" I say.

"Yes. Single, and available, just like you. And I think it's time I officially go on record."

I'm not sure what he means as he holds my hand and continues.

"Gloria, I don't want to play this cat-and-mouse game anymore. I don't want you to look at me and see some irresponsible, wealthy playboy the media has created. The number of years between our birthdates is an insignificant and inconsequential fact that never enters my mind. From this point forward, I would like you to remove these facts from importance in your mind as well."

I'm trying hard to process all this information coming at me, and as if on cue, the background music changes to a beautiful Viennese waltz. Anthony encircles my waist with his left hand and with his right grasps mine in a tender yet strong hold that tells me he knows his way around a dance floor. He expertly leads me in several steps and spins before he returns his gaze to my eyes.

"What do you see when you look at me, Gloria?"

"I'm not sure what I see, Anthony," I whisper. "What do you see when you look at me?"

"More than you can possibly know," he says without hesitation. "I see a vibrant and vivacious woman, a strong and savvy businesswoman. I see a woman filled with compassion and passion, a woman who once gave her heart and soul completely to the man she loved."

I'm not sure how to respond; I don't know what to say as he continues.

"On my way here this evening I saw a horse-drawn carriage on the street, and I thought how lovely it would be to see the wonder of this city from that vantage point with you at my side ... and after spending this time with you, I'm even more certain that I want to experience every exciting and extraordinary event in life with you at my side." He whispers in my ear, "Now, ask me that question again."

"What do you see when you look at me?"

"When I look at you, Gloria, I see my future, our future."

He stops dancing, and like a scene from a classic film, he takes my face in his hands and locks his deep blue eyes on mine as he continues, this time in his native language, which I completely understand.

"I know what is at stake for you if we cross this line, Gloria, and I do not want people to talk until you are ready for them to talk. So until then, we will keep this as quiet as you wish it to be, except between us; between us there is no more need for silence. Between us, the time for pretending is over."

As his lips touch mine, I am swept into an oblivion where time is suspended, where all that exists is one sublime feeling after another.

"Do you know anything about astrology, Gloria?" he asks much later as we are nestled comfortably under the sheets on my bed, as though we have been together for years.

"I live in New Orleans, Anthony; there is a soothsayer, tarot card reader, tea leaf reader, astrologist, and voodoo queen on every block."

He laughs and takes my long braid in his hands and begins to unwind it. "I imagine that is true, but do you take any of it seriously?"

"Not really. Not much, anyway." I trace imaginary figures on his chest with my fingers.

"I knew immediately that you were a Taurus, an earth sign, very grounded," he says.

"You mean bullheaded? Is that what you're saying?"

"Not at all, I was attracted to your strength of spirit and heart. You are not a bull any more than I am a crab. I'm a Cancer, a water sign— very romantic, but guarded. Astrologically speaking, we are incredibly compatible; one of the most compatible duos, in fact."

He kisses me passionately, and when I catch my breath I say, "Well, at least we're compatible on some level, because there's zero chemistry between us." He laughs joyfully as he pulls me close.

He has successfully unwound my braid and runs his strong fingers gently through my hair. "I have never before seen hair so long and so beautiful; it is so luxurious. Do you ever wear it down, not in a braid?"

"Goodness, no. I'm far too old for that."

"No, no, no." He shakes his index finger at me and warns, "You are not too old. What did I say about pulling the age card? It is not permitted. You are not too old for anything you wish to do."

He kisses me again with passion and asks, "Are you too old to enjoy that?"

Not long ago I was beginning to think I was, but there is no denying that the heat being generated between us does not carry an expiration date.

I'm not entirely sure that Anthony is a stranger to this kind of passionate energy, this unrestrained intimacy, but at this stage in my life I'm not gazing at him with the starstruck eyes of a young girl looking for promises or commitment. If our encounter ends here, I will feel a satisfaction that words cannot describe, yet deep in my heart I never want this to end.

Charles is the only man I have ever known in the true biblical sense of the word, and it's been a long time since I have allowed myself to even consider the possibility of falling in love again, and yet in Anthony's arms, the possibility is a very tangible probability.

"You are an unexpected pleasure," I say as he nestles me into the crook of his arm.

"And you, my dear, are an unexpected treasure," he says, holding me tightly.

I've never done anything like this in my entire life, but I have no regret for behaving with such wild abandon. In fact, everything seems utterly and completely right.

"Let's finalize the acquisition, Anthony," I say.

"And which acquisition might that be?" he asks.

"NOLA 2 NOLA. Let's make it happen. I've been ready to accept your offer for a while. What has happened between us tonight has nothing to do with my decision; it just confirmed what I've known for some time—I'm ready for a new journey in my life."

He is pensive and quiet as he lightly kisses my forehead, each cheek, my chin, and the tip of my nose, and then lays his head gently on my chest and says, "The only acquisition I wish to discuss now is the acquisition of your heart, for you have surely taken mine."

When Anthony departs just before sunrise on Saturday morning, I'm feeling anything but old, a feeling that continues as he returns again on Saturday night, and on Sunday.

I'm watching him take a shower in my bathroom on Sunday night as I leave a message with the answering service at the Ochsner Center to cancel my Monday morning appointment, assuring them I will call later to reschedule. I've agreed to meet Anthony at his hotel on Monday afternoon before he returns to Paris.

I'm convinced whatever health problems I had have all but disappeared, as my appetite has returned and the only vestiges of anything queasy in my stomach are the butterflies I feel when Anthony Carlyle opens the glass door, leans out, and shouts over the spray of water, "Hey, gorgeous, where are you?"

CHAPTER 17

— Stephanie —

Monday, January 24

It's been almost impossible to connect with Gloria. I haven't seen her since she practically flew out of Broussard's and then stood me up at the Obit Cocktail event the next day. I'm beginning to see how running *NOLA 2 NOLA* on her own has become increasingly challenging for her, especially since they launched the European edition. She has a great team, but she's ultimately the chief, and it's a huge responsibility. She pushes herself very hard.

In fact, when I finally reached her on the phone a few days ago, she was once again in Paris, meeting with some number-crunchers at Carlyle Communications.

"Does this mean you've actually decided to sell?" I asked her.

"I think so; it's beginning to make really good sense, Stevie. But you have to swear on all that is holy that you won't breathe a word about this to anyone—other than Louis, of course, but make sure he knows this isn't public information yet."

"I get it, girlfriend, I get it."

"I'm serious, Stevie. This is a big thing, and an acquisition like this takes careful timing and strategy. It's a long way from being a done deal, but we're getting closer."

"Closer, eh? Give me all the juicy details. How is Daddy Warbucks doing?"

"Stop calling him that."

"My, my, aren't we testy." I love teasing Gloria about Francois Carlyle.

She thinks she's being coy, but I'd bet the farm, if I had one, that the two of them are getting cozy. But I'll play her game of denial until she's ready to talk about it.

"So when are you coming home? Planning to do any shopping while you're there?"

"I'll be back this weekend, probably Sunday. I have an event at the Louvre tomorrow night; do you need me to pick something up for you?" she teases.

"Sure. How about a da Vinci to go, or maybe a side of Degas?"

"I'll see what I can do." Her laugh is hearty, and she sounds good. "So how is the cookbook coming along? Have you met again with Elizabeth?" she asks.

"Actually, I'm waiting for a call back from her; we've been playing phone tag. Say, did you hear from Emme that I got GW Fins to donate an in-home chef dinner, with wine included, for the Grace House auction?"

"No way! Congratulations, Stevie! We've been trying to get them to contribute. You've got the golden touch, girlfriend!"

We talked for a while about the auction packages I'm working on, and after almost an hour of chitchat we were reasonably caught up on our lives.

"Time to say au revoir. I'll call you when I get back, and we'll go for drinks at Three Muses, okay? I'm about due for a good cocktail and great live music."

"No need to twist my arm. Does this renewed interest in fun and drink mean you're feeling better?"

"It most certainly does! I've been feeling really good, but I'm also very careful about what I eat. I've had enough indigestion and heartburn to last a lifetime. Alas, I've had to permanently say good-bye to butter, cream, fried food, and spice. I've resigned myself to the fact that I simply cannot touch those foods, not even in small amounts. But the end result is that I'm no longer going through bottles of cherry-flavored liquid antacid like Kool-Aid, so I'm thinking I must be on the road to recovery."

"Hallelujah! You were becoming a bit of a killjoy there for a while, a real buzzkill," I tease.

"Tell me about it."

It was so good to hear my friend sound like her old self. And as reluctant as I initially was about her idea to sell *NOLA 2 NOLA*, I'm now thinking it might be the best thing for her. She's been consumed with business the past year, and it's not like she *has* to work. If she actually goes through with the acquisition, it will be good to spend more time with her, like the old days.

I'm assuming she got back in town late last night, and I check my phone when I get up to see if she's sent me a text, but there is nothing yet.

Clearly it's a Monday morning, as my phone starts ringing at the crack of dawn. Well, almost. We've got a roof repair being done, and the contractor called to check on the crew he sent over. Someone from the Vieux Carré Commission called to inform us that we can't hoist the shingles and equipment up the side of the building on the makeshift pulley the workers constructed. The guys won't be happy to know they're going to have to physically carry everything up. I get confirmation calls from two vendors for the silent auction, and my insurance agent calls to give me the update on getting the dings repaired in my car door. And last, but surely not least, Louis calls from Houston, Texas, where he's speaking at the American Academy of Allergy, Asthma, and Immunology.

I've been on the phone most of the morning when Elizabeth calls.

"Grand Central Station, may I help you?" I say when I answer.

"Ha, ha, I can sure relate to that! Do you have a minute?"

It doesn't take us long to decide that after a ton of e-mail and a half dozen calls, it's probably best to meet in person with all of our notes, recipes, and ideas to discuss our next step strategy for the cookbook.

"I hate to ask, but would you mind terribly coming to my place?" Elizabeth asks. "I have several file boxes filled with paperwork, copies of prior cookbooks, and lists of recipes that need to be cross-checked with past cookbooks."

I suppose driving to Old Metairie isn't really that far, and whether I take my car or a taxi, I can always plan some other errands around the trip—maybe a run to Whole Foods or a stop at Perino's. Plus I haven't been inside her McMansion in ages; it's a magnificent place.

"Uh, okay, I guess I can drive over. It's on Mulberry, right? What's the exact address?" I ask, looking for a pencil.

"No, sorry, we're not at that house anymore. The kids and I are at our place on Governor Nicholls."

I had no idea she moved, but this makes it much easier for me, as I can walk there.

"Really? When did that happen?"

"Not too long ago—just after our garden club meeting at Broussard's, actually. Gloria stopped by last week just before she left for Paris; I figured she would have told you."

No, Gloria didn't tell me, but that isn't a surprise, since she didn't even tell me she was going to France this time.

Elizabeth sounds a bit frazzled, and I feel bad for her. She's definitely bitten off more than she can chew, and she seems hell-bent on implementing more and more changes every time the garden club meets. In many ways, she and Gloria are cut from the same cloth; it's been a lethal combination, as Gloria's power as the honorary director of the executive board allows her to approve or veto club president plans with or without membership approval. She has always wielded this power in a judicious fashion, but for some reason she has completely jumped on the bandwagon of change with Elizabeth this season. This isn't a president who is interested in maintaining the status quo.

We agree to meet at her house, and we end our phone call so I can get ready and head over to her place.

When I get there, she escorts me into the luxurious dining room, where stacks of paperwork are strewn all over the table, literally covering the entire surface. Additional cardboard archive storage boxes are stacked on the floor with "G.C. STUFF" written on the outside. I shake my head in amazement.

"Where the heck did you get all of this, Elizabeth?"

"Oh my gosh, from all over! Once I got started, it was like conducting a search for buried treasure. The more I looked, the more I found. Can you believe it? This is the first time in years, maybe ever, that the majority of the garden club records have been assembled in one location!" She points to the table. "I've got sort stacks going for recipes, meeting minutes, correspondence, voting records, financials, membership information, and even a few old to-do lists!" She claps her hands and looks at the collection like a historian looks at rare books.

I do love history, and I must agree that what she's doing is really quite fascinating.

"And just wait until you see this!" She grabs my hand and briskly walks me to her kitchen, where dozens of garden club cookbooks are laid out chronologically on the countertop.

"Can you believe it? Have you ever seen them all together like this?" she squeals.

I shake my head, speechless, as she animatedly continues.

"Look at this one." She picks up a copy of the 1960 cookbook in faded purple ink on very thick and somewhat shiny paper. "This was copied on an old mimeograph machine! Well, it wasn't an old machine then; in fact, it was pretty cutting-edge for the time."

The word immediately brings to mind the smell of the mimeograph, or ditto machine, at my childhood church, where weekly bulletins were appreciated as much for their scent as for their substance. The scent has become embedded in the collective memory of my generation of baby boomers. I remember the countless hours I spent cranking the handle of that machine to help my father print God knows what for his never-ending church committee work.

Elizabeth barely takes a breath before she continues. "I've made an Excel spreadsheet of all the years the garden club has been meeting, including cookbook dates, titles, and the president in charge at the time. Look how many cookbooks we've had!"

She thrusts a document into my hand, and I have to say as I look at the list that I'm very impressed with what she's done.

She excitedly continues. "I'm also cataloging all the recipes used in every edition, and as you might imagine, there has been some duplication of recipes over the years—not that duplication is a bad thing, but we need to be careful how often it occurs. Needless to say, this is all taking a lot of time, but it must be done."

"There was no collective record of any of this before now?" I ask, paging through her detailed list. I'm amazed to see that she's even included a column to indicate who submitted each recipe, and it's quick to see which members take this cookbook very seriously.

"No, there was almost no sense of order! Everything was, and still is, a mess. I've been on a lot of boards and committees since I've been married to Snake … er, Jake, and I've never seen anything more disorganized. Gloria started keeping some records her first time as president in 1991, but even her records are minimal, as this was before the widespread use of personal computer technology. However, I was able to use a lot of her information to begin constructing this database."

"How did you manage to find all this paperwork?" I ask.

"Gloria gave me the names of the members who she felt would most likely have saved paperwork over the years, and between the two of us, we've been amassing this collection since last summer, when she asked me to come on board as president. Believe me, not everyone was willing to relinquish their old files; you'd have thought we were asking them to surrender the Holy Grail, for crying out loud. But Gloria can be very persuasive."

"I had no idea all this collecting was going on."

"Really? I'm surprised to hear that, but that's why I've been pushing so hard for us to consider renting office space somewhere. Do you remember in November when I first introduced the idea to the ladies? Back when this kitchen we're now standing in was flooded, and at the last minute we had to switch the garden club meeting to the John Lafitte Bistro?"

"Yes, I remember."

"Well, I haven't given up on that idea. Unfortunately, that particular building is gone, but something else will come available, and we need to get focused for when that happens! This group really does need more permanent administrative offices, Stephanie. Once we get all this stuff sorted, I can't store it here. Plus, if we take this next cookbook to the level where Gloria and I *think* it can go, where we *know* it can go, we're going to need a central place to conduct the development, marketing, and promotion tasks. We have to stop operating like a backwoods still producing moonshine."

I suddenly get her analogy. I initially thought I understood Elizabeth's broader vision for the cookbook when we talked at the bar in Broussard's, but I can see now that I didn't fully grasp the extent of that vision, her shared vision with Gloria, the level to which they want the garden club to climb. She wants us to skip all the middle floors and go from the ground floor to the penthouse.

I'm captivated by her energy and enthusiasm as she discusses using full color, including photographs and bios, and launches expertly into the technical options for binding, printing, and distribution available. Clearly she has given this a great deal more thought than I imagined.

"Gloria is the editor-in-chief of *NOLA 2 NOLA* for crying out loud!" she says. "Do you have any idea the access she has to publishers and printing resources? She can get us some great pricing, and if we do it right, this entire project can be a huge moneymaker for us every year, instead of just barely funding our annual Christmas party!"

She speaks up before I can voice an objection. "I know the Christmas party is fun, and the toy donations are fantastic, but surely you can see the potential we have to do so much more, to be so much more! Stephanie, please, we really need you to be on board with this lock, stock, and barrel. Please!"

"Well, there's no mistaking whose genetic pool you share, figuratively if not literally." I laugh.

She smiles. "I know, I know. Gloria and I do share a lot of the same ideologies. She reminds me a lot of my mom; they're both very wise and gracious women. I learn so much from her every time we meet."

"So you two are getting close, eh?" My question sparks an immediate, and unexpected, emotional reaction, as Elizabeth's violet eyes tear up quickly and she ushers us back to the dining room.

"I'm not sure I would have made it without her," she whispers. "You know she was the person who came and told me about Jake and … that woman."

"Yes, I know. I was with her at Galatoire's that day."

"Oh, that's right, I forgot." She takes a deep breath, straightens her shoulders, and seamlessly changes the subject as she explains the system she has developed on her table for us to sort out the paperwork from the boxes. We work quietly for a few minutes before she speaks.

"It must be thrilling for Gloria to see the European edition of *NOLA 2 NOLA* take off so quickly. How exciting to be an international businesswoman and get to travel to Paris so often! When is she coming back this time?"

"You haven't talked to her recently?" I ask nonchalantly.

"No, not since she left."

"Well, I'm waiting for her to text me any minute; I'm sure she landed late last night and is already swamped with work."

"Personally, I don't know how she does it all," Elizabeth says, shaking her head.

We continue to go through old files, and Elizabeth soon holds out a sheet of what appears to be very old linen stationary. "Look, Stephanie, here's another handwritten copy of the garden club rules and regulations. This one is dated 1955."

She begins to pace as she continues speaking with the passionate energy of a politician stumping for election. "The garden club needs revised guidelines and written goals that reflect a strategic vision for existing in the twenty-first century. From what I can gather, the official rules and regulations have not been revised since just after the end of the war in 1946." She sits down and looks at me with frustration and continues. "I know you've been against the changes we've been implementing, that you think everything is fine just as it is, but everything isn't fine."

"It's been fine until this season. So tell me, what changed from last season to this one? Other than our club president."

She looks at me thoughtfully and says, "There was scaffolding around your building last year. They were repairing your balcony, right?"

"Yes."

"Why?" she asks.

"Because it needed to be repaired."

"So it was broken?"

"No, the wrought iron railing was loose; we needed to replace a section of rotting wood."

"Why not just leave it as it was? It's an old building; it looked okay from the outside."

"But it wasn't okay; we had to fix the problem before it got worse." As soon as the words are out of my mouth I can see where she's going with this. "But Elizabeth, you can't compare the garden club to a historic building; it's not the same thing."

"Why isn't it the same thing? The garden club is old, like your building, and while it may look good on the outside, it needs repair underneath before it gets worse. We need to pull our heads out of the sand and open our eyes, Stephanie! When something is no longer working as it should, I believe we have two choices we can intentionally make: either ignore it or address it. Then we have to accept the consequences for the choice we make."

"Kind of like you did in your marriage, right?"

It's like all the air goes out of Elizabeth; she lurches back as though I've punched her in the gut.

"I'm sorry, Elizabeth. I didn't mean it to sound that way. I'm really sorry; I didn't mean for my words to sound so—"

"Cruel?" She looks up at me and wipes the tears from her cheeks with the back of her hand. "I'm getting used to that from you, Stephanie; you speak your mind. Either you don't have a very good filter, at least with me, or you just don't care. I'm not quite sure yet which it is."

Her tears are still flowing, and I find myself fighting back my own emotions as the effect of my words sinks in. I notice a box of tissues on the table and hold it out to her as she pulls out a couple of lightly scented pieces.

"I do care, Elizabeth; I'm really sorry I said it that way. It just sounded applicable, in theory, to what you were saying about choices; but you're absolutely right, those were cruel words, but I'm not a cruel person. I didn't mean it to come out that way, really. I'm so sorry, please forgive me."

She wipes her eyes, blows her nose, and leans back in the chair. "No, I'm sorry I snapped at you. You're right about the correlation of the issues, in theory, and I do need to practice what I preach. Like they say, the truth hurts. You were only being truthful. It's just that things are really in flux right now, and I'm struggling to figure out what I'm going to do with my life." She pauses to collect her thoughts, and for once in my life I keep my mouth shut.

"Long story short," she says quietly, "is that I've traded homes with my soon-to-be ex-husband. Jake wanted the big house, and he can have it, along with the big overhead. Don't get me wrong; I'd much rather be here in the heart of the French Quarter anyway, but it's been more difficult than I thought it would be. I guess I just haven't completely wrapped my brain around the fact that the kids and I will be living here full-time."

"I can understand that, but it's an absolutely gorgeous house." I notice that she's used up all the tissues she had, and I once again hold the box out to her. She smiles when she takes the entire box instead of simply removing a couple of tissues. I return her smile.

"So tell me the backstory of this place, Elizabeth. Every home in the French Quarter has one."

She begins to tell me the history of her grand home and the homes around it. She's got a keen eye for detail. She also knows a great deal about historical time periods, architecture, and architects. Additionally, the way she articulates her vast knowledge about the community is mesmerizing. She's a great storyteller and paints excellent word pictures.

"Have you ever thought about going into the real estate business, Elizabeth? Something tells me you'd be really good at it."

"Oh goodness, no, I haven't thought about that. Do you really think I would be good at it?"

What I said in passing turns out to be an idea that we begin to explore more fully as we manage to sort through all the boxes of material she has amassed. We get a great deal accomplished in a couple of hours, and I'd like to think by the time we part ways that I've redeemed myself from my foot-in-mouth disease. In fact, she seemed so interested that I wouldn't be at all surprised if she actually looks into getting a Realtor license.

CHAPTER 18

— Gloria —

Tuesday, February 1

I've been back from Paris for almost a week, and I'm surprised how much I find myself thinking about, and missing, Anthony. Truthfully, there's so much going on in my life that I'm not sure I really have the time or energy to invest in developing a relationship, but there's no escaping the fact that we're having a wonderful time, even if it turns out to be only a passing fancy.

There's also no escaping the fact that I'm going to have to get in much better physical shape if I want to keep up with this fellow. Since our rambunctious romp, my lower back is acting up again, but every time I feel the slight ache, it makes me smile.

Today I'm focusing the majority of my attention on Grace House business, including the upcoming gala and silent auction. I'm meeting with Emme and Elizabeth to discuss ways that Elizabeth can help. I'm so pleased that in spite of the ever-changing scenarios in her life, Elizabeth has continued her volunteer work on the advisory board for Grace House, in addition to her ever-increasing garden club responsibilities. She's quite a young lady. I've also asked Stevie to join us for the meeting, but I'm not sure she took my invitation seriously.

I've scheduled an early lunch with Elizabeth before Emme arrives, so we can play catch-up. It's a beautiful day—a little cool, but thanks to an abundance of sunshine, we're eating outside in the courtyard. Maria has set a lovely table and has prepared a tray of delectable finger sandwiches and icy goblets of sweet tea.

Elizabeth loves architecture and interior design. Every time she visits Vincent Manor, it's as though it's her first time, and her eyes drink in the grand staircase, crown molding, and glistening hardwood floors as we walk to the courtyard.

"I can't imagine what it must have been like to grow up here; this is such a beautiful place. You must love it," Elizabeth says.

"Thank you, dear. Yes, I do love it." We take our seats, and the sound of the nearby fountain is like gentle background music.

"I am always stunned by the cacophony of color in this courtyard," Elizabeth says. She takes a sip of tea. "It is visually stupendous!"

"It's certainly not subtle, is it?" I laugh.

What might seem garish upon description is anything but. The entire south wall of the courtyard is a mosaic of hand-painted Italian tiles in deep, rich shades of purple, gold, and green, in a pattern reminiscent of classic stained-glass cathedral windows.

Patio furniture in warm tones of brown and beige, with multicolor throw pillows, dots the landscape, and canvas umbrellas shoot up from the tables like colorful blooms, all in varying shades of the same purple, gold, and brilliant green. Ceramic pots that sit in seemingly random groupings are anything but, in varying shades of the same three colors.

"How is it again that we adopted that trio of colors?" she asks, genuinely interested.

"When Grand Duke Alexis Alexandrovitch Romanoff of Russia visited New Orleans in 1872, he felt that New Orleans, and specifically Mardi Gras, should have official colors, and he chose purple, green, and gold."

"Bravo to the duke!" Elizabeth holds up her glass of tea.

"Yes, bravo to the duke," I echo.

"Let me see if I remember," Elizabeth laughs. "Purple is for justice, green for faith, and gold for power, right? It is visually stunning, Gloria. Your plants look perfect, like a movie set! I've never seen a more luxurious collection of flowers and plants in a courtyard garden."

"Ah, we can thank Dolores Delacroix for that. She is a landscaping and plant genius."

Maria has served delicious sandwiches, and we quietly eat for a few minutes, enjoying the peacefulness.

When I look up, I notice that she's getting emotional.

My heart breaks for her as I reach out my hand to tuck a stray lock of hair behind her ear. "Oh, sweetheart, I know it might not look like it right now, but I just know you're going to be okay."

"I decided to sell some of my jewelry; I really don't need all of it." She reaches into her Gucci purse and pulls out a deep purple velvet bag and dumps out a stack of jewelry on the table. "There's a lot of truth to the old saying "All that glitter isn't gold." It turns out about 95 percent of my jewelry is fake. But that's not all. Our bank accounts are closed, checking and savings, and he hasn't been making the house payments on either place like he said he was going to. In fact, the house on Mulberry is in the final stages of the foreclosure process; I had no idea. I don't know if Jake even realizes that. The car I have was a gift to me from my parents, so no one can take that, but everything else is gone; it's all gone. My parents know the owner of the bank that holds the mortgage on our Governor Nicholls place, so I think I'll be safe there for the time being, but the expenses are mounting and I have no income. Oh God, Gloria, what am I going to do?"

By the time she utters the last sentence, her angry indignation has turned into a fearful whisper. When I reach out my arms to hold her, she crumbles against me.

"I need to get a job, Gloria, but at this point I don't even know where to start. There's not much call for ex-cheerleaders of my age. Stevie suggested I look into real estate; she said she thinks I'd be good at that. What do you think, Gloria? Is that something you think I could do?"

"Oh honey, I think you can do anything you set your mind to do! But you know, I think Stevie hit the nail on the head with that suggestion! I think you would be a phenomenal real estate agent, especially here in the Quarter. You know your architecture, you know the community, and you certainly have an excellent sense of design and décor. How are you with figures? I mean, do you have any familiarity with commission structures, interest rates, and things of that nature?"

"I'm actually very good with numbers. That's why things didn't seem to add up when I finally started looking at our financial records. Jake always took care of that, along with his manager, who it turns out is just as much of a snake; anyway, that's another story. But as for real estate, I think I could learn what I need to know."

She takes a deep breath. "But Gloria, how soon can someone start earning money in real estate? I need a job soon."

Maria is gentle when she interrupts us. "Excuse me, Miss Gloria, but Miss Emme is here. Where would you like me to escort her?"

"Up to the conference room, please. And tell her we'll be there shortly. Thank you."

"Sweetie, you don't have to stay for this meeting if you're not up to it; I will completely understand." I take Elizabeth's hand.

"No, I'll be okay. I really need to take my mind off this for a while. I'm sorry I unloaded on you."

"Nonsense! You need to process what is happening, and that's what friends are for. I'm going to think about this; I may have some ideas. Let's talk more about this later today or tomorrow."

I put my arm around her as we walk into the house and upstairs to the *NOLA 2 NOLA* conference room, where Emme greets us warmly.

We've been talking about the silent auction for almost an hour when our conversation veers into one of the projects Emme would like to explore with the advisory board, a dream project that could become reality if enough money is raised at the upcoming auction.

She begins to explain her vision with passion. "I know your garden club ladies are aware that our community has a problem. I know they are beginning to understand just how many homeless women and children exist on our streets. But I'm not certain they fully grasp how they can actively do something about it."

"By getting even more involved in the Grace House gala?" Elizabeth asks. "Truthfully, we've got volunteers we don't even know what to do with."

"No, not just in helping to raise money, although that's critical for us," Emme says. "What I'm talking about is actual hands-on work in helping to raise the self-esteem of these women."

"How so?" I ask.

"By offering friendship, mentorship, and guidance to these women."

"Guidance? In what way?" Elizabeth asks.

"In one of the most valuable ways we can offer—through example, through personal involvement, through an investment of time in the life of someone who needs encouragement and empowerment."

"Like the Big Brothers Big Sisters organization?" I ask.

"Yes, similar to that overall concept." Emme nods.

"That is a great idea!" I say, and Elizabeth agrees. "Our garden club members have skills that run the gamut from arts and crafts to business, cooking, gardening, and more. Their talents and life experience could be a tremendous influence."

"Exactly!" Emme agrees. "Did you know that Florence Ingersoll is teaching cross-stitching to three of our gals? She comes to Grace House every weekend; the residents love her."

"That's wonderful," I exclaim.

"But wait; there's more." Emme takes a big sip of water. "I haven't quite fleshed out the variables to this additional component, but I think it warrants further exploration. Let me give you a quick, broad-stroke vision." She is very animated as she continues. "We get calls every day from women who are looking for information and resources. Not just for housing; many women in the community are looking for employment alternatives, which leads to an increased need for education and job training. This issue isn't just limited to our Grace House residents; it's apparently something needed by a much broader audience."

"Oh my gosh!" Elizabeth exclaims. "Gloria and I were just talking about this at lunch. I'm considering my future career options, in light of my new situation, and I'm not quite sure where to start. It would be nice to talk with someone who has additional insight. If this place existed, do you see it as somewhere someone like me could go to get direction and information?"

"Yes! A place women in the community, not just our shelter residents, could turn to; a place where you could connect with other women, get training, counseling, or maybe take a workshop or attend a seminar."

We are unanimously energized and brainstorm for almost another half hour before we realize the time. I walk Emme and Elizabeth downstairs, and just as they head out the front door, Emme remembers something.

"Oh gosh, I almost forgot. One of my biggest concerns right now regarding the gala is leveraging the assets of our volunteers who have expressed interest in acquiring silent auction donations. I know I've said this before, but it's an even bigger challenge now. We must channel their capabilities and energy, as well as track the individual items and packages they are acquiring. They've got great intentions, but right now they're either sleeping giants or loose cannons. Even Elizabeth mentioned this earlier when she said there are garden club members who have volunteered but are without specific direction. If you can find me one qualified volunteer who can handle and direct all these ladies, it would be a godsend."

"I'll see what I can do." I hug her good-bye, watch her walk away.

Emme and Elizabeth have been gone for almost an hour when Stevie shows up at my office.

"Sorry I couldn't make lunch, but do you want to talk about the auction items I'm working on?" she says.

I cut right to the chase in my response. "Emme could really use your help with the gala, Stevie, and not just by acquiring auction items. She's got dozens of volunteers who want to work, but she needs someone to lead them, someone experienced."

"You know how I feel about group leadership politics; it's not my thing. Thanks, but no thanks."

"We really need you."

"It's nice to be needed, but like I said, thanks, but no thanks."

"What happened to you, Stevie?"

"What do you mean?"

"Just what I said, what happened to you? What's with all this 'just say no to group leadership'? You know as well as I do that any successful philanthropic effort comes from a well-organized plan of action, and someone has to direct the band to play in concert."

"Yeah, that may be so, but that someone isn't me. You know I've never been one of those leadership committee types. I'm a worker bee and happy with that. Why does this surprise you now? I've been this way for years."

"I know, and it's incredibly frustrating! You could be doing so much more."

"Why would I want to do more, Gloria? I'm busy enough as it is. Trust me—I've seen my share of queen bee leaders come and go, and I have no desire to draw a big red circle on my chest and wait for someone to shoot an arrow or catapult a boulder at me!"

"Are you really happy with a life of just hosting annual holiday parties?" I ask. "You're a premiere party planner, Stevie; a fund-raising expert."

"What do you mean, 'just'? What's wrong with our parties? Our pirate party is fun, people talk about it for months afterward, and our spring fling, Mardi Gras, and gumbo night events are always a blast! What's wrong with having a good time?" She looks ready to explode, and I've obviously touched on a nerve as she continues. "I'm sorry Charles died, Gloria. I'm sorry you're alone, but I'm not sorry that Louis and I have found something we enjoy doing together!"

"Stevie, there's nothing wrong with your parties, and I'm truly happy that you have sweet Louis to walk alongside you in everything you do, but you're missing the point."

"Which is?"

"There's more to life than having fun. Don't you want more?"

"Gloria, what *more* are you talking about? Does everything we do need to have some higher meaning, some grander purpose? Can't we just have fun for the sake of having fun?"

It's at this moment that I understand something about Stevie with a sense of clarity that I've never before had. It's not that she has turned her back on doing something more with her gifts and blessings; it's that she has made a conscious decision to exist inside the bubble in which she lives, a bubble that has kept her safe for decades.

"What are you afraid of, Stevie?" I ask quietly.

Her face begins to turn red as she stands, slams her hands on my desk and says, "I'm afraid I've wasted your precious time! And I'm afraid that I'm going to be late to meet Louis at Cosimo's for happy hour, so it's time for me to make my exit."

She pulls a paper from her shoulder bag and drops it unceremoniously in front of me.

"Here's my list of auction items. Call me if you have any questions." And she storms out of my office.

CHAPTER 19

— Stephanie —

Monday, February 7

Ihaven't spoken with Gloria since last week. The absurdity that I'm afraid of anything concerning my volunteer capabilities is absolutely ridiculous. She just can't grasp that I've set priorities that don't mirror hers. I have no doubt things will smooth over, they always do, but this time she owes me an apology. She was way off base.

The garden club meeting is at my house on Thursday, and Dolores is busy on the balcony doing her usual green thumb magic. My plants and flowers have never looked as lush and vibrant; I can't wait to show them off to the ladies.

I'm bent over a large planter helping Dolores adjust the new drip irrigation system she's created when the cell phone in my back pocket rings.

"Hey, Stevie, your butt is chiming," she jokes, "but don't let go of that hose until I get this section connected." She expertly completes the job in almost no time, but I miss the call and the voice message icon is already flashing on my phone by the time I get to it.

"It's from Lady McBitch; let's see what she wants." I hit the speakerphone button, and her message plays.

"I'm sorry, Stevie, but after we sent the video clip of the space, John's assistant doesn't think your cooktop and oven will be adequate for his demonstration. We've got to find another speaker ASAP; can you give me a call?"

"Is she serious?" I hit the replay button and listen to her message again.

"She expects me to believe John Besh's assistant doesn't think my stove is adequate? I don't believe that for one minute. I'll bet she screwed something up with the scheduling, as usual. Damn! Who does she expect me to come up with at the last minute?"

"Don't look at me," Dolores says as she searches the lush ivy planters for stray dead leaves to pluck out. "I came to the rescue last month; I've fulfilled my sainthood quota."

The truth is I'm having a love/hate relationship with Elizabeth. There's no doubt she is rather creative, and I'm having a great time developing the cookbook with her, but she drives me crazy with all the drama that seems to accompany all her "leadership responsibilities." I'm getting tired of picking up the pieces of the messes she makes. And I'm sick and tired of Gloria talking about her as though she's the next best thing to sliced bread.

"Hey, why don't you give whatshisname a call—the guy who sells those cool fountains," Dolores suggests.

"Perfect! You're brilliant, Dolores. You should have been appointed queen bee instead of Elizabeth."

"Well, if that isn't a half-baked compliment, I don't know what is," Dolores says, and she sticks out her bottom lip in mock petulance.

Our theme this month is "The Fountain of Love," and after a few calls I'm able to secure as our speaker Richard Burch from Gardens & Gifts, a local garden and aquatic shop—a perfect fit for our theme.

When I call Elizabeth to let her know I've got things handled, Dolores is using her cell phone to take photographs of the balcony, and she snaps a picture of me as I make a snarky face and a somewhat obscene hand gesture toward the phone as I hold it to my ear and confirm the new plans with our increasingly incompetent leader.

"I can't believe that woman." I hang up the phone and reach inside the door to set it on the kitchen counter so I can admire the work Dolores has accomplished and help her gather up her supplies.

"You've really outdone yourself this season, girlfriend. Our balcony is the talk of the town. Gloria's staff photographer was doing a story on the tarot card reader on the corner and took a fabulous photo they're going to use in one of their stories."

"Cool. Hey, speaking of the talk of the town, were you really at Lady

McBitch's pad on Governor Nicholls last week? Julie told Emily that she saw you going inside."

"Yeah, I was there. I'm handling the cookbook again this year, and we're going to do things a little different—imagine that. She invited me over to compare our notes. She's like a pack rat with the garden club files she has amassed; everything was a mess, including her."

I open a bottle of Rombauer Chardonnay, and we have a couple of glasses of wine as I give Dolores the scoop on the LeBlanc family drama. Dolores has an unprecedented vantage point of family drama in her business, and we get caught up on all the juicy gossip in the Quarter before Dolores has to leave.

"Okay, girl, I've got to hit the road," she says, slinging a bag of supplies over one shoulder and grabbing a large basket of other tools with her free hand. "I love how much business is coming my way, but I wish I could somehow haul this stuff over the balcony railings at places like this. I'm getting too old to cart this stuff through houses, up and down stairs, or even in elevators, which not everyone has, Miss Hoity Toity." She gives me a quick kiss on the cheek, and I follow her toward the door.

"I'll see you on Thursday; do you want me to come early and help?" she asks.

"Nah, I think we've got it covered, but thanks anyway."

"What's in the box?" She nods toward the adjacent alcove as we load her supplies into the elevator.

"I finally get to use the three-tier chocolate fountain Louis bought me for Valentine's Day four or five years ago! The ladies will be able to drizzle warm chocolate over fruit and candies."

"Sounds yummy," she says hesitantly, "but I've heard they're a bear to clean; you've got to rinse out all the pieces and make sure every hole is free of chocolate. Mrs. O'Rourke hires someone from her housekeeping service whose only job is to clean the chocolate fountain after her parties."

"Oh great. Take all the fun out of it," I say.

"Adios," Dolores laughs as she waves good-bye while the elevator doors close.

I look at my to-do list and begin checking things off. In addition to the chocolate fruit, I'm serving my favorite chicken gumbo; the recipe is from an old Texas cookbook. For that logistical reason alone, Louis says it can't be real gumbo.

"Gumbo is from Louisiana," he says.

Texan or not, it's good to me, and I know the ladies will love the recipe. It's a perfect choice for a luncheon in February, when the weather in the Quarter can still be a bit cool.

We will also have a decadent chocolate bread pudding that Gloria and I will prepare the morning of the meeting, an annual ritual that I've grown to love.

Gloria grew up in a house with a full-time staff, including a cook, but that wasn't my world. This time-honored tradition we have built together over the years is very special, and I hope it never fades.

The fact that Elizabeth is joining us this year doesn't make me happy, but Gloria didn't give me much choice when she called a few days before our argument to let me know she had invited her.

"I hope you don't mind, Stevie, but I've asked Elizabeth to join us for our annual chocolate bread pudding bake. She's trying to keep a stiff upper lip, but I know the Valentine's Day season is going to be hard for her this year."

I'm growing a bit weary of the "poor Elizabeth" scenarios that Gloria continues to bring up; it's not like she's the only divorced person in the world. But there was not much I could do about her invitation, since she'd already made it.

"Elizabeth said she would also help us set up if we need her," Gloria said.

I declined the help and assured Gloria we have everything handled.

We have a large open living and dining room area, about twenty-five by forty-five feet—plenty of room for our group. We do a lot of entertaining, so preparing and serving lunch for fifty women is not a difficult task.

Louis will turn the kitchen island into a serving station with what looks like professional bar equipment. He plans to move the sofa and slide the dining room table against the wall so it can be used as a sideboard. There will be more than ample space for all the white wooden folding chairs, as well as for the display easel and brochure stand that Richard said he will bring.

The party rental store will deliver the folding chairs the day before, and I'm relatively certain that between Louis, the party rental employee, and me, we will have the house completely set up long before Gloria and Elizabeth arrive.

I'm still a bit ticked off at the newest glitch and can't help but wonder about the validity of the reason.

Did John Besh's assistant really say my kitchen was inadequate?

Well, we'll just show him, won't we?

CHAPTER 20

— Gloria —

Thursday, February 10

It's the day of our garden club meeting, and I'm heading out the door for Stevie's place very early this morning. I receive a text message from Elizabeth telling me an unexpected personal issue has just come up that will prohibit her from coming early to help us bake or set up, and that she will probably be late for the meeting itself.

> I'm also going to send this message via e-mail in case u
> r not checking your phone this early. And I will also cc
> the members.

I doubt this news will bother Stevie one bit, but it will give her more fuel to add to the fire of her growing impatience with Elizabeth. I just hope that Elizabeth is okay. Perhaps the unexpected personal issue is job-related, as I gave her the names of some people to call in the real estate business.

I hail a cab to Stevie's place, and my lower back still hurts a bit as I slide into the seat, which makes me think of Anthony. Although we've talked on the phone several times since I returned from Paris, Anthony doesn't know I pulled my back the last time we were together. I didn't realize it myself until the next day, when I could barely move. The term "cougar" is really quite a misnomer, as I'm feeling more like a decrepit old house cat. Fortunately, the ache gets better every day, and I'm imagining

100 percent recovery by the next time Anthony and I are together. The thought of that makes me smile.

Stevie would have a fit if she knew.

When I arrive, Louis and Stevie already have everything set up, and as I anticipated, she isn't the least bit sorry that Elizabeth won't be joining us to bake.

"She sent me a text message as I was leaving the house and copied you and everyone else on e-mail to let you know," I say.

"I haven't checked my e-mail all morning," Stevie says, "and I don't intend to. This is our special time! Is that a new suit?" she asks.

"Yes, it is. Do you like it?" I spin around slowly like a runway model.

"I love it! Armani, right?"

"Yes, ma'am," I say as I notice her smile at the same time I notice the furrow in her brow.

"Please tell me after all these years that you're not going anorexic on me, like some high-fashion model. You're looking thinner." She frowns.

"That's hardly the case," I assure her.

And it surely won't be the case if I continue to see Anthony, I think, as intimacy isn't the only thing we seem to have an insatiable appetite for. I can't believe how much food we ate the last time we were together.

"I'm serious, Gloria. Louis and I are starting to blow up like balloons the older we get, but look at you—you're doing the opposite."

"Speak for yourself," Louis says. "I'm still at my fighting weight."

"And what fight is that, sweetheart?" Stevie asks. "Brutus versus Cassius?"

"Very funny," he says, and he kisses my forehead. "I think you look great, Gloria. Ready for the big day?"

"Ready, willing, and more than able! Give me direction, Madame Chef." I stand at attention and salute Stevie.

"Here, put this on," Stevie laughs and hands me an apron that looks to be straight out of the 1950s, complete with ruffles, pockets, and an attached wraparound belt. "I figured you'd come dressed for the meeting, but as you can see, I am not. I'll change just before we put the pans into the oven."

She's wearing linen Capris in a soft shade of periwinkle blue and what appears to be a starched white man's shirt with the sleeves rolled up to her elbows.

"Sounds good to me." I slip the apron over my head and wrap the belt around me twice. I notice Louis is now sitting at the counter, drinking coffee and staring at me.

"What's the matter?" I ask. "Do I have something on my face?" I peer into a small mirror hanging near the pantry.

"Are those chopsticks?" he asks, pointing to my innovative hair clips.

"Yes, sir. Very astute." I pull them out, and my thick braid falls almost to my waist. "Charles brought these back from Hong Kong when we were first married. See the ivory inlay?" I hold out one of the ten-inch-long picks for his closer inspection, but I notice his attention is elsewhere.

"Wow, your hair is long!" he exclaims.

"Wow is right," Stevie echoes. "It's been ages since I've seen it down like that. Our hair gets thinner and yours gets longer, no fair!"

"So, now we're fat *and* bald?" Louis smiles and takes a sip of his coffee.

"You two look fabulous, and this hair of mine is a genetic curse, but I can't bring myself to cut it. My mother and grandmother never cut their hair—at least it seemed that way. Long hair was a sign of strength for women in my family."

"Like a reverse Samson and Delilah?" Louis says.

"Exactly!" I laugh and quickly twist the braid into a figure eight on my head and secure it firmly with the two chopsticks. "Voilà!"

"That is totally cool," Louis says.

Stevie shakes her head and laughs. "Why don't you show us what you can do with a knife and fork at lunch today, okay? Because if you get any thinner, I won't be able to borrow any of your clothes."

"Ah, the truth is revealed." I laugh.

"I'm serious, what's your secret? 'Cause I could stand to lose a few pounds, even if Cassius Clay over there is content."

"It's easy. Just stop eating butter, fried foods, rich sauces—oh, and give up cream drinks." I smile.

"Is that all?" Louis laughs. "Piece of cake!"

"Oh, and give up cake too," I say, and we all laugh. "The truth is—I really think I've got an ulcer or a defunct gallbladder. Doc Creswell is doing some tests, but the only way I can seem to keep the hounds of heartburn at bay is to carefully watch what I eat. I had no idea indigestion could be so painful!"

"Tell me about it," Louis says. "Remember when we moved my office, Stevie?"

"Oh my God, that's right! I forgot all about that." She begins to take ingredients from the refrigerator. "His stress level was off the chart, and almost everything he ate gave him indigestion and heartburn."

"Yep. It finally went away when we got settled in, but I can remember there were times when I thought I was going to die. All in all, it made me get better in balancing work and play."

"I hear you, brother!" I high-five Louis. "Trust me—I'm getting much better at that."

"Yeah, I'll bet." Stevie winks at me, and I wonder if she secretly knows what I'm talking about.

"Anyway, I'm really doing great, so stop worrying about me." I point and wag my index finger at them. "So how about we get started!"

"Let the baking begin," Louis cheers, and he tosses a nearby towel on the floor to imitate the drop of a starting flag.

Today Stevie and I are making three huge pans of chocolate bread pudding for the meeting—two for the club and one that we'll split for us. Stevie always tells the story of the time her friend Susie from California came to visit and made the pudding for a dinner party but ate it before the dinner ever took place. It's funny how so many of our memories revolve around food and the friends we've shared it with.

"So do you buy Elizabeth's excuse for being late?" Stevie asks, breaking the first of several dozen eggs into an enormous bowl.

"Of course. Why wouldn't I?" I say while measuring the sugar.

"I don't know, it just seems a bit convenient," Stevie mumbles.

"Convenient? How is handling the fallout of a philandering husband convenient?"

"You're sure that's what's holding her up? She's not the first person to go through a divorce, Gloria. This last-minute 'personal issue' seems like an excuse; that's all I'm saying."

I really don't want to get into another conversation about Elizabeth, and I pick up the single sheet of paper from the counter. "So have you decided yet if we're going to include this recipe in the garden club cookbook this year? You know how coveted the info on this page is."

The food-stained paper I wave in the air resembles a tattered, old treasure map. The creases and folds are crusted with years of coffee stains, ink marks, and notes.

"I don't know yet." Stevie says with a mischievous grin. "Maybe it's time to share the secret, but I'm not sure."

There are more steps to this recipe than meet the eye, and we are halfway through the daunting mixing process when I get concerned about the time.

"Maybe we should have made this yesterday."

Stevie looks at me as though I've sprouted antennae or a third eye on my forehead.

"Nonsense, we've been doing this for years, and there's always plenty of time. Besides, you know darn well that I want the aroma of chocolate baking during the meeting to drive the women wild. You know I want to torture them; that's the point."

"You're so devilish." I smile and shake my head.

The kitchen is clean, the bread pudding is ready to go in the oven, and Stevie has changed her clothes when Richard from Gardens & Gifts arrives with his presentation board covered with lots of photographs, a box of brochures in his arms, and several larger boxes sitting on the floor of the small elevator.

He looks at Louis and says, "Can you give me a hand with these boxes?"

"Sure." Louis is very accommodating.

"Stevie, either one of those would make the perfect accent to any French Quarter balcony," Richard says after kissing both of us on our cheeks. "I just had to bring them to show your ladies."

Louis rolls his eyes; he knows a sales pitch when he hears one. But to his credit as a gentleman, he keeps quiet as he helps move one small table fountain and two larger, but fortunately lightweight, fountains from the elevator to the living room.

Everything is in place when the ladies start to arrive, and Louis graciously offers his services as our bartender.

"Trust me—it makes him feel like a rock star," Stevie laughs as the members greet him with hugs and kisses, which he clearly loves.

The rooms are filling with lots of chatter and the drinks are pouring when I hear Alma gasp as she stares at her cell phone.

"Oh my goodness!" she exclaims.

"What is it, Alma? What's wrong?" I ask.

"Did you see the e-mail Dolores sent to everyone this morning?"

"No, I haven't checked my e-mail all morning; Stevie and I have been baking. What does it say?"

Alma hands me her phone so I can read it myself.

The look on my face prompts Stevie and several other ladies to reach for their phones and begin to check for the mysterious e-mail. Most of the garden club gals have cell phones, but not all of them use their devices for checking e-mail, especially the more seasoned ladies.

Soon almost all the attendees are checking their e-mail on their phones. We look like we're at an iPhone convention.

It doesn't take long to see what has happened. In addition to texting me this morning to say she might be late, Elizabeth also sent me the same message in an e-mail, and as a courtesy to the members, she copied everyone on that e-mail.

After reading that e-mail, it appears Dolores had some thoughts of her own about Elizabeth's message—thoughts she obviously intended to share only with Stevie. But this morning when she sent Stevie her comment, along with a photo, she mistakenly clicked on the Reply All button. Instead of sending her message *privately* to Stevie, she sent it *publicly* to every garden club member.

> From: Dolores Delacroix < DDBB@yahoo.com>
> Date: Thurs, Feb 10, 2011 at 7:30 a.m.
> To: < REPLY ALL >
> Re: Lady McBitch is Gonna be McLate—let's McCelebrate!
>
> Hey, Stevie,
>
> Let's hope Lady McBitch doesn't make it at all. It would be great to have a McBitch free garden club meeting and

not a McTravesty! Your look below says it all, and I would hazard a guess that most of us feel the same when we have to talk with Lady Mc. I think you looked especially attractive yesterday when you had to stop everything and handle yet another of her McScheduling McStakes. ☺

See you soon at the meeting!

Ooodles and poodles of love, D

"Oh, Dolores … what have you done?" I whisper. Then I scroll down and see the photo of Stevie. She is holding her cell phone to her ear, making a face and a lewd gesture with her finger. It is clear the photo was taken on Stevie's balcony.

"Stevie?" I look up and shake my head.

"This isn't what it looks like," she stammers. "We were joking around; I had no idea she was going to send it to anyone."

Just then Dolores steps off the elevator along with a few more ladies, and the hush in the kitchen has a domino effect as it trickles into the living room and the whole house becomes silent. Eerie almost.

Dolores looks around and says, "What's going on?"

"Oh, Dolores," says Alma, "you sent an e-mail to Stevie this morning, with a photo, and you hit the Reply All button and sent it to all of us!"

"Oh crap," Dolores says.

"Good grief, Dolores, you called her McBitch in writing?" Stevie exclaims. "And why would you send a photo of me like that over the Internet? Oh my God, this is awful! How could you do this to me?"

"To you?" I say. "To you? How could you do this to Elizabeth?" I stare at Dolores.

"I didn't know I was sending it to everyone!" Dolores squeaks.

"That isn't the point, Dolores!" I take a deep breath and lower my voice. "A message like that shouldn't have gone to *anyone*. You're an adult; you should know better!"

Dolores and Stevie are sending visual daggers to each other.

Our speaker, Richard, is standing in front of his presentation board with his hand over his mouth. Alma has her hand on her forehead, and

Louis pours himself a drink, shakes his head, and says, "I'm out of here; y'all are on your own now," and exits the kitchen.

My voice is steady and calm as I continue. "I guess it's safe to say Elizabeth won't be joining us at all today, even if she does manage to get whatever personal issues she was dealing with sorted out. And frankly, I don't blame her."

With increased volume I say, "Ladies, please get your drinks and take a seat. Alma, we might as well get this meeting started. I will read the announcements on Elizabeth's behalf, and after the lunch, I'd like every member who is able to remain to stay for a special closed-door session that I am calling as the honorary director of the Fleur-de-Lis Garden Club Executive Board."

Alma rings the bell: *Ding-dink-ding, ding-dink-ding.* I read the announcements, and Stevie introduces the speaker.

"Ladies, we all know and love this man who really needs no introduction, but it's my pleasure to present our dear friend Richard Burch from Gardens & Gifts." She extends her hand toward the easel Richard is standing beside, and when the applause stops, she continues. "We have all been to Gardens & Gifts; it is very convenient to the French Quarter, just a few blocks away on Elysian Fields. You may also know that Richard supplied the lovely fountain that Gloria has by her pool." She smiles toward me, but I'm having none of it as she continues. "Along with the photographs and brochures he has brought for us today, Richard also has catalogs of fountains and yard art available for our courtyards and balconies. So without further ado, I present Richard Burch."

It seems the ladies have forgotten all about John Besh, but Stevie is right; the aroma of the chocolate bread pudding is filling the air, and between that and the earlier e-mail episode, after a while it's hard to concentrate on anything Richard is telling us.

The meeting presentation goes by quickly, and Richard does a wonderful job.

We are more than ready to eat when Stevie announces, "Lunch is served."

The gumbo is a huge success, although everyone is more subdued than usual, owing to the pall that has been cast by the egregious e-mail.

Nonetheless, everyone saves room for the chocolate bread pudding, and I'm glad we made an extra one just for us, so I can share some with Randy and Maria later.

When the meeting and lunch is over, Richard packs up his presentation board and remaining literature. Louis helps him carry everything to his car, minus the smaller fountain, which Stevie convinces him they need for their balcony.

The ladies look as though they've just finished a Thanksgiving feast and can't move, and they compliment Stevie on a fantastic meal, while at the same time appearing apprehensive about what I'm going to say.

I've been formulating the words in my head all through lunch.

"Ladies, if I may have your attention, I think we need to address the unfortunate e-mail situation that occurred earlier. As you know, the last few times we've had guest speakers, there has been drama at the meetings. In fact, this entire season has been filled with unnecessary drama, and if we aren't careful, soon the Quarter will be filled with the buzz about how dysfunctional our group is. I will not let that happen. We have got to get these matters under control. We should be ashamed of our behavior. Our mothers taught us better. This nonsense needs to stop and stop now."

"What are you going to do?" Stevie says, interrupting as she so often does.

I quickly turn toward her, glare into her eyes, and speak in a tone she is unaccustomed to, and one that surprises even me, especially in light of the fact that almost fifty women are listening intently to my every word.

"Oh no dear, not me. The question is, what are *you* and *Dolores* going to do?"

"Me?" A short high-pitched screech comes out of Stevie. "I didn't have anything to do with this!" She points toward Dolores whose downcast eyes show obvious shame and embarrassment for her actions.

I answer calmly. "Then it shouldn't be too difficult to explain to Elizabeth how it is that Dolores felt such unrestricted freedom to send that e-mail to you in the first place. I'm sure Elizabeth is under the impression that the two of you have nicknamed her, and I'm not cleaning up this mess. That's for you and Dolores to take care of. And make sure it's done very soon."

Dolores remains silent and Stevie is uncharacteristically quiet as all eyes are on them.

"Ladies, it's been a long day, and on behalf of our president, I'd like to thank Stevie and Louis for opening their lovely home to us and for preparing and serving a fabulous meal. Our March meeting is our annual field trip, I look forward to seeing everyone at the botanical gardens, and ..."—all eyes follow me as I place my purse on my arm, pick up the extra foil-covered pan of bread pudding from the counter, and turn around to face the ladies—"until then, our meeting is adjourned." I step inside the elevator, which had been propped open, press the button, and the doors slide closed.

* * * * *

I'm not home an hour before Stevie calls. I know she's surprised that I've answered the phone, as she brings up some random subject that has nothing whatsoever to do with today's meeting.

"Do you still want me to walk with you and Coco in the Barkus Parade?"

Mardi Gras has been celebrated in New Orleans since 1857 with many parades, even one for dogs. The Barkus Parade goes through the heart of the French Quarter and raises money for local pet charities. Some of the funniest costumes you'll ever see will be on parade on Sunday, February 27.

"Of course, Stevie; it's our tradition," I say quietly.

"I know it is; I just wasn't sure."

"Stevie, that really was uncalled for. I thought you and Elizabeth were beginning to make some headway in your relationship. Was all that a lie? A faux friendship?"

"No, it wasn't. But I didn't send the e-mail. I was baking with you in my kitchen when it was sent; you know that."

"Merely a formality."

"Huh? What's that supposed to mean?"

"Clearly, Dolores thinks it's okay to speak to you about Elizabeth in a derogatory fashion, which leads me to believe that you haven't done anything to change her perception. And what about that disgusting photograph? Were you or were you not talking with Elizabeth when it was taken?"

"I was," she admits.

"Your actions are speaking loud and clear, Stevie. You might not think of yourself as one, but you are nonetheless a leader, and some people take their cues from you, including Dolores."

"We talked after you left, and Dolores and I are meeting for breakfast in the morning at Stanley's to discuss the problem and find a solution."

"I'm glad to hear it. One of the first solutions needs to be an apology to Elizabeth. I can only imagine how hurt she must feel. She's not a plastic toy, Stevie; she has feelings, and this has been a very hard time for her."

"I know."

"Stevie, you and Dolores need to start listening to how you speak to others; you are sometimes very harsh with your words. You are highly respected by the members, but there is a fine line between fear and respect. Remember—it's not what you say but how you make them feel. And lately you've been making several people feel very uncomfortable."

I can tell Stevie is stunned. I've felt the need to put her in line before, but never like this. There's a tone of utter disappointment and an angry edge in my voice that's unusual for me, and I realize the harshness of my own words.

"I'm sorry if I've hurt you. If I were there right now, I would hug you in spite of how angry I am. You know how much I love you, Stevie; you are like a sister to me."

I can hear that Stevie is overwhelmed with emotion, as her voice cracks when she says, "I love you too, sis."

"We have years and years of history, Stevie—something rare and wonderful that I treasure beyond words. However, all the amazing women in the garden club and in our community are also like sisters. It takes intentional effort to nurture and love all the people that God places into our lives, for however long the season."

I can hear Stevie sniffling and imagine her wiping the tears from her cheeks with one of her crisp designer kitchen towels and then tossing it into the laundry basket.

"So let me tell you about Coco's new costume," I say, signaling a silent understanding and an end, at least for now, to this topic. "I found an amazing outfit that has a plastic jockey attached to a saddle that fits over Coco. It's totally adorable!"

"That's hilarious," Stevie laughs, "a Doberman as a racehorse."

"Not sure how long we'll last, though; she's getting old, and you know how long that parade route is."

The truth is—I needed to blow off steam when I left Stevie's place and I walked home, and now my back is really killing me. I guess I strained it more than I thought. I finally have that follow-up appointment tomorrow for the additional test Dr. Lucerne wants; maybe she can give me something for this backache.

After cancelling my prior appointment at the last minute, I'm a tad embarrassed to see Dr. Lucerne tomorrow, but I'm certainly not going to tell her the reason I cancelled was so I could spend more time in bed with a handsome Frenchman.

CHAPTER 21

— Stephanie —

Friday, February 11

"Well, Dolores, this is a fine mess you've gotten us into."

"Me? I think you labeled her McBitch first," Dolores spouts back.

"But I surely didn't put it in writing for the world to see."

"Yeah … well … that wasn't supposed to happen." Dolores moves the breakfast potatoes around on her plate without eating. "So, what do you think we should we do?" she asks.

"I think we need to meet face-to-face with Elizabeth and let her know that we nicknamed her that when she first took office and kicked out several longtime members. Then *you* need to apologize for putting it in writing."

"Fine, but *you* need to apologize too; you call her Lady McBitch all the time, Stevie."

"I do not."

"Yeah, you do. Maybe you don't really mean it, like maybe it's just a bad habit you don't even realize you have, like those young people who say 'like' every other word, like, you know what I mean?" she says.

Suddenly I can hear Gloria's voice in the back of my mind telling me that people follow my lead even if I don't realize it, and now I totally get what she's been saying. I guess I do need to pay more attention to what I say in front of people. I'm only joking most of the time, but not everybody gets the joke. "You're right, Dolores. I do use that as a nickname for Elizabeth, and it's wrong. I will apologize to her and do my best to stop using the Lady McB slur."

Dolores cocks her head to the side and looks at me strangely before she spears a potato and a piece of omelet and pops it into her mouth. "Okay, so what about the group? How should we handle them?"

"Don't talk with your mouth full," I say, shaking my head at her.

"Don't act like you're Miss Manners." She points her fork at me. "It ain't your place to correct me all the time."

"*Isn't* your place," I say jokingly, and she pretends she's going to catapult a chunk of eggs at me.

"Truce … truce," I say. "I get it. I'm sorry."

We silently eat our breakfast for a few minutes before I say, "I'd like to think the whole thing will just blow over, but I don't think that's going to happen. So maybe we should write a letter of apology."

"Instead of meeting with her in person?"

"No, I don't mean write a letter of apology to Elizabeth. I mean to the garden club."

"I'd rather get poked in the eye with a sharp stick," Dolores says.

"I'm sure we can arrange that." I smile and bat my eyelashes as she shrugs her shoulders in mock resignation. "The right thing isn't always the easiest thing, as Gloria would say. And you know it's the right thing to do."

"Yeah, whatever," Dolores says, and she sticks her tongue out at me like a bad-tempered child, which makes me laugh.

I lift my glass of orange juice. "Let's make a toast."

Dolores picks up her glass. "What exactly are we toasting?"

"Us. We've handled this little faux pas swimmingly well, I'd say. And I think Dame Gloria will be very proud of us." We gently clink our glasses.

Before we finish eating, I leave a message on Elizabeth's voice mail and assure her that the entire e-mail and photo debacle is a gross misunderstanding and practically beg her to let Dolores and me explain and apologize to her in person. I'm very surprised when she calls back within a few minutes and agrees to meet with Dolores and me at the Bombay Club for lunch on Monday.

"Okay, so that's settled. We'll eat our humble pie at the Bombay Club. I love their stuffed shrimp. As for the letter, you wrote the e-mail, so you can write the letter."

"Oh Stephanie, really?" Dolores whines.

"Yes, really. But I'll help you. Send me the first draft—*only me*—and let me read it first."

"Very funny," Dolores sneers. "I get it. I think I've learned my lesson on the Reply All option—trust me."

When I return home after breakfast, I give Gloria a call, but I get her voice mail instead. This is happening more and more these days. "All right, girlfriend, we are fixing it," I say. "Dolores and I are having lunch with Elizabeth on Monday to explain, and Dolores will be sending a letter of apology to the garden club ladies for her inappropriate e-mail. Don't worry—I'm going to proofread it first. Call me later. Love you, bye."

★　★　★　★　★

On Saturday, Dolores sends me a preview of the letter she is going to send:

> Dear garden club members,
>
> Regarding the rude and inconsiderate e-mail that was sent—I apologize.
>
> Sincerely,
> Dolores

I quickly give Dolores a call, and she picks up the phone on the second ring.

"I'm at the Fairfield house, Steph; I can't talk long. What's up?"

The Fairfield house is one of those majestic homes on Esplanade, and Dolores has turned their patio garden into a veritable work of art that consistently makes it a premiere stop on the most prestigious garden club tours in the Quarter.

"I think your letter needs a little more substance, Dolores. Let's talk about it after we meet with Elizabeth."

★　★　★　★　★

Monday, February 14

When I meet Dolores at the Bombay Club, Elizabeth hasn't arrived yet. We forgot all about Monday being Valentine's Day, and we're lucky to get a table, even for lunch.

As soon as I sit down, Dolores says, "I wrote the letter, so you can do all the talking."

"Two sentences is hardly a letter; it's got to say a little more than it does."

We've figured out what to add to the letter when we see Elizabeth come in. She is way overdressed for lunch, and I watch the effect she has on people as she walks across the room to join us. Some pretend not to stare, and others do just the opposite. She nods hello to a couple I don't recognize and waves at another group sitting at the bar.

She's acting like a freaking prom queen on a parade float.

I'm about to make a smart-mouthed comment about Elizabeth's clothing when Dolores quickly moves from across the table and sits beside me, and I silently thank God for derailing my words. I've got to learn to filter my negative comments. I'm secretly proud for keeping my mouth shut.

After stopping at several tables on the way, Elizabeth finally joins us and scoots into the booth across from us.

It's immediately apparent that she and Dolores are giving each other the silent treatment.

"Thank you for agreeing to see us today." I nudge Dolores under the table.

"Yeah, thanks," she adds.

Our server comes by. We place our orders, and I continue.

"We are not going to waste your time making lame excuses; we were both wrong—Dolores for sending the e-mail and photo, and me for ..."

The truth is I have rehearsed this apology numerous times this past weekend, but what I didn't rehearse was her response, and I find myself feeling like a heel as I recite the words and she fights back tears. When I'm done, she thanks me and then addresses Dolores.

"Dolores, I have nothing but the utmost respect for you and for what you do. Beautiful Bloomers is an amazing business, and you have so much wisdom and talent. I had fun visiting with you at the luncheon at Broussard's, but what did I say or do then, or afterward, that made you so mad at me?" she asks with alarming transparency.

"Uh … nothing," Dolores stammers.

"Then how could you turn on me like that? Why would you say, write, such nasty things?"

"Dolores, why don't you just tell her the truth?" I nudge her with my elbow. "Tell her you're still ticked off about her costing you that big account."

"What big account?" Elizabeth crinkles her brow. "What is she talking about, Dolores?"

Dolores only stares.

"The Collette corporate account," I say.

"Is that what this is all about, Dolores?" Elizabeth asks.

There is chilly silence as Dolores continues to stare at Elizabeth, who leans forward and says, "You know I didn't have anything to do with that. You know exactly who it was that cost you that account. You know as well as I do that it was Kevin."

"Kevin? As in your ex-husband, Kevin?" I look at Dolores.

"Is it too early to have a martini?" Dolores asks as she flags down our server. After she orders a drink, she leans back and sighs. "I guess I always knew it was him, but I didn't want to believe it."

"Yeah, we never do." Elizabeth sighs and wrings her hands together.

After an awkward moment of silence, Dolores says, "I really am sorry, Elizabeth. That was a mean e-mail. I was stupid and didn't engage my brain before my mouth—or in this case before my fingers."

I can feel Dolores's sincerity, which I hope Elizabeth feels as well, and I explain how the rude nickname originated and assure her it will not happen again.

"And if it's okay with you," Dolores adds, "I have a letter of apology I want to send to the group. I want them to know that I admit to being a horse's ass and that I was wrong."

"Thank you," Elizabeth whispers.

At the end of the day, Elizabeth forgives us, and the three of us manage to put everything behind us and actually brainstorm ideas about the cookbook and for the new garden club website that is in development.

"I remember the months leading up to the launch of the Beautiful Bloomers website," Dolores says. "It was crazy. But in today's world I couldn't be considered a professional without some kind of Internet presence, so I totally get the need for us to do this."

Truthfully, the ideas Elizabeth has are brilliant, and her words bear more than a little resemblance to Gloria's thinking as she describes the plans for the website.

It's several hours later when we leave, and after a short five-block walk, I'm home. As I step off the elevator, Louis hands me a glass of wine.

"Happy Valentine's Day, and happy happy hour!" he says sweetly.

A bouquet of long-stemmed red roses is sitting on the counter with a "Happy Valentine's Day" helium balloon attached that is bobbing in the air.

I set the glass on the counter, wrap my arms around his waist, and press in hard.

"Do you think I'm a bitch?" I ask him.

"Not right now," he says with a cute little grin.

I give him a slap on his butt, and he boldly teases, "Yeah, baby!"

CHAPTER 22

— Gloria —

Monday, February 14–Valentine's Day

It's been a crazy Monday morning, and it's only ten o'clock, so I can begin to imagine what the rest of the day is going to look like. I can't help but think about the luncheon meeting Stevie is going to have today with Dolores and Elizabeth; I pray it goes well. I jot myself a note to make sure to touch base with her tonight.

Fortunately, my backache has all but miraculously disappeared, and I'm feeling so well that I find myself feeling rather foolish that I agreed to all those tests this past Friday. I have excellent medical insurance coverage, but nonetheless I hate to see money wasted on unnecessary and costly tests.

The three-hour appointment on Friday for the scan and additional tests ordered by Dr. Lucerne took a lot longer than I thought. I had to reschedule a critical appointment with an important *NOLA 2 NOLA* vendor. Fortunately, we were able to reschedule it for today, but now my entire Monday is off-kilter and I'm working in my office with Charlotte to figure out how to play catch-up when our receptionist calls.

"There's a delivery for you, Mrs. Vincent; he's on his way back now."

When she says "on his way back," it actually means he's walking down a short hallway, and just as we get the heads-up, the deliveryman walks into my office. I assume it's a delivery*man*, but I don't know for certain, as a huge bouquet of what appears to be several dozen long-stemmed white, red, and yellow roses is entirely blocking the upper portion of the person carrying the arrangement.

"Delivery for Mrs. Vincent; where can I put this?"

Charlotte and I are momentarily speechless, but she moves to the credenza and quickly picks up a large antique urn and says, "You can place them here." She then signs for the delivery, and the young man exits almost as quickly as he arrived.

The arrangement is magnificent, and the vase is clearly not your ordinary, run-of-the-mill clear cut glass. I immediately recognize it as Waterford; the Lismore pattern is my favorite. Charlotte removes a small white envelope from a clear plastic holder and hands it to me.

"Well, well, well." She smiles. "A Valentine's Day admirer?"

"Valentine's Day?"

"Yes, February 14, today. Valentine's Day, as in 'Will you be mine?'"

We operate months in advance in the magazine business, and there's been so much going on that I forgot all about this Hallmark holiday. But I should have known sweet Anthony wouldn't forget.

"I can't be in town for Valentine's Day," he said the last time we spoke on the phone, "but you will be in my heart."

"You are such a sappy romantic!" I teased.

"But of course! I am French!"

Charlotte leaves me alone to read the card, which is simple but direct.

All my love.

A

I tuck the card inside my desk and send him a quick text message of deep appreciation.

"May I call you later this evening?" he texts back.

I respond with a simple "Of course!"

I'm standing by the brilliant bouquet of roses—three dozen, to be exact—and breathing in the intoxicating scent of their perfume when Charlotte interrupts me.

"There's an Eva Lucerne on the phone. She says it's urgent that she speak with you."

Eva Lucerne? It takes me a few seconds to register that she's referring to *Dr.* Lucerne.

"Thank you, Charlotte. Can you close the door, please?" I say as I reach for the phone.

"Hello, Dr. Lucerne."

"I'm sorry to call your office, Gloria, but for some reason we don't have your cell phone number, and we need to talk about your test results."

"My goodness, that was fast. Okay, so what's the verdict?"

There is a pause before she responds. "I'd rather talk with you in person, if that's possible? I can see you here at my office anytime today before five."

With my day already in flux, it is surprisingly easy to move things around on my schedule, and I make it over to her office and back to mine before my three o'clock appointment. Charlotte informs me the client is already in the conference room as soon as I return. The next several hours fly by.

"Stevie called," Charlotte tells me at the end of the day. "I told her you've had back-to-back meetings all day. She wants you to give her a call so she can tell you what happened at lunch today with Dolores and Elizabeth."

"Thanks, Charlotte."

"Can I get you anything before I head out?" she asks.

"No thanks, Charlotte. I think I'm doing okay. Are you and your valentine going out tonight?"

"Brian is cooking something at home; it's a surprise. You'd swear he thinks he's another Emeril the way he's been carrying on, but the past few weeks have been fun."

In all the craziness of my life, I forgot that her husband fancies himself as somewhat of a chef and has been test driving some of the recipes for the next cookbook. Stevie has him making sure all the ingredients and cooking times are listed appropriately.

"I'm so glad this has worked out; I know he's been invaluable to Stevie."

"It's been an adventure for sure," she laughs, "but I may have to take your lead and lay off the rich foods for a while; I've had my own bouts with indigestion, and it's no picnic."

"No, it's not," I agree.

"So how about you?" she grins. "Doing anything special tonight?" She glances at the roses. "They're gorgeous. I've never seen a bouquet that large."

"They're from a friend," I say.

"I'm sure they are. A very good friend by the looks of it." She laughs.

"Don't get any wild ideas, Charlotte. Now, you get out of here; I'll be fine. I'm going to finish up some of this paperwork and call it an early night. Give Brian my love."

"Will do," she says. "Everyone else has gone for the day; you've got the place to yourself. See ya tomorrow."

I manage to all but forget about my conversation with Dr. Lucerne as I plow through the stack of paperwork in my in-box like a shovel through snow.

In short order, I've written and edited my next letter from the editor, approved feature copy for the deadline issue, and responded to all my outstanding e-mail messages.

As much as I love the magazine, I really am ready to hand the reins over to someone else. It's become increasingly time-consuming, and frankly, I'd rather be doing more play and less work at this season in my life.

Charles knew how to work and play, but I realize I haven't been very good at balancing the two, especially since launching *NOLA 2 NOLA*.

I sit back in my chair, put my feet up on my desk, and stare at the huge bouquet of flowers. I'm surprised Anthony hasn't called, before I realize it's almost three o'clock in the morning in Paris and I'm sure he's already asleep. However, I know he keeps his cell phone ringer on silent when he retires for the night, so I reach for my phone and call. As expected, the call goes directly to voice mail.

"I'm getting ready to call it a day and wanted to personally thank you for the beautiful bouquet, but perhaps you're out painting the Champs-Elysees red on this Valentine's Day evening," I tease. "Whatever the case may be, thank you again for the lovely flowers, I wish you could see them. Good night, my sweet Anthony."

I hang up and take a deep breath, and just as I am remembering the last time we were together, I hear someone's footsteps.

"Miss Gloria?"

"Yes, Maria, I'm in my office," I shout, and I remove my feet from my desk.

"I'm sorry to bother you, Miss Gloria, but there is a gentleman here to see you. He says he does not have an appointment, but he hopes you will see him anyway."

"Oh Maria, you know I don't see vendors without an appointment. Especially not at this time; it's almost eight o'clock at night. Please tell him—"

"He said to give you this."

She hands me a small two-inch-by-three-inch sealed envelope. The linen paper feels rich in my hands as I open it and pull out a single-sided note card on heavy linen paper stock in the same creamy, rich, light cocoa shade. The handwriting makes my heart skip a beat.

> Do you really want to leave me standing _outside_ on your front stoop _alone_ when I could be lying _inside_ on your bed _with you?_
> The choice is yours to make.
> Please make it quickly.
> Anthony

I stand slowly. "Maria, please show Mr. Carlyle to the conference room and let him know I will be with him shortly."

"Yes, Miss Gloria." Maria is halfway down the hallway as I nonchalantly call out, "And Maria, that will be all for the day. I will show him out when our meeting is done."

"Yes, Miss Gloria." She heads down the staircase while I rush across my office to my private powder room, close the door, lean my hands on the porcelain sink, and look at myself in the mirror. I've got the most ridiculous grin on my face.

In record time, I touch up my makeup, brush my teeth, smooth back my hair, and dab some perfume behind my ears. I reach for my lipstick but have second thoughts, opting instead for a clear gloss. I look at the end result in the mirror, glad I'm wearing one of my favorite Givenchy dresses.

It's a short walk through my office, down the hall, and into the conference room, but my heart is racing as I take a deep breath, open the door, and find Anthony standing in the middle of my office facing the powder room, his hands comfortably resting in his pockets and his jacket open.

"You didn't actually expect me to wait in the conference room, did you?"

He closes the short distance between us in two strides.

"Happy Valentine's Day," he says, and he wraps me in his arms.

Our hello kiss feels as though we never said good-bye; we seamlessly pick up where we left off, our bodies melting into one.

"I had planned to take you on a more proper date," he says an hour later as we lie entwined, a lightweight blanket draped over us, our clothing in a pile on the floor. A moment passes. "Are you speechless because you can't believe we are together again"—he kisses the top of my head—"or because you can't believe that we just made love on the sofa in your office? A rather comfortable sofa, I might add." He squeezes me in his arms and smiles.

"Both," I say. "I feel like a schoolgirl! Oh my goodness, Anthony, what if Randy and Maria heard us?"

"We're both over twenty-one." He gently pinches my cheek as he unfolds himself from my arms and stands. I try hard not to stare, but it's virtually impossible.

"Have you eaten yet?" he says as he reaches for my lacy undergarments and hands them to me, then picks up my dress and drapes it over the sofa.

"No, I haven't; I've been running like a madwoman all day."

"Then how about we get some food to go with that exquisite dessert we've just sampled?" He grins and begins to put on his clothes.

"Anthony, it's Valentine's Day in the French Quarter; every restaurant will be packed at this time." I begin to get dressed, amazed at the ease I feel in appearing so bare. "Besides, it's hard for either of us to go unnoticed in this town. I'm not sure it's a good idea for us to be seen together so late, looking like …" I stammer, searching for the right words.

"Lovestruck teenagers?" he suggests. "Or like we're basking in the afterglow of passionate lovemaking?" He raises and lowers his eyebrows seductively.

"Anthony!" I playfully push him and slip my dress over my head.

"I have a better idea. What do you say we forage in my kitchen and see what we can rustle up? Maria always has the refrigerator stocked."

"And how do you explain me if I'm seen in your kitchen this late?" He steps into his trousers.

"I won't need to explain you. Maria and Randy have a kitchen in their quarters; they seldom wander into mine in the evening. However, even if they did, it is perfectly understandable that our business meeting went late and we're getting something to eat. Just be sure to put on all your clothes." I throw him his socks. "A barefoot Frenchmen in my kitchen might be harder to explain."

"Well, we won't be lying about conducting business," he says when we finally manage to get dressed and stop at the conference room, where he grabs his briefcase as we head downstairs. "We can make it official; I brought the latest draft of our agreement."

"Excellent! How is it looking?" I ask as we reach the staircase.

"Very good. I think we're almost there. I'll be anxious to see what your legal team has to say about the new verbiage you requested, I hope we got it right."

"I'm sure you did." I reach for his hand as we descend the stairs and make a beeline for the kitchen.

I prepare us something to eat while Anthony opens a bottle of wine, and we discuss some of the logistical aspects of the acquisition and decide to aim for an end-of-April closing.

"How long will you be in town?" I ask later, as we finish off the wine and Anthony is having a second bowl of Maria's famous chicken tortilla soup at the kitchen counter.

He leans in and kisses me. "I flew in just to see you."

"So you expect me to believe that you have a totally clear calendar to be at my beck and call?"

"I do. At least for tomorrow. I need to fly out early Wednesday morning; I've got to be in Marseille later that day for a dinner meeting."

I see him notice my physical discomfort as I unconsciously rub my stomach.

"Is something wrong?"

"Probably a bit too much spice in Maria's soup. I know better."

"Ulcer or gallbladder?" he asks nonchalantly.

"Pardon me?"

"For almost a year my father pretended he was fine. But he had chronic indigestion and heartburn. Stubborn old coot wouldn't see a doctor until it got so bad he thought he was dying. It was all very dramatic." Anthony chuckles. "Turns out he had an ulcer *and* a bad gallbladder—double whammy."

"Oh my, but he's fine now, right?"

"Father had his gallbladder removed last year; it was a breeze. In fact, he was back at the office the next day. He says now he wishes he'd had it done sooner; he's like a new man."

"Well, as a matter of fact, it seems I may need to bid adieu to my gallbladder as well. I need to have some more tests and look at my options. It's really more of a nuisance than a problem."

"I understand. That's what Papa kept saying."

Being compared to Anthony's father stings a little, but I do my best to shake it off.

"If I'm careful about what I eat, I feel great, so I'm hoping to avoid surgery altogether, especially since we are in Mardi Gras season. But I have one of those "ounce of prevention" type physicians. Very proactive on immediate and aggressive treatment options."

"Well, you just do whatever he tells you to do," Anthony says.

"She," I say.

"Whatever *she* tells you to do. Just make sure you keep me in the loop; is that understood?"

"Aye aye, captain!" I give him a mock salute.

"Unfortunately, I'm afraid I'm going to miss most of the Mardi Gras season," he sighs. "I'll be in China the last week of this month and in Dubai for most all of March."

"I'm sorry to hear that." I pout. "So where are you staying now?"

"I have a room at Melrose Mansion."

"Seriously?" I exclaim.

"Seriously," he laughs. "I checked it out the last time I was in town. It's quiet and close. So close, in fact, that I walked here."

Melrose Mansion is a beautiful historic grand estate that has been turned into a very luxurious bed-and-breakfast inn, and it's just down the block from my home.

"Well, as convenient as that may be"—I frown—"I'm afraid I will be unable to join you there. The owners are very good friends, and I'm rather certain all of their staff know me quite well."

"Well then,"—he kisses my forehead—"we'll just have to use plan B."

"And what might that be?" I return the kiss to his forehead.

"Leave your bedroom window open. I'll crawl through the shrubbery and steal into your room tomorrow night under a shroud of secrecy, like Batman."

"With or without your cape?" I laugh.

"Whatever makes you the happiest," he takes me in his arms. "Your every wish is my command."

We decide to nix the idea of him sneaking into my room, and the next day we take a road trip instead. Charlotte reschedules all my appointments for the day. Anthony and I leave early for Nottoway Plantation, just northwest of New Orleans. We spend the morning touring the massive fifty-three-thousand-square-foot structure, then have a quiet lunch on the balcony of our luxurious suite. The rest of the day is spent making love, drinking champagne, and watching movies in bed.

At one point I find myself in the bathroom doing my best to camouflage my nausea with running water and numerous toilet flushes. When I return, Anthony is sitting on the bed in his slacks and open shirt, holding a white bottle of Maalox.

"The hotel gift shop is a regular pharmacopeia." He grins and starts to shake the bottle. "I warned you not to eat that spicy gumbo. You forget, I told you my father abused his gallbladder for years; he ordered this stuff by the case."

He twists off the cap and pours some in a small crystal aperitif glass he must have snagged at the bar on his way back to the room and holds it out. "Here, drink this and let's watch another movie while your tender tummy rests."

We crawl back into bed as he uses one hand to scroll through our film choices and the other to gently stroke my stomach.

I begin to feel better in no time, and he loses interest in the remote control.

CHAPTER 23

— Stephanie —

Sunday, February 27

Gloria was absolutely right about Coco's new costume being a hit in today's Barkus Parade. Unfortunately, it was so windy that many folks petered out toward the end, including us. But not before we made a critical decision.

"Have you decided yet what you're wearing to the extravaganza?" I asked as we walked in the Barkus lineup.

The Endymion Extravaganza takes place each year on the Saturday before Fat Tuesday, a date that never changes. There are over 125 private balls during Mardi Gras, and the Endymion Extravaganza is one of the biggest. The past few years, it has been held in the Superdome.

With over 2,100 riders, including Louis, on some of the largest floats in the world, and with some of the most recognized rock groups entertaining, it's a huge party that starts at six thirty in the evening and ends around four o'clock in the morning.

Even though this is a night of craziness, it is nonetheless a formal event. The ladies are required to wear dresses that cover their ankles or they won't be allowed in, and the men must wear tuxedos.

Although Gloria owns more gowns than Neiman's, and I must say that I have a somewhat decent collection as well, the Endymion Ball is not about the dress; it's really all about the revelry and the "throws": the beads, plush toys, and trinkets being tossed at you. And it's about the drinks—oh my, the drinks.

This is the one Mardi Gras ball that is like no other. You enter looking like a lady and exit looking like you've been dragged behind a bus. It's impossible to last the night without having drinks spilled on you or someone stepping on your dress, which is why it's ludicrous to buy a new one every year. Besides, few people remember what you wore the previous year anyway. Those who are unfamiliar with the event find it strange that many of us wear the same dress year after year, until it can no longer be worn, at which point we replace it with another and the repetitive cycle continues.

"I think I'm wearing the gown I've worn for the last three years," I say.

"The brown one that's missing half its beads?" Gloria laughs.

"Yep. It's like a Timex; it takes a lickin' but keeps on tickin'! And besides, it still fits."

"Honestly, I can't believe it's that time again." Gloria shakes her head. "I've been so busy it isn't funny, but I'll probably wear the Halston again."

"Good choice." I love her timeless emerald green halter dress that will never go out of style. "And it still fits you, right?" I tease.

"Of course it still fits."

"I was kidding, Gloria. I'm sure it fits, and then some."

I know I'm beginning to sound like a broken record, but I'm starting to get a little concerned about Gloria's weight, and I feel compelled to say something. "All kidding aside, Gloria, we've got to start putting some meat back on your bones; you're going to blow away in a strong breeze!"

"You're so dramatic, Stevie."

"I'm serious, Gloria."

"I know you are, but I really do eat, Stevie; I'm not starving to death. I've just totally given up high-fat and high-carbohydrate foods, and my body is adjusting to a much healthier regimen. Personally, I think I'm looking rather good these days, especially for an old broad!" She hugs me. "I just think you're jealous, dearie."

Maybe she's right, maybe all of us would be leaner if we ate only protein and vegetables, but I don't think Louis or I will be jumping on that culinary bandwagon any time soon.

CHAPTER 24

— Gloria —

Tuesday, March 8–Fat Tuesday

The Endymion Ball took just about every ounce of energy I had, and for the first time in years I didn't jump for beads. In fact, I didn't even stay for the headline band. Truthfully, it's not that I was feeling poorly; I think I'm just getting too old to appreciate the madness of it all. I've been attending the Endymion Extravaganza for decades, and I can remember a time when I could actually hear the bands and enjoy the floats, a time when people could be rowdy without being rude. Things have changed over the years.

Today is Fat Tuesday, and I'm feeling anything but as I try on one outfit after another. Everything is falling off me. I can see Maria in my reflection, staring at me from the far corner of the room. "Any suggestions?" I ask weakly.

"Si. Wear the Queen of Hearts costume, the one with all the padding."

"Good idea," I laugh.

Mardi Gras madness begins today, and at midnight tonight it will end. Fat Tuesday in the Quarter is one big house party. We typically dress up in costumes and go from one friend's house to another all day, eating and drinking. We stop at noon to watch the costume contest in front of the "OZ" bar, then go back to eating and drinking and strolling until seven or so. That's when we usually meet up with friends at the Rib Room for a fantastic meal to help soak up all the alcohol. At midnight the bars close, the streets are cleared, the church doors open, and Ash Wednesday begins.

This is how we do things in New Orleans.

In fact, this kind of revelry is all I've ever known (minus the alcohol) since I was a child.

I grew up in an environment where annual community holidays, events, and celebrations were as much a part of the fabric of life as our annual family holidays were, like birthdays, anniversaries, graduations, and such. Every year, we hit the ground running in January, and I was blessed that my parents fostered a love of the pomp, circumstance, and pageantry of life in New Orleans. Fortunately, Charles was also cut from the same cloth.

These days, between the annual community events, garden club meetings, *NOLA 2 NOLA* deadlines and responsibilities, my executive board duties for Bronzinelle Steel and Grace House, and the everyday stuff of life, my calendar is always more than full. If I'm not careful, there could be something going on virtually every day of every week.

I've been pretty good at balancing things over the years, but life has been a bit more hectic this past year, and especially the past couple of months.

It's been three weeks since Dr. Lucerne gave me her diagnosis, and she's pressing me to make a decision regarding the treatment recommendations she has made. At her suggestion and Randy and Maria's, I got a second and third opinion, and all are the same, which strangely enough brings me a level of comfort, or at least assurance, that I have a general consensus regarding my diagnosis.

However, I'm thinking I'll wait until after the Mardi Gras season to make a decision; there's just too much going on right now.

As Fat Tuesday winds down, I thank God for getting me through the day, because it's been a mighty long one. My Queen of Hearts costume was a good choice, but by the time we end up at the Rib Room, I'm ready to shed the padded layers and get into something far more comfortable— namely, my bed.

"Earth to Gloria." Stevie waves her hand in front of my face. "Helloooooo, are you there?"

"I'm here; guess I zoned out for a minute." I shake my head. "I am so totally exhausted, I'm getting too old for all this. I don't know how you do it."

"She's the Energizer Bunny; that's how she does it!" Louis gives Stevie a wink.

"Oh boy, does he have his rabbits mixed up!" Stevie laughs. "No more champagne for you, fella!" She kisses Louis on the cheek as they playfully joke.

I can't help but laugh as well, because Stevie is dressed as a Playboy Bunny this year, nothing at all like the furry pink bunny that carries a drum and advertises batteries.

She has always been an attractive woman, but she looks absolutely fabulous in the strapless red satin outfit with the tight waist, matching satin ears, a black bow tie, and black fishnet pantyhose.

In all the years I've known Louis, he has never appeared jealous; they obviously adore and trust each other. However, Louis has been very protective of her all afternoon, as her natural exuberance and iconic costume have attracted more attention than usual from men.

"If I didn't know better, I'd say you were twenty years younger than me, Stevie. You look amazing." I flip back one of her bunny ears.

"And you look a little pale, are you feeling okay?" she leans in to ask me.

"I'm fine, just tired. But I've probably had too much junk food and too many cocktails today. I just couldn't say no; it's Mardi Gras!"

Truthfully, I've been fighting back low-level nausea for the past several days, and particularly the last few hours.

"I think I'm going to call it an early night," I say as the server finishes taking our orders and I pass on more food.

"But Gloria, it's not even nine!" Stevie sticks out her lower lip in a dramatic pout.

"I know, I know. But I'm not as young as you, Stevie."

"Oh, good try, girlfriend." She pokes me with her elbow. "Being a few months older than me hardly counts; you'll need a better excuse than that."

I'm too tired to even pretend to invent a better excuse, and after a bit more chatting, I say my good-byes to the group just as the waitstaff begins to bring everyone's food.

★ ★ ★ ★ ★

Ash Wednesday, March 9

It's a beautiful morning, and I've been at my desk for an hour when I decide to attend an Ash Wednesday service at the cathedral. After an easy online check, I discover there are three services today: 7:30 a.m., 12:00 p.m., and 5:00 p.m. I've already missed the early service, but I can make the one at noon.

The church is almost full when I arrive about fifteen minutes before the service begins, and I take a seat in the last pew.

I haven't been inside the St. Louis Cathedral in quite some time, yet seldom does a day pass when I don't drive by it on Decatur or walk past it on my way to Stevie's house.

Growing up, we rarely missed a Sunday service or holy holiday.

Ash Wednesday marks the beginning of Lent, the forty-six days before Easter, a season of reflection and repentance that prepares us for Christ's Resurrection on Easter Sunday.

When Archbishop Aymond explains the meaning of the ashes to those assembled, I feel as if I'm a young girl back in Catechism class at my Catholic elementary school.

Our foreheads are marked with ashes to humble our hearts and remind us that life passes away on earth. We remember this when we are told the lesson from Genesis 3:19: "Remember that thou art dust, and to dust thou shalt return."

His words are powerful, and from my vantage point at the back of the room, I can see a collective agreement as many people nod in silent understanding as he continues.

He talks about how Jesus was intentional in his actions, words, and deeds. He spoke up, and stood up, for others. He spoke of how God's love can bring a revival to our hearts and our community. He said a revival is about God giving to us and us giving back to God.

As the sermon message ends, I can't help but think of yesterday's celebration—how easy it was for all of us to dress up, and stand up, for Fat Tuesday. We will go over the top and out of our way for a Mardi Gras party or a festival, but we are reluctant and uncomfortable when it comes to sharing Jesus Christ in the same way.

I'm thinking what we need is a revival in our garden club and in our entire women's community. I'm envisioning what would transpire if everyone would realize the healing power of faith; if we would stop struggling against the external and internal confusion and simply have faith.

I begin to feel a powerful conviction that any type of revival begins with our own heart first—with our own willingness to face whatever comes our way with faith, hope, and love—and only then can we radiate those feelings to others. And I am energized with a refreshed spirit and a renewed sense of purpose as I get clear direction for my next steps.

It is time for me to face the facts and to put my faith in action.

The taxi drops me at home, and I immediately walk to the sitting room off my master suite to make an important and long overdue call. I leave a message and pray silently while I wait.

"How can I help you, Gloria?" Dr. Lucerne asks when she returns my call within ten minutes.

"I've seen two other specialists and watched all the videos on your website, and I'm ready to go with your first plan of action." I say. "When can we begin?"

"The sooner the better. How about first thing on Monday."

"That soon?" I take a deep breath.

"Yes. That soon."

We discuss the particulars, and once again she assures me that I'm in good hands with her team. Everything is confirmed and my questions are all answered when I hang up a few minutes later.

I'm sitting quietly with the phone still in my hand, relishing the sense of peace that has come over me like a gentle afternoon breeze, when I hear Randy and Maria come into the kitchen after walking Coco. They are talking quietly when I set my phone down on the nightstand and go out to tell them my plans for next week.

I'm exhausted when I call it an early night and retire to my room by seven o'clock. I see there are several voice and text messages on my cell phone from Anthony and Stevie, but they remain unanswered when I turn off my phone and crawl into bed by eight. The garden club is meeting tomorrow at the botanical gardens, and I think I'm going to need all the sleep I can get.

CHAPTER 25

— Stephanie —

Thursday, March 10

I shouldn't be surprised that my early morning call goes directly to Gloria's voice mail. I'm finally comfortable with the fact that a great many people now have her cell number and she periodically puts it on silent so she isn't repeatedly distracted.

"Let me know if you want to ride to the botanical gardens with me today, and I'll swing by and pick you up," I say.

While it's not the same as the almost instantaneous communication we used to share, she's pretty good about getting back to me quickly.

March is our annual field trip month, and the assistant director of horticulture at the botanical gardens will be instructing us on how to plant a butterfly garden. Spring is a beautiful time in New Orleans, and we have an abundance of butterflies and hummingbirds in this region.

It's only a ten-minute drive to City Park from the Quarter. There is ample parking, and the pathways through the formal gardens are always a site to see. Our attendance is typically high when a garden club meeting is held there. This is one of the reasons we decided to make the big announcement about the cookbook at this meeting. The ladies are going to be initially floored at the direction we are taking it, but I've grown confident this is going to be a great success, and I believe that in time they will as well.

Gloria responds to my call within a few minutes with a text message. "Sorry, I have a conference call in an hour. I'll have Randy drive me, and I'll catch a ride back with you. Is that okay?"

"Works for me," I text back. "Just don't be too late. You know this is the big announcement day, and also Miss V. is bringing her pecan tassies."

Because of the location, our food committee has arranged for boxed lunches to be delivered. Although I'm sure the boxes will be decorated with a spring motif, they will include only sandwiches and a bag of chips, and the tassies will probably be the tastiest part of the meal, so they're sure to go fast.

Like me, many of the ladies arrive early, and I can tell they are having a wonderful time as they take a quick tour of the grounds before the meeting begins. Afterward, we will be free to walk around the lily pond and rose beds, some of the most beautiful in the South. We can also walk around the palm garden and into the conservatory. One of my favorite places is the Lord and Taylor Rose Garden, where I'm hoping Gloria and I can take a walk together before we leave.

All said, the entire grounds are magnificent. A couple of our members are regular volunteers here, so we always get extra-special attention.

When the meeting is called to order, a record forty-eight of our fifty members are present; we're missing only Lois Freeman and Gloria, whom I'm saving a seat for next to me.

Elizabeth stands to address the group, and she looks very poised and confident today. She graciously welcomes everyone and makes the usual garden club business announcements as I anxiously look around to see if Gloria has arrived.

When it's apparent that she must move on, Elizabeth looks to me, and I shrug my shoulders and nod my head that I'm ready to go, even though Gloria is not here.

"Ladies, we have a very special announcement to make. Today is a historic day for our garden club." Everyone listens intently to Elizabeth as she continues. "For the first time in our history, we are going to print our annual cookbook in full color and include photographs of each recipe!" The ladies seem excited at the news. "But not only that; we're also going to include a photo of the garden club member who has submitted the recipe—or in some cases multiple photos, as many of these recipes have been handed down through generations—and we are going to include a short paragraph about the person submitting the recipe, and a little about the history of the recipe."

There is hearty applause from some members, while others appear more reserved in their responses; only a few look openly hostile.

Gloria, where are you?

"To share a quick update about what we can expect, I'm very pleased to introduce the person in charge of this year's cookbook, Stephanie Lewis."

All eyes are on me when I stand and join Elizabeth at the lectern, and in light of the circumstances of our last meeting at my home, many audibly gasp in either amazement or relief when we greet each other with a warm and genuine hug.

"Thank you, Elizabeth." I smile. "I agree, this *is* a monumental season for our garden club, and I know you all have many questions. I have worked with the executive board to develop an example of the overall concept for this year's cookbook. To make it easy for everyone, this example will also include written details for how to submit recipes and photos, and all of the pertinent timeline information you're going to need." I hold up a sample so they can see it. "Each of you will be receiving this sample mockup in the mail next week." When the chatter dissipates, I continue.

"As you know, we unveil the cookbook at the last meeting of the season and sell it throughout the summer and fall. Proceeds from the sale of this cookbook fund our annual Christmas party luncheon. But as many of you know, we've barely been able to cover those expenses the past few years. That's why we've decided to take an entirely new and fabulously fresh approach to the project."

I can see some of the ladies are actually sitting on the edges of their seats, leaning in to hear the news as I proclaim, "This year we will be making our cookbook available to a much broader audience through expanded marketing via our first ever garden club website, including an online storefront, and with printing and distribution being provided through a partnership with the publishers of *NOLA 2 NOLA* magazine!" I raise my fist triumphantly in the air, wishing Gloria were here to take a bow.

"So ladies, be on the lookout for the information coming to you in the mail, and start thinking about the recipes that you're going to contribute this year!"

The applause is strong, and I see Dolores give me a double thumbs-up as I return to my seat and Elizabeth introduces our speaker.

Because cell phone usage during meetings is prohibited, I pretend I'm digging around inside my handbag for something as I secretly send another text message to Gloria.

I try to stay focused on the butterfly lesson, but I zone in and out of the meeting, and my disappointment in Gloria's absence is growing.

One minute I hear our speaker mention that the pawpaw will attract the zebra swallowtail, and the next Elizabeth is thanking the botanical garden director and the lecturer and our group is giving them a healthy round of applause.

I'm deluged with questions about the cookbook as I stand in the lunch line, including the obvious one—"Where is Gloria?"

How I wish I knew that answer.

CHAPTER 26

— Gloria —

Thursday, March 10

Maria comes to the study, where I've been sitting with Coco at my feet, trying unsuccessfully to read a book. "Miss Stevie is here to see you," she says quietly.

I've been preparing for Stevie's visit; she is nothing if not amazingly predictable.

"Please show her back, Maria."

"No need, I'm already here," Stevie says as she strolls into the room on Maria's heels.

"Are you okay? I was worried sick about you!" She crosses the room and stands in front of me. "You said you had a conference call; what happened?"

"I did have a conference call. Will you please calm down, Stevie?"

"It was the big reveal day, the announcement of the season, of the decade. Everyone had a ton of questions, and Elizabeth and I thought you were going to be there. I had a seat saved for you."

"I know, I know, and I'm so sorry." I see Maria waiting for instruction and ask her to bring us some iced tea.

"I tried to join you, but I got sick again, Stevie, and I just couldn't go. I had quite a long call with my doctor." I hate to lie to Stevie, but I'm not ready to tell her the whole story.

"I've had several tests lately, and they seem to be inconclusive. Dr. Lucerne thinks my gallbladder is going to have to be removed, and I could have viral hepatitis. We hope to know more next week. I would have told you sooner, but I didn't want to worry you."

"Worry me?" Stevie spouts back while tapping her foot. "We are supposed to be best friends. Why haven't you been confiding in me?"

"I have to be careful, Stevie; I can't have bad health rumors flying around that could affect the sale of *NOLA 2 NOLA*."

"You don't trust me? Who on earth do you think I would tell? I don't understand. I don't understand you!"

Of course Stevie doesn't let me get a word in edgewise as she continues to rant and rave.

"It's almost as if I'm no longer a part of your life. You seem to be avoiding me like the plague. Something is not right. You're keeping something from me. I don't know what it is, but if you ever need a friend, a *real* friend, you know where to find me."

Stevie almost runs into Maria as she storms out of the room, but Maria has quick reflexes and is able to dodge her just before they collide.

"Sorry, Maria," Stevie says. "No need to show me out; I know where the door is."

There is an awkward moment of silence followed by the sound of the front door as it slams shut. I take a deep breath and gently rub Coco behind the ears as she stands by my chair and lays her head on my lap.

"Well, that didn't go very well, did it?" I say.

Maria shakes her head. "No, it did not."

I can see Maria fighting back tears as she picks up the iced tea glasses.

"Please don't disapprove, Maria. You know I can't tell her the truth right now."

"Oh, Miss Gloria, I do not disapprove of your choice. I understand 100 percent. I just wish I could do something more to help you; I feel so useless!"

I gently nudge Coco away, stand, and take the glasses from Maria's hands and place them back on the side table. I can feel her shaking as I put my arms around her.

"Maria, you and Randy are doing so much more than you can possibly realize."

We console each other in a tearful hug.

The fact is, I'm not sure I could put on this brave front with Stevie were it not for Randy and Maria, because these two precious souls are the only people outside of my medical team who know that first thing Monday morning I begin chemotherapy.

CHAPTER 27

— Stephanie —

Friday, March 11

"I'm so ticked off at Gloria right now I could spit nails!"

Louis and I are sitting on the balcony having happy hour drinks.

"I'm sure she didn't want to worry you." He rocks to the jazz band playing on the corner.

"Yeah, that's what she said."

"Well, let's just be thankful they've been able to isolate the problem; you know how challenging the diagnosis process can be. There were times when it took literally months to find the culprit in my patients. Remember that woman from Dallas who drove here every two weeks for over six months before we found out she was allergic to the chemical in the spray air freshener her car wash used?"

"Yes, I do remember that now."

"Even with all these medical technology advances, it's still sometimes a matter of good detective work and the timely process of elimination to get to the heart of the issue," Louis assures me.

"I guess you're right, but I'm still angry with her for not telling me sooner," I say, pouting.

"So is she actually having her gallbladder removed?"

"Not yet; they're trying some new medications and alternative therapy first."

"Well, even if does come down to surgery, it's a relatively easy process these days. With Gloria's constitution, she'll be up and around without registering a blip on her health radar."

"Yeah, but what about the other thing she might have? Isn't that bad?"

"Not the type she has; you said it's viral, right?"

"Yes …"

He goes on to explain this in more detail to me, and I learn that viral hepatitis is more common than folks think, especially in people who do a lot of international traveling, where water and food regulations are not as stringent as they are in the United States.

I'm feeling better at the end of our talk, but no less angry at Gloria for not trusting me enough to tell me the truth from the get-go.

CHAPTER 28
— Gloria —

Monday, March 14

The Ochsner Cancer Institute and Medical Centers in New Orleans are renowned for their clinical research and cancer care for patients. The Gayle and Tom Benson Cancer Center is located in a newly renovated building, with state-of-the-art equipment. Randy drives me and Maria to the center for my first chemo treatment. He knows I'd like to keep my treatment as private as possible, so dropping me off at the front entrance isn't an option. It didn't surprise me when he said that he and Maria had already "scoped out the terrain" this past weekend.

"It's a fifteen-minute drive in good traffic, Miss Gloria, a piece of cake!" Randy says. "And we found the perfect door where you can enter."

"I will take you upstairs." Maria smiles nervously from the front passenger seat.

"Maria, you really don't need to go in with me; I'm not sure how long this will take."

"You take as long as you need; I have a book, and I will sit in the waiting room just in case you need me for something," she says assertively. "Randy will go back to the house, and I will call him when you are ready to leave."

"Maria, I'm sure I can handle this on my own; you really don't need to babysit me."

She dismisses me with a wave and says, "That is a good thing, Miss Gloria, because you know Maria has no patience for babies anymore."

Now I know she's nervous, because she's talking about herself in third person.

Truth be told, as Randy pulls up to the so-called perfect door, I'm a bit nervous as well, and I suppose it will be nice to know that Maria is in the waiting room.

There's no doubt I've got the desire to beat this; I'm keeping my emotions in check, and as for knowledge, I've been acquiring information in spades.

Randy and Maria watched the *Chemo Class for Loved Ones* video online the night I told them about my treatment plans, an experience that prompted Maria to suggest—more like insist—she go with me today.

We walk together and take the elevator to the fifth floor, where she excuses herself. She quietly takes a seat in the tranquil waiting room as I check in with the nurse at the front desk.

I'm escorted to a small but comfortable patient information area, where I'm given an identification wristband that is double-checked for accuracy, and where the first of many health care professionals will explain the entire process and what I can expect at this first appointment.

Name tags and titles are visible on the employees and volunteers, and Sarah is an LPN oncology specialist. Although I assure her that I attended the informative chemo class, she is still required to go over this information with me, and her voice is sweetly melodic as she reviews the process. She further explains, as Dr. Lucerne has done as well, that I'll be receiving my chemotherapy in cycles. I'll alternate weekly chemotherapy as an outpatient at the center, followed by treatment in my home, followed by a few days of rest. These two weeks make up one cycle, which will take a total of fourteen weeks.

"I'll be back to normal by June, and we can put all this behind us," I told Randy and Maria when we discussed my treatment. "I'll be done with all this rigmarole before the last garden club meeting of the season, and before Stevie's and my big birthday bash in July."

I'll be receiving my chemotherapy drugs through a port that will be implanted in my chest and remain for the duration of my treatment.

The implantation of a port system involves a brief surgical procedure. Once the incisions are healed, they tell me I will notice only a small bump under my skin. I will be undergoing this procedure and receiving my first round of chemo today. Sarah checks my weight and blood pressure and records my temperature.

"This scale can't possibly be correct." I stare at the red digital numbers that flash "125" on the panel.

The nurse smiles. "It might be a fraction off, but they test and recalibrate all our scales on a regular basis. You will discover that your weight is an important thing for us to monitor, and you can expect to lose some during your treatment, but our nutritionist will be talking with you every step of the way."

My facial expression must be more concerning than I think, as she asks me, "What is your usual weight?"

"About one forty-five." I'm stunned that I've lost twenty pounds in the past six months. No wonder Stevie has been harping on me so much.

I'm taken by wheelchair to the outpatient surgery center and undergo the painless half-hour process to implant the port. After the surgical procedure, I am taken to a private treatment cubicle with state-of-the-art infusion equipment. The "room" contains a comfortable high-back recliner, a second less-fancy guest chair, a flat-screen television on one wall and a jaw-dropping view from floor-to-ceiling windows overlooking the Mississippi River.

"Oh my goodness, I'm never going to want to leave," I say as I settle into the recliner, where I will remain for the next several hours. I'm trying hard not to stare at the port that has been inserted under my skin just under my collarbone.

"Be sure to watch for signs of infection around your port," the nurse cautions me as she proceeds to administer the cancer-killing chemicals and the slow and silent drip begins. "This can take anywhere from two to four hours for the bags to drain."

"Looks like I'd better plan on being here the better part of every other Monday," I say to Nurse Sarah as the drip continues.

"You are welcome to bring one person with you to your treatment sessions," Sarah says. "All we ask is that the individual is over the age of eighteen and in good health. If your guest has a cold or the flu, it would be best if they didn't accompany you."

"I understand." However, I think that even if Maria comes with me again the next time, I'm not sure either of us would be comfortable sitting together in such close quarters for so many hours. We enjoy each other's company, and we've been together for decades, but this situation is something else entirely. Personally, I do see the potential of accomplishing quite a bit of work during this time, including editing, writing letters, and a host of projects on my ever-growing to-do list that I never seem to find the time to do.

If my treatment goes well, which I'm certain it will, I may decide to eventually bring Stevie, Charlotte, or Elizabeth to future appointments so we can get some things done.

An aide enters my cubicle with a tray of lunch. To my surprise, I nearly clean my plate. "Hope I don't get sick," I say to Sarah as she moves the tray table back from my chair.

She assures me the antinausea medicine will help with that issue, and before she leaves the room, I feel myself start to doze off.

When I awake, Sarah is standing next to me unhooking the tubes from the port, and with a soft voice she says, "Mrs. Vincent, you did very well today. I will let Maria know that you're almost ready to go. Remember—if you have any concerns or questions, please feel free to call. There are also pamphlets and a list of available resources is in your care bag." She points to a canvas tote bag that is hanging from an industrial-size hook on the wall next to the TV. "The volunteers from the center put these bags together for every patient. They include a DVD with information and resources available, hand lotion, mints, and all kinds of useful little things." She peers into the bag, "They've even started adding little booklets of meditations and a recipe book."

I look again at the care bag.

"So, in essence, the center is gifting every 'guest' with a swag bag, right?" I ask.

"Yes, you could say that! All it's missing is a pair of Swarovski earrings or a bottle of Chanel Number Five," she says.

Just then, Maria enters my cubicle with a slight smile and says, "Your chariot awaits."

Maria and I explore the contents of the bag on the drive home, and we're rather amazed at the effort that has gone into assembling it, as well as the thoroughness of the materials provided.

"Oh look, Miss Gloria, a recipe book! May I take this? I want to prepare meals that will help you get better."

"Of course," I say, "maybe we'll find one we can submit for the garden club cookbook."

★　★　★　★　★

Tuesday, March 15

I'm not sure if it's the chemotherapy drugs, the surgical procedure, or perhaps a combination of both, but the next day I feel like I've been hit by a Mack truck.

Fortunately, I'm not feeling nauseated, but I have zero energy, and just lifting my head from the pillow takes monumental effort. I hadn't anticipated needing someone to lean on just to get out of bed or go to the restroom. I'm not sure what I would do without Maria's help.

"Perhaps this will be helpful until you get your sea legs back?" Randy holds out a cane.

Sure enough, the rubber tip looks firm and secure, and I must say, having it to lean on gives me freedom and comfort as I shuffle through the house. "But I will not be seen in public with a cane!" I insist, and Randy and Maria shake their heads in understanding.

★　★　★　★　★

I'm feeling a little stronger when the oncology nurse practitioner arrives at Vincent Manor the next Monday for my in-home treatment. Caron is here for about two hours delivering chemotherapy through the port.

This is how my life will proceed until June—a small price to pay so that my world can return to normal.

★　★　★　★　★

Thursday, March 24

My second treatment at the Center will be this Monday, and while I'm optimistic, I have also realized that if this first treatment cycle is any indication of things to come, I have a long road to recovery in front of me. It's not fair to make Maria handle this on her own, and continue all her other responsibilities at Vincent Manor, even with Randy's help.

It's time I practice what I preach and let Stevie know what's really going on. I'm convinced that I must tell her before my next trip to the center—not just for myself but for Maria as well.

Think I'll call Stevie and invite myself to her place for lunch. It will be good to be within close proximity of Touchdown Jesus when I give her the news.

CHAPTER 29

— Stephanie —

Thursday, March 24

Gloria delights me with her early morning phone call.
"I've been working way too many hours, and I realized I hadn't seen you since the last garden club meeting," she said.

"Technically, that isn't true," I remind her. "You haven't seen me since you *missed* the last garden club meeting and I showed up on your doorstep to call you on the carpet."

"Details, details," Gloria laughs.

"Don't feel bad," I offer, "between the Williams House and putting together the new and improved version of the garden club cookbook, I feel like I have two full-time jobs; it's been crazy! Thankfully, we have text messaging; otherwise, we'd be completely out of touch. How's the stomach? Any word back on whether or not we need to throw a going-away party for your gallbladder?"

"You crack me up, Stevie. We've got a lot to catch up on, and I want to hear all about the cookbook; that's why I have made an executive decision today."

"Oh? And what might that be?"

"I realized that I own the business, and if I can't give myself the day off, who can? So I'm taking the day off! Any chance we can do lunch at your place? I can stop and pick up something."

"Nonsense! There's plenty of food here, Louis is out of town for a couple of days, I'm not on the calendar for the Williams House today, and the timing is perfect! How soon can you get your skinny butt over here?"

I'm so excited that Gloria is coming over for an unexpected and long overdue girlfriend gabfest luncheon. I've made the almond chicken salad that she loves, and I've set two places at the kitchen counter and have a couple of bottles of wine chilling. It's a lovely day, so we might take our lunch out on the balcony, and I've got two lovely teakwood serving trays standing by just in case.

I'm sitting on the balcony waiting for her to arrive, listening to a new jazz band on the corner of St. Peter that started playing early this morning. I'm watching the nuns escort a well-behaved line of schoolchildren from Cathedral Academy across Royal Street and into the cathedral for their weekly Mass. The cathedral bells chime just as I see Gloria's car pull up, and I smile as I watch many of the passersby crane their necks to see who is getting out.

Although we have our fair share of luxury automobiles traversing the streets of the Quarter, including Ferraris, Jaguars, and Porsches, it's not every day you see a Rolls Royce Ghost, and the exquisite lines and beautiful silver-gray color are striking against the early afternoon sunlight.

I watch Randy run around the car and open the back door as he offers Gloria a hand while shouting up to me, "Hola, Miss Stevie!"

"Hello, Randy!" I wave from the balcony as Gloria steps out of the car, a brilliant shock of stupendous color in a cobalt-blue caftan with an emerald-green sash belt. With her cherry-red turban and large Dior sunglasses, she looks mysterious and glamorous. I have no doubt the people watching her are debating a number of famous names as she walks to the door and I buzz her in.

"Why didn't you tell me there was a dress code?" I say as soon as the elevator doors open in my kitchen.

"Don't be silly!" she says, and she reaches for a hug, after which I hold her at arm's length and look her over like I'm appraising a piece of fine jewelry.

"Goodness gracious, girlfriend, what's the occasion? You look straight out of Vogue! You could have given me a heads-up and I would have dressed in more formal attire." I laugh and point her toward a seat at the counter, where she makes herself comfortable.

"Your capris are perfectly fine, and the occasion is lunch with my best friend! I just felt like getting spiffed up a bit today. You know I've been under the weather, and when I looked in the mirror this morning, I scared even myself; I didn't have the heart to scare you too."

"So your stomach is still giving you problems? What did the tests show? Is it your gallbladder, or just control freak perfection syndrome?" I pull a bottle from the wine refrigerator that Louis insisted we have installed and show it to her. "Do you want a glass with lunch? Louis claims it's one of their best." She glances at the label, and I can see she's impressed. "Or would you prefer tea, water, maybe some juice?"

"I would love a glass of wine, especially that wine; make sure you tell Louis I'm very impressed at his selection, but I'm afraid I'm going to pass today. How about some of your famous tea?"

"Tea it is. I'll just put this away for the time being." I slide the wine back into the horizontal slot in the refrigerator. "Maybe you'll change your mind after we eat."

I open the refrigerator and pull out a pitcher of fresh-brewed tea.

"So give me the scoop on the cookbook to end all cookbooks," she says as I pour us tea and serve the salads. "How is it coming along? Give me all the details!"

I launch into an update that lasts throughout our lunch—or at least throughout mine, as I notice she's barely touched anything on her plate.

"Okay, girl, spit it out." I take the last bite of my salad and point my fork. "Clearly something is on your mind."

"Stevie, I haven't been entirely truthful with you."

"Okay …" I put down my fork. "What's up? Are you pregnant?" I laugh and take a sip of tea. "No, that can't be it, because then you'd be gaining weight and eating everything in sight, instead of the opposite. So what's the real scoop?"

When she finishes telling me, I'm not sure how to respond and pour myself a big glass of wine instead.

The jazz band is still playing as Gloria leaves a short time later. The music now sounds far away, muffled, as though I'm slipping underwater and into a bad dream.

I fetch my laptop from the sofa and plug it in at the kitchen counter, watching it boot up the way one watches the sun rise on the horizon. After hours of Internet research, I have learned more about random cancerous cells and chemotherapy than I've ever wanted to know. I pour one more glass of Rombauer Chardonnay.

The sun begins to go down, and I sit in the living room for a long while with the lights off. I don't know whether to allow myself to be sad, mad, or a combination of the two, which is what I know Gloria would advise—"*Balance in all things, Stevie,*" I can hear her say.

When did your voice become so enmeshed in my own?

I'm not sure a day goes by when I don't hear Gloria's wisdom or advice in the back of my mind. She has influenced so much of my life. God is not going to take this sister, friend, from me.

So what if there are cancer cells creeping around inside her body? The doctors have found them in time before they make a home anywhere specifically, and they are treating them in the most aggressive way possible.

I'm so glad when Louis calls later that night.

"Gloria came over for lunch today." I rub my temples.

"That's good; did you girls have a nice time?"

"Not really ..."

I'm torn about sharing this news with him on the phone, but he is a doctor, and he may have some insight.

"She's got some type of cancer, Louis," I blurt out. "She says they don't really know exactly where it's at, only that one of her tests came back showing positive for the 'presence of cancerous cells.' I didn't know that was possible ... to have cancer but not to know where it's at?"

Louis is quiet on the other end of the line, and I suddenly think I'm a complete idiot for telling him this over the phone. It could have waited until he returned.

"Louis? Honey? Are you there?"

"I'm here, Stevie. I should have guessed something was wrong; I'm a doctor!"

"You're an allergist, Louis, and as far as I can tell, she's not allergic to anything except being truthful with me. But thank God she's finally come clean about it. They're giving her chemotherapy treatments, and she says she'll be good as new in a few weeks. The first treatment really sapped her energy, plus she's worried the drugs may cause her hair to fall out, so she wants me to go with her to the next treatment and then to the salon afterward to get it cut. She's cutting off her hair, Louis! Is that a good or bad sign?"

"Calm down, honey," Louis says. "I'm sure a new hairstyle after decades is a very good sign, but just tell me everything she said," he says quietly. "Let's see if we can make some sense of this."

We're on the phone for almost an hour before we both come to the conclusion that the only real danger right now is in our overreacting, which is precisely why Gloria didn't tell me in the first place.

"She's getting the best treatment money can buy in one of the best cancer centers in the nation; I'm sure she's going to be fine. The next few weeks might be kind of rocky for her; everyone responds differently to chemo treatments. I say the best thing you can do is treat her like a normal person; that's what she wants. She's not a freak, she's not dying, and she's not counting the grains of sand in her hourglass of life, so just do your best to be there for her."

Louis is the most level-headed, sensible person I know. His words calm me.

"When are you coming home?" I grab a tissue and wipe my eyes.

"I'll be back Saturday morning."

I'm glad he will be home when I go with Gloria on Monday, because even though I know this journey will ultimately have a happy ending, it would be difficult to walk it without Louis by my side.

The landscape lights come on in St. Anthony's Garden. The shadow of Touchdown Jesus casts a comforting reflection on the Cathedral wall, yet I can't help but wonder how Gloria must be feeling.

CHAPTER 30

— Gloria —

Monday, March 28

Maria seemed relieved not to be going with me for my second treatment, but not because she was uncomfortable in the role.

"It is good for you and Miss Stevie to have time to visit, and I need to catch up with my work here at Vincent Manor."

I'm glad to see that Stevie is back to her old self when we swing by and pick her up on Monday morning. She's standing on the curb in front of her house, and when she sees us turn the corner, she holds her thumb out as though she's hitching a ride and sticks her leg out in a provocative way to get our attention. As always, there are a lot of people on the street, and I wonder what they think when Randy abruptly stops the car in front of her and I open the back door so she can jump in.

"Well, that was too much fun!" she says, peering out through the deeply tinted windows.

"You are too much," I laugh.

"Not according to Louis."

"Ah, so he's back home?" I ask.

"Yep, he got back on Saturday." She reaches into the scoop of her blouse and hands me a business card that is tucked inside her bra. "Here, he gave me the name of one of his colleagues who has medical privileges at the center. He said to call this lady in case you get any adverse reactions on your skin from any of the medications, and especially if you have problems with any of the injection sites over the next few weeks. Apparently you're going to make the junkies on the bad side of Bourbon Street look like choir boys."

I take the card and recognize the name as one of the premiere dermatologists in NOLA.

"Tell Louis thanks. I'll make sure to call her if I have problems." I slide the card into the side pocket on my door. "But things have changed a lot these days; they don't need to poke and prod to find veins for anything. In fact, I've got a direct line, a kind of one-stop-shopping portal."

I flip down the edge of my blouse to show Stevie the area where the port has been implanted, and her eyes go wide.

"Seriously?" She's speechless as I explain the device to her, but she soon has a dozen questions, and I try to answer them as best as I can.

We're almost to the center when I see Stevie looking strangely at the small silk-covered pillow and lap blanket on the seat, and a cleaning pail sitting on the floor.

"Maria thinks I need to have all this, just in case I get sick after the chemo, but I was fine the last time, and I'm sure I'll be fine now. But you know what they say about an ounce of prevention."

"Is worth what? A gallon of vomit?" Stevie jokes.

"Yuck, that's gross, Stevie."

"We don't think so," she says, nodding at Randy, who is trying not to laugh along with her.

"Don't be complicit, Randy." I point my finger at him and smile.

When we get inside, Stevie joins me in my cubicle, and to her credit she is respectfully quiet, although I can tell the questions she has are percolating. When everything is hooked up and the slow and steady drip begins, the nurse excuses herself as Stevie explodes.

"Do you get sick during the treatment?"

"No, they're also pumping in some antinausea meds. I might get sleepy, but it's usually the day after that I'll have issues," I say, trying to sound confident.

"Did she say you weighed one hundred twenty-three pounds?"

"Yes. I was one twenty-five on my first treatment. Goodness, at that rate of two pounds per treatment, I'll be a trim one ten by our party. Will you remind me to call Carolina and let her know to keep the possibility of my new figure in mind as she designs my gown for our birthday gala?"

Stevie's jaw drops. "Are you serious? One hundred and ten pounds?"

"No, Stevie, I'm not serious!" I laugh. "Lighten up, sweetie. I was just kidding. I will not get that thin. Trust me—the shakes Maria has been preparing have ninety grams of protein in them, for crying out loud! And I'm eating every day, just not a lot; but my medical team assures me it's okay, so stop worrying about my weight, will you? Let's talk about the cookbook instead. Did you bring the first mockup with you?"

"Yes, I did." Stevie nods as the corners of her mouth slowly lift and her eyes crinkle.

"Well, don't make me wait; let me see it!"

"I really had no idea Elizabeth was such a pro at graphics software." She reaches into her handbag and pulls out a color copy of what they are proposing as the new layout for the garden club cookbook.

I am completely blown away as Stevie shows me the pages and we discuss their ideas, our options, and the progress they have made on the entire project, including the start of the new garden club website.

The time flies by, and after a little over four hours, we're on our way.

"Well, that was painless," she says as we exit the medical center through our secret back door and she helps me get into the car.

"You haven't been waiting long, have you?" I ask Randy.

"Not at all. Miss Stephanie called less than twenty minutes ago. I just pulled up. Do you still wish to go to the beauty parlor ... er ... the salon?"

Stevie and I look at each other and smile.

"That's a good question, Randy," Stevie says as she turns to me. "What do you say, girlfriend?" She looks at her watch. "We're right on time; are you still up for it?"

"I am."

"Are you feeling okay?"

"I am! Let's go!"

Stevie gives the Stardust Salon a call to tell them we're on our way. We're chatting as if everything is normal when Stevie notices the pail again and asks, "Are you going to need that?"

"I hope not."

"Are you sure? You don't look so good."

"No, I'm not sure ... wait ... I think I need it ..." I clutch my chest and put my hand over my mouth as Stevie grabs the pail and holds it in front of me.

"It's okay, honey, you're going to be okay." Her calming words and the look of panic on her face are more than I can bear, and I break out into laughter.

"Very funnnneeeee, Gloria." She throws the pail on the floor and sits back in a huff. "See if I'm going to help you when you really need it, smarty pants!"

I poke her in the side while continuing to laugh. "Stop it, Gloria! I'm serious. That wasn't funny."

"Yes, it was, and you know it. I'm fine; chill out, would you?" I slide closer to Stevie and put my arm around her shoulder. "I've been giving this a lot of thought, and I think maybe the lesson God wants me to learn is that He wants me to slow down and enjoy time with my friends and family. Tell me, when was the last time we spent four hours of uninterrupted time sitting alone and visiting?"

"Well, it was hardly uninterrupted, and we weren't exactly alone."

"Details, details." I pat her on the knee.

Technically, she's correct; we were never really alone, as the nurses and technicians were frequently checking on the infusion, the pump, and the IV line.

In a few minutes we're back to chatting and acting like schoolgirls.

"I always forget how much I love this part of the lifestyles of the rich and famous," Stevie says a few minutes later as Randy pulls up to the salon and drops us at the front door. "It sure beats driving or taking a taxi."

As we walk arm in arm to the front door, she asks, "Are you sure you're ready for this?"

"Yes, I'm ready."

"Me too," she says mysteriously, and she suddenly stops walking. "Guess what? Never mind, you'll never guess. I made an appointment for me too! I'm getting my hair cut as well, and I've decided to totally change the color. Not sure if I'll do light blonde or maybe a magenta red. What do you think?"

I'm overwhelmed with love for my sweet friend.

"I'm just sorry mine isn't long enough to donate. I wonder how many hairpieces this pony is going to provide?" She grabs my braid and swings it around like a lasso.

I've decided to donate my hair to Locks of Love. This salon is a participating member, and they will be handling everything. With a braid that measures over fifteen inches long, my hair has rarely been cut except for a regular trim, and never colored. I've followed all the instructions for donation; all that's left to do now is cut off the braid. After that, I'll have my remaining hair cut as short as possible without shaving my head. I've decided on a style that is a little edgy, and I have a photo of Meg Ryan at the Oscars folded in my purse to show the stylist.

The owner of the Stardust Salon is a dear friend, and we spoke personally when I made this decision. It was important that he be aware of exactly what is going on.

The salon is typically closed on Monday, but Terry suggested this day and offered to come in with a small team just for me and Stevie.

We both felt like princesses as our transformations began.

When we're almost ready to leave, I call Randy.

"You can come and get us now, but you might not recognize us! Be prepared." I giggle.

After the long appointment, Stevie and I walk from the salon dramatically, like runway divas. When we get in the car, we look at each other and burst out laughing.

"I can't believe we did this!" Stevie shouts.

I'm covering my mouth with both hands. "Louis is going to kill you!"

"Why? He's always loved blondes."

"I feel so liberated!" I run my fingers through my very short hair.

"I can't believe how wavy it is!" Stevie stares at me.

"I know, neither can I!" I crane my neck to look in the rearview mirror. "I guess the sheer weight of my long hair pulled out the natural wave; I had no idea it would look like this!"

Although there's a chance I may eventually lose it altogether, in the interim I think I'm going to enjoy this; it will certainly be easier to care for.

"Stevie, I don't look too ... masculine ... do I?"

"No way!" She looks at me with happy tears. "You are even more gorgeous and glamorous! If anything, you look like a cross between Sharon Stone and Twiggy. Very chic, very sassy!"

"What do you think, Randy?" I see him staring at both of us in the rearview mirror.

"I think you look beautiful, Miss Gloria. And you"—he looks at Stevie—"you look like trouble with a capital T!"

"Oh, goody! Thank you, Randy! Did you hear that, Gloria? Look out, Louis, here comes trouble!" She leans over and whispers, "And look out Francois Carlyle! He is going to flip over your new look."

"How many times do I have to tell you I am not involved with Francois Carlyle?" I say.

"Whatever." She smiles and dramatically shakes her head.

We finally catch our breath when Randy pulls up to Stevie's place.

"Don't get out Randy; I can get the door," Stevie insists. "Glo, are you sure you don't want me to go back to your place with you?" she inquires. "I could stay awhile and help."

"You've done enough today, honestly. I feel pretty good. Thanks for going with me."

"We should have done this years ago—the haircuts, not necessarily the chemo," she laughs. "What were we so afraid of? Change?" Stevie reaches over and hugs me gingerly, as if I'm going to break, "I love you, girlfriend."

"Love you too," I say.

"Hey, is Louis home?" I ask as she gets out of the car.

"Yep, he's home." She looks up toward the balcony and takes a deep breath. "Lord, I hope he doesn't have a heart attack. Do you want to come up and show him our new dos together? Do you feel up to it?"

"I think that's a terrific idea! Let's do it! Randy, I'll just be a few minutes. If they make you leave, just spin around the block and—"

"Sure, Miss Gloria," he says patiently.

The space in front of Stevie's house isn't an actual parking place, and there are certain times of the day when Randy can get away with idling the car and waiting for me, as long as he remains in the driver's seat. But if the meter maids come by, he has to move, and there's a place around the corner he can park if he needs to wait for me. We've been doing this for years, and I seldom keep him waiting for long.

We giggle as we walk to her front door, and I silently thank Touchdown Jesus for the good day as Stevie unlocks her door and we step inside the entryway and then slip into the elevator.

As the doors slide open in the kitchen, we can hear Louis running the blender, and Stevie says, "You wait here; let me show him mine first, and then we'll have your big reveal." She flips the switch on the elevator to lock it on this floor and steps into the kitchen.

"Oh, lover boy …"

I can hear him scream.

"Are … you … kidding … me? I thought you were just getting a little haircut!"

"Do you like it?" she whispers to him in her Marilyn Monroe voice. I'm standing back in the corner of the elevator, but I can see Stevie roll her shoulders and pucker her lips provocatively.

"It's … so … different," he stammers.

Although her cut is new, she's gone from a shoulder-length shag to a more asymmetrical style that is short in the back and long on the sides, it's the almost platinum-blonde color that is far more dramatic.

"Ha, you think this is different? Wait until you see Gloria. Voilà!" She takes my hand and gently pulls me from the elevator as though I'm a showroom display.

Louis is dumbfounded as he stares back and forth at us and watches us as we act like silly teenagers. "You girls are crazy," he laughs.

After a few minutes of staring at us, Louis smiles broadly and says, "I'm making margaritas; would you lovely ladies care to join me before my boring old wife gets back?" He puts his arm around Stevie's waist and pulls her close. "Maybe you can tell me if it's true; do blondes really have more fun?"

She puts her hand on his forehead and says, "I think you have a fever."

"You've got that right; I am a bit hot."

"I think that's my cue to leave; it's getting a bit too warm in here for me!" I laugh. "Randy's waiting outside, and I've got to get back, but I wanted to show you my new look." I give Louis a hug, and he holds on to me longer than usual in an unspoken show of solidarity and understanding.

"You look great, Gloria. Kind of like a rocker chick." He gives me a wink.

"Well thank you, my dear." I play air guitar and shake my head.

I hug Stevie again and hold her tight. "I love you, sister," I say quietly in her ear.

"Love you too," she says, and then I step into the elevator as the doors silently shut and envelop me in a quiet peacefulness. It takes every ounce of energy I can muster to walk down the short alley from her door to the curb where my car is waiting.

By the time I get home, there is nothing quiet or peaceful about me as violent heaves rack my body, and I am so thankful that Maria insisted on placing the pail in the car. I feel absolutely horrible having to use it as Randy pulls into the driveway, but I suppose it's much better than having to shampoo the carpet in the backseat.

Maria rushes out the kitchen door, and between the two of them they manage to get me inside to my master bathroom, where Randy gives us privacy as Maria sits with me on the floor and wipes a cool, wet cloth on my head between spasms and says, "I like your haircut, Miss Gloria! I can even help you wash it now; this will be a good thing, a very good thing."

Her always dependable optimism makes me smile.

CHAPTER 31
— Stephanie —

Friday, April 1

It's been only a few days since our haircuts, but as I sit and visit with Gloria at her place, she looks so perfectly natural in her hairstyle. I'm almost finding it hard to recall her old hairdo, the long braid that was an integral part of her classic look for so many years.

"The gals at the Williams House flipped over my hair, and I had to show them your photo on my cell phone; they're all dying to see your new hairdo in person."

"You and that camera!" Gloria waves her hand. "I forgot you took pictures at the salon. Let me see them."

"You look really good in these photos," I say as we scroll through my iPhone. "You still do. Is it easy to take care of?"

"Exceptionally." She runs her fingers through her hair—a habit it appears she's quickly grown accustomed to.

"So tell me what the *NOLA 2 NOLA* crew thought of your hair? What did Charlotte say?"

"They loved it!" Maria says as she joins us in the kitchen, where we're perched at the counter. "Can I get you ladies some fresh iced tea?" She crosses to the refrigerator as we nod affirmatively. "Why don't you go out on the patio," she suggests. "It's a beautiful day; I can bring your tea out there."

"That's an excellent idea," Gloria says as she stands. "I'll join you there, Stevie, but I'm going to the powder room first. I'll be right out." She crosses through the kitchen to her private master suite.

"Can I help you with that, Maria?" I ask as Maria sets the pitcher on the counter, turns to me, and grabs my hand.

"Miss Stevie," she whispers, "I would never ever betray Miss Gloria; her privacy is very important to me and to Randy. We would protect her with our lives."

"I know that, Maria."

She lets go of my hand and begins to wring hers together, and I can see there is something heavy on her heart.

"What's wrong, Maria? What do I need to know about? You can trust me that I will not betray your confidence."

The words tumble out of Maria's mouth as she talks quickly and quietly, all the while keeping an eye on the door to Gloria's suite.

What she reveals is a total surprise. Gloria had become violently ill after our haircuts—and the nausea continued for almost twenty-four hours.

"She has been in bed since Monday, Miss Stevie! She wasn't even able to go upstairs to her office until this morning. They thought she had food poisoning. Miss Gloria told them she had some bad seafood."

It was more like *C* food, as in 'chemotherapy.'

"I had no idea, Maria, but she looks pretty good right now, I would never have guessed."

"I didn't think you knew, Miss Stevie. I am very worried about her. There is no way she will cancel the next garden club meeting. But what if this happens again? She could be flat on her back in bed from the moment she comes home from the center until the garden club ladies begin to arrive. If that is the case, someone has to be prepared."

Maria is absolutely right; Gloria has been looking forward to hosting the garden club in her home since the season started, and she is determined to follow through, come hell or high water. I assure Maria the information she has confided will remain a secret, and that I will be prepared.

Gloria and I are sitting outside on the patio chatting when she makes a statement that surprises me.

"You are coming to our planning meeting next Wednesday, correct?" she asks.

"Of course I'm coming. It's the last planning session we have before the garden club meets here, and it's been scheduled for months; why wouldn't I come?"

"Just making sure. Elizabeth and Dolores think they're coming for a luncheon meeting to talk about any last-minute needs we may have."

"And we're not?" I tilt my head and furrow my brows.

"Of course we are, but I've also made another decision. I've decided to tell Elizabeth and Dolores about my diagnosis and treatment." I practically hold my breath as she continues. "I didn't want to say anything and worry you, Stevie, but I was feeling a bit under the weather after my last treatment, and I think we need to be prepared in the event my energy is waning during the days leading up to the meeting."

"I had no idea you were feeling poorly after you left my place; I'm so sorry, Gloria. But you look fabulous today!" I take a gulp of tea.

"Right, sure I do." She laughs and leans back in her chair. "But I'm afraid your nose is growing, Pinocchio."

"I'm not lying! You do look fabulous."

"Well, I'm feeling much better than I was; that's for certain. However, I'm not sure how my body will react to the in-home treatment this Monday, and I'll be having my third appointment at the center the following Monday, the same week the club is meeting here. Everything is basically in place, and I'm fully intending to be up and operational, but I would be foolish not to have a backup plan in place, just in case. And I wouldn't want you to be overly burdened, or Elizabeth and Dolores to be blindsided at the last minute."

"That's a wise decision. I think it's an excellent idea to have the girls in our corner just in case." I clink my glass against hers in agreement and say to myself, *Thank you, Jesus.*

★　★　★　★　★

Wednesday, April 6

Although Gloria's home treatment went well on Monday, she looks a little rough around the edges when I arrive at her house a tad early for our luncheon meeting.

Elizabeth and Dolores arrive within five minutes of each other and it's immediately apparent that something is bothering Dolores, she looks clearly distraught. Gloria puts her arm around Dolores's shoulders and leads her down the hallway as Elizabeth and I follow.

"Instead of meeting in the conference room, I thought it would be a nice change to stay down here for this luncheon, if that's okay," Gloria says. "Why don't we take our seats in the dining room, where we can chat a bit before we get started."

Gloria is much more diplomatic than I am, as I cut right to the chase.

"What's up, Dolores? Spit it out before you explode." I sit down and reach for a glass of ice water.

"I got a ninety-day notice to move!" Dolores fights back tears. "I have to be out by July 6. The owners finally got their approval from the Vieux Carré Commission to turn their guesthouse, my house, into an exclusive bed-and-breakfast cottage that they plan to rent by the week. They're going to get more for one week than I pay every month. I don't know what I'm going to do, where I'm going to go."

"You can stay with us until you find something," Elizabeth states without hesitation. The rest of us are all speechless. "Seriously," she continues, "I've been thinking about getting a roommate. We have a huge guest suite on the main level, the kids and I have our bedrooms on the second floor, and the suite is totally unused space. I mean, it's probably not ideal for you in the long run, you probably want your own place, but it could be an option. And I'm sure the price would be right. It's a win-win."

I am totally blown away by the genuine warmth of spirit Elizabeth is showing.

"You'd do that for me?" Dolores scratches the back of her neck and stares.

A lot of water has gone under the bridge since the February e-mail episode, and I can see how proud Gloria is of Dolores and Elizabeth as they agree to meet after our meeting to talk more about this possibility.

"Well, ladies, let's get started, shall we?" Gloria says, adeptly shifting the focus to the upcoming garden club meeting as Maria serves lunch and we review the final checklist.

We quickly discuss the remaining tasks, and all of us agree to spend the entire day here on Wednesday to help with the setup and to arrive early on Thursday for any last-minute projects.

"Other than what we've discussed, there's really not much left for us to do." Elizabeth pages through her notes. "You've got everything so organized, Gloria. It's going to be a wonderful luncheon."

"I agree." I raise my glass in a toast. "And I'm sure the three of us can handle whatever comes our way."

"You mean the four of us," Dolores adds, and she pokes me in the side. "But I understand this is complex math for you." She laughs and counts to four while pointing dramatically at each of us.

"You are correct, Dolores, there are four of us here." Gloria smiles. "And hopefully on Wednesday there will be as well. However, there is a slight chance, a very slight chance, that I may be unavailable." And she begins to share the reason why.

I'm impressed by how well Elizabeth and Dolores take the news; they don't overreact or make this into more than it is, which is the real reason Gloria wants to keep her health situation as private as possible. What she's dealing with isn't as bad as it sounds, but since she's lived so much of her life in the public eye, she understands how these things can be blown out of proportion.

"I really don't want you gals to be worried; I'm going to be fine." She smiles at Maria, who begins to remove our plates. "However, even just the presence of cancerous cells requires the same treatment as a full-blown mass, and this treatment is proving to be precarious. I'm just now realizing the somewhat drastic ebb and flow of this entire process. One day I feel great, and the next, not so much."

Elizabeth and Dolores are more than willing to help however they can, and they agree to be available next week for anything that might come up.

"Thank you, ladies." Gloria leans back in her chair. "I knew I could depend on you. I really didn't want to burden you with all this nonsense, but I didn't want to take you by surprise at the last minute either. In a few months this will all be over and forgotten, but in the meantime it's a bit of a juggling act."

Before we leave, she makes us all pinky-swear that we will not breathe a word of her illness to a soul.

★　★　★　★　★

Monday, April 11

I accompany Gloria to her third treatment, and she's down another two pounds. The joke she made the last time doesn't appear as funny today. At this rate, she really will be skin and bones by the time of her final treatment.

"This is well within acceptable limits," the nurse says when I make Gloria ask about her weight loss.

"See, I told you so," Gloria says, sounding off like an ornery child as the nurse inserts the drip line into the port on her chest.

When the nurse leaves, Gloria jumps right into business.

"There are only a few things left to do." She hands me a copy of her list. "And just in case I need to lie down when I get home today, can you call Brett this afternoon?"

"Of course. Just tell me what you need me to do and consider it done."

Brett Sutton owns Flavorbox Catering, and he also works part-time at his family business, Creole Delicacies, another one of my and Gloria's favorite shops. It's only a couple of blocks from my house, located on Jackson Square. He's going to help cater the garden club meeting.

As she goes over her notes, I can't help being amazed. She's got an IV drip line feeding her poison while she's writing notes on a legal pad and giving me last-minute verbal instructions at the same time. I'm sitting nearby with my own notebook, and I know that Elizabeth and Dolores are ready to swoop in to help in the event Gloria gets benched at the last minute.

However, this is one determined lady.

In one way, having the garden club meeting to plan has been a good thing for Gloria; it keeps her mind off the situation. I know she loves to entertain at her home, and most of the ladies haven't seen all the extensive renovations she has done over the past years, but I hope she isn't overdoing it.

"Well, I think we've got it all handled." I give Gloria a high five as I stand up and stretch. "There's nothing to worry about, except that I need to find the ladies' room. I'll be right back." I drop a quick kiss on her forehead and walk quietly from her cubicle.

The treatment goes well, and Gloria's spirits are high as we get in the car to head back. However, we're only halfway home when I see all the color drain from her face as she doubles over and reaches for the pail.

"Well, if you're trying to pull one over on me again, you're doing a good job." I smile as I hang on to Gloria with one hand, the pail with the other, and glance up briefly to see Randy looking at us in the mirror as he bites his lower lip.

As the waves of nausea continue to crash over her, I can hear Randy call Maria to give her a heads-up on the situation.

"Hey, girlfriend," I joke, as the nausea subsides and I hand Gloria a towel, "remind me to thank Maria for being a puke patrol visionary." She rolls her eyes at me and manages a weak smile before another wave hits.

"Dear God, please let me feel good for the meeting," she prays aloud when we get her home and Maria and I help her get settled in bed.

★　★　★　★　★

Wednesday, April 13

Gloria felt a little better by Tuesday afternoon, but it took until today for her to be up and about, walking without assistance. She is sitting under a patio umbrella on the central courtyard, orchestrating the activity, as Elizabeth, Dolores, and I are in full-steam-ahead mode, working like a well-oiled machine on the finishing touches.

Dolores is working like a Tasmanian devil on the patio, where she's battling a huge hedge of bougainvillea in her warm-weather work attire, a barely-there swimsuit top and shorts.

"Looks like you and that plant have a lot in common; you both live for love/hate relationships," I say as I pass by on my way to get something from the garage.

"Very funny," she says, and she hacks off an overgrown section.

Gloria is growing increasingly stressed as she sees all the activity around her. I have no doubt it's because she's feeling slightly out of control, which is more than slightly out of her comfort zone.

"Dolores, make sure you use those new planters we got."

"Maria, can you show her where they are?"

"Elizabeth, are you handling the name tags?"

"Stevie, where are you going?"

"Crazy, if you don't lighten up, Gloria!" My raised voice causes everyone to look up. "Sweetie, we've got everything covered," I say. "You've planned everything perfectly; don't worry. Why don't we all take a mini–lunch break and have some of that wonderful chicken soup that is simmering on your stove!" I clap my hands. I've forgotten what I was going to get in the garage anyway, so I cross back to the kitchen.

"I smelled it cooking when I was in the kitchen and couldn't resist sneaking a few spoons, it really is wonderful," Elizabeth says.

"Thanks, it's my own recipe," I say as I head into the house to get a bowl for Gloria.

Dolores pipes in. "She thinks it's the magical medicinal cure-all for everything. If I didn't think it would go to her newly bleached-blonde head, I'd agree with her." She takes a bandana out of her back pocket and wipes the sweat from her forehead.

"We should include it in the cookbook!" Elizabeth says. "Or have you featured it in prior years? I don't recall seeing it when I developed the spreadsheet of all the recipes that have been featured over the years. Even so, it should be included again!"

I'm way ahead of her, as I've already planned to include this as one of my recipe submissions.

"You're looking much better," I say to Gloria as I bring her a cup of tea and a small bowl of soup.

"Thanks, but you're a terrible liar."

"No, she's not," Dolores chimes in. "You should have heard her earlier with the fellow who delivered the chairs."

"I wasn't lying to him; we *are* a group of senior citizen ladies! Give me a break; I got us a huge discount on the rental!" I bat my eyelashes.

"You gals are a hoot." Elizabeth looks up from her calligraphy work and shakes her head.

"Wow, those look great, Elizabeth," I say, looking over her shoulder. Truthfully, I've never seen freehand calligraphy done with such fluid ease. These name tags are going to be lovely, and it takes me back in history.

"The day I met Gloria I remember thinking how absurd it seemed that this crazy club of hens would put so much stock in name tags." I quickly wipe my eyes. "Like they were mini-Picassos with safety pins."

"How long ago was that?" Elizabeth asks as she returns to writing the names.

"Over thirty years ago," Gloria responds quickly. "I remember the day like it was yesterday."

"You do?" I raise my eyebrows.

"Of course!" Gloria takes a sip of her tea. "You walked into your first meeting like a confident cat out on a stroll, but I could see you were really a kitten shaking in her boots."

"Like a fish out of water?" Dolores says.

"Or a leopard without spots?" Elizabeth adds.

"More like a yin without her yang," Maria unexpectedly says as she carries out a tray of food for everyone.

"Yes. I like that, Maria." Gloria nods and places her hand gently on top of mine. "And we've been balancing each other out ever since."

"Lunch is served," Maria says as she rescues us from the emotional moment.

"That's good, because I need a break." Dolores hoses off the dirt on her arms, then her legs, and then turns the spigot on her head.

"Good grief, Dolores; this isn't your shower," I say. "Have some decency."

She gives me a mischievous smile and slightly pulls her swimsuit top to expose her right breast. I let out a shout and exclaim, "Puppies and kittens, puppies and kittens!"—a phrase we use in the south to help our brain focus on something more pleasant.

"Well, that's something you don't see every day," Elizabeth says quietly.

"And let's all thank God for that!" I say as Dolores grins, Maria shakes her head, and all of us chuckle, including Gloria.

Dolores playfully pats me on my back as she sits down with us at the table for a lunch of soup, crackers, and sweet tea.

After we're finished and Maria takes the empty bowls, Gloria slowly stands.

"I need to rest for a few minutes; is that okay? I'll be back, I promise." Before disappearing inside the house, she stops on the threshold and turns. "I love you gals; thank you so much for being here."

We all sit silently for a few seconds after Gloria disappears into the house.

"Time's a-wasting, girly-girls." Dolores stands and points her finger at us like an angry schoolmarm. "Get the lead out and get back to work." She winks and sashays back to her project as Elizabeth and I return to ours and the gentle sounds of the fountain and the singing birds accompany us.

CHAPTER 32

— Gloria —

Thursday, April 14

It's the morning of the garden club meeting, and I'm standing at my bathroom sink and opening one pill bottle after another. I've decided to premedicate myself before I even step out of my room. I'm going to take an antinausea pill, an antidiarrhea pill, and an antianxiety pill. If I had an antireality pill, I would most likely take it as well.

I've also decided not to drink real coffee today; I'm going to sip on decaffeinated herbal tea instead. I don't want to eat or drink anything that might upset my stomach, which at this point in time is pretty much anything and everything I put in my mouth. I'll eat after the meeting, after everyone is gone, if I can.

I don't want to take any chances today.

This month the garden club will be discussing roses, my favorite. I have fourteen different varieties on my property. You can never have too many roses.

Our caterer, Chef Brett, arrives in plenty of time and takes control of the kitchen. He and Maria hit it off immediately, and today he will be preparing my favorite, shrimp and grits, and Maria will be making a simple yet fabulous salad with fresh tomatoes from our garden and parboiled asparagus, topped with crumbled feta cheese and a balsamic-and-olive-oil dressing.

Perino's has sent their rose expert, Cynthia McDow, as our guest speaker, and I enjoy spending time with her before our guests begin to arrive. Cynthia is thrilled to see so many exquisite roses growing all around Vincent Manor. I have climbers on the privacy walls and gated walkways, rose bushes outline the perimeter of the main house, and several different species of long-stemmed roses grow around the newly renovated carriage house.

When the ladies start to arrive, Cynthia greets each guest individually and graciously presents each one with a stunning long-stemmed rose, taken from an elegant basket nearby. Yet in spite of all this special treatment, the whispering still begins.

This is the first official reveal of my new haircut, which is most likely the cause of all the whispering. Then again, perhaps it's because I'm a tad thinner, and I can understand why this fact might be misconstrued as meaning more than it actually does.

I'm relieved that a core group of my dear friends know the truth, because quite frankly, all this secrecy is making me weary. I find myself thinking the best thing may be to come clean, to tell them all the truth and let the chips fall where they may.

I give this serious consideration as the ladies are being served mimosas and white sangria around the pool. What a fantastic day; the weather is perfect. April is a great month to hold an outdoor meeting— lots of sunshine and warm temperatures. I'm thrilled with the turnout. Everyone seems to be enjoying themselves, and so many have given me such wonderful compliments on my new hairdo. I'm sure Stevie is getting her share as well, as her new look is a real shocker. She's always looked young, but the shade of blonde the hairdresser used is very flattering on her. It makes her look even younger and more mysterious; I bet Louis is loving it.

Elizabeth and Stevie are standing by the pool chatting. It amazes me how far they have come in their friendship. Stevie looks very chic in what she refers to as her uniform. In warm months, Stevie usually wears a silk T-shirt and five-pocket pants by Christopher Blue. The spring colors look so good on her, and now with that blonde hair, it's a striking combination.

As I look around, it appears we're off to a great start, and I'm very proud of the team who helped to make this possible, especially over the last few days, when I was unable to fulfill my own responsibilities as we came in to the final stretch. Without Stevie, Elizabeth, Dolores, and Maria pulling together, things would not be going as smoothly as they are now.

Our members are enjoying visiting and exploring the grounds, and seeing all the renovations we've made on this magnificent old compound. Charlotte is joyfully giving tours, and I'm so thankful she's going to be with me throughout the summer after all.

Instead of being transferred out of state next month, Charlotte's husband was given a last-minute opportunity by his company to go to Shanghai for the summer, after which he will return to the States, where he will be in line for an even better position. Charlotte will be staying with her in-laws until he returns, and when she asked if she could remain in my employ instead of leaving next month, I was ecstatic. When I confided my health situation to her, I shouldn't have been surprised that she wasn't surprised. Charlotte is bright, intuitive, and my right-hand gal in so many ways; she had been putting the pieces together for a while.

All my favorite friends are here today, and I am blessed beyond belief. I feel an overwhelming sense of joy. It's one of those moments when you really see what life is all about, it's a gift—a fantastic, wonderful gift.

Then I hear the faint sound of the broken bell—*Ding-dink-ding, ding-dink-ding*—and the meeting is being called to order. Alma introduces Elizabeth as she takes the podium and greets us.

"I'd like to thank Gloria Vincent for welcoming us into her home." She leads the applause. "We know you have a lot going on, and we appreciate your graciousness." After a standing ovation that truly humbles me, she continues. "Ladies, I need to remind everyone that the deadline to submit your recipes and photos for our cookbook is May 12, the day of our next garden club meeting. Everyone should have received a copy of the mock-up design in the mail." She holds up the sample copy. "But if you haven't received your copy, please see Stephanie Lewis after the meeting; she has extra copies." Stevie stands up, waves, and flamboyantly shows off her new hairdo as many of the ladies laugh and applaud.

"Thank you, Stephanie." Elizabeth smiles. "I'd also like to remind everyone that next month we will elect a new president and one new executive board member, so please start thinking about nomination selections."

She then explains how the current board will make calls and send e-mails to scout out members that might be interested in filling the positions. A name will be placed on the ballot if the member agrees to fulfill the responsibilities of the role. The members will then cast their ballots at the next meeting in May, voting to choose from among those nominated. The votes will be tallied and the results announced that same day. When Elizabeth is done explaining the rules, everyone is nodding with the understanding of the process. I catch a glimpse of Stevie, who cocks her head and raises one eyebrow. I can tell something is going on in her pretty little head, and given her mischievous nature, there's no telling what she has planned.

"On a less formal note," Elizabeth says, "I hope to see all of you at Jazz Fest!" She pumps her fist in the air as applause breaks out yet again.

Jazz Fest is one of many music festivals in New Orleans; however, it's probably the largest, and this year the outdoor festival is expected to attract four hundred thousand guests over its two entertainment-filled weekends. With twelve stages, the festival takes place the last weekend of April and the first weekend in May.

Each year, Louis purchases three Big Chief tickets for one of the weekends. Big Chief tickets are outrageously expensive, but Louis is a music freak who spares no expense. He is so good to Stevie, and me. With those tickets, we will be sitting in covered elevated stands with private bar service and extremely clean and upgraded porta-potties—a very big deal at a festival this size; there is never a line.

Louis is planning on attending the first weekend of the festival. He's looking forward to seeing Gregg Allman and Jimmy Buffet. Stevie is excited to see Robert Plant. Me? I'm just excited to be going, period.

After a brief Jazz Fest pitch, Elizabeth introduces Cynthia McDow, who immediately captivates the audience with her presentation, and it's during her talk that I suddenly feel a deep conviction to make an announcement. Elizabeth nods without question as I whisper my request to her.

At the end of the speaker presentation, Elizabeth thanks her and says, "Before we have lunch, our gracious hostess has something to share," and she motions for me to come forward. Once again, I'm overwhelmed by the rousing applause.

"Thank you for that warm welcome, ladies, but first let me say how beautiful you all look today! Every one of you is beautiful, inside and out." I extend my hands and applaud them as they join in. When it quiets down, I continue.

"Ladies, I want to thank all of you for coming to my home today, but most of all, I want to thank all of you for being my family." As I gaze out at the group, I can see expressions of mutual admiration and of mild confusion, and I need to take a deep breath before I continue.

"It's because you are family that I want to share something with you today."

I'm interrupted by a voice from the audience that I recognize as Stevie's as she shouts, "Something more than your fabulous new haircut?"

"Yes, something more than my new hairdo"—I laugh and twirl around—"but something nonetheless related, in a round about way." I wink at Stevie as she gives me a nod; it doesn't surprise me that she senses what I'm about to do.

"Ladies, I want you to hear this today from my own lips, not from whispered conjecture or rumors that may come as time goes by. I want you to know that I am undergoing a short series of treatment at the Gayle and Tom Benson Cancer Center to treat some cancerous cells that were discovered in a recent series of tests." An audible gasp erupts from the crowd, and I gesture for the ladies to allow me to finish before they make assumptions.

"Girls, I'm going to be fine, but I would be foolish to think that the word isn't going to start to spread. Unfortunately, the chemotherapy treatment has some side effects, including what appears to be an unhealthy weight loss, but I can assure you it is, in fact, quite normal. Truthfully, I am *not* on death's doorstep and I do *not* have some rare type of inoperable cancer. So if you hear someone talking about my health, particularly if what they are saying is wrong, feel free to speak as someone who has heard it directly from the horse's mouth, and whenever possible, to set the record straight."

"You can count on us." Dolores points her finger in the air.

"We've got your back," Miss V. unexpectedly calls out, leading several of the ladies to shout additional words of encouragement.

"So, now that you've seen me and my sassy haircut and heard the real truth, you can rest assured that I'm going to be fine, and I want you all to know how very much I love you. Those three little words are never said often enough. You will be hearing me say them a lot more often, and I hope you will all join me in saying them more often as well. And without further ado, I think Chef Brett has something he would like to say."

The chef stands and loudly declares, "Lunch is served."

I silently thank God for the superhuman strength to keep my emotions in check as I navigate my way through the ladies who are now standing on their feet, clapping wildly and shouting words of affirmation, encouragement, and, yes, love.

This turns out to be one of our best meetings ever. It's also been a good day for me, as I've found renewed energy, no doubt coming from my empowering family of sisters.

At the end of the meeting, the ladies are leaving and I notice they're all hugging one another. And what's that I hear? Ah yes, those three little words.

CHAPTER 33

— Stephanie —

Saturday, April 30

It's been two weeks since Gloria revealed her haircut and health to the garden club, and I'm still being inundated with calls. I've been assuring everyone Gloria is doing great, and I imagine we'll run into several of them at Jazz Fest this weekend, where they'll be able to see this for themselves. Gloria called last night from a dinner meeting and said she definitely feels up to the annual excursion.

"My body has finally turned a corner," Gloria said on the phone. "After my fourth treatment on Monday, I was only down for one day, and I feel fantastic! In fact, I just had a glass of Dom Pérignon and an exquisite medium-rare chateaubriand with asparagus spears and baby potatoes. I've got to get back to the table; I'm with a group of corporate stuffed shirts, and I'm calling you from the ladies' room."

It was so good to hear Gloria sound upbeat, energized, like her old self. I've watched her rally around the flag these past several weeks and I'm inspired by her outlook and attitude.

"It's been a crazy day," she said before she hung up, "but it might be a long night, so I just want you and Louis to know you can count me in for tomorrow. Send me a text when you two head out the door, and I'll be waiting."

Louis has been up since the crack of dawn; he's as excited about Jazz Fest as most eight-year-olds are about Fair Day. This year they are expecting excellent attendance, due in part to great weather.

I'm waiting for Louis to come downstairs when I decide to call

Dolores. She answers on the first ring. "Hey, girl, I can't talk long, Louis and I are heading out the door, but can you meet me next week for dinner?"

"Sure, when and where?"

"How about Tuesday around six at the Grapevine Bistro. Louis will be out of town that night, and I'm going to need to eat somewhere."

"I love that place," she purrs, "it supplies me with great eye candy— three delectable pieces, to be exact."

"Oh, for heavens' sake, Dolores, that trio of bartenders are young enough to be your sons."

"Don't ruin it for me, Stephanie; I can still dream."

"You mean fantasize, don't you?"

No matter how popular the media has made cougar-type relationships, the thought of an older woman with a younger man just doesn't seem right to me. I guess I'm still old-fashioned, and I think it's kind of creepy to see a woman with a man who is fifteen or even twenty years her junior. Yuck! Fortunately, I know Dolores is only kidding; she would never really hit on any of these guys.

Suddenly Louis prances into the kitchen. "Are we ready to go?" He claps his hands.

I hold up one finger and mouth the words "Give me a sec."

"I've got to go, Dolores. I'll see you next week."

"Hey, quick before you go, how's Gloria?" Dolores asks.

"She's great. We're on our way to pick her up now."

Louis is tapping on his watch and waiting impatiently as I talk. "Sorry, Dolores, I gotta go. Louis is getting anxious; he can't wait to get to Jazz Fest and start eating." I gently poke Louis in his trim tummy as he rolls his eyes.

I hang up the phone and follow Louis into the elevator. "Call Gloria and tell her we're on our way," he says.

"I'm way ahead of you," I say, and I hit send on a prewritten text message that tells her to be on the lookout for us. "Let's go!"

Once we've parked the car, our Big Chief tickets give us easy access to the Acura Stage, where most of the headliners play. This is about the only place besides her home where Gloria ever dresses somewhat casually, usually wearing T-shirts and capris, albeit the T-shirts were from Anne Taylor or Giorgio Armani. This year is no exception, but she's added a lightweight long-sleeved blouse to her ensemble, and I can clearly understand why.

She's always eaten like a bird, but the chemo has really killed her appetite, and it shows. Her collarbones are jutting out like the arms of an oversize clothes hanger, with the silky cream-colored T-shirt gaping around her neck. When she turns around, I can literally see the individual vertebrae in her spine, and I gasp.

"What's the matter?" she asks. "Are you okay?"

"Uh, I'm fine; it's nothing. I was just stunned by the crowd; there seem to be more people here every year," I say lamely as she nods without question. I would be more concerned if her color wasn't so good or her energy not as high. The truth is—weight notwithstanding, this is the best I've seen her in weeks. *If I didn't know better, I'd say she was …*

"OMG!" I stare at her. "You're getting a little action, aren't you, girlfriend?" I wink.

"What do you mean?" She tilts her head and squints.

"You know exactly what I mean! Spill the beans! Your dinner meeting last night—exactly whose stuffed shirt were you getting into?"

"Stevie!" she screams. I see the pink color in her cheeks go quickly to red as she turns her face.

"I knew it!" I say. "I knew it! You little vixen, you are seeing him! So Daddy Warbucks *is* in town, eh?"

"Keep your voice down, and how many times do I have to tell you there is nothing going on between Francois and me."

"Yeah, right."

I'm willing to let go of the subject, at least for now, while Gloria and I pick the perfect seats in this high-dollar reserved section where there really aren't any bad seats on the elevated platform area. Louis takes off almost immediately to survey the food vendors. Once we get comfortable, I look out over the ground floor of the arena to watch the sea of people carrying blankets and territorial flags, wandering helplessly in the dirt, scouting out places to camp for the day.

"Give us your huddled masses," I say, "but I'll take first-class seating any day of the week!"

"You're such a snob, Stevie." Gloria pokes me with her bony elbow.

"Oh yeah, and you're not? Why don't you wander down there and try to find somewhere to sit." I motion toward the throbbing sea of humanity. "Then tell me how much of a snob I am. And while you're at it, try to find a restroom down there."

"Okay, okay, you're right. I'd much rather be here"—she puts her arm around me—"even if you are a busybody with an overactive imagination."

Louis returns with his arms full of what's sure to be anything but a lo-cal lunch, and Gloria and I help him unwrap and lay out all his food treasures in our space so we can eat before Cyndi Lauper starts her show.

Over the next four days, we will consume more food and alcohol than our total body weight, at least Louis and I will, but that's life in NOLA—fun, food, and music, in abundance, and often!

Music is blaring from the loudspeakers and the anticipation is mounting in the crowd when I notice a familiar face and nudge Gloria.

"Is that Daddy Warbucks?" I squint my eyes.

"Where?"

"Right there"—I stand and point—"at two o'clock."

Gloria follows my finger, and her eyes light up as she confirms the presence of Francois Carlyle.

"Is that James Carville he's with?" I ask.

"Stevie, sit down; you look like a tourist." She pulls me back to my seat.

"Looks like sonny boy has some new arm candy," I whisper. "Isn't that Miss Louisiana?"

Sure enough, it's the beauty queen with her arm locked with Anthony Carlyle's. I watch as Gloria slides down in her seat while trying not to look at the group of distinguished men passing by, surrounded by several burly security guards.

"So you did know they were in town?" I bat my eyelashes and smirk.

"Yes, I knew they were in town. We had a big meeting yesterday. I haven't had a chance to tell you about it; I was waiting to get situated. Do *not* cause a scene, Stevie."

"I think they see us!" I wave wildly at the younger Carlyle, wondering if he'll remember meeting me at the Napoleon House with Gloria months ago.

"How could they not?" Gloria quickly reaches into her pocket for her lipstick and applies it like a pro in two swoops without even looking and then runs her fingers through her hair to fluff it up.

As soon as he sees her, Francois Carlyle practically bolts over to Gloria, wraps her in a bear hug, and plants a kiss on each cheek. "What a pleasure to see you again."

"Again?" I discretely mouth the words to Gloria.

Francois is grinning like a Cheshire cat as Gloria introduces us and he warmly shakes my hand. Ms. Louisiana is holding on to Sonny boy's arm like a tick on a yard dog as he says hello to us, shakes my hand, and extends the same European cheek kiss to Gloria. He introduces us to his flavor of the week, who will never be mistaken for Miss Congeniality, and he is clearly embarrassed by the spectacle his father is making as he fawns over Gloria. To her credit, Gloria seems unfazed by his demonstrative display and then greets James Carville like an old friend. She makes a quick comment about his show; I always forget how connected this woman is to old-guard Nola royalty.

After everyone is introduced and a bit of small talk is conducted, Francois looks out toward the huge audience and exclaims, "I love this country!"

"The country as a whole, or the country of Nola?" Gloria smiles and gently pats Francois' arm.

"Both!" he says as the group laughs. "Please forgive us, *mon chéri*"— Francois squeezes Gloria's hand—"but we cannot stay. My dear friend wanted us to see the festivities, and now we must head back. However, I look forward to seeing you soon." He once again kisses her on both cheeks, as does sonny boy, who still appears somewhat disturbed by the entire situation.

"I do love your hair like that," Anthony says to Gloria, much to the dismay of Miss Louisiana.

"Thank you." She runs her fingers through her hair. "It does make it infinitely easier to get up and go now."

"I know exactly what you mean," Anthony says as he mimics her move with his own hair and laughs.

The group departs just as the performance begins, and in no time we are caught up in the music.

★ ★ ★ ★ ★

After several hours, Gloria is holding up pretty well, but she and I have never been ones to spend the whole day here. Usually we pick and choose the concerts we want to see and go back and forth from my home to the festival. Our Big Chief status allows us this luxury. The times when we are not at the festival, you can typically find us back at my place in the Quarter, enjoying a glass of iced tea or wine with our feet propped up, people-watching from my balcony. Which is where we are now. We took a taxi home and left Louis at the festival.

"You know I love Vincent Manor," Gloria says, "but why my ancestors didn't build something right here in the heart of the Quarter like this is beyond my comprehension. This is the hub of everything!"

I nod. "Maybe so, but your ancestors were visionaries; they knew what they wanted. We don't have a pool, a garage, a patio garden, or a conservatory."

"Minor details, my dear." She holds her glass of tea in the air to toast. "You have the thing that counts the most now. Location, location, location!"

"Okay, girlfriend." I lean back in my chair and put my feet up on the shared ottoman. "Enough of the small talk; give me the scoop on Daddy Warbucks."

"Will you please stop calling him that? It's very disrespectful." Gloria shakes her head as the corners of her mouth turn up. "Besides, that's no way to talk about the man who owns the company that now officially owns *NOLA 2 NOLA* magazine. I signed the papers last night; the acquisition is final."

CHAPTER 34

— Gloria —

Monday, May 2

Jazz Fest was amazing this past weekend, and I'm not the least bit tired today. In fact, I woke up early raring to go, and I was planning to meet with Charlotte after my treatment to fine-tune our strategy for our part in moving the *NOLA 2 NOLA* offices from Vincent Manor to the CBD. Plus, the steering committee for the Grace House Gala is using our conference room for a planning meeting later today, and I was hoping to sit in on that as well.

However, the day might not play out as I initially hoped.

Caron is unavailable today, and the substitute nurse practitioner sent by the home health care service to administer my treatment is slower than molasses in January, and at the rate she's going, I'll be lucky to get into my office by sunset.

"Are y'all in a hurry?" she drawls as I find it more and more difficult to contain my impatience. Watching her is like watching a movie in slow-motion. I don't often get frustrated with people, but this situation is getting more than a little ridiculous.

"Actually, I am somewhat pressed for time today," I admit. "Please forgive my asking, but you have done this before, right?"

She waves her hand and laughs. "Of course I have; I just want to make sure we get everything correct."

"Will you excuse me for a moment?" I pick up my cell phone and exit the sitting room. It startles Maria when I enter the kitchen and quickly hold my finger to my mouth. "Shhhh," I whisper, "I need to make a call;

don't let her follow me if she comes out." I point toward my room, and Maria nods as I walk into the foyer and make a call to the agency.

I discover that Caron had an unexpected family emergency but she'll be back to work tomorrow. I don't want to disparage the substitute nurse they have sent in Caron's place, especially when I find out that she is highly qualified and has been with the agency for over a decade. I stretch the truth just a little when I explain that something has come up on my end and ask if it will totally disrupt the course of the treatment if we delay today's infusion by twenty-four hours.

"Just this once, Mrs. Vincent," the scheduling nurse says, "but it's important to remain on a consistent schedule." I convey my complete understanding and express deep appreciation for the way she has accommodated me.

When I return to the kitchen I give Maria a quick overview, and she is more than willing to let the nurse know that I have an important business need to address, which is true, and that I have already called the agency to reschedule with someone else for tomorrow.

I head upstairs to my office feeling as though I've been given a gift—a gift in the shape of an entire Monday morning that I can devote to something other than the routine medical process that has jeopardized my time every Monday morning for so many weeks.

However, this isn't just any Monday morning. It's a special day—a bittersweet day, but a day I am nonetheless excited to see arrive.

Charlotte is surprised to see me, but we waste no time before jumping right into the matter at hand. As of last Friday, *NOLA 2 NOLA* is officially owned by Carlyle Communications, and their team will now be handling all operations and management responsibilities. Our only responsibility is to make sure that everything listed in the acquisition contract as part of the sale gets from point A, which is Vincent Manor, to point B, the new offices in the CBD.

While the staff has known about the pending acquisition for a while, relocation plans could not commence in earnest until the papers were officially signed. The new editorial offices include new furniture and new computers, all networked to state-of-the-art publishing and printing technology. The majority of our work now will be to make sure that all hard-copy files and archive material is packed and sent, and that data transfers are conducted from our computer hard drives to the new mainframe system. The most extensive project is to relocate all the supplies and equipment from Phillip's studio above the carriage house—a project that I have no doubt will be conducted with the utmost care and attention to detail.

The entire *NOLA 2 NOLA* move will be conducted in stages over the next several days, with everything completed by May 11, which I see on the calendar turns out to be the day before our next garden club meeting.

The morning flies by, and Charlotte and I have carefully reviewed the relocation strategy and discussed some alternative ideas for using the soon-to-be-vacant space. We take a quick lunch break downstairs, where Maria has prepared a burrito for Charlotte and a protein shake smoothie for me, and we're back upstairs in the conference room by the time the members of the Grace House Gala Steering Committee begin to arrive.

CHAPTER 35

— Stephanie —

Tuesday, May 10

I suppose one of these days I'm going to have to grow up. This year Jazz Fest really did me in, I'm still recovering. Louis and I hadn't planned on attending the second weekend this year, but at the last minute we were invited by friends who had Big Chief tickets that weren't being used, so we took them up on the invitation. I had already committed to important back-to-back engagements this Tuesday and Wednesday, plus houseguests this weekend. I knew I'd be exhausted at the end of the weekend.

And I was right. I couldn't imagine I would be in any condition to accompany Gloria to her fifth chemo treatment on Monday.

"Don't worry, Stevie," Gloria said when I called her Sunday morning. "I'll be fine; I just started a new book, and it will keep my mind occupied. Enjoy your guests today, and sleep in tomorrow."

Which is exactly what I did.

Maria called late on Monday night at Gloria's request to give me an update. She had accompanied her to treatment that day, and after some "mild nausea," Gloria was sleeping peacefully.

Louis had an early flight this morning and will be in Atlanta for several days, and I'm excited about having dinner tonight with Dolores. I've got a fabulous idea that has been brewing in my brain for quite a while, and I want to share it with her.

Six o'clock doesn't get here quickly enough; I'm starving. When I get to the Grapevine Bistro, Dolores hasn't arrived yet, and I take a seat at the bar, as that's where we'll probably eat anyway. Jeffery automatically brings me a glass of Heavenly Seven chardonnay; Louis and I are regulars here—maybe too regular.

Dolores will be pleased to see that all three pieces of her favorite eye candy are working tonight. Jeffery is tall and handsome, very suave like Ricky Martin. Gerald is a real man's man and a great neighbor; he once surprised me with coffee beans from a specialty store he visited while on vacation. Then there's sweet Devin, who is wickedly smart and cute to boot; he and Louis usually banter back and forth with their sports knowledge. We know them, and they know us. However, I think Dolores scares them. They're not sure if she's a cougar or an alley cat.

I take a sip of the exceptional wine and hold my glass up to the guys, who are all standing within close proximity behind the bar, and say, "Gird your loins, fellows! I'm waiting for Dolores, not Louis."

After a bit of harmless joking with the guys, the crazy lady finally arrives.

"Hey, wild thing, what took you so long?" I kiss her on the cheek.

"You forget, Stephanie, I'm a working girl," she says with a tad more volume than necessary as she gives Jeffery a wink.

Oh brother, here we go.

Devin hands Dolores an extra-dirty vodka martini as she sits down, and she looks at him coyly from under her lashes and says, "How nice you remembered that I like it dirty."

Devin's blush is immediate. The boy needs rescuing, and I quickly butt in. "Devin, I'd like to order a cheese board to start with."

"Yes, ma'am," he replies, and he quickly moves to the end of the bar to place the order.

"What's the hurry?" quips Dolores.

"No hurry, just hungry. Can't have wine without something in my stomach."

"Speaking of stomach, how is Gloria doing?"

"She had her fifth chemo treatment yesterday. I talked with Maria last night, and she said Gloria was feeling okay."

"You didn't go with her?" Dolores asks.

"Not this time, but she really doesn't need anybody to hold her hand; she's doing fine. She'll be good as new in no time." I lean in toward Dolores. "But that doesn't mean she hasn't been affected by the cancer and the chemo. I don't think she's been making very good choices these past few months concerning the garden club. That's why we need to take matters into our own hands. She'll thank us in the long run—trust me."

I reach into my Salvatore Ferragamo handbag that Gloria gave me for my last birthday. She gives me great gifts. I pull out a couple of folded sheets of paper.

"What's all that?" asks Dolores.

"Your future, and the future of the garden club." She wrinkles her nose as we take a few sips of our drinks.

The cheese board arrives in record time as I lay out my plan.

"The nominations for garden club president are this Thursday, and Elizabeth is pushing hard for Julie Ann for president. We both know that won't be good. We need someone older, wiser, and a whole lot more professional to do this job. I think you're a perfect blend of all three. Although what profession you're in might be questionable, especially with that outfit."

She's wearing a Juicy Couture two-piece workout suit in Pepto-Bismol pink.

"Hey, I'm off the clock; I can wear what I want. Anyway, why don't you do it? Why don't you be president? I'd vote for you in a heartbeat."

"Thanks, but this is not up my alley."

"Oh, and it's up mine?" Dolores raises her eyebrows.

"Yes!" I put my hand on her back. "You're a professional entrepreneur with a full-time business in the Quarter; you'd be much better at it than me. I brought a copy of the membership roster. I split it in two and highlighted names for each of us to call. I don't care if Julie Ann makes the executive board, but we *can't* have her as president. You need to make some calls and let these ladies know that you'd like their support. I'll do the rest."

"Are you sure about this? Gloria will slap you naked and hide your clothes when she finds out."

Her comment makes me laugh. "I highly doubt that, Dolores; just trust me on this. I've agreed to allow my name to be added to the ballot, but I have absolutely no desire to be president, or even an executive board member. When you win, Julie Ann will come in second and automatically be on your executive board, and as the third-place runner-up, I'll be free to help you. I know you can do this!"

Just then, Jeffery leans in and says, "You ladies look like you're up to no good. Are you ready to order dinner?"

"Yes, we are!" I put the papers in Dolores's hand, and she folds them up and tucks them into the front of her bra. *Like that bra needed any padding.*

"Yes what—up to no good or ready to order?" he asks.

"Both!" Dolores and I echo in unison as we review the menu and make our selections.

The bistro chef is a wizard. He has to be, as he works in one of the tiniest kitchens in the Quarter yet manages to turn out the most fabulous dishes. We've never had a bad meal here.

Dolores finishes her martini and signals for another as we eat dinner. "Do you really think Gloria is doing better?" She takes a bite of steak. "I've worked on her plants several times since we had our meeting at her place, but she rarely comes outside to say hello like she used to."

"I wouldn't take it personally; she's been really busy. There's a lot going on at *NOLA 2 NOLA*. Gloria sold the magazine."

Dolores practically chokes on her food. "What? When?"

"The day before Jazz Fest, but she's been considering it for a long time, even before she started treatment. She said I could tell you since the deal closed, but don't say anything about it yet, okay? A press release should be going out soon, and it's going to be public knowledge any day, but things have been really crazy for her."

"What is she gonna do? I mean, is she retiring or what?"

"Trust me—she's got more than enough to keep her busy, but it would be a shame if the garden club reins get passed on to someone like Julie Ann; it could mean the downfall of the group, and I know that isn't what Gloria wants."

"Yeah, I wouldn't think so," Dolores pushes some vegetables around on her plate.

"You know as well as I do that Gloria has always burned the candle at both ends, but now she gets worn out so easily, and it's really hard on her. That's why she's not thinking straight about what's right for the garden club. But she's almost done with chemo, and once this is over she'll be able to eat normally again, regain her strength, and put back on some of the weight she's lost. Until then, we have to do what's right, and what's right is having you as our next garden club president!"

After dinner Dolores and I say our good-byes and head home. I have only a half a block to walk, and I'm surprised to see that Dolores is riding her bike; she doesn't quite look like a cyclist. But then again, she doesn't quite look like a garden club president either.

CHAPTER 36

— Gloria —

Thursday, May 12

Responsibility has always weighed heavily on my shoulders, and I used to think there was no better way to balance that burden than by wearing one of the heaviest and quite possibly most profound pieces of contemporary jewelry I own, an original cuff bracelet by Paloma Picasso. I have always loved the feel of the heavy metal on my wrist.

"You look like Wonder Woman," Charles used to say to me whenever I wore it.

Every time I put it on, I feel powerful and a little off-balance at the same time. It's always a good reminder that I'm not Wonder Woman; I can't spin like a whirling dervish and create a different place, a different time, a different reality.

It's always reminded me that my life is what it is, a grand and glorious adventure.

I still feel that way, except now this lovely bracelet keeps falling off my bony wrist. I'm going to have to wait before I can wear it again, until after my treatment, when I'm able to eat anything I want and can put on some weight. I return it to my jewelry box and look for something else.

I must also look for something else besides different jewelry to wear. Now that I have sold the magazine, I must look for a new adventure. I need to change my perspective on some areas in life. First up is my perspective on Anthony—dear, sweet, precious Anthony.

Although he has not pressured me in any way, I know he wants me to begin seeing him in a different light. I know he wants to take our relationship to the next level, but I'm not quite sure what that next level is.

We talk almost every night, and since the announcement about the acquisition went public yesterday, we've spoken a half dozen times. We agreed weeks ago that in addition to the crackerjack publicist they have on staff, Francois will be the point person for media sound bite interviews. I'm lying low for the time being because I'm well aware that the camera isn't my best friend these days.

I'm prepared to field questions about the acquisition from the ladies at the garden club meeting today. But mostly I'm excited about the nominations and about my special announcement. I haven't even told Stevie yet, and I made Emme and Elizabeth promise to keep the secret until today's meeting.

On my drive to the Court of Two Sisters, I see Stevie walking and ask Randy to pull over.

"You can let me out here. I will walk with Stevie the rest of the way."

I'm relieved when he doesn't question whether I "feel up to it" or try to dissuade me from going, like an overprotective father. Yet something tells me he won't be far behind, hovering somewhere.

Stevie sees us pull to the curb and walks over to meet us. As I get out of the car, a puzzled look comes over her face.

"What's wrong?" I ask.

"Aren't you going to be warm in long sleeves? It feels like a hundred degrees out here."

"I did have a sleeveless dress on today, but when I caught my reflection in the hall mirror before I left the house, I was shocked. And if I'm shocked, you can imagine what the ladies will think. I look much worse than I feel, and I don't want them to talk, so I put this on instead. I'll be fine. It's actually cooler than it looks; silk is like that."

"Well, I think you look stunning," Stevie says, and she wraps her arm tenderly around my waist as we walk.

"Bless your heart, but that's not entirely true." I smile.

She wags her finger and does a rather poor impression of me. "It is true, and I'll have none of that negative self-talk."

"Tell me I don't sound that bad."

"Almost." We laugh, and before I know it we're at our destination.

"Well, here we are." Stevie smiles broadly. "Let's go eat and elect a new president and executive board." She winks.

"I know that you know we're going to nominate you," I say.

She quickly turns to me and with an impish smile says, "Yes, I know."

"And that's okay with you? You're ready to take the helm if you get voted in?"

"Let's just cross that bridge when we get to it, okay?"

We will be crossing that bridge a lot sooner than she expects, as I've convinced Elizabeth not to nominate Julie Ann, so the only person being nominated today will be Stevie. She's going to make a fine president, even if she doesn't realize it yet.

I'm excited that we're meeting here today. The Court of Two Sisters gained its popular name from two sisters, Emma and Bertha Camors. They operated a variety store from 1886 to 1906 on the premises that is now a restaurant.

When we planned this meeting for May, we decided not to take a chance with the weather, and so we booked the indoor Terrace Dining Room. Yet even though we aren't sitting outside, we can still enjoy the outdoors without enduring the elements, or the honeybees. The wall of glass that separates our luncheon from the outdoors allows us to enjoy the view of the three-tiered water fountain, the jazz quartet, and, of course, the huge two-hundred-year-old Wisteria vine in full bloom.

Because of New Orleans' tropical weather, plants grow like weeds here. Flowers that bloom for four or five months in northern Louisiana bloom here almost all year, with exquisite bursts of color.

Soon we find our seats and the server pours Stevie a tall mimosa. I put my hand over my glass to let him know I'm not partaking today. "Iced tea?" he asks, and I nod.

The room is filling up, and we are quickly directed to the fabulous buffet.

When we get back to the table, it's hard not to notice that I have very little on my plate, especially when Stevie and Dolores have their plates piled so high that their food is literally defying the laws of gravity.

"Word has it that a special dessert has been prepared for our meeting,"

Dolores says as she sprinkles salt on her mashed potatoes "It's going to be served after our speaker completes his presentation."

"Where did you hear that?" Stevie asks.

"I don't know; around, I guess." Dolores shrugs.

"I haven't heard anything about that," I say. "But the chef is known for his desserts, so it could be any number of things. How exciting."

While we are eating, the bell rings: *Ding-dink-ding, ding-dink-ding.*

Elizabeth stands to speak. "Ladies, we have a lot to accomplish today, so I'd like to get the meeting started. Today is the deadline to submit your recipes and photos for the annual garden club cookbook. If you want your special recipes to be included, make sure you send them to Stephanie before midnight tonight. If you have any questions, see Stephanie after the meeting today." Stevie stands and waves as Elizabeth continues.

"Everyone was given a blank ballot form when you arrived. It looks like this." She waves a three-inch-by-five-inch piece of yellow pastel paper in the air. "I will write the names of the nominees on this board." She points to a whiteboard that has been set up on an easel at the front of the room. "There will be no limit to the number of nominees; however, there are only two positions to fill—that of president and one executive board member. The person with the most votes will be named president, and the second runner-up will assume the board member role. The name you are writing on your ballot is the name of the person you wish to have as president for next season. When you have completed your ballot, fold it in half and drop it in this basket when I come by your table." She holds up a bright red wicker basket. "I will come by your table in fifteen minutes to collect the ballots. Are there any questions?"

The room is strangely silent, which should have been my first clue.

"Okay then, let's open the floor for nominations."

Right on cue, Miss V. stands and says proudly, "I would like to nominate Stephanie Lewis." The ladies applaud as Elizabeth acknowledges the nomination and confirms acceptance from Stevie.

"Do we have any other nominations?" Elizabeth asks.

I know Stevie is expecting Julie Ann to be nominated as well, and I can't wait to see her surprise when she discovers that isn't going to happen, that her name is going to be the only one on the ballot, thus making her a shoo-in for president.

To say I'm the one surprised is an understatement when Alma suddenly stands and says, "I would like to nominate Dolores Delacroix," and the roar of the applause is nothing short of spectacular, a clear indication that something is rotten in Denmark.

Elizabeth acknowledges the nomination and confirms that Dolores not only accepts the nomination but is also willing to carry out the full duties and responsibilities of the office, to which Dolores replies, "You bet your sweet bippy I do!"

To everyone's surprise, there are no additional nominations for president.

"I thought Elizabeth was going to nominate Julie Ann," Stevie stammers.

"Well, it appears you thought wrong." I gently place my hand on her leg, lean in, and whisper, "Don't worry, Stevie—you will make a great president; and I think Dolores will be a very good executive board member. We are going to have a wonderful time next season!"

There are no additional nominations, and with only two names written in large block letters on the white board, Elizabeth tells everyone to vote wisely and enjoy their meal as she sits down to finish hers.

After fifteen minutes, Elizabeth begins to walk from table to table, retrieving the ballots in her wicker basket. It appears some of the ladies are having a hard time deciding whom to vote for, and it takes Elizabeth longer than usual to collect the votes. As she passes our table on her way back to the podium, Elizabeth reminds Alma and me to meet her upstairs to count the ballots once she introduces the speaker. She returns to the podium and calls everyone to attention.

"Ladies, thank you for joining us today and for participating in our voting process to crown the next Ms. Garden Club USA!" She pumps her fist in the air like a cheerleader, and I can see Stevie roll her eyes as the ladies applaud Elizabeth's contagious energy and excitement.

"However, before we make that special announcement, we are fortunate to have a very well-informed and well-connected employee of Harold's Nursery here to speak to us today—none other than Harold's own nephew, Daniel McRaney." She motions for Daniel to step up, and as he takes his place next to Elizabeth, I place my napkin on the table and stand up.

"Well, girlfriends, that's my cue to go count ballots. I wish you both the best of luck."

Dolores is clearly the dark horse in this race, and I have no doubt she is well aware that Stevie is going to be our next club president. I only hope that Stevie is actually prepared to accept the role; I have a feeling she didn't think she would stand a chance against Julie Ann, considering her close ties to Elizabeth, and I could tell she was genuinely surprised when Julie Ann wasn't nominated.

As I walk away from the table I can hear the whispers, but this time it's not about my weight or about the vote; this time the whispers are all about the good looks of our speaker. Daniel is young and well built, probably from all the digging and lifting he does, and his bronze tan, beautiful blue eyes, and blond hair make him somewhat of a GQ celebrity, especially among a group of ladies who are 'of a certain age.'

Daniel pulls some pamphlets from his backpack and starts his presentation with a compliment to our members. "Well, you couldn't have picked a better spot; this is a perfect location for our topic today— beautiful summer colors."

Daniel has been speaking for nearly thirty minutes when Elizabeth, Alma, and I return to the dining room.

When his talk is finished, the three of us join Daniel at the podium and Elizabeth thanks him for speaking. Dolores shouts over the applause, "Honey, you can speak to me any day of the week!"

We've grown accustomed to Dolores's unfiltered and sometimes crass comments, but I feel sorry for this young man as he nervously smiles, quickly gathers his belongings, and scoots out of our sight.

I can see from the corner of my eye that Stevie is smiling at me, but there's no way I'm going to make eye contact with her; I'm far too angry. No wonder she was so confident and cocky; it seems she's been working overtime behind my back. I'm certain of this because of the landslide decision made today; there's no way this would have happened otherwise.

"Ladies, the votes have been counted. Let's put our hands together for our next garden club president, Miss Dolores Delacroix." Elizabeth begins the applause, which starts strong but quickly becomes uncomfortably sparse as Dolores responds like a hysterical contestant who has won a spot on *The Price is Right*, as she jumps up and down, hoots and hollers, and high-fives anyone willing to reciprocate.

"Thank you, Dolores." Elizabeth continues. "And let's also welcome Stephanie Lewis as our newest executive board member." Stevie is slow to stand, and although the applause appears steadier for her, I get the distinct impression the members are feeling anything but comfortable with what has occurred this afternoon.

It hurts me deeply that Stevie would intentionally do this, but it breaks my heart more to think that she would do it while having a clear understanding of the ramifications of her actions. I have to believe that she doesn't fully grasp what she has done; that she doesn't realize the scope of her manipulation and what it could do to this club.

Instead of returning to my table after the results are announced, I take a vacant seat nearby as Elizabeth makes her closing remarks.

"As you all know, we only have one more meeting in our garden club season before we take our summer break, and it's a very important meeting, as this is when our newly elected officers will be sworn in. But that's not all; we will also be premiering our new annual garden club cookbook and launching our brand-new website and storefront! And if that isn't enough, we have another special announcement."

She motions toward me and says, "As many of you know, Gloria Vincent has recently handed over the reins of her award-winning magazine *NOLA 2 NOLA*, to Carlyle Communications, an international publishing conglomerate. And as many of you saw when we toured Gloria's lovely home at our garden club meeting last month, the *NOLA 2 NOLA* staff had considerable office space in Vincent Manor—space that Gloria has graciously offered to us for garden club administrative offices!"

I'm ecstatic when the ladies seem genuinely happy to be taking this step, because it's a step that has been a long time coming.

"That said, make sure you don't miss our June meeting at Amelie's." Elizabeth clasps her hands together. "And before we close today, there's one final thing. I know many of us are already planning our summer schedules, so I want to make sure you all have Saturday, July 16, circled in red. This is a very special sixtieth birthday bash at the Foundation Room for two of our very special members. Stephanie Lewis will celebrate her special day on

August 14 while we are on summer hiatus, and Gloria Vincent will celebrate this landmark occasion in just five days, on May 17. As our honorary board member and the ancestor of the woman who founded the Fleur-de-Lis Ladies Garden Club of New Orleans, Gloria Vincent is our own national treasure. So please join me in wishing this incredible woman a happy birthday."

I am stunned when, clearly on cue, the chef and his crew push a serving cart into the room that is topped with a huge sheet cake covered in purple fondant and delicate cascading wisteria, orchids, foliage, and gold ribbon, the trio of colors that form the tradition of the Quarter, and with a tasteful number of candles—one for every decade. Everyone in the room joins in as Elizabeth begins to sing, "Happy birthday to you, happy birthday to you ..."

I am humbled, honored, and, for once in my life, relatively speechless as I look out to see the ladies jump to their feet as they sing and clap. I blow out the candles to the sound of more applause, and as I hug Elizabeth I look over her shoulder to see Stevie standing toward the back of the room looking none to happy. I'm guessing she wasn't privy to this surprise, and while I'm really angry at her for stacking the votes, I feel sorry that she feels left out of this celebration. I motion for her to join me, but she shakes her head.

I'm not sure whether it's a good thing or not, but I don't cross paths with either Stevie or Dolores before I leave the Court of Two Sisters almost an hour later.

★ ★ ★ ★ ★

"Look, Maria"—I place the carefully wrapped dessert on the counter when I finally return home exhausted and elated—"I brought you and Randy birthday cake! It was so beautiful; you should have seen it!"

"Oh, Miss Gloria," Maria exclaims, "the colors are so pretty, so vibrant!" She sticks her finger in the icing and tastes it. "Ooh, very sweet, very good!"

I tell her all about the meeting and the results of the voting, and she just shakes her head.

"Do you know if Charlotte is still in?" I look at my watch and cross the kitchen to the elevator.

She nods. "She is still upstairs."

"I have a little bit of steam left in me, Maria; I think I'll head up to my office until dinner."

"Yes, Miss Gloria."

My back is aching, so I take some ibuprofen before I go upstairs. As soon as I open my office door, Charlotte meets me with eyes wide open.

"You received a package from Carlyle Communications; it's in a very big box."

I unwrap the box, and inside is an exquisite replica of a majestic clipper sail boat encased in glass with a note attached in what I recognize as Anthony's handwriting. I can feel the blood rushing to my face as I read it. Charlotte isn't saying anything, and her professionalism prohibits her from asking, but I know she's dying to know what the card says, and I boldly hold it out to her.

Come sail away with me. I love you. xoxo

"Oh my God!" Charlotte screeches.

"Shh, don't get Maria up here."

We both laugh just as Maria calls out in the distance, "Is everything okay, Miss Gloria?"

"Yes, everything is just fine," I call back.

Charlotte is acting like a giddy schoolgirl. "What are you going to do, Gloria?"

"What do you think I should do?"

"I say, go for it!" she exclaims without hesitation.

"Really?"

"Really. It's clear to me you two have been an item for months," she says, and I raise my eyebrows. "Don't worry—I haven't told a soul. But you always tell me to seize the moment and step out in faith; that's what I think you should do now. You deserve it; go have some fun."

I've been thinking about Charlotte's words all evening. Maria and Randy have retired to their quarters for the night, and I crawl up in my big, comfy bed and reach for my phone just as it rings.

"Hello, handsome," I say.

"There is no more mystery with caller ID," Anthony laughs.

"None." I smile. "Just don't ever have someone else call me from your cell phone, because that could get awkward."

"Only if you answer provocatively, and I do not think that 'hello, handsome' constitutes provocation."

"Why, because it's empirical fact that you are handsome?"

"Very funny, my sweet. So did you get my package?"

"I did."

"And?" he sounds like a young boy whose anticipation is killing him.

"And … I will give it thoughtful consideration."

"Thoughtful?" he says.

"Okay, serious consideration."

"Serious?" he challenges.

"I'm not sure what comes after thoughtful and serious, Anthony."

"Yes. That's what comes after thoughtful and serious consideration. Just say yes. I've been looking for you all my life, Gloria Vincent, and I'm not going to let you go now. We have only just begun this journey together."

"You sound like an old song from the Carpenters."

"Who?"

"Never mind." I laugh.

"Speaking of old songs, I downloaded the perfect ringtone for when you call me."

"Okay, so what song did you find?" I lean back into my stack of comfy pillows.

"Listen," he says, and when I hear *You Are So Beautiful*, I am overcome with emotion. I once told him it was one of my favorite songs.

"I fixed the phone so your name and number do not appear, just the beautiful melody and the sound of my heart beating as one with yours. You think that sounds corny, don't you?" he asks.

Although his words may sound corny, I have no doubt his sincerity is completely genuine.

"Sweet dreams," he says softly

We hang up; I reach over and turn out the lights.

Sweet dreams indeed.

CHAPTER 37

— Stephanie —

Friday, May 13

I know Gloria is upset, and the first thing for me to do today is talk to her. I just need to convince her that Dolores will make a fine president. I'm glad when she takes my call and we make arrangements to have lunch today at her house.

I'm walking out of my house by eleven thirty, and the warmth of the sun hits my face as I look up and see Touchdown Jesus, always a wonderful sight, day or night.

As I walk toward Esplanade, I run into one of the French Quarter's quality of life officers. The City of New Orleans has a large and growing homeless population, but thanks to organizations such as the Metropolitan Crisis Response Team, and of course Grace House, emergency aid and housing will reach a good many of them. We speak for a minute and then I excuse myself; I don't want to be late.

Maria points upstairs to Gloria's office. As I mount the stairs, I'm struck by how unusually quiet it is, and as I enter what used to be the main hub of *NOLA 2 NOLA*, all that remains is furniture, empty file cabinets, and artwork. Except for Charlotte's area just outside of Gloria's office, all vestiges of personal touches are gone. I'm not exactly sure what space has been allocated for garden club business—perhaps one of the private offices, rooms that before the renovation used to be bedrooms.

"Wow, it's like a cemetery in here!" I exclaim.

"I heard that," Gloria says as she comes out of her office. "Are you saying I look like the walking dead?"

"If the shoe fits," I tease. Gloria shoots a rubber band from a nearby desk at me. I'm encouraged by her playfulness, but the corners of her mouth remain fixed, horizontal, and the space between us feels awkward.

The fact is, she does look frail, although she covers it well with accessories and the right clothing. Today she's wearing a sundress with a loose knit cardigan wrapped around her shoulders. She looks like she walked out of a magazine.

My eyes travel over the area. "I never realized how big this space is. How come you didn't tell me you were offering nesting rights to the garden club?"

"How come you didn't tell me you were fixing the votes?" She crosses her arms.

"I didn't fix the votes!"

"What do you call it then?"

"I call it taking a chance on the underdog. Dolores will make an excellent president!"

"Seriously, Stevie?" She squints her eyes and then quickly says, "Wait," and holds her palm out to me. "Don't answer that; let's start over."

Gloria closes the space between us and gives me a somewhat hesitant hug, "Hi Stevie. It's good to see you. How about we go downstairs for some outside dining?"

We walk downstairs and out onto the patio. The pool looks so inviting that I'm tempted to remove my shoes and dip my toes. The large umbrella provides us with ample shade, and the warm light breeze is a gentle reminder that summer is just around the corner.

Maria is right behind us with cold and refreshing lemonade. Perfect for today.

"You have the most beautiful patio. Dolores has done such a fabulous job." I take a sip. "She's a very gifted person."

"Yes, she is quite gifted, in *this* area." Gloria waves her hand at the luscious greenery that sprouts abundantly and continues. "Dolores has more knowledge of plants and flowers than anyone in the club, including you and I combined, and she undoubtedly has the stamina and willpower to succeed in business endeavors no matter the odds. But mark my words when I say that I do not feel group leadership is an arena where she is going to thrive. It's like tossing a grade-school girl into a college-level classroom and telling her to "get with it!" It's cruel. That said, I have to ask you, Stevie, why have you so forcefully thrust her into this position?"

"I didn't force her! She agreed to do it, and she was voted in!"

Gloria doesn't take her eyes off me as she leans forward and fixes her steely gaze on me.

"Exactly whose idea was it, Stevie?"

I want to shout, "Does it really matter whose idea it was?" But I realize that it does matter and that perhaps I've made a terrible mistake.

"Uh … mine," I say.

"And I suppose you offered to help her with the responsibilities, correct?"

"Uh … yes."

"So let me get this straight, Stevie." Gloria leans back in her chair. "You're going to help her secure the meeting locations because she doesn't have the connections—you do. You're going to help her develop the yearly notebook because her administrative skills aren't quite up to speed. Oh, and you're going to make all the phone calls, give all the meeting announcements, and write all the e-mails because her communication skills are, should we say, a tad raw?" She pauses and crosses her legs. "So tell me, Stevie, what exactly is Dolores going to do as president?"

I'm afraid I don't have an answer for my friend, and I'm afraid her wisdom has once again surpassed my wit, but I need her to know that my intentions were honorable.

"I know you wanted me to be president, Gloria, but not everyone has leadership qualities like you. I have never wanted that kind of responsibility; that's not why I joined this club. You know I'm a hard worker and can handle any task. That's because I'm a worker bee, not a queen bee. That would be you." I give her a little smile.

"So because you don't see yourself as a leader, you have taken on the 'anonymous' role of garden club president with Dolores as your marionette?"

It feels like the air has been sucked out of my lungs when the realization of her words sinks into my brain as she continues.

"Stevie, you underestimate your abilities; you always have. You are capable of handling a lot more than you realize. But I understand that something is holding you back. After all these years, I'm still not sure what it is, but deep down inside *you* know and God knows, and between the two of you I'm sure you'll work it out." She takes a sip of her lemonade.

"But that doesn't solve the current situation, does it?" I swirl the ice around in my glass.

"No, it doesn't."

We agree that I need to meet with Dolores and discuss this, and the more we talk about the situation, the worse I feel for Dolores, because in spite of her bravado, I have a feeling she is shaking in her boots over this. It wasn't fair of me to put her in this position. In the big scheme of things, I'm feeling pretty rotten about what I've done; and, the weight of Gloria's disappointment in me makes me feel like a heel.

"Do you forgive me?" I ask.

"Of course, silly." She puts her hand on mine.

"Do you still love me?" I whisper.

"Oh Stevie, of course I do! If my love for you was dependent on some of the choices you make, we'd have been toast years ago!" She laughs.

"Thanks a lot." I roll my eyes at her.

"You are most welcome." Her lips turn up in a little smile.

"Speaking of choices"—she folds her brocade napkin, sets it on the table, and stands—"I've got an important one to make, and I could use your expert advice. Do you have time? I want to show you something in my office."

"Sure." I slide my chair back and follow her inside the house.

Our heels click on the hardwood floor as we walk up the stairs and down the hallway. I follow Gloria into her office, where she points to a beautiful model of a clipper ship sitting on her sideboard.

"Well now, that's an interesting piece of art." I walk over to look at it more closely.

At about three feet long and two feet high, the intricate replica is really quite spectacular, but it's unlike anything else in her collection.

"It's a bit different from your other pieces, but I can see where you might—"

"I didn't buy it, Stevie. It was a gift."

"Really? It's quite some gift."

She hands me an embossed card with the Carlyle Communications crest at the top that reads "Come sail away with me, I love you. XOXO."

"I knew it! You bum!" I playfully slap her arm. "I knew it wasn't all innocent! So how long has this officially been going on?"

"It's not official; we prefer to keep it private."

"Okay, so how long has this unofficially been going on?"

"Several months?"

"Months? Are you serious!"

"He wants me to sail to Bora Bora with him." She looks like a fragile woman, but her words are strong and sure, and she is beaming with excitement.

I can't remember the last time I've seen her like this; I'm not sure I ever have.

"I'm happy for you." I put my arms around her and give her a gentle hug. She's lost so much weight it's scary, but I know she'll come around once the chemo stops, because when I look into her eyes, there's a sparkle that says she's full of life. She really cares about this man.

Suddenly I connect the dots. "Oh my gosh, you've been sleeping with him, haven't you?"

"That's a tad personal, don't you think?" She seductively looks out from under her lashes and grins.

"I knew it! I can't believe you kept this a secret from me!" I look down at the card again.

"Hold your horses!" I stare at the card. "When he says 'I love you,' does he mean I love you, I love you? The real I love you?"

"As opposed to the fake I love you?" Her eyes crinkle at the corners.

"Wow, this is unbelievable. It's a lot to take in."

"I know." Gloria sits down on one of the wing back chairs in her office and clasps her hands on her lap.

"Well." I sit on the chair next to her. "Do you love him?"

"I think I just might," she whispers.

"Wow. Wow." I'm not sure what to say. It's a lot to process. Then I see Gloria look over at the grand ship and bite her bottom lip.

"Well, I say you should go for it!"

"That's funny; Charlotte used those exact words."

"She knew about this before me?"

"Take it easy, Stevie; I just told her yesterday when this was delivered."

"Okay, so how soon after your last treatment before you can travel?

I think a boat trip with Francois Carlyle might be just the right thing for you. I can't wait to hear the tongues wag about that when it happens! This gets more like the Jackie O. story every day!"

The idea is starting to grow on me when I notice she's looking at me strangely.

"Stevie, I've been seeing Anthony Carlyle, *not* Francois."

To say I'm dumbfounded is an understatement.

"Uh ... I ... oh," I stammer. "You're kidding, right?" I stare openmouthed.

"No, I'm not kidding."

"Anthony Carlyle and you? You and Anthony Carlyle?"

"Yes." She nods. "Is that so unbelievable?"

There is no way I can wrap my brain around this right now; I'm afraid I'm going to say something stupid and unforgiveable.

"Wow, I'm speechless; that's a lot to swallow. Ooooooh, I didn't mean it!"

Great, Stevie, open mouth and insert foot and anything else you can find.

"Stevie!" Gloria squeals.

"Sorry, sorry." I glance at my watch and jump up. "Well, girlfriend, on that note, I'm afraid I'm going to have to think about this for a while. Don't worry—my lips are sealed." I make the motion of zipping my mouth.

"Uh, Gloria, I didn't realize how late it is. I really do have to head out, but let's talk more about this later, okay?"

"Okay," she sighs, and she stands.

"Seriously, Louis and I are going to Irene's for dinner with Brenda, and Tim and I need to go change clothes and spruce up. I didn't realize I'd been here so long."

"I understand." She gives me a peck on the cheek and waves me toward the door. "Give them my love," she says as I all but fly out the door and down the stairs.

This is almost impossible to comprehend. Anthony Carlyle must be fifteen or twenty years her junior! Is she serious? She's going to be the laughingstock of the Quarter when people find out.

I'm crossing Governor Nicholls when I see Elizabeth's Range Rover parked in front of her house. It's packed with stuff, and the back hatch is wide open. I wonder if *she* knows about Anthony.

I walk toward her house as she's coming out through the gate. She's surprised to see me.

"Stephanie, what are you doing here?"

"I saw the car wide open and thought I'd say hello. I just left Gloria's; I'm on my way home. What are you up to?" I try to sound friendly.

"My divorce was finalized last week, and I was officially awarded this house in the settlement. I'm moving the rest of my things in from the big house."

I'm not sure what to say, as "congratulations" doesn't seem appropriate. "Good riddance" would be applicable, but that doesn't feel right either.

"I'm sorry, Elizabeth. Is there anything I can do?"

She looks at me with piercing eyes and simply and firmly states, "Yes, stop acting like a spoiled brat. Your shenanigans yesterday were unbelievable. What part of your brain can conceivably think that Dolores is capable of leading that group?"

"Obviously I'm not alone; she was voted in by our members."

"Really, Stephanie? Is that how you're going to play this?" She marches to her car and grabs another box. "You know as well as I do the only reason the majority of the garden club ladies voted for Dolores was because you told them to. You did whatever you had to, to get your way. Shame on you!" The veins in her forehead are popping out, and I'm taken aback by her words.

"You know, you could have told me about the surprise birthday cake. She *is* my best friend."

"Seriously? You could have fooled me." She sets the box back in her car and perches on the edge of the hatch; it appears as though she's fighting back tears. "Stephanie, do you have any idea how much you hurt Gloria— and the club itself?"

"She's fine. Don't you think you're overreacting a bit? I told you I just left her place; we talked about the situation. We're going to fix it. Everything is going to be okay."

Elizabeth looks up at me and shakes her head as tears spill from her eyes. "Everything is not going to be okay." Her lower lip quivers.

I can see how insensitive I have been to this girl. I just left Gloria's, where I had to apologize for my bad behavior, and now, ten minutes later, I'm apologizing again. What is the matter with me? Clearly she's distraught about her own situation.

"Elizabeth, I'm so sorry about your marriage, the divorce. I can't imagine the pain you and your children are going through. All of this upheaval has to be hard. Please believe me, I'm really not an insensitive bitch. Is there something I can do? I will help in any way I can."

"Is that what you think this is about? Me? All of this?" She waves her hand at the house and the boxes in the car and almost savagely wipes the tears from her eyes as she stands and faces me. "Gloria has become my best friend too, and I didn't tell you about the surprise cake because I figured you'd find a way to put the brakes on it because it wasn't *your* idea, because it didn't fit in with *your* personal property rights over Gloria's life!" I take a step back as she rocks forward on the balls of her feet like a wild dog being held at bay by a restraining leash. "But I couldn't stand the thought of waiting until your star-studded birthday bash to show her how much she is loved, because she probably won't be there!"

"Of course she's going to be there; don't be silly. We've been planning it for months."

"She's dying! I think Gloria is dying!"

"That's not true. She's doing much better. Why would you say such an awful thing?" I stammer. "You don't know what you're talking about."

"I do know! I lost my aunt to cancer last year, and Gloria has the same symptoms, she's getting the same treatment. She obviously has something more than 'random cancer cells'; she looks the same as my aunt did before she died!" She takes a deep breath and gives in to the cascade of tears as she turns, reaches up, and slams the car hatch shut. "I love her too, Stephanie! And I hate to see her like this. It hurts a lot, and I don't know what to do."

She turns and runs into her house. As the front door slams shut I can't help but feel incredibly sorry for her. She has confused Gloria with her aunt, a woman she obviously cared a great deal about. I feel bad that on top of everything else she is dealing with, she is still grieving the death of her aunt.

Gloria isn't going anywhere, except maybe to Bora Bora with a wealthy boy toy.

CHAPTER 38

— Gloria —

Tuesday, May 17–Gloria's Sixtieth Birthday

I awake to the smell of freshly baked apple cinnamon bread, immediately thankful that my in-home treatment yesterday hasn't left me nauseated. I can already tell this is going to be an amazing day.

Thank you, Lord, for sixty glorious years!

I can hear Randy and Maria plotting something outside my bedroom. Just then the door magically opens and Coco comes sauntering in wearing a cone-shaped birthday hat and a colorful scarf tied around her neck.

"What excellent taste in accessories you have!" I rub behind her ears, and she gives me my first official birthday kiss of the day.

By the time I shower and dress, Anthony has already called twice, and I'm heading out of my suite and into the kitchen when Stevie calls and sings to me.

"Happy birthday to you, happy birthday to you, happy birthday old lady, happy birthday to you!"

"Thank you, maestro. But if I'm an old lady, what does that make you?"

"Younger than you." She laughs. "Louis and I will be picking you up at five thirty; I'm pretty sure he is more excited about this than you are."

Tonight my dear friends are taking me to Commander's Palace for a birthday celebration dinner. I'm really going to have to pace myself today. After chemo treatments, I'm well aware how quickly things can turn on a dime.

"Okay, gotta go," Stevie says. "I'm sure you're going to be Miss

Popularity today. I just wanted to be the first to sing to you, to make sure you start your day out right."

"Thank you; however, might I suggest voice lessons before you decide to take your show on the road?"

"Ouch! Tell you what, I'll make you a promise."

"What's that?"

"I'll practice before our party so I can carry a tune that day in Grammy-award fashion."

"I'll hold you to that promise." I laugh.

"Tonight is going to be fun, Gloria, but I'm telling you, our big birthday bash is already the talk of the town. It's going to be the event of the summer!"

"I'm certain it will be, with you at the helm," I laugh.

Tonight is only part one of the celebration to commemorate our sixty years. In true southern belle fashion, we will drag this birthday event out for several months. It will culminate in a grand soiree at the elegant Foundation Room. Right now the July 16 party seems a long way off. Right now I just want to get through today. My one-day-at-a-time focus has been working out pretty well for me, and I don't want to jinx it.

The deliveries begin just as I hang up the phone. I see the Old Metairie florist van pull into the driveway.

By the end of the day, my house will look and smell like a funeral parlor. By sunset it will seem that every garden club member, philanthropic group, and company vendor who has ever advertised with or had stories in *NOLA 2 NOLA* has sent flowers, fruit baskets, and gifts.

The simple card that comes from Anthony early in the day touches my heart the most:

My Darling:
It is impossible to place a value on what you mean to me. In lieu of flowers, which I have no doubt you do not lack in your home today, I have made a donation to Grace House in the amount of $10,000 for every decade you have graced this planet.
All my love.
Anthony xo

When I look outside and see Emme's and Elizabeth's cars parked on the street, I'm excited, and I head upstairs to share this incredible news with them. They didn't waste any time moving their things into the old *NOLA 2 NOLA* offices, and it already feels like they've been here for ages.

I hear the girls in the break room talking, and the smell of fresh coffee hangs in the air like succulent perfume.

How I miss coffee.

"Happy birthday!" they shout as I come through the door, making my heart skip a beat with surprise.

"Oh, gosh, are you okay, Gloria?" Elizabeth asks, rushing to my side.

"I'm fine; you just scared the living daylights out of me, that's all."

"Sorry! We were waiting for you to come upstairs to give you this." She points to a lovely gift bag on the table. "It's from both of us"—she points to Emme and then herself—"but you can't open it until I get back; I need to meet someone at CC's in five minutes. Will you be around for a while?" I nod my head. "Good, I'll be back to the office within the hour." She waves as she heads toward the stairs. "I do love to say that—'the office.' It has such a nice ring to it!"

After she disappears, I walk around and look at what they've done.

"I must say, you've both settled in quickly. I'm very impressed."

"Trust me," Emme says, "we're the ones who are impressed. We've been up here for dozens of meetings, but we never paid attention to the actual space—the way everything has been planned and designed. It's amazing! Thank you for this opportunity, Gloria."

"You are most welcome; it's a pleasure to have you gals here."

I meander over to her desk. "Emme, have you received anything from Carlyle Communications?" I nonchalantly ask.

"Carlyle Communications?" She checks her list of auction donors and sponsors. "I don't think so."

"No, I'm sorry, not for the auction. I just discovered that Mr. Carlyle made a donation to Grace House in honor of my birthday. I want to make sure it doesn't slip through the cracks."

As though a gift of $60,000 ever could.

"How thoughtful of him," Emme says. "I'm tracking donations on a separate list." She hits a few keystrokes on her keyboard. "We've been receiving donations for a couple of weeks in honor of your big day; eighteen checks came in just today! Look at this list."

I walk behind and peer over her shoulder at the Excel spreadsheet she has pulled up on her screen.

There are dozens of donations ranging from $25 to $1,000, and I shake my head in amazement. "Oh my goodness, I had no idea."

She scrolls to the bottom and points. "Look at the total, Gloria."

I'm stunned by the amount donated by so many people. "I'm going to want to write each one a thank-you note," I say, "so please make sure Charlotte gets that list."

"Yes, ma'am. But I don't see Mr. Carlyle's gift; do you know when he mailed it?" She looks intently at the list as she conducts various data sort options and comes up fruitless.

"I could be wrong, but I doubt it was mailed. Check for a wire transfer directly to the bank from an account in France."

"Really?" She appears confused. "A direct deposit? I didn't know anyone could do that on their own—without prior authorization, I mean."

I can't help but laugh at her comment, and I resist the urge to tell her that Anthony is hardly just "anyone," and I can't wait until she sees how much money he has donated. His gift alone could pay off the mortgage on one of our Grace House shelters.

"Oh my gosh!" I'm startled by her sudden outburst as she moves her face closer to the screen to see the list of deposits she has pulled up. "Is this amount correct? Did they make a mistake? This can't possibly be right."

Sure enough, a deposit of $60,000 is showing up from Le Banque France, and I rest my hands on her shoulders as I stand behind her and look at the screen.

"There's no mistake. It's correct. Ten thousand dollars for every decade."

"Yahoo!" She jumps out of her chair and nearly knocks me over with her exuberance. She grabs me in a bear hug and then almost immediately checks herself for what I assume she thinks is a breach of professionalism and pulls away.

"I agree 100 percent! Yahoo!" I yell at the top of my lungs, pump my fist in the air, and give her what I hope is an even bigger hug as she jumps up and down.

I can't wait to tell Stevie about this donation when I see her at dinner tonight. But then again, I'm not quite sure how she feels about the Anthony situation. Other than her call this morning, we haven't talked since she was here on Friday. I've been trying not to think about her reaction to my personal news or about the President Dolores situation, although I know we'll have to address both soon.

CHAPTER 39

— Stephanie —

Tuesday, May 17

"Hurry, Louis; I don't want to be late."

"Slow down, Stevie; we have plenty of time. You know we won't have to wait on Gloria; she's always punctual." He gives me a sarcastic grin.

Sure enough, as soon as we pull into the driveway, the side gate opens and Gloria makes her way to the car. She looks stunning, absolutely beautiful; but frail—very, very frail.

"Louis is our chauffeur tonight." I nod toward Louis.

"At your service, ladies." He dips his head.

Gloria and I are a couple of Chatty Cathys all the way to Commander's Palace.

Once inside, we are quickly seated.

The service is impeccable here, as is the food. Our orders are placed and the wine is poured. Louis and I look at each other, raise our eyebrows, and grin.

"I know you were probably wondering if you were getting a gift from us."

"Stevie, this is all the gift I need—dinner with my two most favorite people in the world at one of my most favorite restaurants. Nothing could top this." She reaches over to hold our hands.

I turn to her and say, "We have a surprise for you, and it will be delivered to your courtyard tomorrow."

Louis quickly pulls an envelope from his jacket pocket and hands it to Gloria.

"What is this?" she says in a higher-than-normal pitch.

"Just a little something we had to dig around for. No pun intended."

Gloria slides a photograph from the envelope. Her eyes open wide with surprise.

"Is this for real?"

"Yes, ma'am. It's the gift that keeps on giving." We all bust out laughing.

The photo is of a forest pansy redbud. Gloria and I have a mutual friend in Southlake, Texas, who has several of these beautiful trees in her front yard. We both love the way the leaves shimmer like silver dollars. Gloria says the leaves dance when the wind blows.

"Since I'll probably never own one, I figured this is a gift we can share. It will be on your property. You can nurture and maintain it, and I can enjoy it."

Gloria smiles at me and says, "Oh, of course, Stevie. I adore these trees. Where do you think I should put it?"

"These redbuds love shade and lots of moisture. Perhaps at the north wall; the house should supply ample shade from the afternoon sun. I'd also advise a soaker bag through the summer, at least for a few weeks."

Gloria looks at me and slightly cocks her head. "Well, dear, you certainly know your trees."

"Not really, only the ones I love and the ones I hate." I give her a half grin.

"You are so bad, Stevie."

The main course is served, and Louis begins devouring his rack of lamb. I'm savoring my steak. Gloria was smart and called ahead to inform the chef of her special dietary needs. I'm not sure what it is he prepared for her, but I'm glad I'm not eating it.

I decide there's no time like the present to go ahead and bring up the "Dolores" issue.

"Gloria, Dolores and I have met, and after a very lengthy conversation, we have a solution, if we can get your blessing." Gloria looks intrigued. "We'd like to implement something new in the garden club. We'd like to be the first co-presidents. What do you think?"

She glares into my eyes. "What's that I hear? You want to change something?"

I roll my eyes. "Yeah, I knew that was coming."

Then her reaction pleasantly surprises me.

"I think that's a great idea, Stevie. This might be exactly what the club needs. With Elizabeth's plans to increase membership, this could entice more women to get involved, especially if they can share responsibilities. I'll call an executive board meeting so we can have this approved by the June meeting. I'm very proud of you, Stevie. You and Dolores really came through on this one."

The entire evening at Commander's Palace has been incredibly enjoyable. Louis excuses himself to go visit a table where some of his rock camp buddies are dining.

Gloria takes a sip of her hot herbal tea. "You've been rather quiet about our last conversation at my house, Stevie. It isn't like you." She looks out from under her lashes. "You know what—who—I'm talking about."

"I really don't know what to say about that, Gloria. Truthfully, I've kind of put it out of my mind."

"Okay, so while you've been putting it out of your mind, do you think I'm out of mine?" she asks.

I start to blurt something out, but she can see an unusual level of restraint, and I change my mind.

"I think you are a big girl and you need to do what you feel is best. I just don't want to see you get hurt by him or by public opinion."

"Oh, for Pete's sake! Is that what you're worried about? That people will talk? Oh, honey, people have been talking about me since I was born. That's the least of my concerns."

"And you believe he's sincere in his affection?" I ask.

"Not really, he just wants me for my luscious body." She winks.

"Gloria." I reach out and touch her arm.

"Yes, I believe he is sincere. That's not what worries me."

"Then what?" I look puzzled.

"He's a wonderful man, and I've fallen head over heels for him. He has brought life to places in my world that I thought were dead. But"—her lower lip trembles—"if he remains with me, he will never have children, and I think he would make a wonderful father. In many ways, his life is just starting, and mine? Well, who knows."

CHAPTER 40

— Gloria —

Monday, May 23

I've persuaded Stevie that it will be fine if she doesn't accompany me to the center today. I'm pretty sure she's secretly relieved. I haven't been totally honest with her about all the tests I've had or the test results.

The fact is, I haven't been totally honest with myself either. I weigh in at 112 pounds. The red digital numbers are like a wake-up signal to my brain.

"Do you know if Dr. Lucerne is in the center today?" I ask the nurse. "I'd like to talk with her if that's possible."

Sarah conducts the usual tests: blood pressure, temperature, weight. "Actually, your doctor has ordered a CT scan before we start treatment today, and she plans to see you after today's infusion. Will that work for you?"

"Yes, of course. But are you sure about the scan?" I ask.

"I'm sure. This is the radiology order." She hits a few keystrokes, and the order comes up on the screen. She confirms my name and today's date and points. "Yep, it's scheduled for this morning, and it looks like your ride is here."

A handsome young man from the radiology department rolls a wheelchair into the room. I've learned it does no good to insist that I'm capable of walking. I look at his nametag and sit down in the chair. "Are you old enough to drive, Adam?" He laughs as we head down the corridor, stopping briefly at the lab, where my blood is drawn for some additional tests.

I've soon completed the CT scan and am resting comfortably on the recliner in a treatment cubicle as the medication drips through the IV line. Dianne, one of my favorite nurses, asks how I've been doing.

"The nausea has subsided quite a bit, but I have zero taste buds left. Nothing tastes good. I'm forcing myself to drink protein shakes, but I'm a little worried about my weight."

"Unfortunately, that's one of the major side effects of chemotherapy drugs. They destroy your taste buds while they destroy your cancer. But talk to Dr. Lucerne about your concerns when you see her today."

Dianne reviews my medications and dosages.

"Dianne, can you also make a note that my lower back is still giving me trouble? I'm not sitting at my desk nearly as much as I used to, but it doesn't seem to be getting better. And I'm not sure if this has something to do with one of the new medications, but my skin is itching all over."

"I'm entering that info right now," she says while continuing to type.

Today's treatment seems to take forever. I guess I'm just ready to get on with my life. I'm ready to say good-bye to the side effects of the chemotherapy and all the medications. I'm ready to eat, drink, and get fat and sassy! Frankly, I'm ready to throw caution to the wind and go to Bora Bora with Anthony.

After my treatment is finally over, I'm sitting in one of the comfortable chairs in Dr. Lucerne's private office. I'm paging through a book I picked up from the side table when she enters.

I'm always impressed by her handshake. It's firm and professional, yet warm and kind. She takes the chair next to mine, and we chat for about five minutes. I am immediately concerned when she transitions into doctor mode.

"Gloria, I have the results from your CT scan. I also ran more blood work"

I'm completely surprised by this news. "Well, that was fast."

"I am concerned, as are you, about your weight loss."

I lean forward and wince in pain.

"Is it your back?" Doctor Lucerne asks.

"Yes, but I'm okay; it must have been the way I was sitting. I've gotten used to this backache over the years."

"Gloria, the CA 19-9 is a blood test that measures the level of antigens, the substances that cause the immune system to make a specific immune response in the blood serum of a person with pancreatic cancer."

I hear myself take a deep breath. I've known from the start I had more than just "the presence of cancerous cells," and that the point of origin was *in* my pancreas. Yet hearing Dr. Lucerne say the words "pancreatic cancer" is a reality check. I think I hoped in some distorted way that if I didn't actually say the words, then the facts wouldn't actually be facts and somehow the chemotherapy would magically make the cancer disappear. After all, we hear stories like that all the time, right?

"So what's my level?" My throat is dry.

"When we started treatment, your level was already significantly elevated at 500 units per milliliter."

She fixes me with an intense gaze and talks in a soft and melodic cadence that conveys both tremendous authority and genuine compassion.

"Gloria, there's no easy way to say this. Your current CA 19-9 is over one thousand units per milliliter, and the scan has revealed that the present course of treatment isn't working. The tumor in your pancreas has continued to grow, and the pain you have in your back is directly related to the pressure of this growing tumor."

Dr. Lucerne is sympathetic and caring as she leans forward and takes my hand. "Gloria, this cancer is very aggressive. It has spread to your liver, and there are significant spots on surrounding organs as well. I'm so sorry. Your cancer is too far advanced for any type of surgery. We will do all we can to help you. There are people who have defied the odds, but the prognosis for your illness doesn't look good." She squeezes my hand and says softly, "I want you to know that I will help you through this."

If I could organize my thoughts in this moment, I would admit to the good doctor that I've created scenarios in my head of what I would ask her in this situation. I've envisioned how I would flow seamlessly into a rational conversation with her about my feelings, questions, and the choices I needed to make. In those fantasy scenarios I am always composed and supremely stoic as I address the real possibility that I might die much sooner than I expected.

Yet in this painfully real moment I cannot find my voice to discuss these things. I can only look into her eyes and trust her to help me, and trust God to see me through it.

"I imagine this must be one of the hardest parts of your job," I say as I squeeze her hand. She does her best not to reveal her true emotions.

"Gloria, I know this is a lot to assimilate, and we can talk about other options: clinical trials, experimental treatments, and medications to manage your pain. Right now we have to immediately address the jaundice."

"Guess my spray tan isn't working, eh?" I nervously smile.

"The tumors are putting pressure on your bile duct, and it is almost completely swollen shut. We've got to go in and insert a stent so your liver can drain properly. We can do this in an outpatient setting. I'd like to check you in and keep you overnight."

"Now?" I stammer.

"Is that possible?" she asks quietly.

"Can it wait, even for a day? I ... I ... I need to process this, I need to prepare, I need to tell someone."

Actually, I'm not certain what I need to do first, only that I'm not ready to do this today.

"I understand, Gloria, but I need you to understand this is critical. We can address this and treat it, but I need you to understand the consequences if you walk out of here and pretend this isn't happening."

We agree that I will check in first thing Wednesday morning for the procedure and that I will return immediately if I experience changes in my current condition before then.

I've called Randy to pick me up, and I pause for a time in the lobby to appreciate the comforting sounds of the water features and take in the expansive view of the great Mississippi. I've lived such an amazing life. Somehow, I'll find a way to deal with this current situation, but I'm not yet ready for God to call me home.

When the elevator doors open on the lower level, Randy is waiting and gallantly extends his arm. "Your ride awaits, senora." He smiles as I link my arm into his.

I'm so thankful to Randy for discovering this alternative entrance. It has afforded me the ability to worry less about the need to wear my public game face. Not that my public and private personae are so vastly different, but there have been times when it has taken every ounce of fortitude I can muster to keep the hounds of nausea hell at bay.

Fortunately, this is not one of those times, as my stomach is unusually calm, which surprises me considering the news I just received.

When Randy opens the car door, it's not as easy as it used to be to slide in.

"Randy, have you gone and turned our lovely Ghost into a low-rider? It seems much closer to the ground these days." He chuckles and gingerly helps me inside.

I'm mostly silent for the ride home as I concentrate on my breathing and will myself and my stomach to remain calm. I go over and over Dr. Lucerne's words in my mind, not yet willing to allow them to pierce my heart.

I can see Randy occasionally look at me in the rearview mirror, and when I catch him I smile.

"I'm doing okay," I assure him.

When we pull up to the house, Maria is standing by the door, a huge smile on her face. Although I'm not sure what kind of secret code system they have, I've been aware since my second treatment that Randy communicates via text with Maria on our return trips, letting her know how I'm doing, what to expect when we arrive. They are never lengthy messages—he knows how I feel about texting while driving—but they are clearly in cahoots, and whatever their covert system, today he has obviously informed Maria that I'm not retching in the backseat like a frat boy on pledge night.

Dear Maria, you have been such a blessing.

I watch Randy walk around the car, give her a quick kiss on the cheek, and say a few words before she heads back inside and he opens my door.

It's even harder to get *out* of the backseat today than it was to get in, and I'm thankful for Randy's strong and steady arms as he helps me not only from the car but up the walkway to the house as well.

"It's always nice to have a handsome gentleman on your arm." I pat his sleeve and smile at Maria as she stands just inside the kitchen door, waiting for us. "You've got a keeper here, Maria." I wink.

"Yes, Miss Gloria, most of the time that is true."

"What do you mean 'most of the time'?" Randy growls in mock anger.

It's good to be home. The sight and scent of the birthday flowers and plants that have spilled over into the kitchen lift my spirits. It's been almost one week since my birthday. How quickly life can change.

"Can you folks have dinner with me tonight?" I ask Maria and Randy before I head to my bedroom to rest.

"Absolutely," they say, almost in unison.

Maria prepares a wonderful stew for their meal later that evening.

"This is delicious, Maria," says Randy.

I look over at Randy's bowl and see that his contains huge chunks of meat, most likely Maria's famous rich savory beef, and I lean over his bowl and breathe deeply, silently praying that the aroma won't turn my stomach.

"Oh my goodness ... that smells sooooo good!"

"You are welcome to have some," Randy offers.

"No! Maria says sternly. It is not good for Miss Gloria's tender stomach right now."

"She's right, Randy, but thanks anyway for the offer." He nods. "I do love your stew, Maria, and all the special meals and shakes you have been making for me, but I miss beef. I miss chicken. I miss sushi, Cajun gumbo, barbecue hot wings, and fried shrimp. I miss solid food, period!"

I get up and open the wine refrigerator and pull out a bottle without even looking at the label and set it down hard on the counter. "And I miss wine. Red, white, cheap, or expensive, it doesn't matter. But you know what? Even if I did throw caution to the wind and have a glass of this, I wouldn't be able to taste it! The only thing all this damn chemotherapy has managed to kill are my taste buds, and I want them back! I want my old routine back! I want my life back!"

When I finish my tirade, Maria and Randy both have concerned looks on their faces.

"I'm sorry." I sink back down in my chair.

They say you can run but you cannot hide. My time for hiding has come to an end as I tell them the results of my blood test and scan, including the urgent need to have stent placement surgery this Wednesday. I tell them everything, including the sobering official diagnosis.

"The doctor says I have stage-four metastatic pancreatic cancer."

Maria tries valiantly to fight back tears, and Randy's big hands swallow mine as he tries to comfort me. "We will get through this."

"I'm not sure how all this is going to play out, but it's very serious, and I have a feeling it's going to get worse before it gets better. I don't want this to sound like I'm giving up, because that isn't the case. I still have one last chemo treatment in this series, and Dr. Lucerne is doing some research on a clinical trial she heard about. But before we go any further, there is something I must tell you."

"You can tell us anything, Miss Gloria," says Maria, taking my hand. "You know that."

"I do know that, thank you. This is something I've been meaning to tell you for years—and I mean that literally. But for some reason I never got around to it. I want you to know that no matter what happens to me, you will both be provided for."

Their reaction goes from confusion to an uncomfortable clarity.

"Don't talk about such things!" Maria dismissively waves her hand.

Randy stands up and pushes away his chair. "I know I speak for both of us when I say that has never been a concern. Our only wish is to take care of you and Vincent Manor for as long as you need us," he says firmly, and Maria nods in agreement.

"I'm sorry if I offended you. I love you two so much, but before we get caught up in whatever it is we'll be facing, I need to know that you know where you stand. Please. It will make things easier on me knowing we have had this conversation. I won't talk about it again, I promise. Let me tell you what is already written in my legal documents. Please."

Randy sits back down next to Maria. "If it will make you feel better."

"It will, thank you." I take a sip of water. "I know you're aware that I am the last member of the Bronzinelle and Vincent families. There are no heirs to inherit my estate. I've decided to bequeath Vincent Manor to one of the historical societies. But whatever it becomes, it will still need full-time caretakers, and you will be offered those positions for the duration of your lives. The bottom line is that you will both remain an integral part of Vincent Manor for as long as you wish."

Randy is a big, burly brute of a man, yet I can see it takes every ounce of energy he has to keep from giving in to his emotions. Maria tries to speak, but her tears are flowing like Niagara as her husband puts his arm around her. Randy gently rubs her back as Maria wipes her eyes, and then he turns his gaze on me.

"Thank you, Gloria; that is very kind and generous. But with or without that, we will be here as long as you need us. We will not let you down."

"Thank you. I never doubted that. I love you both so much."

They envelop me in a tearful embrace that leaves me feeling both exhausted and refreshed. This duality of opposites is a strange feeling—one I will come to understand more as the days go by, when fear and trust, anger and peace, and sadness and joy walk side by side.

"Does Miss Stevie know?" Maria eventually asks.

"Not yet. She wasn't at my treatment today, thank God, but I won't keep this from her. I have to be in the hospital on Wednesday, so I need to tell her tomorrow." My mind begins to spin with things I need to do.

"Maria, I need to check in to the medical center early on Wednesday, and I won't be back until midday on Thursday, if everything goes well. I should probably plan to take the rest of the week off, but I've got a meeting at Bronzinelle Steel and several other things on my calendar I'll have to reschedule. I need to meet with Charlotte—oh, I need to tell her what's going on too."

Maria opens a nearby drawer and pulls out a five-inch-by-seven-inch lined notepad and pen and prepares to write.

"Tell me what you need, what you want."

I'm not sure there is rhyme or reason to the things I rattle off, but to her credit she writes furiously and doesn't question a thing.

"I'm going to call Stevie before I go to bed and see if she can come here for breakfast tomorrow, and pray I still feel as good then as I do now."

I can't believe how physically good I feel, and I hope it isn't just shock. I hope I don't have a delayed reaction that kicks me in the butt in the morning.

"I could call Miss Stevie right now," Maria offers, "if you would like? It might be easier for you."

"Good idea." I nod. "Thank you."

Maria is on and off the phone in less than two minutes and confirms that Stevie will be here at eight thirty tomorrow.

Lord, help me.

CHAPTER 41

—— Stephanie ——

Tuesday Afternoon, May 24

Maria greets me at the front door. "I will take you upstairs, Miss Stevie; that's where everyone is."

Today is surreal. I'm still reeling from the unbelievable facts Gloria disclosed when she invited me for breakfast. I've been walking around in a haze of disbelief and shock all day. Thank goodness I had time to share my concerns with Louis before he left town. Of course I agreed to return when Gloria called, but if this has anything to do with the bombshell she's already dropped, I'm not sure I can take it. How much does she expect me to process in one day?

"What happened? Is Gloria okay?" I grab Maria's arm a bit tighter than intended and release it just as quickly.

"Miss Gloria is fine," she says, trying to assure me.

"Then what's this about? Who's here?" I ask as I head toward the stairs.

"I made some little chicken salad sandwiches, and there's some of that truffle cheese you like. There is also tea and coffee."

I hear voices and laughter as I climb the last few stairs, and I'm a tad out of breath as I reach the top.

"Come and join us, Stevie," Gloria calls out as she sees me come around the corner. I take a deep breath and enter the room.

The first person I see sitting at the large conference table is Elizabeth. Things between us have been strained since our run-in on the street. However, we've managed to continue our collaborative work on the cookbook and website. Fact is, she is somewhat correct about her assumption, but I still refuse to believe that Gloria won't beat this. The only other person in the room is Emme, so perhaps this has something to do with Grace House.

Gloria is seated at the head of the table, looking every bit the part of a successful CEO. Given the news she shared earlier this morning, I can't help but wonder if she's thinking straight. I'm not certain I'd be thinking at all if our positions were reversed.

In spite of the fact that she's fighting for her life, Gloria still exudes an aura of power combined with a grace and goodness. It's reassuring to see her back in this environment. However, when I see a wheelchair sitting in the corner near the elevator, I'm suddenly reminded that things aren't like they used to be. When I look closer at Gloria, I am afraid they never will be again.

She looks pale and gaunt. Her usually prominent cheekbones are even more pronounced, giving her a skeletal look. Because I'm now aware of why her skin tone is turning yellow, I'm even more concerned. I put on my game face and smile.

"My, but aren't we looking rather bohemian." I give her a peck on the cheek and step back.

"Carolina had this made for me; don't you simply adore it?"

She's wearing a deep purple silk caftan with a long flowing scarf tied around her head. I've always loved that Gloria doesn't intentionally name drop, and I wonder if anyone else knows she's talking about Carolina Herrera, a well-known designer.

Gloria has always worn elaborate turbans and scarves, and the familiar look is comforting to me. She's been keeping her hair short since we got our drastic new hairdos a few months ago. She never lost her hair, as do many people who are on chemo.

"Forget what I'm wearing!" Gloria shouts. "Look at you, gorgeous, making a grand entrance as always!"

I spin around, showing off my new jumpsuit.

"Sorry I'm late," I say. "I had to get Louis off to the airport."

"I understand he is on his way to Las Vegas for Rock Camp this week, playing guitar with someone named Eric Johnson or something," she says.

Emme and Elizabeth laugh as Gloria motions to the chair on her right. "Sit here, I've saved this for you. I think you know everyone. But first grab yourself something to eat and drink."

She *thinks* I know everyone? Now I really am worried.

I grab a delicate gold-banded porcelain plate and fill it with an assortment of goodies, although my eyes are bigger than my appetite at this point. As I take the chair next to Gloria, I can smell her perfume, Creed Fleurissimo.

"I'm so glad all of you could join me today!" Gloria says, clasping her hands with childlike joy. "My absolute favorite people are in this room, and I mean that from the bottom of my heart." She takes a deep breath and continues. "As we begin, I need you to know that for the time being, everything I'm about to say must remain confidential. I know I can depend on all of you to honor that request."

"Of course," we all say, almost in unison, as she continues.

I can't tell if Emme and Elizabeth feel it, but as soon as Gloria begins to speak, I feel the air in the room suddenly get heavier, and it seems as though an unseen visitor has stepped uninvited into this inner circle.

I become acutely aware that I am deeply frightened, and instead of giving in to the wave of fear that threatens to strangle me, I give in to a wave of uncontrollable emotion.

I begin to weep.

"I'm sorry," I say.

Gloria's patient look says it all as she reaches over and places her hand firmly atop one of mine.

"Oh my God, I am so, so, sorry, Gloria." I shake my head as tears cascade down my cheeks. Elizabeth reaches over and sets a box of Kleenex down in front of me, none too gently, and Emme is fidgeting with a button on her jacket.

"I'm sorry, Gloria. I didn't mean to disrupt things, to be so disrespectful."

"I understand, Stevie." She continues to squeeze my hand. "I'm the one who should be apologizing, I didn't think about how deeply our morning meeting might have affected you."

She continues to hold fast to my hand but turns her attention to Emme and Elizabeth, as they look quite puzzled.

"Ladies, I have good and bad news to share with you. I wanted Stevie to be here to experience the good news, because she has already been privy to the bad news. But I wasn't thinking clearly; I didn't consider that it might be hard on her to hear it again. I was being grossly insensitive."

I look at my friend and pray that she understands the depth of my sincerity, especially since she's heading for surgery early tomorrow morning.

Gloria winks at me and proceeds.

"Okay, then I will cut right to the chase and address the elephant in the room. As you know, I've been undergoing chemotherapy treatments for the past several weeks. However, I haven't been totally honest with you. Dr. Creswell discovered the presence of some random cancerous cells when he conducted tests this past fall, but further tests showed the cells had an origination point located in my pancreas, where a small tumor was discovered in February. The chemotherapy has been in an effort to shrink the tumor so I could undergo surgery to remove it."

Emme bites her bottom lip, and Elizabeth gives me an I-told-you-so look as Gloria places her hands in her lap and continues. "I discovered only yesterday that the tumor is putting pressure on the bile duct, and this unsightly shade of yellow you see under my fading spray tan is actually jaundice. I will be undergoing a minor surgical procedure tomorrow to have a stent put in to help my liver drain properly."

I've remained calm throughout her disclosure. Elizabeth and Emme realize this information isn't coming to me as a surprise.

To their credit, or to Gloria's innate ability to downplay and manage crisis, neither of them are dissolving in overt displays of emotion. After answering a few of their questions and assuring them she is going to be fine, Gloria takes a sip of water and continues.

"There is no doubt in my mind that we serve a God of miracles. Everything is going to work out according to his plan. I feel compelled by my current health situation to stop dragging my feet about some ideas I've been contemplating. Rest assured these are not ideas that suddenly came out of the blue. What I'm going to share are thoughts I have been mulling over for quite some time. However, my sudden unexpected health situation has prompted me to address them now."

"Why? Is the procedure tomorrow dangerous?" Emme asks. "I mean, forgive me for being so blunt, but—"

"No, no, dear,"—Gloria waves her hand—"it's not dangerous at all; in fact, it's typically done on an outpatient basis. The only reason I'll be remaining overnight is because my doctor knows I won't have the good sense to stay off my feet and rest afterward." She grins. "I'm not worried about kicking the bucket on the table tomorrow, truly. I just had a personal epiphany that I really ought to share my ideas with you gals to see if you're even interested, and I figured there's no time like the present." She slaps her hands on the table and leans forward. "So, do you want to hear what I'm thinking?"

The room is so quiet one could hear a pin drop as we all nod and she continues.

"Elizabeth, I've watched you handle adversity, opportunity, and tragedy over the past several months, and I've come to admire and respect your tenacity. You've almost single-handedly brought our garden club into the current century. Plus, the work you are doing on the cookbook and website is nothing short of miraculous. You aren't afraid to assess a situation, make a firm recommendation, and take action."

"Thank you, Gloria," she whispers.

"I also know you are at the top of your class in real estate school. That's why when you get your real estate license I want you to consider coming to work for me, for the Vincent Estate. The fact is, Elizabeth, I've got real estate holdings all over this city, all over the state, and I've paid a fortune over the years to brokers, agents, consultants, and the like to help me buy, sell, trade, and manage all this property."

We are all mesmerized by what Gloria is saying.

"I'm not disclosing this for any other reason than to give you a big-picture vision. The Vincent Estate Trust currently owns multiple properties valued at somewhere in the neighborhood of fifty million dollars or so."

There is an audible gasp from all of us as she continues.

"I'd like to develop a small company for the purpose of maintaining, acquiring, and developing the real estate investments and holdings of the estate. I'd like you to consider the position of CEO of this division."

Elizabeth's violet eyes grow wide, and her hand flies to her chest.

"Make sure to breathe, dear." Gloria smiles and continues. "The position will include a yearly salary including commissions, benefits, and flexible hours. Your private office will be up here on this floor. You can choose any of the vacant editorial offices along this hallway." She points. "As I said, this is a broad-spectrum vision, and more finite details will be developed and forthcoming, but I'd like you to be thinking about this as you complete school and take your real estate license exam. I want you to know this opportunity is going to be available, if it interests you."

"Seriously?" Elizabeth shakes her head in disbelief.

"Seriously. But don't feel you need to respond now. I understand there is much to consider."

"Are you kidding?" She cups her face in her hands and shakes her head. "Of course I'm interested!"

Gloria's eyes sparkle. "Well, okay then! You give it additional thought, and we will talk more about this in the coming weeks."

Gloria turns her focus to Emme, who is smiling broadly and patting Elizabeth on the back. I'm not sure if the gesture is one of kindness or if she's keeping Elizabeth from hyperventilating. For all the drama that Elizabeth and I seem to have in our relationship, I'm strangely happy for her. Given her precarious situation, this is an ideal position. I have to agree with Gloria that she's a very talented gal, even if she does tick me off from time to time.

"Now, Emme. I know the administrative offices you have for Grace House are sorely insufficient. I don't want you to think of this as a temporary situation; I want to offer you permanent space here at Vincent Manor for the development department of Grace House."

Emme is visibly grateful as Gloria shares more of her thoughts about growing the Grace House outreach.

"As for you, Stevie, since it appears that you and Dolores will be key players in the garden club next season, I want you to be aware that I plan to give the garden club more space on this floor. The two of you can conduct your business with more resources, and more comfort."

When she is finished, Gloria looks exhausted.

"I can see you're all pleased by these announcements, but to be truthful, I'm a bit tired and need to rest now." She stands. "I don't want you to be worried about me tomorrow. Please don't feel the need to visit; it's a simple procedure. I'll be home on Thursday. However, I've asked

Stevie to be in touch with you via text throughout the day to give you updates." That's news to me, but I nod in agreement as Gloria turns to me.

"Stevie, would you come with me downstairs?"

I stand, and she links her arm through mine.

"Ladies, you are welcome to remain as long as you like; feel free to have more refreshments. You both have keys to lock up when you leave."

Elizabeth and Emme jump to their feet. They take turns thanking and hugging Gloria, and wishing her well. With our arms encircled in a group embrace, Emme says a short, sweet prayer.

As we walk slowly toward the elevator, I look over my shoulder to see Emme and Elizabeth standing very still as they watch us depart. When they see my eyes, they both wave and mouth the words "thank you." I'm not quite sure what they're thanking me for, as it's Gloria who is responsible for their good news. Then, as she leans on me for support, that's when it dawns on me: I am responsible for Gloria. She is depending on me, and Emme and Elizabeth are thanking me for taking care of her.

But I'm still upset that I didn't know the level of her illness, that she didn't trust me enough to share it sooner. I'm angry at God for letting this happen. I'm confused about what to say or do, how to think or feel.

Mostly, I'm scared stiff, until Gloria squeezes my arm.

"Well, that was fun!" Her eyes glisten, we step into the elevator, and the doors glide shut.

CHAPTER 42

—— Gloria ——

Wednesday, May 25

R andy, Maria, and Stevie accompany me to the Medical Center for my early morning check-in. I did my best to dissuade them, but they were having none of it. With my energy at a premium these days, I need to choose my battles wisely, and I decide this isn't going to be one of them.

My registration, pre-op examination, and OR prep are orchestrated like a theatrical production. I move seamlessly from area to area with a crew of highly professional technicians monitoring the production: nurses, assistants, lab technicians, anesthesiologists, and radiologists.

By the time they wheel me into the surgical suite, I'm pumped so full of relaxants and pain medications that I'm certain I'm levitating a foot off the table. I'm also pretty certain I say something horribly inappropriate to the two male aides who slide me from the gurney to the operating table.

When I awake from the operation, I can hear people whispering before I see them, and when I open my eyes, I need to blink several times before I remember where I am.

"Welcome back, sleepyhead." Stevie holds my hand and gently pushes a strand of hair off my forehead. "You are going to be blown away at how fast your color has changed. We've been watching since you got back from the OR, and it's amazing!"

"How long have I ..." I lick my dry lips as Maria approaches the other side of my bed and picks up a paper cup and a plastic spoon.

"Would you like some ice chips, Miss Gloria?"

I nod, and she spoons the refreshing ice into my mouth.

"You got out of surgery a couple of hours ago," Stevie says. "You've been up here in your room about an hour. Do you remember the doctor coming in and talking with you?"

I shake my head.

"Well, let me give you an update," she says. "You aced the procedure with flying colors. The stent is in place and clearly doing whatever it's meant to do, as you no longer look like an Oompa-Loompa."

"They also removed the port," Maria says quietly.

"Oh, thank goodness! That thing has been driving me crazy." I refuse to see this news as a sad ending. Dr. Lucerne talked to me before she scheduled my surgery. We agreed that another dose of chemo wasn't going to do any good.

I reach for the bed controls that are incorporated into the side rail and push the button to elevate my head. Stevie adjusts my pillows, Maria straightens my blanket. Randy is seated on a sofa near the window.

"Good to see you up." He smiles and nods his head.

"It's good to be up." I wink.

Hours later, Randy and Maria have returned home to feed Coco, and Stevie is still camped out at my bedside in a chair she pulled over from the sitting area. I'm not sure if she's resting or sleeping, as her head is nestled in her arms on the edge of my bed.

I reach out and gently stroke her hair as she slowly turns and blinks.

"Guess I dozed for a minute." She smiles. "How are you doing?" she whispers.

"I'm good, Stevie. How are you doing?" I continue to stroke her hair, and I can feel her body start to tremble and see her eyes fill with tears.

"Oh Stevie, I would have told you sooner, but I didn't want you to worry. I didn't want you to walk on eggshells around me, or treat me differently. And I guess in a way I figured if I didn't think of the cancer as an actual tumor, I could pretend it was something else, something the chemo could destroy. I'm sorry I laid all this on you so suddenly."

I doubt Stevie can even see me at this point, as her eyes are so cloudy from tears. I hand her a box of tissue from my bedside table and let her cry.

"Girlfriend?" I ask when her sobs have subsided. "I'm really going to need your help."

"Anything," she says as she blows her nose, "just name it. We're going to get through this. You are going to beat this, Gloria."

★ ★ ★ ★ ★

Monday, May 30

I've been home for three days and I'm still feeling like a truck ran over me when Maria rushes into my room and closes the door behind her.

"Mr. Carlyle is here, Miss Gloria." It takes a few minutes for my brain to register what Maria is telling me. "Miss Charlotte has escorted him upstairs to the conference room. I didn't know what else to do. He insisted on seeing you; he said he knows you are home. What do you want me to do?"

She is clearly flustered, and I suddenly realize this is very new territory for Maria. She has only ever known me to be involved with one man, Charles. And although I have not fully disclosed everything about our relationship to her, she's smart enough to put the pieces together.

"He doesn't know I'm sick, Maria; I haven't exactly told him. He kind of thinks it's my gallbladder."

"Do you think he doesn't know it's something more? Love isn't that blind."

"Who said anything about love?"

"Oh, Miss Gloria, I was born during the day, but it wasn't yesterday. Now, how about if Maria helps you get ready so you can talk to your young man?" She grabs a brush from my dresser table. "Maria can do your hair."

Uh oh, she's talking about herself in third person; I'm in trouble.

"How can I do this?" I say, the panic coming through in my voice. "I've just taken my pain meds; there's no way I can go upstairs right now. And besides, I look like a zombie! Look in my eyes, Maria; do I look like a zombie?" She looks close then steps back and turns me toward the bathroom.

"Your eyes look fine; your breath, not so much. Go brush your teeth and throw some cold water on your face. I will find something nice for you to wear. Vamoose!"

In short order I'm dressed in a floral maxi dress with a lightweight sweater, hair and makeup done. Maria pulls out a necklace and earring set in blue and purple amethyst. It goes perfect with the colors I'm wearing.

"Okay, where should I meet him? In the study? The courtyard? Perhaps at the dining room table?" We decide on a more casual location, where Maria can nonchalantly pass through from time to time to see if I'm doing okay.

In record-breaking time I'm primped, prompted, and positioned.

The granite countertop in the kitchen is a great idea, as I can place my feet on the rungs of the barstool. The three-quarters height of the counter allows me not only to lean but also to use it as leverage should I need to stand. I'm not handicapped; I can still walk, though I am a bit weak. The pain meds make me woozy. I've been using the cane or a helpful arm since I got home from the hospital; this counter will be my helpful arm.

As Maria helps me get situated, she comes up with a plan.

"If you find it is too much and you need to end things, tell me to check your calendar to see if your meeting with Mr. Smith is for today or tomorrow."

"Mr. Smith?" I'm confused. "I don't have a meeting with a Mr. Smith."

"I know that, Miss Gloria! It is a code so I can rescue you! And if things are going wonderful and you want Maria to disappear, tell me I'm free to run my errands. Randy and I will get out of your hair for a while. Okay?"

It's all I can do to keep from laughing hysterically at the entire scenario, but I appreciate her sincere concern. "Okay, Maria, I think I've got it. Mr. Smith keeps you in the room and ends the meeting and 'errands' gets me privacy. Got it! What other covert operations do you have up your sleeves?"

Maria chuckles and leaves to go get Anthony.

As I wait for them, I look down to see my mother's hands resting on the counter, so worn, so capable. Her tapered fingers are slender but substantial, strong but somehow still feminine. Her parchment-like skin is translucent, the veins like roadways on a map. However, my mother has been on the other side of heaven for years, so whose hands are these? The breath catches in my lungs when I realize I'm looking at my own hands.

When I see Anthony enter the room, I am overcome with emotion.

All thoughts of carrying on this elaborate masquerade are dashed. There is no way I can do this; I don't have the strength.

"I'm sorry I kept you waiting, Anthony. Maria and I were going to have some tea. Would you like to join us?" Maria doesn't skip a beat as she walks to the sink and begins to fill the teapot. "And Maria, after you get the water on the stove, can you please check with Charlotte to see if my meeting with Mr. Smith is scheduled for today or tomorrow?"

"Yes, Miss Gloria." She puts the teapot on the front burner and turns the knob. "I will be right back."

As soon as she leaves the room, Anthony wraps his arms around me. My return embrace is not as warm, and he steps back and looks into my eyes.

"What's wrong, Gloria? We have not spoken much since your birthday. Did my gift offend you?"

"Oh no, Anthony! It was wonderful!"

"Then what is it? You do not return my calls or my texts. It's as though you've disappeared."

"I'm sorry, truly; I've just been so busy. So when did you get into town?" I say lightly as we hear Maria coming back down the stairs.

"Please, Gloria, no small talk. Look me in the eyes and tell me to my face that you have not been avoiding me, that something isn't wrong between us."

I don't want to hurt this precious man, but I don't want to lie to him either.

"I can't do that, Anthony," I whisper as I look down and mindlessly twist my bracelet.

He steps away from me as Maria enters the room.

"Miss Charlotte said your meeting with Mr. Smith is today, and he should be arriving any minute."

"And that would be my cue to leave," Anthony says. "It was good to see you, Gloria." He kisses me lightly on each cheek and turns to Maria. "Good bye, Maria, it was nice to see you again." He takes her hand and places a polite and gentlemanly kiss on the back of it and then crosses the kitchen and lets himself out the back door.

Maria shakes her head. "*Ay dios mio*, he is a man in love."

I rest my chin in my hand and stare wistfully out the window as his car disappears. "Don't be silly."

"I may not know a great many things, Miss Gloria, but I do know love, and that man"—she points out the window—"he has it for you."

That may have been so at one time, but I fear I have just doused any flame Anthony Carlyle once had burning for me. My heart breaks with the memory of his face as he walked out the door and, in all probability, out of my life.

In the grand scheme of things, this is for the best. I don't want him to see me like this.

"Please help me to my room, Maria. I need to lie down."

CHAPTER 43

— Stephanie —

Thursday, June 9

"Wow!" Louis startles me with his compliment as I finish getting ready. "You look nice today. You're wearing a dress?"

"Yes, sir," I acknowledge. "This is a Suzi Chin; I love the way her line fits me."

"I love it too, but did my wallet? How much did that great look set me back?"

"Don't worry—I'm worth it."

Louis crosses the room to my side. "I'm really sorry about Gloria not making it today." He squeezes my shoulder.

"Yeah, me too."

Up until yesterday, Gloria had every intention of attending the garden club meeting today, but just as I was getting ready to leave Vincent Manor last night, she changed her mind.

"I can't do it, Stevie," she said as she looked at me in her dressing table mirror as I finished brushing her hair. "I don't have the energy to see them, not now. I can barely walk from my bed to the bathroom."

"Then we can take the wheelchair!" I told her. "Randy can load it up, and we—"

"No, Stevie." She grabbed my hand. "I don't want everyone's memory of the last meeting of the year to be of me in a wheelchair."

"But you have to go, Gloria."

"Stevie, I can't. I can't see them right now; I'm all cried out. You have to convey my apologies. You have to be there for both of us tomorrow."

I eventually came to grips with her decision as I walked home from her place, and the huge shadow of Touchdown Jesus that greeted me last night was especially comforting.

$$\star \quad \star \quad \star \quad \star \quad \star$$

"Do you want me to go with you?" Louis asks as I head out for Amelie's. It's a sweet offer, one he knows I'm not going to accept. I thank him, grab my purse, and give him a more-than-friendly kiss just before I step into the elevator.

"Congratulations again on the cookbooks!" he shouts as the doors glide closed.

The cookbooks were delivered last Friday, and they really are stupendous. I'm excited about showing them off today, and truth be told, the new website is fantastic. Gloria was right; it really is a monumental day for the garden club. I'm sorry she won't be with us to experience it, but I'm determined to be joyful and gracious, which is how Gloria would be, and how she would want me to be.

It's a short walk to Amelie's, and just a couple of blocks before I enter the courtyard, I can already hear the sweet sounds of the trumpeter, Mario. What a perfect day for a courtyard luncheon.

Our end-of-the-season meeting is always more of a social event than the others; there's no formal program. We display and sell the cookbooks and install the new board. This year our installation is decidedly different than it has ever been, as Dolores and I have been officially named as co-presidents. We will share the responsibilities next season, another garden club first.

It truly is a day of celebration: new officers, new cookbooks, a new website, a new administrative office, and a new beginning for us all.

I've explained and significantly downplayed Gloria's absence to the ladies; only Elizabeth and Dolores are aware of the specific details, and they completely understand. It's a bittersweet moment when Alma picks up the bell and gives it a hard shake: *Ding-dink-ding, ding-dink-ding.*

Elizabeth stands and welcomes the ladies. She makes a few brief comments, then wastes no time calling on me.

"It is only fitting that Stephanie Lewis unveil our new cookbook, as it wouldn't have happened without her hard work. It took months to gather all the recipes and interesting historical tidbits she has added. For the first time in our history, we are making our cookbook available to a much broader audience via our new website and storefront. I think everyone who purchases a cookbook will find these facts and features most interesting. Join me in welcoming, and thanking, Stephanie Lewis." She leads the applause as I walk up next to her.

"Thank you, Elizabeth; I really enjoyed working on this project. I appreciated the freedom to add the 'lagniappe.' I had a great time helping to design the cover and interior layout this year. It was a daunting task, but we got it done. Alma and Miss V. have agreed to be our salespeople today; they will be sitting at the table by the hostess stand to check you out. We have a limited supply today, so I expect them to be gone before our meeting ends. We will have a second printing, and those copies will be available for purchase on our website at www.welcometothegardenclub.com."

The ladies are visibly impressed when they see the cookbook. It's gorgeous.

Soon it's time for the formalities as Elizabeth calls Dolores up so she can read the Oath of Office to both of us. I can't help but smile as we repeat after her. I wish Gloria were here to see Dolores's face. This is no doubt one of the proudest moments of her life. I never thought I'd say it, but I'm more than a little excited to be sharing the position with her.

When Elizabeth is finished, we are sworn in. As mutually agreed, Dolores will be making the key acceptance speech, and she stays at the podium.

"As your new co-president, I'd like to acknowledge what a fantastic job this past year's board has done." She leads the group in applause, then directs her attention to Elizabeth.

"Elizabeth, although some of us may have had our doubts, you proved us wrong, and you have a lot to be proud of. You showed us what dignity is all about." She reaches out and extends her hand to Elizabeth and then hugs her warmly before she continues. Her voice is gravely, raspy and rough, but her sentiment shines through brilliantly.

"I know I'm the dark horse in this group. I know I'm a bit rough around the edges compared to some of you gals, and that I rub some of you the wrong way. I get that." She steps out from behind the lectern. "But

I want y'all to know that the garden club is my family. And while some of you are *listening* to me, I want to make sure that y'all are *hearing* me, because I have something important to say." She squares her shoulders and continues.

"In 1843, Isabella Bronzinelle saw a need in the French Quarter, and she filled it. She didn't see a need to be politically correct. I know I'm not the most qualified, or the most educated, or even the most fashionable, but in my heart I know that I'm the most ready to assume this role."

I can't believe my ears. There was no coaching on my part for this, and my mouth is open like a codfish's. "You go girl!" I say very quietly as she finishes her speech.

"I'm not here because I want the title, the prestige, or the business, although I do welcome the business," she laughs. "I'm here because I want your respect. I'm going to do what it takes to honestly earn it. Thank you."

She returns to her seat next to me. There is a jaw-dropping silence before the group is on their feet and applauding, including me.

It's been a wild year, more excitement that this club has ever seen, but we made it through. We are all a little stronger and a little wiser for it. I feel as though we learned to appreciate one another. We've learned to count on one another more. We've learned that life can change in the blink of an eye. It's important not only to stop and smell the roses, but also to stop and share the love you have for the precious people in your life. Gloria's illness has changed us all.

The luncheon has wrapped up, and Dolores can't quit hugging everyone. Elizabeth looks at me and smiles. We can't stay here any longer; the staff needs to start setting up for the dinner crowd. As agreed upon, I'm going to head over to Gloria's house to give her a play-by-play update, but I'm going back to my place first to change shoes; I forgot to bring my flats.

I can hear Louis talking to someone on the balcony when I get home; perhaps he's on the phone. When I walk outside, he jumps up and yells.

"Surprise! We're having happy hour; where have you been?"

I look over to see Gloria lounging on a wicker chair with her feet propped up on the ottoman, pillows wedged around her for support, sipping a glass of wine. She looks like Audrey Hepburn, so chic, so fragile.

"Hello, girlfriend, glad you could make it; fabulous weather, don't you think?" she says, holding her glass up to me in a toast.

I am thrilled to see her; it's been ages since Gloria was here, not since Jazz Fest. I kiss her hello, then wrap my arms around Louis and whisper in his ear, "Thank you, thank you, thank you."

I'm startled by Maria, who seems to come from nowhere, hands me a glass of wine, then refills Louis's glass.

"Are you sure you don't want to come live with us?" Louis says to Maria. "We have a much better view than the dive where you live," he teases.

"I'm sure, Dr. Lewis." She grins. "But thank you."

I settle into a comfy chair, tucking one foot under me. "The girls said to tell you hello; everyone missed you." Gloria smiles as she takes a sip of wine. "Hey, are you allowed to have wine?" I tilt my head.

"Well, I'm technically not supposed to be drinking alcohol, especially with the pain meds I'm taking, but I'm not driving or operating heavy equipment. I'm only having this one small glass"—she takes another sip—"so I'm giving myself permission."

"You're a doctor, Louis; what do you say? Is it okay?" I ask.

"I say that Gloria is a big girl and she has a doctor who I'm pretty sure has already counseled her on the dos and don'ts of alcohol." Louis tips his glass to her.

"You are absolutely correct." Gloria laughs. "And she said, off the record of course, that a little wine wouldn't hurt."

"Then a little it is!" Louis exclaims as we clink our glasses.

I begin to tell them all about the garden club meeting. "You will never believe what Dolores said; she was fabulous!"

When I'm finished with the garden club update, it's obvious that Gloria has something to say. She looks at both Louis and me and says calmly, "I need your help."

"What's on your mind, Gloria?" Louis sits back in his chair. "How can we help you?"

"I'd like you and Stevie to be the executors of my estate." She takes another sip of wine and looks out through the railings as a beautifully decorated horse-drawn carriage comes down the street. "Oh, look! It's a bridal couple; she's wearing her gown."

Truthfully, Louis and I aren't paying much attention to what's going on down on the street. "Sorry, I seem to have a short attention span these days," she jokes.

My throat tightens up with emotion. "We thought you might ask us this."

"We've already talked at length about it." Louis leans forward, puts his elbows on his knees. "It would be an honor to do this for you. Just tell us what you want and what you need us to do."

The jazz band is playing "Somewhere over the Rainbow," and everything feels surreal to me as she continues.

"Thank you. I knew I could depend on you two. Brad, my attorney, is updating my will. I'd like us to all sit down together in the next week or two and go over the basics of the distribution of my estate. I'd like to discuss my intentions with you and answer any questions or concerns you might have while I'm still thinking clearly."

Louis is completely calm about the discussion we're having, but me, not so much.

"Of course, just tell us when." Louis pours us another glass of wine, but Gloria puts her hand over the top of her glass, shakes her head. "I've got two symposiums scheduled this month, but Stevie knows the dates I'll be gone. You gals figure out what works best, and I'll depend on my lovely and efficient wife to get me there." He winks at me.

"Thank you," Gloria says. "I've got a great legal team, and I think we've addressed all the aspects of my estate. It's rather clear what I want to happen concerning my property and finances. I trust that as the executors of my estate, you'll make sure these things happen to the best of your ability."

"We will." Louis nods.

"But there's more; it's not just that." She shifts her position. "I also need you to serve as my health care proxy. You'd be holding dual power of attorney as executors of my estate and for my health care."

My bottom lip begins to quiver, but when I look at Louis, it's as if he's being asked to drop her clothes at the dry cleaner.

"No problem, we can do that," he offers without pause or question.

"I want to officially designate the two of you to speak for me when I cannot speak for myself. I'm hoping that by discussing this ahead of time we can get beyond all this and move on to enjoying the time we have—and I hope it's a lot of time." She sets her glass down on the table.

"Of course, I completely understand." Louis crosses his legs at the ankles. "You're being very wise to address this now; Charles would be very proud of you."

I'm speechless as they talk back and forth as if they're discussing the weather.

Gloria looks at me with deep concern. "I want to make my wishes known about how I want to be treated. I want to be able to enlist the aid of the medical profession so that comfort and dignity are what I take with me to heaven and what my loved ones remember in my final days."

"Oh Good Lord, Gloria." I shake my head. "Are you really going to try to control the way you want to die too? Seriously? I suppose you're even planning your funeral service." I smirk, but I can't believe my eyes when I see a sheepish grin start to appear on her face.

"No way! You're not … are you really? OMG! This is totally crazy, Gloria."

I stand and yell, "You're both crazy! I'm going inside to get some cheese and crackers."

Once I'm inside the door, I press my back against the wall and silently suck in great gulps of air as I fight to push back the tears that are welling up inside me. They cannot see me, but I can see, and hear, them clearly.

"Well, that went well," Gloria says as she picks up her glass and finishes her wine.

I put my index finger to my lips when I see Maria sitting in the living room staring at me and watching the activity on the balcony as well.

"Don't worry about Stevie," Louis says. "I'll talk her down from the ledge; you just put everything you want and don't want in writing and make sure Brad has all the correct legal documents for us to sign. We can all get together and go over every single item so we are perfectly clear about your wishes. You can depend on us, Gloria."

Louis reaches over, takes her hand. I motion for Maria to follow me as I tiptoe to the kitchen through a cloud of tears.

I'm staring inside the refrigerator, trying to decide what to serve, when Louis sticks his head inside the door and calls out.

"Honey, Gloria is going to take off. Can you ask Maria to call Randy for the car?"

"Si, Dr. Lewis, I am calling him now." Maria quickly hits a few buttons on her cell phone keypad and then drops it back into her pocket.

"Wow, that was fast," I say.

"We have a system," she admits.

We both look up as Louis and Gloria come inside from the balcony. Gloria is holding on tightly to Louis's arm. I lean over and whisper to Maria.

"I'm thinking maybe you and I need to get a system too. The road could get a little rocky." She nods in silent agreement.

Maria has walked ahead to join Randy at the curb by the car as Louis and I saunter at a slower pace on either side of Gloria, appreciating the love we have for each other and knowing in our hearts that life is changing.

★ ★ ★ ★ ★

Friday, June 10

I feel an incomparable wave of love and deep respect for my dear friend, my precious sister, when I join her for lunch the next day at Vincent Manor.

"I do believe in miracles, and being proactive does not mean I have given up," she said to me shortly after I arrived. "But if the time comes when God calls me home to be with my sweet Charles, I want to be home in my own bed, in my own house, with those I love nearby. I want to know that *all* my wishes will be carried out, for others in my life and for myself. There's a lot to do, and I want to do it while I still can; and Stevie, I need you to help me."

"You can count on me, Gloria; I'm sorry if I was a tad ... rude last night. You have to admit that it's kind of an awkward conversation to have."

"You are right, it is. But it shouldn't be. Let's have lunch in the den, shall we?" She takes my arm, and we walk down the short hallway to the elegantly appointed room.

"I haven't been in here for quite some time. I forgot how hunt-club it looks."

She laughs as we perch ourselves on stools at the mahogany bar. Maria serves my favorite spinach, walnut, and strawberry salad. Gloria is drinking some kind of god-awful looking green juice. "What is that, Gloria? Oatmeal? Porridge? Gruel?" She throws back her head and laughs.

"After you left yesterday, Louis told me that you've had a written will since you were a teen; is that true?" I take a bite of the scrumptious salad.

"Sweetie, I've had a last will and testament since I turned eighteen; it's part of the territory in my family. In fact, if more people would look at this document as a beneficial aspect of life, it wouldn't be something that is feared or delayed until a crisis occurs. Which is the absolute worst time to be making critical decisions. One shouldn't leave the destiny of their personal affairs, or affects to chance."

"Are you telling me you actually have a list of where you want all your stuff to go?"

"Are you telling me you don't?" she exclaims.

"Uh ... no ... I don't. I suppose Louis gets everything if I go first, but I haven't really given much thought to specifics; it's all rather morbid."

"I don't agree with you, Stevie; it's not morbid at all. It's smart and sensitive."

"Sensitive? How's that?"

"Think about it. Should you have your heavenly homecoming before Louis, the last thing he would need is to figure out what to do with your personal things! Do you want him walking into your closet every day, smelling the perfume on your clothes and wishing you were still there with him?"

I smirk. "Actually, yes, I do."

"You are insufferable." Gloria tosses a swizzle stick at me and takes a sip of her green smoothie. At first it is difficult for me to talk about this. I'm pretty tenacious, but I'm not as ready to send Gloria out into the heavenly realm as she seems ready to control the way she gets there.

I mean, seriously, it's not typical to say, "Hey, would you pass the salt and let's discuss your end-of-life care wishes."

Yet no matter how atypical the discussion might be, after a while I begin to realize that Gloria is right. The more we talk about our feelings—about her needs, wishes, and requests—the easier it becomes. It begins to make sense.

CHAPTER 44

— Gloria —

Saturday, July 16

It's hard to believe the big day is here at last.

Stevie calls early. "How are you? How are you feeling? Make sure you take a nap today."

"Yes, ma'am," I say in my best little girl voice.

"Very funny. I'm serious, Gloria; don't wear yourself out today, and make sure you wear your boogie shoes tonight."

"Yeah, right."

"You promised you'd dance."

"So I did."

"Hey, I just found out that George Clinton and Funkadelic are performing a late-night show at the House of Blues," Stevie says, "and they're going to serve a late-night dinner in the Foundation Room after our party. We can stay if we're up to it."

"Oh good heavens, that will make for a long night, but I'll do my best. Let's play it by ear, okay?"

I wouldn't let Stevie cancel our party; she worked so hard to plan it. The invitations were the cutest I've ever seen; she has learned to do so much with Photoshop. We managed to keep the guest list down to our age, sixty, and the band she hired, Party on the Moon, is one of my favorite local groups. It will be a fun night.

One more event, God, just one more.

I've been preparing special little notes and gifts to give as party favors to everyone who will be attending our birthday bash this evening. My mother always said, "It's not what you say that people will remember; it's how you make them feel." And my hope is that my friends will feel how very much I love and appreciate them. Maria has helped me wrap literally dozens of gifts and mementos, and Randy will be taking them to the Foundation Room later today.

Anthony has been calling almost every day, but I'm not returning his calls or texts. I'm convinced that in the long run this will be better for him.

Stevie and Louis have been so worried about me that they cancelled their annual week at the beach. They have been going to Pensacola Beach every summer for as long as I've known them.

And this year I missed the annual Running of the Bulls. I usually attend with Stevie and her kids, as they always plan on being in town the second weekend of July every year to participate.

In actuality there are no real bulls present, at least not in the literal sense. Instead the runners are chased by roller derby girls swinging large plastic bats. It's such a wonderful and hilarious event to watch.

Since the doctor gave me the report, my mind has accepted the diagnosis, but my body is still fighting it.

These days I spend "good days" in my office upstairs, thanks to the elevator. For those days when I can't manage so well, I've got a makeshift office in my den on the main floor. That's where I am when Brad Winslett, my attorney, arrives and Maria escorts him in.

I didn't tell Stevie I was meeting today with Brad to deal with life head-on. It's the day of our big birthday bash, and I know she has carried the weight of responsibility for this celebration from the start. I couldn't, wouldn't, derail her from her course.

In spite of the topic, I'm looking forward to his visit. Brad is always a joy to see.

"Hello, Gloria," he says warmly as I stand to give him a hug.

"Brad, thank you so much for coming over. I feel special to have an attorney that will make house calls."

"Well, that's because you are special." He speaks softly with a smooth, deep voice and takes a seat next to me as he reaches into his briefcase for a file. "I brought all the documents for you to sign. I made all the revisions and stipulations you requested. I have to say, this will be quite an undertaking for Stephanie and Dolores; you must have a lot of confidence in these women."

"I do." I take a few minutes to look things over and pick up my pen.

"Maria, I need you to witness my signature." Brad is surprised when Maria materializes seemingly from nowhere. I knew she was nearby, as she is always within an earshot of me.

Maria is standing next to me with her hand on my shoulder as I begin to sign the papers, and I can hear her start to sniffle. While signing the document, I reach up with my left hand and hold on to her hand as she starts to shake. "It's okay, Maria; it's all good."

"Oh, Miss Gloria." And the tears start to flow.

"Maria, please don't cry. We don't want to make Brad print all this again, now do we?"

"No, Miss Gloria, we don't." She leans over and signs her name as a witness.

Maria walks Brad out to his car. I head back to my master suite. After a long nap and a leisurely time spent primping for the party, I'm feeling quite energized as I look in my dressing table mirror. *Not too bad for sixty.* *Je vas danser 'a soir.*

Once again, Carolina came to the rescue and designed a gorgeous multicolored silk poncho to wear over my hot pink gown. Maria had to alter the gown so it didn't fall off me, and she did a wonderful job, but the dress is strapless, and at 110 pounds as of my last weigh-in, there's no way I'm wearing anything that revealing. The semisheer overlay looks absolutely fabulous. I feel very Studio 54-ish.

Randy double parks and walks me through the Decatur entrance, where Matthew, the restaurant manager, greets me and escorts me to the elevator.

"Miss Stephanie is already here and giving the band instructions," he says with a grin.

"I'm sure she is." I swipe my card so the elevator will take me to the third floor.

Sure enough, when the elevator doors open, I can hear Stevie's voice.

"Make sure you play Beyonce's 'Single Ladies'; that's her newest favorite song. And remember to play the Michael Jackson selection, and don't forget 'We Are Family' by Sister Sledge."

That crazy girl.

The place is beautiful. Stevie had the most fabulous arrangements made. Tall glass containers filled with flowers and glitter-covered willow branches reach almost to the ceiling. Glitter confetti sparkles from the tabletops. The Foundation Room slipcovered all the chairs with a plum-color silk with gold ribbon wrapped around the back of each chair and tied in a french knot. Truly exquisite.

"Gloria, I hope you are as pleased as I am with the setup," she says. "I asked the staff to put the carving station at the end of the buffet line, and we will use the dining area to eat and visit. The band will be in the lounge area, where the dance floor is."

"Everything looks perfect, Stevie; you've outdone yourself." I wrap my arm around her waist.

She claps her hands, and her eyes sparkle. "Thank you. It is lovely, isn't it? I can't wait for the band to play. I've asked them to start around eight thirty, and we've got them until eleven, if we last that long."

"I'll do my best," I assure her.

"Oh, and there is a table filled with gifts over there." Stevie points to a table in the far corner. "Matthew said you had them delivered earlier."

There is a beautiful white damask tablecloth draped to the floor under the gifts that Randy dropped off earlier.

"Yes, they are surprise party favors." I smile.

"Okay, but maybe you should have at least told me so I could factor it into the program."

"Then it wouldn't be a surprise!" I tap her on the nose. "Don't worry— it's just a little something I prepared for our friends, and I only need a minute to say something before dinner is served."

Within minutes our guests begin to arrive. Everyone is dressed to the nines and in a festive mood. They are very cordial as they greet me, and I know they all want to know how I'm feeling, but only a few dare to ask.

Stevie calls everyone to attention and delivers a lovely greeting just before the buffet table opens, and then she hands the microphone to me.

"I want to thank you all for taking the time to share our special celebration with us tonight." I once again put my arm around Stevie's waist. "When I was growing up, my mother always gave me a special gift on her birthday, something personal to her, not bought new at a store. Those memory tokens ranged from jewelry to photos, poems, and everything in between. Mother always said it is much better to give personal items away while you are alive. They have more meaning to the ones receiving them." The room grows noticeably quiet at the mention of mortality. I wave off any negative connotations and point to the table in the far corner. "There are memory tokens for each of you. They are individually addressed, so please make sure to pick up your party favor before you leave this evening—my birthday present to you. Now, with that being said ..."

"Let's par-tay!" I yell, and I pump my fist in the air.

The band is great, and the old disco numbers seem to resonate with this crowd, as many of us are showing our age. All except Stevie, that is; she has a reservoir of energy that doesn't quit. I always forget what an incredibly good dancer she is. Stevie knows I'm a huge Michael Jackson fan; the band played several of his songs. They played a special set that energized me and the guests in an almost supernatural way, then Stevie danced a solo to *Thriller* as we circled around her. Seriously, the girl can move!

Stevie and I are taking a break at a quiet table near the back of the room, and I've surreptitiously asked Louis to hover nearby to temporarily ward off any guests who might approach us for the next few minutes so we can have some privacy.

"There's one for you." I grin.

"One what?" She cocks her head to the side.

"A party favor!"

"Really? You didn't have to do that."

"I know I didn't have to; I wanted to." I take a small box from my handbag. "I want you to have this."

"Gloria, this isn't my birthday; hold on to that until August." She puts her hands out to block the gift.

"Oh, don't worry—I have another gift planned for your actual birthday, but this is for making our celebration possible, for being an amazing friend, and for putting up with me for so many years."

"Well, it just so happens that great minds think alike, because I have something for you too," she announces. "But I couldn't find the right gift wrap, and you don't get my present until later."

"Okay, so in the meantime, open yours!" I hand her the package that Maria wrapped so beautifully, and she cradles it in her hands like a delicate piece of china.

"Charles gave it to me twenty years ago, and it's always been very dear to me." In spite of the music and revelry around us, I can hear her take a sudden breath.

She gingerly unwraps the box and opens it slowly. The sparkle in her eyes is priceless, and I can completely understand why my mother loved to turn the tables on her own birthday. Giving at a time when people do not expect to receive is so fulfilling.

Stevie gently lifts the beautiful charm necklace from its velvet-encased pillow. It is covered in hearts of all sizes and made of different materials. There are small gold hearts with gemstones in the center—some with diamonds and some with emeralds. Some are made of colored glass, and some are fashioned from other precious metals.

"It's from a designer named Anne Koplik," I offer. "All her vintage-inspired pieces are handmade. Trust me—this is always going to be a conversation piece when you wear it, so prepare yourself."

"Oh my goodness! It's gorgeous, Gloria." Her eyes become cloudy as she inspects the charms closely, each one appearing more intricate than the last. "I don't know what to say."

"Well, now that's a first!" My heart is full as I watch her expression unfold like a flower.

"Go ahead, put it on. Louis told me what you were planning to wear tonight, and I knew it would look stunning with that dress!"

She carefully wraps the piece of wearable art around her neck, and I can see her hands start to tremble, but she finally gets it hooked.

"Oh, Stevie." My hand goes to my own heart. "It's absolutely beautiful on you, and you're absolutely beautiful wearing it." As I extend my arms to give her a hug, I can no longer contain my own emotion, and the tears spill from my eyes. "I want you to think of me every time you wear it. I want to always be in your heart, because you will always be in mine."

The evening is a huge success, and it wouldn't have happened without Stevie. She and Louis boogie to a couple more dance songs before the band slows things down and begins to play *Nobody Does it Better* by Carly Simon. Charles and I loved that song; I can't help but think that it might not be long before I will see him again. I feel like bursting into tears as

I head off the dance floor, at which point I feel a nudge on my shoulder and turn around.

Louis is standing with his hand out. "May I have this dance, birthday girl?"

I see Stevie from the corner of my eye, and she's grinning from ear to ear. I can't refuse Louis; he is such a sweetheart. Stevie got lucky when she found this man.

We've only begun to dance, but I feel like Louis is holding me up. The slower pace and familiar song relaxes me, and I'd love to go home now, but I promised myself to make it to the end.

I'm resting my head on his chest and swaying to the music when I suddenly feel Louis tense his muscles, shift his position and throw back his shoulders. I straighten up to look at him, but he is looking over my shoulder and smiling. I follow his gaze just as Anthony joins us and taps Louis on the shoulder.

"May I cut in?" He holds out his hand.

Louis stops but does not let go of his hold on me.

He protectively asks my permission. "Gloria ...?"

"Yes, it's okay, Louis. Thank you for the dance, my sweet silver fox." I hold him close and kiss him on the cheek.

"The pleasure was all mine, sweetheart." He gently places my hand into Anthony's and strongly grasps Anthony on his shoulder and says, "You take care of her."

"You have my word," Anthony says to Louis while his eyes are fixed on mine.

Fortunately, it's the end of the evening, so most of the paparazzi have filed their stories and called it a night. But as I dance with Anthony, I can see from the corner of my eye that there are still a few people who are trying hard not to pay attention to us. I don't recognize any of them as media journalists, but frankly at this juncture I couldn't care less. I'm just so happy to have Anthony's arms wrapped around me.

"Gloria, my plane is still trying to clear customs at the airport; I'm here because Randy came and got me."

"Randy brought you here?"

"Don't you even think about getting angry with him, Gloria. He loves you like a daughter."

"Randy and I are almost the same age," I say.

"Age is irrelevant, remember? Feelings will always trump age."

He holds me close and whispers in my ear. "I know people are looking at you, at us. I am willing to continue playing the part of your business associate, but I am weary of the game, my love, and all I want is to feel your lips against mine, to forget that anyone else exists outside of you and me. My heart, my soul, my body, aches for you."

As we move together slowly on the dance floor, the decision is instantaneous, without worry or concern for public perception. Our passionate kiss sends a clear message to those who are watching our every move, that we are obviously much more than business associates.

He holds me tight with one hand and gently cups my cheek with the other. "Gloria, I know this sounds crazy to you, but I love you; I am certain of it. It has been a very long time since I have felt this way, and if the feeling is not yet mutual, I plan to spend the rest of our lives together convincing you."

He kisses me in a way that brings memories flooding over me, to the young blush of romance, when Charles first stole my heart.

"I think I need to sit down after that." I lean my head against Anthony's chest and take a deep breath. I don't want him to see how weak I really am. "It looks like Stevie and Louis are having a nightcap at the bar; why don't we join them for a moment?"

"I will grant your wish, because this is your special evening"—he wraps his arm around my shoulders, and we walk toward the bar—"but let it be known that I really want you all to myself." He kisses the top of my head, and I can feel my cheeks get warm, especially when I look up to see Stevie and Louis looking our way.

"This was some night, girlfriend!" Stevie says. "The Foundation Room did a superb job; everyone was so impressed!"

"Good evening, Mrs. Lewis." Anthony kisses the back of her hand. "You look exceptionally stunning this evening. Is that an Anne Koplik piece?" He admires the gold charm necklace she is wearing.

"It is!" She holds her glass up in honor of his keen eye. "I do believe we started our relationship this way, Mr. Carlyle." She laughs as Anthony helps me up on one of the tall barstools and stands protectively behind me as he motions for the bartender to pour us champagne.

"Uh … your *relationship?*" Louis raises his eyebrows as the men shake hands.

Stevie begins to explain. "The first time I met Mr. Carlyle—"

"Please, call me Anthony."

"And I'm Stevie."

"Uh, no, you're not," Louis interjects. "With all due respect, Anthony, my dear wife's name is Stephanie."

"I understand completely." Anthony nods at Louis.

"Oh Lord, testosterone!" Stevie laughs and winks at Louis. "As I was saying, the first time I met Anthony, he complimented me on a Weiss brooch I was wearing, one of mother's pieces. I was quite impressed."

"My mother always said that while clothes are indeed important, you can tell a great deal more about a woman by her perfume and jewelry," Anthony says as his arm encircles my waist.

"My mother said the very same thing!" It never ceases to amaze me how much Anthony and I have in common.

Louis makes the first of several toasts when I realize the bar is beginning to fill up.

"Tonight's show at the House of Blues must be getting ready to start," Stevie remarks.

★　★　★　★　★

"I'm exhausted; I'm afraid it's time for me to go." I start to stand, and Anthony gently helps me off the barstool. He's always a gentleman, but he's been extremely gentle this evening, especially considering how things ended the last time I saw him, and I wonder what's going on—how much he knows.

"Well, we did it, sister!" Stevie reaches over and wraps me in a tender embrace and whispers in my ear, "I hope you don't mind that I couldn't find the right gift wrap for your present."

I briefly furrow my brow in confusion before I understand what she means.

"You!" I look at Stevie and then fix my stare on Anthony.

"That's why you're here. She told you to come," I say.

"She didn't *tell* me to do anything," Anthony says. "She invited me to a party, and I graciously accepted. Now, why don't we get out of here?" He grins.

"Yes, why don't you?" Stevie says. "Louis and I are going to stay."

"We are?" Louis tilts his head.

"Yes, dear, we are. Now, you two run along." She dismisses us like we're schoolkids, and I can't help but appreciate her good intentions as we say good night.

"Stevie, I've had such a wonderful time; everything has been magical. Truly magical."

It's almost eleven when Anthony escorts me downstairs to my car, and I expect more resistance when I tell him I need to call it a night, but he gently kisses me good night and steps back to allow Randy to take my arm and help me slide into the backseat.

I've never been gently passed between so many gallant and dashing men—first Louis, then Anthony, and now Randy—like I'm a breakable porcelain doll. I am so blessed to have people in my world who love me, and as I fix my eyes on Anthony as he watches us pull away from the curb, I think it has been such a long time since I felt loved in this way, but my heart is overcome with equal parts of exquisite fullness and heartbreaking despair.

CHAPTER 45

— Stephanie —

Sunday, July 17

The day after our birthday bash, it is like someone has let the air out of Gloria's sails, and I think it's all my fault.

"I'm sorry, Gloria," I say when I visit her at home the next day. "I thought you would be excited to see Anthony. I guess I didn't think it through enough."

"I know, I know," she says quietly, and she pats me on the leg as I sit on the edge of her bed.

"It was good to see him, at first. He is such a kind and loving man."

"I think he really cares for you, Gloria."

"I know he does, Stevie, and I care for him, but there's so much more to it."

I can see that now.

She refuses Anthony's calls all morning, and in desperation he calls me later in the day.

"I'm not blind, Stephanie, I can see she is not well. Please ... how sick is she?" he begs.

"Very." Is all I can manage to say without betraying her trust, and I feel horrible that my good intentions have turned out to be so painful for them both.

"She told me it was something else. I didn't know." His voice cracks. "I thought she was avoiding me because I said, did, something wrong, something foolish. Stevie, I must see her, be with her. I am coming over there now."

I do my best to respond gently. "Anthony, if you burst in trying to see her today, you will break her heart. I know that isn't what you want. She doesn't want you to see her this way."

"Then what can I do? How can I help?"

"Go back home for now. I will stay in touch, I promise."

We hang up, and I sit very still for a long time. This isn't fair. I'm finding it hard to understand God's plan in all this.

* * * * *

Monday, July 18

The response from our celebration, and from Gloria's memory token party favors, has lifted Gloria's spirits. Calls, e-mail and hand-delivered notes begin to pour in bright and early, and her funk from yesterday vanishes.

I promised Gloria weeks ago that we would meet here today to discuss her plans for Vincent Manor, and I'm so happy to see that she is revitalized by all the attention her surprise gifts have created.

I'm sitting at her kitchen counter going over notes on my laptop computer, and Maria is cutting up fruit as we listen to Gloria tell one caller after another the story behind the memory token she selected for each of them. The stories are poignant, poetic, and often personal. I'm only now grasping the full measure of what this means to Gloria and to the recipients.

During one call I whisper to Maria, "How long have you two been working on this?"

"*Ay dios mio*, Miss Stevie, this has been going on for several months. She had the guest list, and I would see her reading it. Every so often she would bring me a basket of gifts to wrap with yellow sticky notes on them. She was very serious about this."

Maria looks over at Gloria, and there is a discernable sparkle in her eyes.

"There's only one Gloria," I say as I follow her gaze.

"Yes, Miss Stevie, only one."

Eventually Gloria and I get down to business.

"Stevie, I have put a lot of thought into the changes to be made. I want your honest opinion and a list of any concerns that you think I should consider."

I can't help but think to myself, *She'll be a CEO till the day she dies.*

"The time may come, Stevie, when I won't be able to answer your questions about the decisions I have made, and so I welcome questions." She takes a breath and shuffles through some papers. I can't believe the love that I feel for my dear friend at this moment. While every part of me wants to scream in protest at this travesty, I know in my heart that it is right, it is proactive, and it is so Gloria.

"The majority of Vincent Manor will be placed into a trust shared by the Fleur-de-Lis Ladies Garden Club of the French Quarter and the Grace House Shelter of New Orleans, with the primary purpose being to develop a French Quarter women's enrichment center. The former offices of *NOLA 2 NOLA* will be allocated for shared use by the governing board of the FDL Garden Club and the developmental staff of the Grace House Shelter.

"The former *NOLA 2 NOLA* studio space above the carriage house will be allocated as the headquarters and primary office of fund-raising and development for the enrichment center and the garden club, which includes the publishing and distribution of the yearly garden club cookbook. I want you to be in charge of everything that goes on in that building." She looks at me our of the corner of her eye, as though checking to see if I'm really listening.

"Yes, ma'am," I reply. "Really, how can I say no to you now."

She gives me a smile, and we continue to discuss details for another hour or so.

"A new position of executive director for the French Quarter enrichment center will be entrusted to Dolores Delacroix, including the provision of an on-site apartment and a monthly stipend. Duties and responsibilities are listed in a separate document, such as overseeing administrative responsibilities, and conducting and coordinating educational enrichment classes for women in the French Quarter who desire to adopt the mission and vision of the organization. I want her to continue to take care of our gardens and use them as examples to teach not only the ladies of the garden club but also the women in our community."

"Speak of the devil," I say, "I think I hear her in the garden. I'm getting tired; don't you need to go take a nap or something?"

Gloria looks a little confused, but no one knows me like she does. I'm starting to feel overwhelmed and emotional. I've been keeping it together so far, but the floodgates are about to open.

Dolores comes bouncing into the room. "Did you see how beautiful the plumbago looks?"

Gloria gazes out the window. "Everything looks beautiful to me."

"Stevie, why don't you and I continue this tomorrow? I think I'd like to discuss a few things with Dolores."

Knowing now that she did read my mind, I gather my laptop and the binder she gave me to study and kiss her good-bye. As I start to leave, I give Dolores a heads-up.

"You might want to take notes, girlfriend."

★　★　★　★　★

Tuesday, July 19

The days pass quickly, with many good ones for Gloria, but also plenty of not-so-good ones.

The burden of carrying this weight of knowing what to do (and what not to do) is discernibly lifted when Dr. Lucerne refers Gloria to Monique. Monique is a nurse who works in tandem with the cancer center to offer patients palliative care. For now, she is seeing Gloria three times a week, but those visits will slowly increase, and at some point, she will become a full-time live-in caregiver.

Monique comes to help Gloria, and all of us, navigate the rough waters of balancing quality-of-life concerns during treatment, as well as end-of-life care. She will become the glue that holds all of us together, the proverbial angel-in-disguise.

I know Gloria has been in pain throughout this whirlwind transformation, but the first time I saw her experience pain, real pain, it was almost unbearable to watch. Monique gave her Percocet, and it slowly started to help.

Just managing the medications alone requires someone with Monique's expertise and patience. Gloria is taking a lot of medications, and not just for pain.

"I was so against it when Charles wanted to turn these rooms into a master suite, but he was a man of vision. He said I would thank him later when I was old and gray." She looks up. "Thank you, Charles. Now I want this room to be comfortable for everyone, not just for me."

Gloria has been blessed in many ways, not the least of which is the level of financial freedom she experiences. She fully understands that what she is doing isn't something afforded to most people who are traveling this course.

Her king-size bed was the first thing to go, and when it and the oversize matching nightstands were replaced by a state-of-the-art computerized hospital bed, a tall multidrawer nightstand, and a rolling tray table, the room seemed to double in size.

An adjoining room that once held a hodge-podge collection of Gloria's things is now a beautifully appointed guest bedroom for the live-in hospice nurse.

On a wall that once held an original Chagall oil painting, there is now a large flat-screen TV. Gloria has never been a huge fan of television, but she's starting to enjoy it. It's also been good for her as she spends more and more time in her bed.

One day, after watching Dr. Phil and the Oprah Winfrey show, we began to discuss those ah-ha moments people have—those moments when the epiphany is reached, the lightbulb suddenly goes on, and you finally say, "I get it, I get it." Those moments when even a talk show host can help you find clarity.

"I've been thinking a lot about ah-ha moments lately." I lean back in the plush recliner and dip my spoon into the single-serving container of Ben & Jerry's Mint Chocolate Chunk ice cream. "What it takes for some people to finally reach them."

Gloria reaches over to the controls on her bed to elevate her head and looks at me silently.

"You've been telling me for years that I have leadership potential."

"And so you do," she says.

"That's just it Gloria; it doesn't amount to a hill of beans if *I* don't believe it, no matter how much you tell me that *you* believe it. But I think maybe I've had one of those lightbulb moments." I finish off the ice cream and set the container on the end table. "Wanna hear it?"

"Of course." Gloria smiles.

"You've been quoting Eleanor Roosevelt to me for years, saying that no one can make us feel inferior without our permission, and I suddenly realized that's what I've been doing. I have been giving myself permission to feel inferior. I've always enjoyed volunteering. My mom taught me the value of giving. She loved to volunteer at our church, at my school, in our community center, and even at the hospital. She was on every board and committee imaginable, always ready to be a leader, and you know why?"

Gloria shakes her head.

"Because being a leader defined her; it gave her a title, a position—it gave her worth." I take a big sip of water and continue. "My mother loved giving herself to other people, but for some reason I felt I could never measure up. I know she loved me, but would she love me if I failed? Once I became a parent, I started to understand unconditional love. Of course she would love me, but would others? Could I handle that kind of pressure? I realize now that I've been afraid—afraid of failure. However, in these past few months, you've shown me what real courage is. Watching you endure pain and uncertainty has made me realize how foolish I've been. Life is too short to live in fear." I take a deep breath and once again lean back in the recliner. "That's my epiphany, my ah-ha moment. Maybe I should send Dr. Phil and Oprah a thank-you note." I click the mute button on the remote control to restore the volume, and I focus my eyes, if not my attention, on the screen.

We get caught up watching the end of *Divine Secrets of the Ya-Ya Sisterhood*, one of our favorite movies. When it's over, I collect my things to head home for the day. As I give her a kiss good-bye, Gloria grabs my hand.

"I love you, Stevie."

I smile. "Love you too."

She squeezes my hand with more strength than I thought she had. "You know how to lead Stevie, and you know how to love." She takes my hand and places it on her chest. "You just need to trust your heart to be willing to let go and let God give you the strength to do the things that he's already equipped you to do. He has already made you a leader, Stevie. He has already made you an encourager, a visionary. You just have to trust yourself, and him.

Before I leave, I agree to go to church with Gloria on Sunday. I have a scathingly brilliant idea that will make it a perfect day.

★　★　★　★　★

Sunday, July 24

I see the outside of the cathedral and the verdant St. Anthony Garden every day from our balcony, but I always forget how incredibly gorgeous the inside of the St. Louis Cathedral is, how breathtaking and majestic everything is.

Few cities in the world are quickly identified by a building; Paris has its Eiffel Tower, New York the Empire State Building, and the city of New Orleans is instantly recognized by our cathedral and its position overlooking Jackson Square. The Cathedral-Basilica of St. Louis, King of France, is the oldest Catholic cathedral in continual use in the United States.

The Sunday Mass is quite beautiful, and the father's message of God's mercy combined with the liturgy fills me with emotion.

When the service is over, we wait patiently for the congregation to start to clear out.

As we prepare to leave the cathedral, I urge Gloria to walk in the opposite direction of everyone else.

"You're going the wrong way; we need to exit these doors, Stevie," she whispers, trying unsuccessfully to pull me in the opposite direction.

"No, actually, we don't." I gently take her arm as she notices one of the altar boys holding open a door at the back of the cathedral—a door that is usually locked.

"It wasn't as hard as I thought it would be to get this special dispensation, or whatever it is you folks call it. You're a pretty well-known girl, in case you didn't know it." I smile.

There is a light breeze, and the scent of flowers is in the air as we cross from the awesome expansiveness of the St. Louis Cathedral into the peaceful and utterly private St. Anthony's Garden—an area that is seldom open to the public.

"Just knock on this door when you wish to leave," the young altar boy says to me. "There is no hurry."

"Thank you, young man," I say, and Gloria is speechless as the door closes behind us and we enter the courtyard.

"Oh, Stevie." The tears cascade unashamedly down her cheeks as she stares out at the lush garden. "It's been so long since I've walked here."

"Then let's not waste a moment getting started!" I take her arm, and we begin to walk slowly on the red brick pathway that encircles this little island of green, with its noble oak, sycamore, and magnolia trees in the shadow of the wall of the sanctuary.

St. Anthony's Garden is an intriguing sight to tourists and a continual delight to residents. It is also somewhat my own backyard; we look up at my balcony and admire Dolores's handiwork in the lush baskets of ivy cascading over the railings.

"She really is very good at what she does," Gloria says. "It's beautiful."

"Thank you. I couldn't agree more."

"She has worked so hard to develop her business. She was completely devastated, and totally broke, when Kevin left, rather like our sweet Elizabeth," Gloria says. "But look at her now! I am so proud of her. Won't she make a wonderful teacher and mentor for young women who are turning their lives around?"

When we reach the base of the marble Sacred Heart of Jesus statue, we are without words as we stare up.

"It certainly looks different from this vantage point, doesn't it?" I say.

"I remember standing in this very same spot when I had my first communion; I was so in love with Jesus." She rubs her hand gently on the stone base and presses her cheek on the cool surface. "I was seven years old then, and I can remember it like it was yesterday."

We take a seat on a concrete bench, and she begins to tell me all about that day and more.

"Stevie, I've had a wonderful life; all my dreams have come true." It's hard for her to talk; it seems hard for her to find the air needed to push out the words, and I lean over to hear her.

"All of them but one … I always dreamed about being a mother. When our daughter was born, Charles and I were over the moon; she was our gift, our treasure, our blessing. Sadly, she was born with a rare blood disorder; we soon learned that every day we had with her could be our last. The day she died, I held her in my arms. I held her fragile little body as she took her last breath. It was the hardest thing I have ever done in my life. But Stevie, it was also the closest I have ever been to God. In that moment when Abigail left our world, I saw the face of the one who was taking her home to be with him. He was good. I knew he would love her for eternity."

It's hard for her to see me, as her eyes are filled with tears; but she can feel my hand in hers, and she squeezes it tighter. "Let him take me, Stevie. Let me go and be with my sweet Charles, and with my precious baby, my Abigail. I love you, Stevie."

I wrap my arms around her, and we both begin to cry. *Why? Why her?* We hold each other tight, and I can feel her heart bounding against mine. I pull back to stand and gently lift her to her feet. She grasps my arm to steady herself. We both wipe the tears from our faces and try to compose ourselves, aware that there are people looking through the fence at us.

As we are about to leave and are waiting for the altar boy to answer my knock, Gloria turns to look back at the garden and tilts her head up at the statue.

"If anyone made a touchdown today, it was you, dear sister." And she wraps her arms around me in a very tight hug. "This is a precious gift that I will hold in my heart forever."

CHAPTER 46

── Stephanie ──

Cancer presents itself in many different ways. In Gloria's case, it presented itself quickly, fiercely, and with a "take-no-prisoners" attitude.

Monique calls me at a quarter after six in the morning to tell me that Louis and I need to get there ASAP.

When we arrive, she is alive but not responsive. I lie down next to her and stroke her hair and hold her hand, just being close to her to let her know she isn't alone.

You can plan and prepare all you want, with the best intentions, but in a single moment life can change.

Gloria is surrounded by the ones who love her most—me, Louis, Randy, and Maria—when she takes her last breath. I can't help myself as I weep openly like an inconsolable child. Maria is holding it together better than any of us, and she stops the hands on the clock. Coco is lying on the floor at the foot of her bed. It's obvious she knows what's going on. I reach down and run my hand over her head; she breaths a heavy sigh.

With tears streaming down his face, Louis says a few beautiful words about how Gloria influenced his life and what a wonderful lady she was. Randy proceeds to lead us in a very heartfelt prayer. Maria is reciting a Rosary in Spanish. Louis rubs my arms and gently pulls me into his embrace and softly whispers, "Let Monique do her job now."

When we step back and turn toward the door, I see Elizabeth coming down the hall. She immediately breaks down crying. Louis and I rush to her.

Maria goes into work mode and starts preparing a pot of tea. Elizabeth eventually pulls herself together and starts the phone chain.

Bad news always travels fast.

★   ★   ★   ★   ★

Monday, August 8

Her funeral is simple and beautiful. The sanctuary is full. There are as many people as there are roses. Louis and I take our time visiting with her many friends and colleagues. Phillip walks up to me with an eight-by-ten-inch envelope. "Hello, Stephanie." He greets me with a kiss on each cheek. "I have something very special for you."

I open the envelope, and I am overcome with so much emotion that my throat tightens; I can hardly breathe.

Words cannot describe the precious photographic images I hold, as Phillip explains.

"I was on a shoot at the Faulkner House when I saw you two," he says. "I hope you don't mind."

The Faulkner House is next to St. Anthony's Garden, and Phillip had captured several photographs of Gloria and me walking arm in arm in the garden. Also, he took a close-up of us with our cheeks pressed against the cool stone of the base of Touchdown Jesus and holding hands just before we left the garden.

The photos send me over the edge. They are the last photographs ever taken of me and Gloria together.

As we start to leave, I see Anthony waiting for us by the door, and I extend my hands for a hug. He wraps his arms around me, and tears gently stream down his cheeks. He slowly removes a crisp white linen handkerchief and wipes his tears.

There is something truly special about French men; they don't seem to harbor the same need for maintaining an air of stoic bravado as their American counterparts; their emotional walls do not seem to be as high.

With his voice cracking, he states, "Her dying has left an empty hole in my heart, my life. I'm finding it very difficult to understand why God would give such a beautiful gift only to take it away so quickly. Why would he fill my heart with such love and joy and then leave it so utterly and completely empty?"

I place my hand gently on his shoulder. "Charles was the love of her life. But Gloria learned through her relationship with you that God can fill every void if you let him. You made her very happy, Anthony. You showed her how to love again."

"Ah, *mon chéri*, it was she who showed me how to love."

★   ★   ★   ★   ★

Sunday, August 14–Stevie's Sixtieth Birthday

The sunlight is finally starting to slip through my bedroom drapes. I've been awake for hours. I can't help but think of Gloria today; I miss her so much. I'm startled when the doorbell rings so early in the morning. Louis is unusually responsive as I nudge him to go answer the door.

"Come on, Stevie, for crying out loud, I'm tired; let me sleep." He pulls a pillow over his head.

Fine. I'll let you sleep. See if I care.

I grab my robe, shuffle downstairs, and press the intercom button.

"Delivery for Stephanie Lewis," a male voice says.

"Give me a minute, please; I'll be right down."

Who would be making a delivery on a Sunday?

I take the elevator downstairs and look out the peephole and see a man dressed in a uniform and carrying a clipboard, so I open the door.

"Stephanie Lewis?" he asks.

"Yes …"

I'm startled when he yells over his shoulder. "Go for it, guys."

I'm standing at the door, dazed and confused, as I see a crew of men begin to unload several boxes stamped "Fragile" from a large truck.

Deliverymen in the French Quarter are much like taxi drivers in Manhattan; they know how to navigate the terrain, and you don't mess with them. I'm standing at the door, and before I can say "hold your horses," they walk past me, place the boxes inside the elevator, and walk back out.

"Wait—" I stammer. "What is this?"

"Delivery. Didn't we establish that, ma'am?" the big guy with the clipboard says as he smirks and heads back to the truck.

I'm somewhat taken aback by his gruff manner, and I'm trying to process what's going on, as six large boxes have been stacked in my elevator in record time.

"Wait, wait!" I hold my hand up. "What is all of this? Where is this delivery from?" I call out to the big guy who is talking on his cell phone just as I look over to see the deliverymen gingerly unloading Gloria's beautiful art deco dressing table from the truck, followed by a large flat crate that I would lay odds contains an original Françoise Gilot painting.

I quickly look over my shoulder at the boxes in the elevator, and tears fill my eyes. I have no doubt they contain a most exquisite collection of Waterford crystal, and I remember Gloria's promise to me so many months ago.

Suddenly clipboard guy is off the phone and standing next to me.

"The delivery must be from a convent or something," he says. "All it says on the order is 'Sister Gloria.' But the guy up there just called me, and he said for you to release the elevator so he can unload it." I follow his pointed finger to see Louis standing on the balcony, completely dressed and holding a cardboard sign that reads "Happy Birthday, Sister!"

I would know Gloria's block printing anywhere, and I'm overcome with emotion.

It takes several trips in the elevator to get everything upstairs, especially since each of the pair of priceless oriental side chairs has been wrapped in multiple layers of thick furniture-pad blankets.

"I can't believe you managed to keep this a secret!" I alternate from smacking Louis on the arm to hugging him so hard he can hardly breathe.

"What do you mean? I'm a good secret keeper." He grins. "But it almost didn't happen. There was a glitch in the delivery, and I was on the phone all day yesterday coordinating this."

"Thank you; it's the best birthday present I could get …"—I nestle my head on his chest as he wraps me in his arms—"other than to have her back."

"I know, sweetie, I know." He kisses the top of my head.

Live and love like there's no tomorrow.

Special thanks to Allison Bottke. Without her, this book would never have happened. She was my writing coach, editor, and mentor. There are not enough words to express the depth of my gratitude. Please visit www.allisonbottke.com to learn more about this gifted woman.

Thanks also to Caron Jacobs, who kept a close eye on my punctuation and never let me quit.

To Isabelle Jacopin, thank you for creating the perfect image for the cover of my debut novel. (Isabelle is a local artist that divides her time between New Orleans and her studio in France.) For information on Isabelle, contact her through facebook @ Isabelle Jacopin

Made in United States
Orlando, FL
28 May 2022

18273921R00212